THE
C
OF THE
HEXAD

THE AFTERLIFE SAGA
BOOK 7

STEPHANIE HUDSON

The Cult of the Hexad
The Afterlife Saga #7
Copyright © 2020 Stephanie Hudson
Published by Hudson Indie Ink
www.hudsonindieink.com

DEDICATION

I dedicate this book to everyone affected by Alzheimer's and Dementia, which includes my own family. So this one is for my wonderful Nan, who is loved dearly.

Lost Inside

I know who you are,
I have seen your face,
It's wandering in my mind,
Lost in a wondrous place.

I speak about you fondly to all who know,
The places I find and the places I go.
I reach out to you and take your hand,
To bring you with me to discover my land.

The land in which my memories will find,
A loving heart, one given in kind,
A hopeful day just like the rest,
We will seek together on our quest.

Because I will love you even when I'm not here,
As I hold your hand and you look back in fear,
So please remember my mind is not lost,
It is simply a place you cannot cross.

I am just wandering around in my world,
Where one day I wait for you by gates so pearled,

Because we will make it through this together,
On a high flying day, like birds of a feather.

So don't be sad if I ask for your name,
I'm just lost in my world that's no longer the same,
But my memories are sweet and they hold you so dear,
Forever and always, year after year.

FOREWORD

But before that…it's time for a quick…

Important Insight from the Author,

Hello lovely Afterlife fans, this is a little note from me explaining about the craziness you are about to read. Firstly, I should start by saying that yes, this is the right book and no, I haven't lost my marbles…*not yet anyway*. Although at the beginning of this book, you may believe you have. But have no fear, for I can assure you it will all start to make sense soon.

Secondly this is the part where I have to ask you to trust me on this one as the more you read, the more it will start to unravel and make sense. It is also vital to the rest of the story and is just another massive piece of the puzzle that helps to complete an even bigger picture.

This book will twist your mind and having you questioning where the story came from, and where it could possibly go. Before BAM, it hits you with the truth! It is an epic mind warp and a journey both reader and our heroin experience together in search for what is real and what is fiction.

It's a wild ride, with more twists than you can shake a cat at...but please don't shake cats, we like cats. ;)

So please sit back, trust me and enjoy, I promise, our sexy Draven and Lucius are both in this one and as always, at the ready to save the day!

Love Steph x

PS...Now it's time for the real Prologue!

WARNING!

This book contains explicit sexual content, some graphic language and a highly addictive Alpha Male.

This book has been written by a UK Author with a mad sense of humour. Which means the following story contains a mixture of Northern English slang, dialect, regional colloquialisms and other quirky spellings that have been intentionally included to make the story and dialogue more realistic for modern-day characters.

Please note that for your convenience language translations have been added to optimise the readers enjoyment throughout the story.

Also meaning…

No Googling is required ;)

Also, please remember that this part of a 12 book saga, which means you are in for a long and rocky ride. So, put the kettle on, brew a cup, grab a stash of snacks and enjoy!

Thanks for reading x

PROLOGUE

'Time.
'Faith has its tight grip on our lost time like endless sands we
cannot touch. Oceans of hopeful space between us mean
nothing if the ship cannot sail and Courage is lost in the
darkness without the stars to guide us.
One by one the crimson moon will take our sisters of the earth
on a never-ending journey of stolen power.
The cups will fill, blood will flow and nine by nine will fall to
the Hexad.
Time is power.
Power leads to destruction.
Destruction brings forth the end of Time…our time.'

"Draven!" I shouted out his name instantly looking for him in the dark. Like gripping onto the anchor my mind needed to keep me from losing myself to the storm this supernatural force wanted to drag me to.

Ever since getting back from Hell something deep inside of

me told me only one thing mattered and that was…something was coming. Something strong attacked my mind when it was at its weakest in sleep. When I was at my most vulnerable and couldn't focus on anything but the voices. They spoke to me of another life and another time of which was now. It was almost as if I was living parallel to my dreams.

I couldn't understand it but by the time I would wake the memories unravelled like vapour streams into the dawning sky and were lost until the next time night fell.

I didn't want to worry Draven so remained silent on these strange nightmares I couldn't decipher. And besides, it wasn't as though I had much information to give him, even if I had wanted to explain. It was as if every time I could feel the dream coming to an end I would desperately reach out and try to grasp at the details with my fist. I could feel my fingers curl around something sharp and cutting but I would ignore the pain in sight of the truth I was searching for. But the blood I could feel dripping down my wrist would dry and flake to dust as I opened my hand and found nothing, before I woke.

"I'm here sweetheart." Draven's soft voice caressed my fragile nerves and helped wash my hands of my guilt…a guilt I didn't understand. It cleansed me like I was being both blessed and baptized in a lake of truth. Where these thoughts were coming from I couldn't say but it was as though I was back to the beginning. It was like I was looking at myself in the stream that day I found Frank's uncle's cabin, only now when I saw myself, I saw the figure of Draven standing strong behind me keeping watch.

Upon opening my eyes my visions of our reflections in the water were replaced by the man I loved…

My husband.

"Another dream?" Draven asked and I raised an eyebrow wondering how long he had known?

"We have been married nearly eight months now Keira, do you not think I know when my wife has a troubled mind?" I rolled my eyes making him laugh. He always made it very hard to be moody when he looked so damn handsome.

"Know it all." I muttered causing his laugh to vibrate around our home… 'Afterlife'. It was a strange name for a home I would admit but I thought it was more than fitting considering what we had been through. The way I felt was that I had been reborn since meeting Draven all that time ago and this was the Heaven I now lived in. It was as though the very building itself embraced me into its depths like a mother's waiting arms…so why did I wake feeling like I missed it when living it?

"Keira?" Draven asked out of concern.

"Make me forget, Draven." I said and instead of the right questions asked he simply nodded like he knew. He knew what I needed right now and it was the same as always. Eight months is a long time to be lost with only a hand to hold in the dark dreams of what should have been.

Draven kissed me, softly at first and then as he rolled my body under his and the desperation we both felt started to bloom. It opened up between us like the first rays of sunlight caressing the horizon and teasing the sky with light. Golden naked skin lay over me like a blanket of warmth, protecting me against the bitter cold reality that would take me back there.

"No, Keira… *I will make you remember.*" Draven said and exhaled the warmth hearing those words made me feel. I placed both my hands on his cheeks and brought his lips back to mine. I opened up to his touch and the taste of him bursting across my tongue. I felt myself becoming lightheaded as I relished every second I had in his world.

Such strength he held over me should have frightened me and somewhere in the world I knew it did but here *she* couldn't touch me. No, right here I was untouchable, if only for the few seconds the cosmos allowed us. And here, in his arms, I would *never* fear Draven…no, I only feared myself.

I closed my eyes tight as his kiss touched the deeper parts of my soul and my tears fought to break free as I wished harder than last time that his touch would finally take root and keep me here. But I knew who was watching. *She* was always watching. Sometimes I would look back at here and scream at her. Sometimes I would plead with her, beg even. I would shout, hurl abuse, throw things and threaten against what she didn't understand. Because that lost, weak little girl didn't know me. She didn't know this life and the gift I had found. She knew nothing of what the touch of a loving hand could bring. She knew nothing of the strength behind every action fighting for it would mean or make you do.

She knew nothing.

But I knew.

I knew it was coming…*I always knew.*

Because this was the point I would always realise the haunting truth behind my dreams, behind the truth. That hand I reached out in a vain attempt to grasp back some understanding of a life I kept dreaming about was pointless. Because it wasn't *her* life I was trying to hold onto and understand, it was this one…It was *my* one.

This was the dream and that hand, that bloody hand reaching out and gripping tight was mine. It was mine trying to drag me back there. Back to that place I hated. Back to a place where nightmares were real life being lived through and this, my heaven, was the dream I escaped to.

So keeping my eyes closed was pointless because whether I saw her or not she would take me from Draven like some thief haunting the shadows. I had been kidnapped before, God knows

I had and survived it time and time again but what do you do when it's yourself that is the kidnapper? How do you fight yourself in a battle only one of you believes is fighting?

Feeling Draven kissing my neck was trying to combat my sombre thoughts but not enough to stop me from opening my eyes and facing the inevitable. Tears ran down into my hairline as soon as I saw her above me watching like a frightened doe in headlights. It was clear she didn't understand what she was seeing and when Draven's wings erupted from within him, her eyes widened and shock always replaced the fear.

She didn't understand what he was, that much was clear. So maybe I needed to show her. I put my arms around him and pulled his hair making him growl. He pulled back to look at me and just as his eyes flashed violet blood he kissed me once more. He saw me looking at her and growled again.

"Ignore her." His demon demanded and I closed my eyes against the pain that he knew. Then before that pain could rip me in two he rolled me over so I was above him. He entered me in the same move and I threw my head back in rapture of being taken this way. He commanded my body the only way Draven knew how and I felt my pleasure building like a hurricane.

I rocked my body the way I knew he liked and he thrust up harder knowing the way I liked it. It didn't take long until we found the peak of our pleasure together because he knew as well as I did that we didn't have long left.

Time was precious and it was broken. And one look into her eyes as I threw my head back, staring at her the exact moment I came around Draven's manhood and she knew it too. The mirror she was watching me through cracked. The ceiling of our four poster bed began to shatter and for the first time in eight months I had gotten through. The glass reflected my life back to me in broken pieces and that was now the world she saw me through. I had made her see that her world, well…it was broken too.

Because it had been stolen. Because her world belonged to me. It was mine and one thing was for damn sure…

I wanted it back!

CHAPTER I
WHICH ONE IS HELL?

I woke up panting and trying to catch my breath like it seemed I did most mornings these days. Last night's dream seemed to be the most real yet. For the last eight months I had been suffering from these types of nightmares and each one grew in intensity. The theme remained mostly the same and it was a haunting thing to have to witness when night after night I saw myself trapped, scared, angry and devastated.

"Are you awake?" I almost groaned out loud but thankfully stopped before I got myself into even more trouble.

"Uh…yeah." I said tucking my hair behind my ear which was a habit of mine.

"Oh dear, was it another bad dream?" My mother asked as she pushed my door open and I gave her a small smile as my answer. Her frown soon replaced what I had come to know as fake concern.

"Was it about that man again?" She asked scowling disapprovingly at me, as if I had any control over it. The worst mistake I made was talking to my sister about it when not making absolutely sure no one was around at the time. My cousin had a nasty habit of getting people in trouble that was for sure.

"Mother." I said pulling back the covers and stuffing my feet into a pair of well-worn tartan slippers that I had owned for years.

"No Katie, your uncle and I have had just about enough of this. It upsets us to see you so distracted for days after. We think it's time for you to see someone about it." I groaned wondering how many times now I had heard this all before. I didn't know why it was, as I had never seen one before, but I hated the idea of seeing a psychiatrist. The very thought of talking about my dreams with anyone other than my sister made me scratch at my arms like I had a rash or something. But no, it was only ever the same old scars that I had lived with ever since the accident.

I shook these solemn thoughts from my mind, casting them away with the last sticky remains of the dream.

"Mother we have been over this." I said being strong for once.

"Yes I know, but your uncle knows someone and thinks it is best..." I rolled my eyes as I faced the wall getting fresh underwear out of the top drawer. If she had caught me that would have been another lecture.

"No." I said slamming the drawer shut in an unusual stand against my family. It was as though when I saw that girl in my dream, that other version of me, something in me snapped eight months ago. Just the very sight of her in my mind's eye sometimes made me strong. It made me want to be more like her in some way. Not the trapped and kidnapped part but the feisty side of her...that's what I admired. She was strangely like some sort of role model to me, one who unknowingly helped me get through this suppressed life I had been forced into. I didn't know what I would do if I didn't have my sister Arianna in my life.

"Now Katie, be reasonable." I rarely said no to my mother as let's just say she wasn't the most forgiving of people and considering how religious she was I always found this surprising.

"I said…"

"I don't like your tone Missy. Now I said you are going and that is final or you will have your uncle to answer to and you know his temper." My mother said and I jumped when she slammed the door and I heard the latch lock into place. This was my family's answer to most things. Lock me in my room like I was a teenager, not the grown woman I was.

Most of the time I didn't care as I enjoyed being alone unless Arianna was the one sneaking into my room. No, it just meant that I was given the time needed to analyse my dreams in peace. Not that this particularly helped as I could never fully understand the meaning of them but I felt like I owed it to her to at least try. It was strange the way I thought about her as a real person and not just another side to myself. I knew it was crazy but it was like looking in the mirror and pretending your reflection is some other person living a better version of your life.

Apart from looks we had very little else in common. She was beautiful and reminded me of the goddesses we had been taught about in class. Although I would switch off in our teachings when they said to shun such creatures as beauty only brought trouble.

Well I guess they weren't wrong if my cousin was anything to go by, I thought bitterly. It wasn't as if I was jealous, far from it as I preferred to have a warm heart and kind soul over beauty any day and as my sister often told me, I was blessed with both. I would only blush and laugh the compliment away like I did most things. But oh what it would feel like to be more like the girl in the mirror. For a start, what would it feel like to have those captive hands holding me instead of her?

I shuddered just thinking about him. And what last night's dream had brought me. I had felt myself getting so close to it. As if I had been reaching out trying to chase the unknown. That feeling a woman has when being with a man like that. It had been so hot and carnal. So forbidden and if any of my church members knew what thoughts really went on in my head, then oh my, wouldn't I be known as the wild child. Shunned wasn't a strong enough word to cut it.

Banished more like.

Because they didn't know what or who I dreamed of. They didn't see what I saw. They didn't see another version of my naked body being taken on an altar in wild abandon. They didn't see me giving myself to not just a man...

But a Demon with wings.

"Hey Sinner girl, you been chastised again?" Arianna 's voice shook me from my dangerous thoughts. I looked round after realising I must have been staring at Hell for a good twenty minutes now. It was a replica of the painting 'The great day of his Wrath' by an English artist by the name of John Martin. It was something I found myself spending far too much time staring into thinking about the world I lived in. It was a depressing image and one that was put there for that very reason, I was sure.

It showed the end of the world and a great eruption where both mankind and mountains fell together into the pit of ultimate despair. It often made me shudder to look at but I had to admit that in times of my own despair I found something unexpected in the sight of such destruction. For there at the bottom, amongst the other doomed souls and as the world crumbled into fiery depths below, one figure sat there and simply cried as she waited for her death.

So I would look at that lone figure whenever I felt lost in a life I didn't feel as though I belonged in and thought…well at least it could be worse.

"You're not looking at that God awful painting again are you?" My twin sister asked as she came to sit on my side of the bed and we both faced the wall that held the one reason for our sins, sins that we seemed to commit without even knowing it. Even though we were twins we were as far away from each other as fire and ice, in both looks and personality.

We both had long blonde hair that we were forced to wear tied back into tight and often painful buns at the base of our necks. We were both pale and we were both short being only five foot three but that's where the similarities ended. Arianna had a pair of cute dimples either side of her lips and when she smiled I often felt that as long as they were showing then everything would be okay.

Her eyes would shine like blazing topazes and gave away her mood no matter how she tried to hide it. They were definitely the windows to her soul and that soul was nothing short of beautiful. Her lips made the perfect cupids bow and she had often been reprimanded for wearing lipstick as they always seemed to have a natural red tint that never went away.

We were both curvy creatures and thankfully looked nothing like our mother who was painfully thin and looked far older than she was. But whereas I was heavier on top, Arianna was heavier in the bottom, with curvy hips that she couldn't help but sway as she walked. I would often have little daydreams about what it would be like when we were freed of this place and could do the simple things we knew the outside world took for granted. Things like shopping for new outfits before going out for an evening and letting our hair down in more ways than one, I thought as I felt the digging pins in my neck holding all my hair into place.

I had gotten dressed shortly after my mother had closed the door on me and the itchy woollen shirt under the hideous sandy coloured burlap dress they made all the woman wear was already making me sweat. I swear it was only forced upon us as another form of torture for us to endure. The summer months had been Hell.

"Do you ever wonder what it's really like down there?" I asked making my sister scoff at the question and scratching at my dress being reminded of what we were both still looking at.

"God, its worse than I thought…you have stable duty again don't you?" I laughed once and then shook my head.

"They're going to make me talk to someone this time." I said looking down at my lap and ignoring the pang of hunger I usually got when being locked in my room.

"You had another dream?" I nodded and closed my eyes against his image as if seeing him in my mind as often as I did actually caused me pain. I didn't understand this addictive behaviour and why I couldn't find the strength to let it go…to let *him* go.

"Ah…I see."

"What am I going to do Ari, this is getting out of control?" I said covering my face with my hands and feeling ashamed, the way we were brainwashed to think. I felt my sister's hand at my back and it took little force to lean into her embrace for the much needed comfort I craved right then.

"We will figure this out Kay and if we don't, then at least we will be out of this shithole soon." I snapped my head up and shot a panicked look to the door.

"Ssshh, you don't want them to catch you saying that." I warned knowing what our punishments were like. She just shrugged her shoulders and said,

"Don't worry Kay Bear, there's no one home…some important meeting at Elders Mount or something, so we are safe." I had to smile at her nickname for me that had stuck ever since my love of Carebears when I was a kid. And for some odd reason whenever I thought back to my childhood toys the image of a green haired girl came to mind. I had to wonder if it wasn't some distant memory my mind was searching for. Maybe some eccentric neighbour or someone from the school we used to go to. Either way I doubted it was someone my mother would have known, not with green hair and a body full of colourful tattoos.

"Yeah for now but what about Rory?" I asked leaving the image of that girl and getting back to our spiteful cousin knowing the last thing we needed was a repeat of what happened only a week ago…the bruises had only just started to fade.

"Yeah well if that bitch wasn't pregnant then she wouldn't have dared, Uncle or not!" I shuddered at the thought of *his* wrath but decided not to remind her of our joint punishments during her rant.

I wished I could have been more like her. Ari didn't seem to be afraid of anything and I felt bad a lot of the time that she spent so much of her energy looking after me. Well okay, so it wasn't like we were kids anymore but sometimes I think she forgot that.

It was as if since that fateful day that drunk driver crashed into us she took on the role my father no longer had the chance to fill. He had died instantly and I would have been next if it hadn't been for my sister, who dragged both me and my mother out of the car. She had saved us both that day but we both knew the mother we shared had also died in that accident. It was the most sinful of thoughts but we both wished it had happened that way so that we could simply mourn the woman we once loved as our mother. Instead the brutal reality was that the love we once had was lost long ago along with the fading memory of our father and hate had quickly replaced it.

It was a sad truth our new lives had been forced to learn the very first day we were brought to the Hexad Colony. If I thought my sister and I had been close before the accident then what happened after was to forever cement that love and devotion for the rest of our lives. If it hadn't been for Ari then I really don't think I would have survived being forced to live here and no doubt Ari felt the same. To the Elders our 'wilful ways' as they called it, had to be beaten out of us for good and they had been trying to do just that for the last seventeen years.

"Hey, come on Kay, it won't be long now." Ari reminded me that we only had a month until we finally got our time to leave like the others had. It was shortly to be our joint birthday in just over a months' time and everyone who reached their twenty fifth birthday got the option to leave the Hexad Colony. I don't think Ari and myself even spoke once about which choice we would make, no it was more of a case of counting down the days.

The day we lost our father was the day we entered our own personal Hell. I looked up at the only painting I was allowed on my walls because its sole purpose was to show me what would happen to my soul if I disobeyed the Elders' teachings. My sister had a similar painting in her room by the same artist and its title was just as depressing as mine being 'The Destruction of Sodom and Gomorrah'.

"I don't think he was a happy man, do you?" Ari asked nodding at the painting and I had to laugh as she referred to the artist.

"Maybe he lived here for a spell." I said this time making her laugh.

"It's a possibility." She replied nudging me and that was it. That was all it took to drag me from my distracted mind and back to the reality we needed to focus on.

"I don't see why you get to dream of the kind one." I

muttered pretending to be sulky. When Ari didn't fire back with a witty reply I turned to look at her and was surprised to find her blushing. For the last eight months we had both been plagued with dreams of another life and let's just say that the man in Ari's dreams was a lot less frightening than the one in mine... or so the way Ari told it. But that wasn't the only difference between our dreams. Ari experienced her dreams as herself, which I can imagine added to the deep blush that had crept its way across her usually milky cheeks.

The man she dreamt of she only ever described as kind and loving towards her which was why we called him 'The Angel'. But as for me, well that was a different matter entirely. My dreams were always as some useless bystander who was left to watch helplessly as another version of myself remained captive in some dark and handsome man's bedroom. I had often woke silently screaming and panting to catch my breath as the sight of her destitute cries got too much for me to bear.

I didn't know why this was happening to us but for me at least it always felt like my other self was trying to tell me something. Maybe she was trying to let me know how I could save her from the dark man. It was strange the pull he had over her and the pull he had over me for that matter. It was as if whenever he was out of the room she would try everything to try and reach me. She would cry, she would scream, one time she even threw a chair to get my attention but there was never any sound in my dreams.

Then he would enter and it was as if she did everything in her power to try and hide the fact I was watching. He never saw me and given the power it was obvious he had in abundance I was more than glad of it...or was I? Oh, who was I kidding, I had often wondered what it would feel like to have him look at me at least once the way he looked at her.

I had once dreamt that after only minutes of entering the

room he found my other self in nothing but a small towel after showering. One look was all it had taken before he ripped the towel away from her, bent her neck and bit into it as though his ravenous thirst for blood had been too much to wait. Her knees buckled and I let out a silent gasp just before he caught her then carried her to the bed all the time still with his fangs firmly embedded in her neck before he firmly embedded something else of his inside her.

I wasn't naive to what happened between a man and woman in love inside the bedroom. But having not experienced it myself did mean that when these certain dreams occurred I was left with a torrent of mixed emotions. Confused, flustered, embarrassed, torn but most of all, unbelievably aroused.

I was ashamed to admit that seeing what I was forced to often left me feeling disgusted with myself. The fact that I managed to get turned on by watching him take her the way he did. But even more disturbing was how much my captive self seemed to not only enjoy it but crave it. It was all so confusing but most of all frightening to witness. There was no denying how much he scared me but my reactions to him added to that fear tenfold. He seemed to possess the power over the mind and that was one of the most frightening possibilities of all and one of the reasons we had named him…

'The Demon'.

"You had another dream as well…didn't you?" I guessed when I saw her twisting the same dress I wore around in her hands. It was a nervous habit of hers and one that didn't happen very often. Mainly when I asked questions like this one. My own nervous habit on the other hand was tucking my hair behind my ear or playing with the ends, one that definitely happened often seeing as I was far shyer than my twin.

"Yes but I don't want to talk about it this time." She said, which was unlike her.

"But…"

"Do you want to tell me about yours?" Well she certainly had me there.

"There you go." I frowned at her smug face at guessing that I wouldn't.

"Don't worry, we will sort this out."

"How?" I asked as I had long ago given up on these dreams ever fading into distant memories.

"I have a plan." She replied waggling her eyebrows at me and I groaned out loud. I was just about to ask what I knew would most definitely mean trouble, when we heard voices outside my window. We both signalled to each other at the same time, smiling as we usually did whenever we did something at the same time, like twins often did.

"Trust me." She whispered as she got off the bed and walked softly to the door. I gave her a nod knowing that there was only one person on this planet I trusted and it was her.

"One month honey and then we will be free." Ari reminded me and then held up the ring of keys giving them a little shake. I knew she had swiped them off the hook in the kitchen and I rolled my eyes at her humour, making her wink.

She left me, quickly relocking my door and I held my breath as I usually did until I knew she had replaced them back in time. The clue in this was that I didn't hear my mother's high pitched shock of horror that her daughter could do something so insolent.

I heard Ari's feet on the staircase before I heard the front door open and I closed my eyes against the feeling of loathing I felt every time I heard my mother's voice from behind a locked door.

I knew it wasn't right…that *she* wasn't right. I remembered what my life was like before this horrible place and when you have lived a taste of the good, wholesome and normal, well let's just say that it then shines a brighter light on all the wrong you're forced to live with. All the wrong you're forced to be a part of. I never feared Hell for all the reasons the elders taught us to fear it… no, I fear Hell for all the things they taught us to do and we were foolish to believe in. I fear the Hell I was living in right now and Arianna was right…

One more month of Hell and we were free.

CHAPTER 2
MADNESS SEEPED THROUGH

"I'm trying to help you...*I want to help you.*" I said tapping the glass I always saw her through, only now that glass was slightly cracked around the edges. Did this mean something? We had both tried to break the glass on various occasions, thinking it just as simple as then being able to walk through into each other's world but it had never worked. So what had changed I didn't know but looking at her now she seemed even more broken than before.

It was another one of those times she simply sat on the bed and stared out into the night with tears streaming down her pale cheeks. She looked so sad I almost preferred it when she was angry just so that I too didn't have the same reasons to cry as I did now. It looked as if someone had just taken her world away and I frowned knowing who. I swiped away my tears feeling angry at the same injustice that was forced upon us both.

He had no right just to take her against her will and keep her locked in that room until he was ready for her body again. Could he not see what he was doing to her? I wished we had found some way of communicating but in all this time not one word had been spoken between us.

Oh, we had tried in the beginning but nothing had worked. She had written things down on paper from the Demon's desk but no words had shown. We had both tried to over pronounce our words so that we might lip read them but her mouth would blur and it didn't take a genius to guess mine did the same.

I had given up telling her that I would try and save her. Sometimes I spoke about the Colony and how long we had left until I could search for her. I had nothing to back up the ways I would accomplish this other than my blind faith and determination. Not because this girl looked exactly like me, even in ways not even my own twin did but because I had been living her nightmare right alongside her for so long now, that I couldn't actually remember a time before I dreamt of her.

The stranger thing still was when I spoke to Ari about this she said the same thing about her Angel. She had no idea what he was called and like the man in my dreams, I too had no clue as to what his name was either. But there were some things I could be certain about and that was he definitely wasn't human.

Ari didn't speak much about her dreams and for the first time in our life my twin and I were keeping secrets from each other. The funny part was that I knew we did this for the same reasons…the same *sexual reasons.* The only difference I guess was that the man in my dreams did things to the other version of me, whereas Ari's Angel did his things to her personally.

The sight of the door opening dragged my eyes back to the room and I felt my heart kick into a new beat at the first sight of him. It was the same as always. The very second I laid eyes on him I was gone. My mind would only focus on the most handsome monster I had ever seen. Carnal thoughts would flood my sensibility, rendering it as useless as if my hands were banging on the glass.

He wore a dark suit this time and I actually swooned against the frame of my private window pane. I never took my eyes off him whenever he entered the room and I wasn't the only one that he would overpower with his intimidating presence.

My other self would watch him the same way I would, which was as though every time could be the last. Secretly the thought actually caused me pain and I never understood why. I was both terrified and infatuated with him. In fact if the other girl in his life didn't look like my exact double then the agony of seeing him with another woman every night would have driven me even more insane than I most likely already was.

I saw him speak and could tell instantly he wasn't happy about something. His tensed square shoulders said as much even without seeing that formidable frown on his face. He removed his suit jacket and casually threw it over one of the chairs in the room like it no longer mattered. I spared a glance at the figure of me to see her swipe at her tears before turning to face him. She never cowered away from him and I had to admire her spirit. If that had been me I would lower my head and only move when he ordered me to.

I narrowed my eyes and saw a little tick in his cheek that I had grown to recognise as him being slightly amused. She must have said something that made him have to fight the urge to smile. Those were my favourite times when looking at him. There was nothing more beautiful in this hidden world than *that* smile. If I hadn't seen what he had done to her in the past, the brutal and raw ways he had taken her body, then I could have believed he too was *my* Angel.

But the creature he transformed into when angry or lustful couldn't be ignored. It was beauty captured by the beast alright and I too was right there in that locked cell of my own mind to witness it all. Because when I turned away from the church window and looked around the dark room all I saw was an iron chamber with a door that led straight back to *my* Inferno. One that would only open when my time here was done and it would force me through the gates of what I loathed to call home.

The secret part of me wished I could just step into their world, free the girl and take her place. At least then I would discover what it felt like to be touched that way by a man, no matter how terrifying the thought was. Sometimes I would see the way he looked at her and there I would witness the proof of his love and devotion, one buried there so deep I knew nothing could uproot it. But then why did he keep her locked there?

I had never seen her anywhere but this room and every single time she had been trying to tell me something. She would even try and get to me when he wasn't around, so what else could it mean other than her trying to escape and needing my help to do so?

I had replayed so many dreams over and over in my mind and the only conclusion was that he was obsessed with her and used his powers over her. That was the only way to make sense of why she would willingly go to him and make love to such a man who upset her so much. I mean good Lord, she let him feed from her for Christ sake! And speaking of which he was just loosening his black tie from his crisp white shirt when he started to approach the bed.

He ran a single finger across her bare shoulder where her loose t shirt had slipped to one side. I shuddered for her, almost feeling the same touch for myself. This often happened and was shamefully how I nearly experienced my first orgasm.

I remembered it like one would with an early childhood memory. It was weird the way it felt like the first one I ever truly believed in, as if all the rest had been the dream and this one was the only one that had really happened. It was like a switch had been flipped eight months ago and the hate I and Ari

22

both had for the Colony had multiplied to new levels, until leaving was all we could think about.

I remembered waking up and crying out at just the exact moment my other self did in the dream as we neared our release together. But for me it never came and it only left me feeling empty and cold.

She looked up at him and I saw him shaking his head softly at her as he wiped away a stray tear. It looked so caring that you could almost believe they were just two people in love and I was the intruder. But then she ripped her face from his and stood up to walk away from him in anger. He let his hand fall and turn into a fist, one that thankfully I had never seen him unleash on her yet. She came to stand opposite me with only this thin pane of glass between us but it could have been a vaulted door for the strength it held.

We both raised our hands together and placed them over each other. I looked up into her eyes and saw my own staring back at me. Our tears fell in sync and we both lowered our heads at the same time as the pain became too much to bear. Then one word escaped my lips that I had no control over…

"I'm sorry."

"What did you say?!" My head snapped up the moment I heard my own voice but knew it hadn't come from me. My other self was staring at me like she couldn't believe what was happening. Had she just heard me? Had I just heard her?

"You…you can hear me?" I asked tentatively and her mouth dropped open.

"Yes! Yes I can!" She shouted and I saw the man shift across the room at an impossible speed. I took a tentative step back in fear of him being this close. She saw my reaction to him and shouted,

"No! Don't go!" I stopped in my tracks as she ordered. Then

I saw his lips moving but couldn't hear him and she turned her head to speak back to him,

"Why can't you hear her and I can?" She asked him and he nodded towards the cracks that had appeared around the edges of the glass. In our last dream before this the whole of the glass had shattered just as it finished. Did this mean something was coming? Did this mean we were meant to break the glass completely in order to speak to one another?

"I need your help Keira! Please…free me…free…LOOK OUT, BEHIND YOU!"

"AHHH!" I screamed as hands suddenly grabbed me from behind and painfully dragged me backwards through the door that was my life.

"NOOO!" I shouted kicking out and wrestling with the hands that held me down.

"Wake up you stupid child!" My mother's voice pierced through me and my last and fading vision I took with me was my other self trying in vain to break free from the arms that held her from behind. Arms that stopped her from breaking free and trying to get to me. As the door slammed shut on that image I thought I heard the sound of a small amount of glass cracking even more and could only pray to the Gods I would find it to be true.

"Mother?" I said after being shaken awake.

"Get up! You will be late for your chores if you do not hurry." I closed my eyes against the wave of emotions that dream had flooded me with and I let my head fall back against my pillow.

"Did you not hear me?!" My mother yelled and for just a few more precious seconds I blocked it all out.

"I did, but I don't think they did in Kentucky…was that what you were aiming for?" I said and then gasped right along with my mother. I couldn't believe I had said that and I covered my mouth as if it would help.

"What did you just say to me?" She hissed and I knew I was in big trouble now. Okay so I could either say sorry and grovel or just roll with it and accept my punishment with dignity. I took a deep breath and in my mind said, oh bugger it!

"I am sick of you speaking to me like I am a child and just walking in here thinking you own me!" I said whipping the covers back and getting up to face her. The shock on her face was almost laughable and I might have done so if my heart hadn't been racing.

"You little Bitch!" She screamed and then before I could dodge her she was at me. She lashed out at my head and clocked me right on the side with her fist. The blow knocked my head to one side and before I could recover from the ringing she had grabbed my ear, like so many other times before. She used it to get me to walk with her and I squealed in pain.

"Well upon my word, you have gone and done it this time Missy!" My crazed mother shouted walking me to the basement.

"NO! Not down there! Anything else! Not down there!" I screamed in vain and twisted only to find another blow to my face. I slumped to the ground and gave my mother the time to find the right key. I tried to crawl away from her not caring about the pain but only about the horror that awaited me down there.

"The Elders will hear about this Katie." She said before she kicked me in the abdomen, putting too much pressure on my solar plexus for me to be able to breathe properly. My diaphragm was still working through its painful spasm when she dragged me up and pushed me down the stairs. I felt each bang down and only managed to stop myself from rolling further when I was already half way down. I was lucky I didn't feel anything break other than receiving a nasty bump to the head that I could feel bleeding from my temple.

"You will pay for this...one day soon... You. Will. Pay!" I spat out the threat back up at her from the staircase now smeared with my blood. The shock was written across her face and as plain to see like our lying Bible. Suddenly the thought of hitting her with it came to mind and I couldn't help it when I started laughing like I had lost my mind. I don't know what had gotten into me but it was like I had brought some of my dream self back with me.

She frowned down at me like she knew the reasons for this outburst but instead of saying more she simply crossed herself like this was what she was programmed to do, not what she wanted to do. Was it all a religious act with my mother? Why had I never noticed this before? But more importantly...

Why had I never thought to ask myself this before?

She slammed the door and left me in the darkness, with only a current of strange thoughts to keep me company. I winced as I lifted my bruised body from the staircase and felt around in the dark so I could find my footing when I stood. There was no banister and the last and only time I had been punished down here, I had fallen off the edge and cracked a rib on my way down. Well at least that hadn't happened this time, although my head certainly pounded enough to remind me of what pain felt like.

I don't know what it was about being locked in a basement but I was terrified of it. And the sickest thing about this punishment was they knew it. I was the only one I had heard about that received such a punishment and as far as I knew it hadn't even been used as a threat to the others. I had no idea how they knew I had been as terrified as I was considering I had never said a word. Not even to Ari, so how did they know it was my ultimate fear?

It wasn't as if anything had happened to me in the past for me to be so scared but even now it was hard to get past the fear long enough to make my body work. The last time I had spent my time sat on the top step with my hand on the door. I remember when they finally opened the door seeing the light for the first time in two days. The first thing I saw was the bloody smears on the wood and when I looked down at my hand I saw my red raw bleeding knuckles where I had tried to punch my way out. Needless to say the wood won the fight.

That day they had broken me and I vowed I would never do anything that would land me back in this nightmare. Well little good that did me I thought with a groan.

I closed my eyes and focused on the pain in both my stomach and my head so I wouldn't panic. The last time I had hyperventilated until I passed out, only to wake to the sound of Ari's voice bringing me back. I remembered her outrage and arguing with our mother on the other side of the door but it was all in vain as she had received ten lashes for the offence. So she had found another way to help me through and that's where I needed to get to now.

There was a window down there, I remembered that much.

"Come on Kay, pull your shit together." I said out loud, which actually helped calm my shattered nerves. Getting up took longer than it should have but with the added fear of falling off the edge I finally started to make progress. It was only when my foot touched the ground and came off the last step that I allowed myself a sigh of relief. I don't know why or what had changed since last time but it felt like I had been through so much worse than this that it gave me a strength I didn't understand.

The window was covered with an aged piece of cloth that allowed in the tiniest amount of light through the threadbare holes. It was enough to feel my way there and after tripping only once, I finally reached it. I yanked the material from the dirty glass, ripping it from the rusty nails and felt better as soon as the looming darkness was taken away. The light danced on the particles of dust that floated in the air and I reached up on tip toes to see through the window. It was too high for me to see much so I looked around for something to stand on, which was when I saw it.

"What on earth is this?" I muttered when coming across what looked like a primitive prison cell without the bars. There was an inflated bed which was covered in a thick layer of dust that had obvious not seen a warm body in a while. An empty child's plate and a plastic spoon were left on top of it with an old spider's web waving at me in the air like a draft was coming from somewhere.

It was an eerie scene alright but one made even creepier by the broken music box that lay on its side. I swallowed hard and let my dangerous curiosity pull me closer to the broken shards that lay scattered around the tiny ballerina, one that had stopped dancing long ago. As I stepped closer I felt my hands start to shake as something was sickeningly wrong about all of this.

I stood over the box and looked down without moving as I tried to make sense of it all and the nauseating feeling looking at the broken glass brought me. Part of me didn't want to move or was too scared to do so, but it was as if I needed to know what was going on and something in this scene would show me. So I bent on one knee, feeling as though I was disturbing history by touching the box.

I noticed the ballerina's arms were broken off and as soon as I set it back down the broken sound of the Nutcracker's Sugarplum Fairy started to play. That tiny tinkling sound hit me like a bulldozer and all I could smell was blood. That stomach-turning scent of copper wafted up my nose as if the room was flooding with it.

I looked around but saw nothing that would produce that smell but then I remembered my head and touched the sticky patch that must have explained it. I shook my head as if this would help me wash away the feeling that I had seen this all before but that was impossible. The last time I was forced down here I had stayed in the darkness and saw nothing of the room. I only knew there was a window because Ari had spoken to me through it, trying to coax me towards it. Needless to say my fear had won that day.

A bright light flashed on the floor and I looked down to see that the biggest piece of the broken mirror had caught the light from the window. I frowned down at it and was about to turn my attention back to the window when something stopped me. It was as though I had no mind over my actions as I bent and grabbed it. I held it up to look at myself and instantly screamed.

"NOOO!" I shouted at the image of my other self looking back at me but it wasn't seeing her that made me react this way. No, it was the shadowed figure reflecting back at me, one that stood at the top of the staircase with nothing but the light behind him framing the horror.

I looked back at the fear and tears in the girl's eyes… *my eyes*. It was then that I knew this was her nightmare I was witnessing and just when I thought I couldn't take much more I noticed the blood. At first a single droplet emerged on the glass and trickled across the reflection of our eyes. But soon I had no other choice but to view our faces through a red veil of crimson. I screamed again and threw the mirror shard down, letting it smash in the corner of the room.

I jumped and looked down at my shaking hands only to see our joint nightmare wasn't over. My hands were covered in blood and as I lifted my hands up, I noticed the deep slashes cut into the flesh on my forearms.

I could hear my screaming and feel my head violently

shaking back and forth, but the other side of me could hear nothing this world had to offer and my body was frozen in time. I just looked down at the horror of my mutilated arms and I knew.

I knew what she had done to try and get away from the Demon.

I knew what she had done to us…

She had tried to kill us.

CHAPTER 3
CAN YOUR DREAMS KILL YOU?

"*K*ay…*Kay?*" As soon as I heard my sister's voice the vision of blood disappeared. It was just like someone up there had snapped their fingers or flipped a switch ending the gruesome sight.

"Kay, come on!" My sister hissed in panic. Hearing this was enough to get me moving. I looked around getting back to my original plan and trying to find something to stand on. I almost wept with joy when I saw a step ladder. I grabbed it and rushed to window knowing that Ari could get into trouble if she was seen. I pushed it up against the wall and after taking that first big step to avoid the broken slat, I was there. I pushed the window and muttered a 'thank you God' when it opened with only a little elbow grease.

"Ari!" I said to her feet that were level with my head.

"Come on, I'm getting you out of here." I smiled at her determination and said the only thing that needed to be said.

"Oh, Hell yes." I then put both my arms through the small space and dragged my body the rest of the way gripping onto the grass. Ari helped me up and after giving me the once over she gritted her teeth against the anger she no doubt felt at seeing what our mother had done to me.

"Let's go." I nodded and after making sure the coast was clear we ran for the barn. The Colony was a pretty remote place, one that was flat, full of fields and therefore easy to spot runaways. However if you could make it past the vast open space then you could easily get lost in the surrounding woodland that framed the Colony.

I was about to ask about being caught when one look at my twin and I knew I just needed to trust her. So when she took my hand in hers I just let my worries go and let my feet carry me away. We ran towards one of the older barns, that these days held nothing but old rusty farm equipment and surplus hay. I wanted to ask why no one was around but thought it best not to stop mid getaway for a chat.

Thankfully the doors weren't locked and were only held together with a heavy chain wrapped around the handles. We crept inside making sure not to let the large doors give us away as it creaked on its aging hinges. Once we were inside we both leant our backs to the door and took a moment to catch our breaths.

"I hate to be the killjoy in this great escape but what now?" I asked after leaning forward to make it easier to breathe.

"I overheard our Bitch of a mother telling Uncle that you would be locked down there until tomorrow night. As soon as I heard that's what she had planned I knew I couldn't let it happen again." I gave my sister a sad smile before concern outweighed my relief.

"But you could have been caught!"

"Nah, I let the horses out of their stables, so that should keep them busy...now stop worrying and come on, I have a surprise for you." I stopped myself before bombarding her with loads of questions and number one on that list was 'what if they knew it was her'.

I followed her through to the back of the barn until we came to a rickety looking ladder that led to a mezzanine level. I ignored the next question I wanted to ask and just went on up. Once I reached the top I saw that this was obviously where they stored most of the hay. I looked back at Ari but she just nodded to a small triangle window that was the only source of light. I climbed my way over the bales to see someone had made what looked like a straw fort.

"Did you do this?" I asked in awe.

"Okay, so it's no New York penthouse but welcome to your new home...for two days at least." I looked around the hidden space finding blankets, pillows and best of all, a basket of food. She had even placed a small pile of books next to the make shift bed with a small flashlight resting on the top. I wanted to cry out my thanks and weep at the feet of the only person who loved me in this world. I said it once and thought it a million times before but I just knew I would never have survived without my twin.

In the end I didn't cry and crumble to her feet. No, I simply stepped into her body, put my arms around her and then whispered in her ear,

"I love you."

"I know you do, Kay Bear."

"How did you have time to do all this?" I asked in awe. She looked back at me and the confusion was clear to see.

"How long do you think you have been down there?" Now it was my turn to frown at her question.

"I don't know, ten, fifteen minutes tops...Ari? What is it?"

"Kay, you were down there for hours."

～

Shortly after that Ari left so she could sneak back into the house and act like she had no clue what had happened. I spent that time eating the leftovers from last night's meatloaf dinner with a piece of stale bread that would go unnoticed for that very reason. I also spent the time wondering how on earth I had lost so much time down there.

I was trying to get my head sorted out and figure out what these dreams and visions actually meant. Had the figure at the top of the stairs been a vision of my Demon? Had that hellhole been where he had kept her?

I turned my head to one side and frowned at my own thoughts. It seemed the most logical explanation but if that was the case then why did that idea not sit well with me? Actually the thought made me sick to my stomach and not just because I found it hard to believe anyone could do that to someone they loved. Now this was one thought that made me laugh out loud considering the things my own mother *did to me.* But it was something else within me that felt so wrong just thinking that it could have been *him.* Or was that just all part of his mind control?

"Hey, I'm back."

"Jesus!" I shouted, jumping a mile when Ari popped her head over the top of the ladder.

"That's a sin you know." She said but as soon as the words were out I no longer heard them being spoken just now by my sister.

"What did you say?" I asked on a freaked out whisper. I saw her lips start to move but then softly the world around her started to change.

"That's a sin you know." A different voice overrode my sister's, replaced suddenly by a man's deep and sensual voice. It spoke to me and my hand went to my chest feeling it thump erratically under my palm. I felt my lips start to move and I frowned at the voice I heard playing back at me, one that was full of confidence and feisty playfulness.

"This is never going to work if you keep creeping up on me and nearly scaring me to death!"

"Kay...Are you alright?" I heard my sister's voice as if it was being spoken at the end of a tunnel.

"I...I..." I shook my head and closed my eyes at the painful pressure building at my temple.

"And what do I get in return?" The man's voice asked again and this time sounding just as playful as mine had. My eyes snapped open despite the pain and I gasped without making a sound. My mind tried to force my body to do as it was told and that was to turn around and run. But none of that happened. Not now...it was too late for running because there he was.

Stood right in front of me.

I looked down and let the shorter parts of my hair fall forward only to see my hand outstretched as if trying to take something from him. He had something in his hand and was keeping it from me, holding it behind his back. He playfully looked down at me given the vast difference in height and I felt myself bite my bottom lip, something I had never done before. He raised one eyebrow and smirked when seeing the evidence of what his presence obviously provoked from within me.

"And here was me thinking that you were the type to just take whatever you wanted...oh well." I said shocking myself enough that my instincts would have had my hands flying to my mouth in regret. But that never happened. Instead I turned my back to him only to find his speed was nothing short of superhuman.

He was stood back in front of me by the time I turned and grinning at me like he...well, like he wanted to take a bite out of me! He held out what looked like a small phone and my hand reached out to take it with no choice on my part.

I knew it was a mistake, I was screaming that mistake out at myself but it was all in vain. He grabbed my body, pulling it forward so I had no choice but to go to him. Then he spun me around so he was at my back and I felt my neck being arched to one side. Oh God, he was going to bite me! He was going to feed from me and then there would be no going back.

I would be his forever.

I looked up as my head was forced into the position he wanted me in and the sight I saw was like someone dumping me into an icy river. A large mirror stood in front of us, one that was framed in the exact replica of our church's main window. I couldn't understand what I was seeing but more so the sight of me as my other self, the miserable part of me in the broken window that was no longer looking so desolate. No, she was long gone and in her place was a girl that only needed one word to describe her…

She was *free.*

The blissful look on her face said there was nowhere in her world that she would rather be than in his arms. It wasn't the frightened face of my world. It wasn't the suppressed girl's hands that gripped onto his arm, holding him to her. It wasn't the confining coarse dress covering a body quivering at his touch. It was her, not me and for once I hated it!

"I want it to be me." I said and just for a few seconds her image flickered to mine. As soon as this happened I realised my mistake as it wasn't me that he wanted…

It was her.

His arm tightened painfully around my torso and anger overtook his once lustful face. His eyes found my frightened ones staring back at him in the mirror and they ignited into a deep purple fire that blazed at the sight of which girl he held captive in front of him.

"It can never be you!" He hissed through gritted teeth and

36

then it happened. Time seemed to speed up and in a blur of movement I only had enough time to see my doomed fate in the form of dangerous fangs flashing white before I felt them bury themselves into my jugular…

My Demon wanted to kill me.

"Katie!" I heard the name but for the first time it no longer felt like my own.

"What happened? Are you okay?" My sister asked as I felt myself collapse to the straw bed in what felt more like defeat than exhaustion.

"Katie?"

"I don't know." I answered honestly wondering if I would ever be okay again. That lasting image of the Demon I was becoming obsessed with, trying to destroy me was one that I knew would haunt me for the rest of my days. It was almost as if he blamed me for something…*or someone?*

"What happened just then, you started to go all weird, like you were hallucinating or something?" Ari asked handing me a cup of water she had just poured from a flask. I took great gulps of my water before answering her as it suddenly felt like I hadn't drank anything for days.

"I don't know, it's never happened to me before…well before today that is. Something you said must have triggered a vision, like being in that basement did." Ari frowned at me, folding her arms.

"Okay, start talking Kay." She demanded sitting down on an opposite hay bale. I didn't think talking about it was a good idea but I found that once I started that I just couldn't stop. I told her everything starting backwards with the vision I just had.

"She spoke to me Ari."

"She spoke to you? But I thought you said…"

"Yes I know but something must have happened.

Something… *broke through…"* I said this last part leaning forward and in a whisper as though the reasons just hit me.

"…The window." I added before she had chance to ask me what.

"The one you see your dreams through?"

"Yes and the very same one that's in our church…could it really all be inside my head? Could my mind really be making all this up because I will tell you Ari, it really doesn't feel that way."

"I know. It doesn't for me either. I was thinking about this earlier and I have a theory." I took the last few sips left of my water and said,

"Well thank God one of us does," over my metal cup.

"What if there is something more going on around here, you know apart from all that prophecy, Chosen One crap?" I closed my eyes again as if hearing all the Colony's crazy wacked up shit caused me actual physical pain.

The Six 'Fathers' or 'Elders' as they were also called, were like the leaders of the Colony and each had their own family household surrounding one communal farm. Mostly the Colony remained self-sufficient, growing its own food and our energy coming from solar panels and wind generators.

However there was a blacked out van that would turn up once a week with what we gathered to be more supplies. We never saw what was being unloaded as we knew that as soon as the van was seen on the boundaries of our land we had to disappear inside our rooms. Only the elders knew what came and went in the unmarked van and no one questioned the Elders…*ever.*

"Well needless to say that neither of us believes a word they preach and all this rubbish about Rory being the 'Chosen One' and carrying the prophecy inside her is just another way to control us." I said knowing that nothing about this place was even on the radar of being normal.

Our cousin Rory was a grade A bitch and there was no other way of putting it. But the Elders believed that she had been chosen when she woke up one day pregnant. Our Uncle, Rory's father and leader of the Hexad Order just deemed it so one day and that was that, we had a new Queen Bee in Crazyville. No one knew how she got pregnant in the first place but rumours were born, even in a place as strict as this. Some of us believed it was one of the Elders themselves who had knocked her up but of course none of us ever dared speak our minds.

"Yeah, but it's not just that. Don't you think it's weird that one girl has been allowed to leave every month for the last eight?" Ari asked and to be honest I hadn't even thought about it until now. All the 'Fathers' had extended families with not only children of their own but some were even grandfathers.

"I guess." I said wondering what she was getting at.

"Don't you think in a Colony this small the chances of having ten girls all becoming twenty five in the same year is… well, *very* unlikely." Well putting it like that then yeah, the chances of that happening were…

"And to add to those impossible odds is the fact that each birthday has landed on a full moon, as in, the exact day!" Ari carried on and like she said it added even more proof to those impossible odds.

"Why hadn't we thought about it before?" I asked now thinking how obvious it had all been to see.

"I think it has something to do with our dreams. The last dream I had my Angel was trying to tell me something and the dream ended with him pointing to the full moon outside his window." Even though there was nothing sexual in what she was saying I knew there had been a heck of a lot more to this dream, well that was if her crimson blush was anything to go by.

"It was after that when I started to think about why this place is even here or why we are even having these dreams? And now both of us in the same night managed to break through and in one way or another, we communicated with them…it has to mean something, it just has to." I could see now how much this was affecting my twin and I don't think I realised up until then just how much her feelings mirrored my own. We both knew there was something more to these visions and each new day just seemed to lay more evidence to that conclusion at our feet.

"I agree." I said comforting her and placing my hand over hers that she rested on her knee. I knew my twin, better than I knew myself sometimes and I could see in her beautiful blue eyes how much of a toll this was taking on her. Ari was strong, much stronger than I but these dreams seemed to be grinding her down, almost making her desperate…or was it because our joint time was nearing for when we could leave.

"It's Bethany's time to leave next isn't it?" I asked making sure I had it right, as losing time in this place was easily done.

"Yeah, tomorrow night is her leaving ceremony…why?"

"Because now we suspect something isn't right, it would be a good opportunity to keep a look out for anything …don't you think?" Ari's smile told me she completely agreed.

"Well that is if I am let out from house arrest by then or you might be flying this detective mission solo."

"No way, mother wouldn't dare keep you from a ceremony, not when the Elders teachings are all about strength in numbers when it comes to worshipping the Gods." This I guessed was true, so all I needed to do was make sure I was back in that hole before nightfall tomorrow. As if reading my thoughts Ari said,

"Don't worry about it, everyone will be too busy on the

other side of the house to see you sneak back in. You know what it's like when someone leaves, 'elbows deep in dough and pie making for us little woman' and 'fields need a' ploughing for God's righteous men'." I had to laugh at the different voices she put on for each example. The squeaky woman's voice sounded very similar to Bethany, the girl who was lucky enough to leave tomorrow night and the man's was overly deep, the way our pompous uncle always spoke in his sermons.

"Right, I'd better be getting back before mother thinks you need a cellar buddy and tries to stuff me down there as well." I rolled my eyes thinking with that woman there was a first for everything and I would put nothing past her as long as it was cruel and unloving.

I stood up with my sister and grabbed her hand just before she was about to leave.

"Thank you Ari."

"What for?" I looked around the small straw shelter that looked more homely than my stark room ever did and said,

"For all this, but most of all for getting me out of that place...the vision I saw down there..." My shiver was enough to describe how traumatic it had been and Ari pulled me in for one last hug.

"One month."

"One month." We both whispered at the same time, repeating it like our very own survival mantra.

"Maybe we should have T-shirts made for the big day?" Ari laughed at me before pulling back and motioning with her dress.

"What, and lose these lovely stylish and oh so comfortable dresses...are you mad?" She mocked making me laugh.

"Good point."

"I think we hold off the T-shirt ordering until it can say, 'Freedom Forever'."

"I like it and a lot catchier than 'One Month'." I agreed, thankful at least we could joke about our dire situation. Because facing facts, if we weren't laughing, we were crying and I think our tears had dried up long ago for the both of us.

I watched my sister leave and could only hope she wasn't caught. It seemed these were my main worries these days...oh who was I kidding, these were my worries everyday living in this God forsaken place. I had lost faith in what we were taught a long time ago as I could never believe this was the kind of life anyone would want for their family, let along the Gods that supposedly made us.

Of course a lot of the others here would never have shared our view and believed in whatever they were told without question. They were told that we were chosen for a higher meaning. That the six Gods of the Hexad were to be worshipped at all times and in turn they would grant us favour when it was our time to be welcomed into heaven. None of this had ever sat well with me and Ari but we learned very quickly to keep our mouths shut when it came to our opinions.

It wasn't that we weren't religious but it was as if somewhere deep down we *knew* the truth. Almost as though we had been told or even shown the proof. I didn't know if this was because we had both been seven years old by the time we came here and this meant we had all the memories of a life before this.

We remembered what it was like to watch TV and eat sweets. We remembered what it was like to play games and find comfort in our favourite toys. To have family BBQ's with delicious home cooked food and be surrounded by friendly neighbours.

So when we were forced into this life, it had just meant feeling like you had been ripped away from your old one. One that had been good and pure and something to rely on. Because you never missed the little things until they were taken from you. The resentment you feel towards those who refuse to give you back that life is insurmountable. And with every passing year it grows filling you with a kind of hatred you never knew you could possess.

Which only meant one thing...

Giving you the power to survive.

CHAPTER 4
AN ICY FEAR

Two days of solitary time had been just what the doctor had ordered and as long as I wasn't imprisoned down in that dungeon then this had felt more like a holiday than a punishment. Of course, my mother didn't know that and would no doubt expect to find what she had the last time she dished out this sentence. Well the last laugh would be on her if she thought to find me that way ever again. This time my dignity wouldn't allow it.

I smiled at the thought of the disappointment I would see written across her face when she opened that door to see me unaffected by the experience. Thanks to Ari I had been well fed and had a comfortable and peaceful night's sleep.

In fact I went to sleep that night looking at the moon shining bright through the small triangle window that was situated above my make shift bed, thinking about what life out there could offer us. At first I had been too scared to fall asleep in fear of what I might see. I knew I was being a wimp but after yesterday I thought it for a good reason. So when I woke to the glaring sun coming through the same window I was surprised to find I'd slept the night through without a single dream.

Now I only had minutes until I knew it would be time to leave my simple sanctuary when Ari came to get me. It had me wondering if Ari had also had a dreamless sleep and if that in itself wasn't a message of things to come? I felt myself becoming increasingly anxious as the seconds ticked by. I didn't know how I knew it but tonight would be different, I could just feel it.

I had already packed up all the evidence of anyone being here just in case it was found. I buried it under one of the hay bales until we could get rid of it at a later date, as we didn't want to take any chances. Not now we were so close to freedom. In a lot of ways it felt like being in prison and the month leading up to our release date was like being on parole. Although going by that logic, then yesterday's antics weren't going to do me any favours in that department.

I looked outside the window to see it wouldn't be long before it would be getting dark and the leaving ritual would begin.

"Come on Ari, where are you?" I asked out loud.

"Alright Steve McQueen, keep your hair on." Ari said scaring me when she seemed to come out of nowhere. One of my dad's favourite movies was the Great Escape from the 1960's, so I knew why she called me this. I remembered it being on in the background often as me and Ari played with our Barbie dolls on the living room floor.

That had been when we were a real family. Back when our mother had been loving and kind, reading us stories before bed and letting us lick the spoon when baking. When we would go on family holidays and enjoy days out together. But after my father died, it was as though my mother had become a different person. She simply piled us both into a car the second my father was cold in the ground and drove across the country to her brother's Colony, here in Lancaster County, Pennsylvania.

"I was worried." I admitted.

"You know that causes wrinkles, right?" I rolled my eyes as she laughed.

"Come on, we'd better get you back. Mother's busy ordering people around as usual."

"And Uncle?" I asked hoping he too was out of the way.

"I haven't seen him since sermons this morning but Thomas said something about a meeting at Father Jacob's Homestead this afternoon." I frowned at this but Ari just shrugged it off as normal.

"Come on, it will be fine."

"I don't know, I guess I just have a weird feeling is all." I said holding myself around the stomach like I could feel the snake of doubt coiling around tighter and tighter down there.

"I do too if I'm honest but either way, we have to get you back." I gave her a small smile, feeling slightly better that Ari felt the same as I did. I guess it was a weird twin thing but if one of us didn't agree with the other, something kind of felt off balance.

"No guts, no glory." Ari said taking my hand and giving it a squeeze. I nodded, squeezed her hand back and repeated what had once been our family's moto thanks to our father being in the army.

"No guts, no glory."

We made our way down the rickety ladder and ran to the barn door at the other end. Ari held up her hand motioning for me to stop before I opened the door.

"What's wrong?" I whispered watching as she placed her palm on the door as if waiting for a signal from somewhere. She frowned once before shock widened her eyes.

"Quick! Get back, get back now!" She warned and we both ran back for the ladder as if our lives depended on it.

"Get up them, go, go!" I didn't need to be told twice, that

was for sure. I grabbed the splintered wood and climbed getting to the top and over the edge just as I heard voices. I turned round to see Ari's head right behind me but when I heard the wood snap her head disappeared.

"Ari!" My desperate call was answered with an umpf sound where she had hit the floor. I ran to the edge and looked over to see her limping out of sight.

"Hide!" Her warning was clear…

They were coming.

I did as I was told only hoping she was both okay and out of sight from those that were now opening the door. I had ducked down behind the bales of hay just hoping they couldn't hear my heart pounding out its fearful beat as I could. However, I still couldn't help but sneak a look as I knew they wouldn't be able to see me from down there, not at this angle.

Two men that I only usually ever saw at feasts had walked in the barn and opened the doors wide before motioning with their hands for something to come through. At first I thought it must have just been for some old farm equipment, like one of the machines that must have broken down during use. They usually remained here until they got round to fixing them or until the right parts were delivered, that I gathered came with that mysterious van that showed up once a week.

However. what the next two men heaved in had me scowling in confusion. It was a giant metal X shape attached to a wooden frame and on one side had two wheels, so it could be tipped and pushed in as it was now. It must have been pretty heavy considering the struggle the four of them all had getting it in.

The only one I really recognized was named John and he took off his cap once it was in place to wipe the sweat from his brow.

"Did the Fathers say what this was to be used for?" He asked one of the others who was stood closest to him.

"It was made clear not to ask but…" The other man took a step closer to John and whispered this next part.

"…I am sure it is needed for tonight." John looked shocked for a moment and looked as if he was going to say more when the man he had been speaking with warned him to say no more with a simple head nod to the others. Their behavior made me wonder if there weren't others in the Colony that had the same questions as I and Ari did.

I never realized it as much until now but seeing these four the way they were had me also wondering how much of the Colony was divided between those that choose this life and those that had been forced into it like we had.

There had been times, especially in the last eight months when people had arrived here and not taken kindly to this way of life. They hadn't lasted long within the Colony but by all accounts given, they had been allowed to leave again as they were within what was called the 'Deciding age'. If they were not then they would remain here under a 'guardian' family in the hope of one day converting their corrupted minds to the ways of our Hexad Gods.

Those of course that were the ripe old age of twenty five and chose to leave were classed as unworthy in the eyes of the Hexad, the Colony's six Fathers and cast back into the unclean world as it was known. They were then known as the Fallen Bloods, the ones unable to be saved and were seen to the Colony's border never to return…the lucky bastards I though bitterly.

However on the rare occasion there were those named the Righteous Bloods that were welcomed to stay as they thought of this place as their salvation. These were quickly elevated in their positions and rose up in the ranks quickly. So it was no wonder that the Colony was divided but the trick was knowing who was who, as speaking against the Colony was classed as a heinous sin. It was one of the reasons Ari and I never spoke to the others in fear that there was a Righteous Blood lurking in the shadows, waiting to catch us.

Some would actually act like the Fallen, just to lure you into a false sense of security before the entrapment was complete. Through this, plans of escape had been prevented countless times and those punished were too traumatized to ever try again, let alone speak of it. No, they simply had to wait their turn and hope the years in this place were both kind and swift.

Thinking on these thoughts had me wondering why it was only the women who had the ceremonies when their time came. Thinking back, I don't ever remember saying goodbye to one of the men when they left or it even being spoken about. People just seemed to 'disappear' from this life. I suppose it helped that we were encouraged not to become too close to people other than immediate family and even then it wasn't expected.

The reasons they gave for this, for people in our age bracket especially, was it wasn't looked upon favorably if you were known as being friends with someone who could choose to become one of the 'Fallen'. You would often be shunned for having bad judgement and this could go on for years.

The Colony was a lonely place to live in at the best of times but being shunned was like living on a deserted island full of natives that hated you being there. It was a depressing existence that was for sure.

And now looking at these four, you could see there was a definite division in the ranks, as for a start, no Righteous Blood would ever question one of the Fathers. It looked like this John and his friend were clearly counting the days until they could become the Fallen, just like we were.

I looked at John again, knowing it was definitely the guy

Ari had pointed out once. He had a red and angry line leading down from the side of his temple to the middle of his cheek, one that was still healing from his fall. The story Ari told me was that John had been found unconscious in the woods that surround the Hexad lands and brought here to be saved. He woke remembering very little other than his name and that he had been out searching for his friends when a storm hit.

Having no shelter and unable to find his way back in the dark he fell, hitting his head and therefore losing his memory. From the way Ari told it, it seemed that our Uncle had taken quite a shine to him, believing he would fit in here nicely. She also told me that she overheard a conversation mother was having with one of the other 'mothers' about how Uncle believed he had been sent here for a higher purpose. She then went on to say how Uncle thought him to be a fine suiter for his daughter, Rory as now the Gods had made her 'The Chosen One' she would be in need of a good husband.

As far as I had just observed, I think my Uncle was counting his chickens before they hatched. The guy looked ready to bolt at the first opportunity and that was from way up here. Saying that though my Uncle was a scary man and one I wouldn't want to have to say no too, especially when it included his precious daughter.

But it wasn't the usual personality traits of a scary man that had you lowering your head when he walked past you. It wasn't like he had a quick temper and roared in your face if you did anything wrong. He didn't scream or shout or even appear angry when he was. That was what you feared the most…

The unpredictability of it all.

There was never a warning to what my Uncle would do. He would remain the same no matter what he was feeling. So it was that eerie calm that you feared the most. That simple silence and controlled look of disdain that left you feeling like deadly, bitter ice was creeping along the ground and making its way slowly up your body. That not knowing of when he would lash out suddenly without warning or even without reason. You would just look up from the floor from where his blow had delivered you and all you would see is him staring down at you smiling. It quickly became a look you loathed but above all, one you tried everything in your power to avoid.

So no, I couldn't help but feel sorry for John and what my Uncle no doubt had in store for him.

Shortly after their conversation came to an abrupt end due to the other Righteous Bloods getting closer, they all left the barn. Ari wasn't stood next to me but I knew we both sighed our relief at the same time. We left it a few more minutes before moving from our hiding places just in case one of them decided to come back for any reason.

I was just happy that we hadn't been caught but one look out the window told me that could very easily change, especially if we didn't get a move on. We had wasted enough time as it was, having to wait for those four to wheel in that monstrosity. What was it even for? But more importantly, were they right, was it for tonight?

"Are you okay up there?" I heard Ari ask just as I was stepping over the hay.

"Yeah but forget about me, are you okay…did you fall?"

"I did but no damage, so we're okay but if we don't hurry that is likely to change." I looked down at the ladder and was glad it wasn't a complete right off otherwise getting down was going to be fun…as in, the variety that wasn't actually fun at all.

Thankfully though I only had a bit of a jump when reaching the bottom and was soon stood next to Ari who was patting the dust from her dress.

"Let's try again should we?"

"Let's." I agreed and we both walked back to the door to try our luck again. Only as it turned out lady luck was obvious on vacation, it was that or she was on the time of the month and therefore wasn't feeling very charitable because the door wouldn't open.

"Oh shit!" Ari said pushing on the door and only hearing a rattle of chains for her efforts.

"Here's let's try together, maybe it's just stiff on the hinges." We both pushed but it was no surprise when we got nowhere.

"They must have locked it behind them this time!" Ari said after banging on the door in anger.

"What are we going to do?" I asked her back as she turned away from the source of our misery.

"I don't know but the one thing I do know and that is we are so dead if we don't get our asses outta here and soon!" Well she was right about that. We both looked around the room as if the answer to our prayers would appear in the form of a flashing exit sign.

"Wait! What about the window?" I said looking up at the triangle that was as least big enough for a body to fit through.

"Do we know what's on the other side?" I shrugged my shoulders knowing there was only one way to find out.

"Alright, you look up there and see if there is a way down on the other side, I will stay down here and check to see if there isn't a hole or something we could break through."

"Okay, but we'd better be quick." I warned with the feeling of dread getting heavier on my shoulders by the mounting seconds I wasn't back in that basement. Ari agreed and we both went our separate ways. I ran for the ladder and after two failed attempts at heaving myself up over the broken slats, I had finally managed to drag myself to the top. I scrambled over the hay and then dragged one of the bales so it was directly under the window for me to climb up on.

"Any luck?" Ari's voice behind me made me jump and I nearly slipped off the hay.

"I'm just about to check, but I guess if you're up here then you didn't find anything useful."

"You guessed right. It might be an old barn but there has to be something said for whoever built it." Like usual I rolled my eyes at Ari's humour before checking out our last hope at getting out of this mess.

"Please, oh please, oh please." I muttered as I stepped up to the window now I was at the right height.

"Yeesss!" I said fist pumping the air like I used to back when I was a kid.

"I will take that as a good sign." Ari said as she climbed up to join me.

"Think you're up to a bit of climbing?" I asked in a hopeful tone.

"Like I have a choice." She grumbled pushing open the window and releasing the stale smell of old, dusty hay. I took in a deep breath of fresh air before looking down at the sloping roof, realizing that there must have been a small room off the main part of the barn.

"That's where I hid when they brought that 'thing' in." Ari informed me.

"And it looks like it will be helping us again. Do you want to go first?"

"I would say rock, paper, scissors but I don't think we should push our luck, do you?" Ari said already choosing to go first and swinging her legs round and out over the frame.

"Probably not." I agreed and took her hand to help steady her as her feet found the roof. She lowered the rest of her body down until she was crouching and then slowly started to slide down, using her hands to steady her pace. I decided it looked like a good enough technique, so when I swung my legs over, I did the same as she did.

Once we both got to the edge we knew we would have to jump the rest of the way but considering it was only the height of your average garden shed, I knew it wasn't going to be too hard.

"Ready?" I asked.

"No."

"Good. Let's go." I said jumping, knowing she would do the same.

We landed on the soft grass without damage and once we checked the coast was clear, we set off for the house. It was lucky that the back of the house was facing the old barn and that the window I had crawled out of was also on this side. It wasn't long before the last of the twilight had gone, making things even more difficult in finding our way. This of course wasn't the only reason it was a race against the clock as our mother had made it clear she was only letting me out just before it was time for the leaving ritual.

"We're going to make it." Ari whispered when we came to stop behind a wood store just near the house. We checked first that no one was around and then made another last run for it. We both skidded on the grass as we stopped ourselves abruptly, so as not to make a sound by banging into the side of the house.

"You ready for this?" Ari asked me and I scoffed.

"Were you ready to jump?"

"Good point. Now go!" She said as she was bent down holding the window open for me.

"Sir, yes sir." I replied before doing as I was told and sliding on in there. The ladder was still where I had left it, which was my first good sign. Once I was in I looked back up at Ari and gave her a wink, which was all the encouragement she

needed to get going. The last part of this plan was to simply wait for my jailor to come and get me and no one would be the wiser.

I knew we couldn't go through with all this again. I couldn't put Ari in danger like that… I just couldn't. But I also knew that no matter how much I warned her of the risks that she would only do it all over again, even if it meant she would get caught right alongside me.

So that's why I knew that from now on we both needed to make sure we made no more mistakes. We had too much riding on being allowed to leave in a month's time.

Just one month.

After years of suffocating with what felt like the Fathers' hands around our necks we would finally get a chance to breathe clean pure air for the first time. Air that hadn't been polluted by lies and blind devotion of the worst kind. The kind that infects the mind and poisons the good right out of people.

The type that *killed our mother.*

I closed my eyes against the anger that one thought invoked within me and exhaled as I turned my back to the window letting go of my bitterness…for now anyway. But that's when I felt it. Those hands around my neck squeezing the breathable air from my lungs as panic started to seep in.

My eyes snapped open and I took in the dark room trying to make sense of the cold dread. Was it the vision? Was it my old fears coming back to haunt me? Then it hit me as a voice penetrated the room and all other fears before now seemed lost in a sea of insignificance.

"Hello Katie."

That's when I felt it…*That's when I felt the ice.* So I said the only thing my fear would allow me…

"Hello Uncle."

CHAPTER 5
A CRIMSON MOON

S at here now staring at the Divine Judgment passed down by God was as unnerving as awaiting my own judgement. Studying the two neighboring cities as they were completely consumed by fire and brimstone offered little comfort and I was starting to hate the painter John Martin. I shook my head for where my thoughts were leading to for the millionth time, wondering where Ari was.

Once I was caught red handed I had expected my punishment to have been delivered down there in the basement, however this didn't happen. After finding him sat at the base of the staircase in the dark and on a rusty school chair waiting for me, I had expected him to lash out when he stood. But to my surprise and trepidation my Uncle had done nothing but motion for me to precede him up the stairs. I had done so slowly, waiting for the physical 'catch' that getting too close to him could mean. But he had simply let me go to climb the stairs only to find my mother waiting for me.

I don't know what was more surprising in fact, to find I wasn't half beaten yet by my Uncle's hand or that my mother remained silent during the whole thing. She just handed me a black bag and led me to my sister's room which was in the attic. I had hoped to find Ari in there waiting for me, but it was empty.

"Where is Ari?" I asked but my question was ignored.

"Get dressed. The Ritual starts soon." These were my mother's parting words to me as she slammed the door, locking it behind her. I dumped the bag on the bed, finding every scrap of clothing I owned in there. I wasn't sure what their game was by putting me in here but when I looked around the small room it didn't take me long to find the thin mattress that had been thrown on the floor. Part of me was delighted that I had been moved up here but the distrust in me quickly killed all hope that losing my own room was my 'punishment'.

I tipped all the clothes out onto the bed and grabbed the only other dress that I owned. It was a thick black woollen dress that was only to be worn during the leaving ritual. I laid it out and after fishing out fresh underwear I started to undress. I walked to the chipped ceramic bowl that sat on a wooden desk next to a battered copper jug.

The crude washing station was situated under the window and stood only in my underwear, I began to shiver. But it wasn't the cold that penetrated my skin that caused this. And even when I poured the freezing water into the bowl, picked up the slither of soap and began to wash did it affect me. No, it was none of these things that racked my body to shake and forced the tears down my cheeks. It was looking out into the night to see the full moon high above the barn. The abandoned barn I had found solace in to escape the pain I would now feel tenfold. Because I knew something was coming. Something bad would find us of that I had no doubt and the lights coming from that usually dark barn told me as much.

They knew…*everything.*

So here I was, sat awaiting another cold moon to shine and

illuminate the horrors to come. Sat here staring at the sight of destruction wondering what my own would be. The only hope I could hold on to was that they didn't know Ari's part in all of this…but if that was the case, then where was she?

I flinched when I heard the bolt slide back on the door behind me.

"It's your turn." My mother said and my lip curled in disgust before I faced her. I didn't say a word but when I stood I straightened my back and showed no fear, something I knew from one look at her she was disappointed with.

I wanted to shout and scream at her. Inside my mind I turned my head to face her as I walked past and snarled the words 'You're sick!' but my lips never moved. In another thought I lashed out and attacked her smiling the whole time. In fact, every step I took closer towards her I had time to play out a number of scenarios in my mind, none of which I would do but I certainly found it helped.

I followed her down through the house and for the first time I realized just how stark it was. There were no pictures on the walls or ornaments dotted about the place. I was suddenly hit with the vision of another home, one filled with warmth and character. Family pictures decorated the walls, along with art work that I knew came from a family member and was placed there with pride. Then there was an attic room, much like the one Ari and I now shared. Only this one was exactly how I imagined decorating my own room, should I ever get the chance to own such a thing. A bed with a thick purple quilt bursting with scatter cushions to match looked like it would feel like heaven. Books were laid out without worry of being found by prying and judging eyes. A small heap of worn clothes were left without fear of a reprimanding hand and the sin of jealously hit me hard. That was the life I wanted, the life I craved so badly that it almost felt like *my life* stolen from me.

I shook the confusing thoughts from my mind as I continued to walk the depressing proof of this life, one that I lived instead of the one I wanted. I didn't think I had seen a single flower enter the house and amongst all the grey, a flower would have been something you wouldn't have forgotten. It was like a soulless island void of colour, hoping that the world beyond couldn't touch it with its beauty, in fear it would lose its intense power of misery.

We reached the front door and as I touched the door frame I noticed the only decoration I had seen, which was a simple wooden cross nailed to the wall. I don't know why I was drawn to it the way I was, as I had never noticed it before.

"Come on, stop stalling!" My mother snapped and as soon as the words were out, the cross spun on its nail and swung round so it was upside down. I knew this to be the Petrine Cross and one that was a sign for the Antichrist. I looked back to my mother and for one split second saw a monster staring back at me.

It was like my mother's human face was fighting with the demon inside of her. As though her shadow was coming alive and trying to free itself from the confines of her body. The demon shook all around her and vibrated away from her face, showing me another demonic one screaming to break away. Its eyes were distorted holes dragged to one side as it tried to pull itself free. The mouth was the same, open wide in what looked like a death call, one void of any features that would be classed as something coming from a human. No teeth, no lips, nothing to suggest other than the true nature of this beast belonged in Hell...

And it was coming from my mother!

"What are you staring at, you insolent girl!" She barked making her face snap back to normal and when I looked back to the cross I saw it too was back to its usual position. Was I losing it? Had that all been in my head or was something of a higher power trying to tell me something. Even if this was so, I didn't need a vision like that to know I shouldn't be trusting my mother, or following her as I was doing. But I had little choice. I needed to find Ari and I had the worst feeling in the pit of my stomach that was exactly what I was going to find right behind my mother's steps.

"Nothing." I mumbled wondering what my face had been like when seeing her like that. It had been as if her skin had excreted an evil vapor, one that was forming another side of her...*the true side of her.*

I continued out through the front door looking up automatically at the moon. It was as if one of the gods was holding a flash light down at the earth and homing in to watch this new horror play out. Well as far as I was concerned he was free to jump in and save my ass at any moment.

Although nothing they preached to us suggested for one moment that the Gods cared for us, if anything they were perceived as more cruel than anything else... that, of course was if the stories told were to be trusted. In fact, Ari and I believed this wasn't the case at all and we were only led to believe these things as another form of control. Just another way for them to use fear as a tool to get us to do as they saw fit. It was sickening to think about it but the warning signs were all there as plain as day.

So I closed my eyes for a moment as if trying to absorb the power the night held. I needed to be strong. *Ari* needed me to be strong. So I opened my eyes and screamed! I screamed out in utter terror as that brief strength left me. I felt my body start to shake and convulse with a fear like no other. The sight before me was Hell and the work of the Devil and it was no longer below us but surrounding where I stood.

Bodies all around me were strapped to X shaped frames and

they were screaming. All eight girls were naked, bleeding and on fire with their flesh melting from their bones. None of them had passed out like you would have believed or at least died from all the smoke they surely inhaled. No, it was as if they were being forced to stay alive until there was nothing left. And then one by one with their last dying breath, they each held out one arm that the flames couldn't touch and pointed a finger at me. I shook my head walking backwards as they each blamed me for what was happening now.

"No...! *No, no*...NO!" I first shouted my denials before screaming them. Then one by one the light went out, leaving one black charred body after another, until no flames surrounded me. I let out an almighty scream, damning the Heavens above only to find my reply was a full moon that turned red...

A crimson moon.

"I won't tell you again!" For once the sound of my mother's voice was welcome as it transported me back from that Hell, one I didn't understand. Why was I being shown these things? What was I supposed to do? It felt like there was something the Gods wanted me to stop but without seeing these thing in the real world then I remained clueless.

"Where are we going?" I asked as we walked away from the direction of the barn.

"To the feast of course." I faltered in my step and looked back at the barn to see the lights were still on. I knew walking away from it was a mistake but when my mother grabbed my arm and yanked me to follow her, I felt I had little choice. But wait? Did I really have so little choice...what would she do...kill me?

"Run...run to her, Keira." A voice spoke to me as if searching me out from the back of my mind. *Keira*, I had heard that name before? Where had I heard it...think Katie...think,

Keira? But wait, that wasn't my name. Then why had it come from my thoughts as easy as thinking to breathe?

"No." I found myself saying out loud. My mother, who still had hold of my arm, gripped me tighter and turned her head to look at me in disbelief.

"What did you say to me?" Her voice changed into something terrifying but for once I wasn't scared of her. I yanked my arm free feeling the scratch of her nails tearing at my skin.

"I said NO!" I repeated leaning into her face and witnessing the change from anger to shock. I decided not to wait around for her to retaliate but instead I turned on my heel and did what my heart told me to do.

What I *needed* to do.

I ran towards the barn with everything I had in me knowing deep within my soul that something was happening. Something that had to be stopped! I needed to get to that barn before it was too late.

Before…

"*Ari!* Oh god no. Ari I am coming!" I shouted when I heard her screams coming from inside the barn. I reached the doors and wrenched them open not realizing that they had been locked from the inside. I don't know where my strength came from but right at this moment I welcomed it, even if its source was borrowed from the very Devil himself!

I suddenly came to a standstill there in the doorway and the sight that met me was without a doubt the very core of where my nightmares lived. Ari was naked and strapped to the X frame we had seen being wheeled in there earlier that day. Her back was marred with bloody lines from the whip that one of the Righteous Bloods held in his hand.

He had been torturing her and she had been gagged until recently as I could still see the bloody twisted material, slipped down to around her neck. Her wrists and ankles were red raw from her efforts in trying to escape. But this wasn't the only thing that turned red raw as a bloody mist overtook me, something sharp and twisted… and I snapped.

"That's it Bitch, scream for me…*I like it."* He whispered in her ear after forcing her head back by her hair. So I quietly stalked closer and grabbed an old rusty pitchfork that was lent against a beam. I was moving with only half my mind as my own as though another part of me was possessed. I felt like my limbs were drumming with an energy like no other. As though my blood was singing with every step we took and before I knew it I was crossing over to the dark side.

I grabbed his hair from behind, wrenched his head back with that same strength borrowed and whispered,

"Scream for us Bitch… *we like it."* And then I forced the pitchfork up under his chin, impaling his head on the wooden pole. Blood spurted from his mouth and forced his lips and cheeks up like he died smiling. It was a haunting sight but one the other side relished in and instead of screaming at the sight of what my hands had done, they simply dropped his head like waste, letting his body follow.

"Katie?" Ari asked, barely able to lift her head up to look at me.

"It's me Ari…I'm here now."

"What is going on in…?" I heard my mother's voice coming but before panic seeped in a strange impulse kicked in. I flung my arm out and looked just in time to see the doors to the barn slamming shut before my mother could enter. I saw the chain I had snapped wrap around the handles like a snake and hold there against my mother's banging. I had no clue how I had done that, or any of this for that matter but I knew now was not the time to waste in wondering.

"Are we going to die now, Kay Bear?" My sister asked

finding my eyes for the first time and I held her face in my hands to answer her.

"No, Ari, we already died here...*now it's time for us to live.*" I then kissed her on the forehead and went about getting her down from the ungodly device. I hated heard her hisses of pain and they grated along my spine like fingernails dancing on my backbone. Once I got her down and let her weight fall into me I knew now there was only thing left to do.

"Wait here. I will be back." I ran to the ladder and this time climbed it with no problems. I found the stuff I had stored, grabbing the blanket and water flask that still had a few mouthfuls left in it from when Ari had refilled it for me. It was a lot darker up here but at least I could see what I was doing thanks to the oil lamps that had been placed below. By the time I got back down to Ari I knew we didn't have long before our mother had no doubt told the Fathers we were in here.

"Wh...what are we... going to do?" My sister's hoarse voice croaked out the question. I knew there was no way we could escape, not yet anyway as Ari was in no condition to run cross country, let alone stand up on her own.

"I have a plan. It may sound insane but we have no choice." She nodded once and said the only words I needed to hear...

"I trust you." After these words of encouragement, I got moving. I tried not to gag when I had to put my foot onto the Righteous Blood's head and pull him free from my own implement of torture. I then dragged him as much as I could up against the X frame and put the whip back in his hand. Then I rushed back to Ari just as we started to hear voices approaching.

"We need to scream Ari. Do you hear me? We need to make as much noise as we can so that everyone from the feast hears us. We need everyone, not just the Elders or this will never work." She understood what I was trying to say and at the same time we started to scream for help.

"HELP US!"

"HE'S TRYING TO KILL US!" I added banging on the door knowing it would hold with the chains still in place.

"Everyone will hear them." I heard my mother's voice say to someone in warning and sure enough she was right. The next thing we knew we could hear others coming to our aid.

"HELP US, WE ARE TRAPPED AND HE'S TRYING TO KILL US!" I shouted again and then I knew it was time to get rid of the evidence...the only way I knew how.

"Still trust me?" I asked as I held up the oil lamp I had unhooked from the nail.

"Torch it." Ari replied making me smile. So I did just that. I threw the lamp aiming at the dead Righteous Blood's feet, satisfied when it exploded around him.

Soon the flames engulfed him and for a few horrifying moments I was taken back to my vision, knowing now what it had been trying to tell me.

They wanted me to do what I couldn't do for them.

To become...

My sister's savior.

CHAPTER 6

BAPTIZED WITH FIRE

As I had planned, by the time we got the doors open everyone from the Colony was stood round the barn to witness our escape from death. We had waited until most of the flames had consumed the body before releasing the door from its chains and burst out of there at just the right moment before the mezzanine level collapsed.

Some of the people were already trying to fight the fire with buckets of water and two people were pulling hose pipes over ready to provide aid. All I could think about was how I hoped there would be nothing left of that building, however I knew the ash would be gone long before the horrific memory of what happened there ever did. But our only solace was that the Fathers, whether they had been involved in this or not had to at least act horrified that one of their own could do such a thing.

"What happened, child?!" One of the Elders named Godfrey asked. He was one of the eldest of the Fathers and had had a granddaughter leave the Colony only a month ago. The strange thing was that none of the Fathers ever seemed upset that their family members had decided to leave and forever be then known as the 'Fallen'. Why was that? But more importantly, why was I only asking myself this now?

"It was one of the Righteous Bloods! He kidnapped my sister and tortured her…" I said and decided now would be a good time to test out a theory I had, so I continued, warping the truth.

"…He said he was doing the Fathers' work and that they told him that she needed to be punished!" I made sure to catch the troubled looks between the Fathers that did little to ease my mind and convince me they hadn't been involved. I knew what was coming next as they couldn't have the rest of the Colony believing such a thing. After all, forgiveness for acts like these from those who are supposedly picked by the Gods would have been going a step too far and would have been all they needed to tip the balance of belief.

It was getting clearer to those who were on the cusp of rebelling and this would have been all they would have needed. And one look from the guilty Fathers told me as much. It was surprising all that you could see when you had your eyes opened by so many acts of cruelty. It only takes one for you to break but just because you do, it doesn't mean you become weak as there was definitely strength in knowledge. Or so I was beginning to find out.

"That's outrageous! He must have fallen to the ways of the Devil…" Godfrey was the first to deny the claim and then Father Davis spoke,

"Yes, yes…that makes sense as he used fire to cleanse his work and the flames to teach us of his wicked ways." He then crossed himself making others do the same. I looked to my mother who stood at the back near my Uncle. It was only when she started to receive questioning stares that she was then prompted to finally act like a Mother should and was pushed towards us both by my Uncle's hand. He must have seen the whispers starting and knew he had to act.

"Oh my dear daughters! Thank the Gods you both survived!" She said grabbing us both and pulling us into an embrace. Ari cried in pain and I pulled my mother off her. I heard her 'umpf' noise but cared nothing for how it looked. I was tired of playing by their rules.

"She needs a doctor, she is injured!" I said knowing there was no way we would be allowed to leave and find an actual hospital. But at least it meant that right here and now, in front of all these witnesses a healer would have to be provided and that meant sanctuary for the both of us, at least for the meantime.

Because I knew as soon as we were back in that house, the caring act would stop and God only knew what those two would do to us. I knew my mother had been involved after what she said to me up in Ari's room. 'It's your turn' had been my mother's words, which had definitely sounded more like a promise.

The new feelings I had for my mother now were a loathing of the likes I had never felt before. I hated my Uncle for sure and the way he had always treated us but as far as I was concerned, we were never his blood. Our mother however was the woman who gave birth to us and nurtured us as infants. Ari had even saved her life and this was the thanks we got! This was all the love we were shown, disappointment that we had escaped possibly a death she had a hand in. Oh yes, it was worthy of loathing alright.

Thankfully my pleas were answered when the Colony's healer made her way through the crowd. I didn't know her first name as out of respect to those older than us, we only called them by their last name.

She was married to Mr Collingwood, one of the farmers who

obviously had never been interested in working up the ranks within the Colony so to speak. However, his skills at growing bountiful crops each year was what rewarded him with great respect and I gathered this was enough for him. They had never had children but every encounter I had ever had with Mrs Collingwood had told me that she was warm and kind, two traits that were definitely a rarity around here. She had come from a medical household as her father had once been a Doctor in Lancaster, so naturally she was the first choice when appointing a healer.

"Give her to me, I will care for her." She said coming to the other side of Ari as if ready to take her weight. So I handed my sister over to her, listening to my gut feeling as I knew I had made the right decision. It wasn't as though I had many options to do much else but at least this time I wouldn't be letting her out of my sight.

"I am coming with her." This was a demand that spoke volumes as to my mental state, considering it wasn't often you would dare demand anything from an Elder. She nodded once obviously knowing how much I needed this.

"No! You will come with me Katie, your Uncle and I need you to explain what happened to us in private." I visibly cringed and Mrs Collingwood didn't miss it.

"I am afraid Cynthia that Katie might have smoke damage, so she too will need to come with me to be cared for." Mrs Collingwood said coming to my aid and calling my mother by her first name. This was making it clear that they were on equal ground. I wanted to smile at the awkward position my mother had made for herself, considering she had no grounds for refusing her. After all, it was that or show the whole Colony how little she actually cared for her girls.

"Oh…uh… yes, yes, I mean of course." Watching my mother stumbling on her words was what I could officially class as the only highlight of the day. Mrs Collingwood and I both walked away with Ari between us and left the sight of the burning barn behind us. Poor Ari was close to passing out by the time we got to Mrs Collingwood's homestead and when she was finally lowered onto a bed she was panting in pain.

I refused at first when being asked to leave the room and insisted that I be allowed to stay. Ari gave me a sad smile and took my hand in hers.

"Go on, I will be fine." I knew why she said this and I would have done the same in wanting to spare Ari the sight of my pain. Both of us always had this natural urge to put the other first because of our bond, so I knew what was best for Ari. Once the door was closed I found myself a seat in the living area and looking round I realized just what a home should feel like. Even in this dire situation or who knows, maybe even because of it, I started to see the world, this world for what it really was...

Bleak. Unnatural. Fake.

It felt like the lie of all lies. But what had happened back in the barn, now that had been the truth. I could see that now. That the person I thought I was all this time, the quiet, shy and fearful girl that had never been made to feel like a grown woman was actually someone strong. I knew what I had done, in killing that man and taking a life, should have had me cowering in fear for what the Gods may do but I wasn't. If anything it had felt like my power had come from them. That my other self had led me to Ari and not only pointing the way but also taking over and doing what needed to be done.

It scared me how natural it had felt and when I looked down at my hands now, I saw that they were shaking. What was wrong with me and who was I becoming when I thought that murdering a man was natural for me? But then a simple flash of the nightmare of seeing Ari, who I loved most in this world, being hurt like that...well then, that murder became justice.

It was as simple at that and when you were forced to live in these simple times, then what other option did I have? It wasn't like we could go to the cops and report a crime.

"Katie, you can go in there now." Mrs Collingwood startled me and looking at the wooden cuckoo clock hung on the wall, I realized I had been convincing myself of these facts for over an hour. I stood up, ignoring how stiff I felt and walked back into the room Ari was in.

"Her back was pretty cut up but I cleaned them up as best as I could. She was lucky she didn't need stiches but I think there will be some scarring. Which reminds me, I noticed that she had some bad scars on her back from another incident..."

"We were both in a car accident when we were younger. Ari hurt her back and I hurt my arms." I said stopping her before she thought this type of thing had happened before. The fact that it had and hadn't left any scars wasn't something worth mentioning. After all, it wasn't as if she could do anything about it considering our Uncle was the leader around here. Besides, she had done so much for us already, more than she knew in fact, so I didn't think it fair laying even more problems at her door.

"Ah, I see." She said and then she patted me on the shoulder and said,

"Go and be with her but I want you both to try and get some rest. No one will bother you tonight." She turned to leave when I stopped her.

"I can't thank you enough...your kindness...and..."

"Hush now or you will make this old lady blush." She said waving off my gratitude as though it was nothing, but did she not understand that in a place like this, it meant everything. She closed the door on us and I approached the bed. Ari looked peaceful and I didn't want to disturb her, so I went to sit on a nearby chair.

"You know you have always been terrible at trying to keep quiet." Ari said opening one eye and smirking.

"That's why I lost at hide and seek when we were kids." I replied, scooting my chair closer to the bed.

"Ha! Well it didn't help when you hid behind a curtain with your feet showing." Ari laughed and it was a beautiful sound considering what she had just been through but there was something about what she just said that forced a vision out of me.

I was in a luxurious marble room, with the biggest, grandest fireplace I had ever seen. But I seemed to be in a panic and was scanning the room for something. It was only when I saw the curtains that a plan must have formed. I then looked for another way out and when I found it I ran to it. Then strangely, I opened the door and was surprised when I didn't go through it but instead ran back to the heavy red and gold curtains that were hanging to the floor. I stepped behind one and tried to control my heavy breathing. Then my heart almost stopped when I first heard footsteps before another door opened.

"She couldn't have gone far I can still feel her near...FIND HER!" As soon as I heard his voice erupt with anger I screamed, feeling this time that my heart *did* stop.

"You just had another one didn't you?" The sound of my sister's voice jarred me from what felt like the past and my tensed muscles could finally relax back into the chair.

"Yeah." I said still panting.

"Now it's happening when we are awake."

"You too?" I asked oddly finding comfort in this new knowledge.

"Yes but I don't know why. It's almost like the closer we get to something, the stronger it gets." This made sense as it felt the same with me, almost like a...

"Like a beacon." I said making her cry out her agreement.

"Yes! Exactly like that!" Okay so both shouting that out wasn't exactly like we had just solved all our problems, no if anything we had just added a bucket load more questions to the pile. But one thing remained clear through it all,

"We need to get out of here, Ari."

"Agreed." She said whipping back the covers and wincing with the movement.

"We can't go now, plus Mrs Collingwood said we would be fine here for the time being. We need a plan." I said making sure she didn't do herself even more damage by getting out of bed. Ari had always been the strong one. When I was little I used to think she was invincible and to look at her now, after the beating she'd just received, I could believe it once again. When she dragged us out of that car the authorities couldn't believe that a seven year old had achieved such an incredible feat. And to top it all off she too had been injured and like me had the scars to show for it.

When our dad had swerved the car to avoid a truck that jack knifed when it had hit black ice, he had lost all control. The car had flipped countless times and I just remember the glass exploding all around us. The unusual scars on Ari's back had doctors scratching their heads as to how she had received them as all she could tell them was that it felt like she fell and hit something hard. As you can imagine this merely confused them further. My own scars occurred when Ari had dragged me from the car on my front, by my hands and the glass had done the rest.

As a child she had simply wanted to get me from the car as quickly as possible as the wheels were still turning and she got scared the car would drive away with me trapped inside. Of course now our memories told us the tree it had hit wouldn't have allowed that to happen but her fears were for good reason as the car set alight just after she saved our mother. Our father had died on impact and the sight of his bloody body still haunted us to this day.

So having scars on my arms didn't bother me at all. Because every time I looked at them I was reminded of two things. One was that we were put on this earth to live each day like it was a gift given and two, was that there were no limits to what loving someone could mean or make you do.

"So what is the plan?" Ari asked and it was strange as it seemed that in a short time we had swapped roles. Ari was normally the one with a plan and the one that led us through that plan with no fear. So when did I become the fearless leader?

"You saved me." Ari said as if reading my thoughts, which wouldn't have been surprising seeing as we were twins.

"I murdered someone." I whispered stating the obvious.

"No, you saved someone...*me."* I knew what she was saying and put that way I would do it all again because it came down to simple primal rules of survival. It had been either him or Ari. Because there was no doubt in my mind that he would have killed her and me too as it seemed my time would have been next if my mother's words were anything to go by. No, I had no choice and Ari's words simply reminded me of that fact.

"So what's the plan badass, Kay Bear?" I smiled and said only one word,

"Escape."

Mrs Collingwood remained true to her word and not one person disturbed us the rest of the night. This wasn't for lack of trying though as my mother had tried to get us taken back home. But after a long argument from Mrs Collingwood, mother finally had to agree that what was best for our 'health' was more important than my mother's 'emotional' state. Her argument for needing us home so badly would have been laughable if it hadn't have highlighted the seriousness of our need to leave as soon as possible.

There was only one reason my mother seemed desperate enough for us to be back in that house and it wasn't anything to do with our health or her 'emotional state'. It was for the type of punishment you don't come back from.

We decided it was now or never as we both knew the likelihood of making it to the end of the month was never going to be a reality. Thankfully when the storm hit that night it seemed luck was on our side as we were less likely to be seen making a run for it. I had been worried at first on how Ari would cope after her injuries but as usual, Ari just acted like nothing was wrong. This was proven when she was up and out of bed as soon as we heard Mr and Mrs Collingwood call it a night.

The problem we had was we didn't know if our mother and Uncle would have anyone watching the house. But in the end it was a chance we would have to take. So under the cover of darkness we sneaked out of the Collingwood home and made a run for it into the surrounding woodland.

The run had been hard, harder so for Ari due to the extreme pain this must have put on her back. By the time we reached the cover of the trees we were also soaked from the heavy rain, but we didn't care as we had made it past the hardest point. Here in the darkness and under the cover of the forest we had more of a chance to remain hidden until we could at least find a road.

We had no idea how far we would have to walk, which was why I had no choice when it came to stealing a loaf of bread and some carrots from Mrs Collingwood's larder. At least I'd found a scrap of paper and a pencil so that I could write a sorry note, hoping she would understand why. Although after dealing with my mother I think she had an idea what was going on, so wouldn't be surprised by our actions, not considering the door had been left unlocked as if giving us the go ahead.

"We made it." Ari said bending over to catch her breath like I was.

"Yeah, let's just hope that was the hard part." Ari agreed and we carried on slowly as the small flashlight Ari had also taken from the house wasn't providing much light. This was also a good thing as we didn't exactly need to be letting people know where we were should they come looking for us.

"As least these trees offer some protection against the rain." That was true but the damage had already been done as we were both shivering from the cold wet clothes we now wore. Mrs Collingwood had also been kind enough to give us both a set of old clothes she used to wear when she was younger. Apart from smelling a bit musty from being stored for so long, they were a lot warmer than my woollen dress or Ari's forced naked state.

We continued on and I had to wonder about how easy it had been making it this far. People who had escaped before had also run into the trees and I didn't know whether it was a good sign or not the fact they had never been seen again. There were only two scenarios I saw the reasons for this and one was that they had gotten lost and most likely died out there in the wilderness. And the other, a more hopeful one was that they got so far and then found a road to civilization.

"What do you think it will be like?" Ari asked me and I took this as a sign she needed to take her mind off the uncertainty we faced.

"The outside world?"

"Yeah."

"I think it will be like breathing for the first time." I answered honestly. Her deep sigh told me she felt the same.

"Do you think it will have changed much?"

"Yeah, but in a good way."

"Do you think I will finally get a chance to learn how to drive?" This had been one of the things Ari most wanted to do in life. She loved the thrill of speed and danger in a sense. She was always climbing to the highest point in any tree and beyond what anyone else was willing to go. She was always the first to try anything and no matter how dangerous it seemed, she was there. She was a natural born leader and always managed to set an example to others that you shouldn't be afraid of the unknown. And that was precisely what we were doing now by taking that leap into the unknown.

The unknown to freedom…it certainly had a nice ring to it.

We talked some more about what we would do when we finally got out and one of the things was getting in a car, after Ari had passed her test of course, and just driving across the country. We fantasied about what we would see and what we remembered of our family trips as kids. The places we would revisit and how we would both try and find work as waitresses in the towns we stayed in until we had enough money to hit the road again.

It may not have sounded like much of a dream to other people but to us it would be our own little slice of heaven on Earth. Because that's what this place did to you. It made you crave for the little things in life and made you realise what was important. And for us, it was simply the freedom to do whatever we chose to do with our lives, without being beaten for even thinking it.

It was to eat real food and marvel at the taste without being called gluttonous. It was to chat until all hours of the night without fear of being caught and be loud and laugh and dance and do all the things we found beautiful in the world. No, we knew we didn't dream big, but we dreamed beautiful and that's all that mattered.

We continued talking like this and instead of us getting tired from all the walking if anything, it encouraged us to push harder without even realising it.

"Ice cream." Ari said as we had moved on to a torturous game we used to play by naming all the things we missed and couldn't wait to do again.

"Socks." I said thinking back to really comfy warm socks that used to have bright patterns on.

"A cup of tea." I said, and it came out of nowhere as I never drank tea.

"Tea? But you never…"

"Ssshh, get down!" I hissed pulling her down into the bushes and grabbing the flash light from her to turn it off. I heard a noise up ahead and soon a different light flashed once in the trees.

"Oh no, they found us" Ari whispered, and I held my breath hoping and praying this wasn't it.

"Is that what I think it is?" I asked when we both heard a strange noise. Strange because we weren't used to hearing it anymore and also because you didn't expect to hear a car in the middle of the forest.

"Maybe we are closer to a road than we thought."

"Maybe." I agreed but I wasn't so sure. I waited a moment longer and decided to take a look. Raising my head slowly above our cover I saw nothing but the dark forest looming on for as far as the dark night would allow. There were no lights anywhere and the sound of the engine had long gone. Was Ari right, could we be near a road? Well there was only one way to find out.

"Come on, let's check it out."

"Okay, let's go." Not surprisingly Ari agreed and we both cautiously at first went in search for what we could only hope was a road and not the Fathers coming to look for us. At this point we didn't have much in the way of options as it wasn't like we had a map or knew which direction to head in. No, we were going on blind luck, so if this had just been a sign of where to go, then we were taking it.

"Look Kay, is that what I think it is?" I moved closer and closer taking Ari by the hand until we stepped out of the tree line and onto a road.

"Bingo!" I said jumping and squealing with delight into each other's arms. We looked one way and then the other, deciding to press on the way we started and hope it led to a main road as this was just a dirt track but at least it was a start. It was also obvious it was being regularly used as you could still see the fresh tyre tracks in the mud when we shone the light down.

"Let's see where this goes." I nodded in agreement and we set off once more, only this time it was a lot easier thanks to the track we followed. Manoeuvring through the forest hadn't been easy, especially at night but the worse thing in our position was that it had been slow, something we just couldn't afford to be. But now, being on this road, we could feel ourselves getting nearer to achieving our goal and we were buzzing because of it.

"I see lights." Ari informed me on a whisper and for one small moment I let myself hope for them to be the lights from a small town or even a motel, anything to prove we had done it. But the closer we got the more we realised this dirt track only led to a small cabin in the woods.

"There's still a track that leads past the house, maybe that's the road out of here." I looked to where Ari pointed to and saw she was right, there was a track but it was obviously one that was hardly ever used.

"Let's check out the cabin first as someone might live there that could help us and look, at least they have a car." I pointed to the large truck that had been parked around the side.

"Okay, but I think we should sneak up and look through one of the windows first, as we don't know who's in there."

"Let's hope for a little old lady who's feeling charitable." I said making Ari chuckle.

"At this point I would go for an axe wielding hillbilly that has passed out on whiskey and we can just swipe his keys." She said this time making me chuckle but still raise an eye brow in question.

"What? We're fugitives now, anything goes...plus I might get my chance to drive sooner than I thought." She winked at me and then walked on leaving me shaking my head laughing.

The closer we got the more it became apparent that it was unlikely that it was lived in, although I guessed the car suggested otherwise. The place was run down and that was putting it nicely. But the lights were coming from the windows below which told us it must have had a basement. We crossed the road and sneaked up to the cabin as quietly as we could but when we heard a woman's scream we both dropped to the floor.

"Oh God, what was that?" Ari whispered next to me and I shrugged my shoulder just hoping it wasn't the axe hillbilly Ari had been kidding about. When we heard no more screams I motioned for us to move again and check it out. After all there could have been someone trapped in there who needed our help.

We got so far and started to hear voices. It was strange at first, like someone was humming or singing quietly in an eerie voice but then we soon realised it wasn't one voice, it was many...and they were chanting.

I pointed to the basement and we moved closer to the small rectangle window that was almost level with the ground. The sound was much louder now and it was clear it was a group chanting something in a different language as it certainly wasn't in English.

I really didn't want to look and from the horrified

expression on Ari I wasn't the only one. But we both knew we had to look as after hearing that girl's scream we had no choice.

So we both crouched down either side of the window, remaining out of sight and on mouthing *one, two, three,* we looked.

It wasn't an axe murdering hillbilly...

It was much, much worse.

CHAPTER 7
DESPERATE HANDS

Blood.

That was what I remembered most about the crash. All the blood. It dripped down from my father's body half hanging from the broken windscreen. It poured from my sister's back, soaking her pink t-shirt in a strange V shape. It even pooled under my mother's head as she lay unconscious on the grass. But the most blood I had ever seen had come straight from my veins and poured down my arms into my hands. I remember cupping my hands together in some naive hope of catching it, thinking maybe they can put it back into me.

But now when I thought back to that memory it would forever be attached to something far more sinister. Because *this,* right here and now was the most blood I had ever seen and it was sickening.

"Oh God..." Ari muttered after being sick. I didn't know how I managed to keep my own stomach in check at the sight of what could only be described as Demons feasting.

When we finally looked our first thought had been to scream, which was why both our hands flew to our mouths to trap the instinct within. We knew now what none of the others knew really happened within the Colony and most importantly, where their children really went when they left.

It had all been a lie.

A deadly lie.

Because there was Bethany, naked and strapped up like a sacrifice and being drained of her blood for the monsters to drink. Her body had been beaten before her throat had been slit, bathing her own body crimson. She was tied to some kind of tilted wheel and the grooves carved around it looked to channel the blood down to a symbol below.

The symbol was what was known for us at the Colony as the Hexad. It was made up of four triangles, two smaller ones at the top and two longer ones at the bottom, giving it six points that were supposed to represent each of our Gods.

But the six robed men that stood there now, with a cup in each hand drinking from the girl's blood were no Gods! I wanted to spit on the ground at the thought of it and the heinous lies they had told. Because even without seeing their faces we knew who these six monsters were.

The Fathers.

And we had watched as each of them had held a chalice cup under the six points of the Hexad, where the blood overflowed and then toast to another successful month. We had no clue to what it all meant but watching them drink together had been Ari's limit of keeping her food down.

"We have to do something?" Ari said wiping her lips on the back of her hand.

"We have to get out of here." I said knowing that was the only option left. She frowned and was about to argue when something in the room made us both look. The six Fathers all finished the last of their stolen blood and then one by one they ripped back their hooded robes, revealing themselves...*for who they really were.*

"No, it...it can't be..." I muttered in disbelief but it was Ari who actually gave them their name.

"Vampires?"

This was my limit as I fell back from my crouched position unable to take anymore. I started to walk backwards like a crab on my hands and feet in despair. Ari stayed at the window like she was watching what else was happening but all I could think about was... It was all true. That all this time we had been ruled by Devils being disguised as Gods incarnate. All so they could feed from us and lead us like sacrificial lambs to the slaughter.

We saw it right there in their bloody eyes and demonic faces. Their lengthened fangs still stained from their feast. We saw the truth as they all laid down their cups and chanted out what could have been their victory.

"We have to go...*now!*" Ari said dragging me up from the ground and pulling me away. She pulled me over towards the car and as if she knew it would be open she yanked on the door.

"What are we doing?" I asked as she stuffed me inside but shut the door before opening the driver's side.

"What we have to." She said and then before I could ask how she was planning on driving this thing without knowing how, she started up the car and we were off down the beaten track.

"Ari, how are you doing this?!" I asked looking at her in amazement as she drove like she had been doing it all her life.

"I don't know but something just told me that I could. I heard his voice Kay, I heard it again and it told me to get in the truck and drive!" I believed her. How could I not after what we had been through, especially in this last few days. Was this what our visions were trying to tell us? Had they been trying to lead us here all this time and show us the truth?

"I heard them. Oh God this won't stop! I heard what they

have planned Kay!" Ari was panicked, like she knew what was coming and she had to tell me everything as quickly as possible.

"Tell me! What is it?" I asked never feeling fear like it.

"It's us! It's only ever been about us! Don't you see, it's all been a lie…"

"What are you talking about it?!" I asked looking behind us and thankfully not seeing another car following us.

"Our whole lives Kay…it was never real…*we were never real!"* Hearing this was like being suspended in ice unable to move from fear of freezing to death. Every inch of my skin was covered in bumps and all my hair stood on end like I was already trapped in that icy water.

"That's…that's *impossible."* I said shaking my head as the hopelessness washed over me.

"Think Kay, is it, is it really so impossible?! Think back to your dreams, think back to the girl! What is she trying to tell you?!" Ari shouted after swerving to miss a tree and a branch snapped back against the side of the truck's frame, making me jump.

"How do you know this? What happened? What did you see, Ari? Tell me!" I said asking a million questions and Ari was just about to answer at least one of them when she noticed something in the mirror.

"Oh shit, they're here! They found us!" She said and I looked back to see nothing but shadows…but wait, those weren't trees.

"What's happening?"

"You need to get out of here, you need to find a way inside your dreams and lead you to the girl, they are the only ones that can help. You need to find a way to save us all, Kay." If I was shaking my head before then now I was really shaking my head.

"What do you mean me…Ari you're coming with me!"

"Shit!" She shouted just as the light on the truck illuminated the sight in front of us. It only confirmed what we feared all along.

"By the Gods! No one ever made it out did they?" Ari didn't need to answer. Not considering what we were both looking at. And not considering the size of that stone wall blocking us out from the rest of the world.

We were trapped…but most of all…

We had *always* been trapped.

Ari swerved the truck at just the right moment making it slam the side into the wall. Our bodies jarred sideways and I hit my head on the glass. Pain erupted but it wasn't enough to stop me from moving when Ari told me to.

"We need to get on the roof, quick!" I followed after her, pulling myself out of the driver's side window and using the window frame to climb up on the roof of the car.

"Grab that branch to pull yourself up…hurry, they will be here any second." I did as I was told and I let Ari hold my legs and heave me up enough to reach it. I then used it to walk the rest of the way up the wall until I reached the top. Once I did I got on my belly, anchored my legs and reached my hand down for Ari to grab.

"Jump up!" I shouted down at her but she was just stood on the roof looking out as if readying herself for what was coming.

"Ari grab my hand!" I shouted again but she wasn't listening. I started to panic so said the only thing she would listen to.

"Right I am coming back down there!" This got her attention. She turned her head slowly at first, as if an eerie calm had overtaken her.

"They won't kill me, not yet…they need me to keep up the shields, that's how they have done this for so long. Eight girls… eight months… You need to trust me Kay."

"No! What are you saying, just come with me!" She wasn't making sense!

"I can't, that's not what I am here for…I know that now. I was always meant to save you. To keep you safe until this day came…You're the one Kay, the one they're really afraid of, that's why they needed you. They needed you for the end."

"Ari, you're not making sense! Come on!" I begged with tears streaming down my face but why wouldn't she listen!

"Bring them here Kay…bring them here and save the world. It was what we were always meant to do. Bring them here…*and save me.*"

"Bring who here! Please Ari, I don't understand!"

"Bring your dreams here…they are looking for you…just let them find you Kay…let *him* find you."

"WHO?" I screamed out my sobbing frustrations at her.

"Your Demon." No! She couldn't possibly mean…no, she was scared, she only said this because she feared for my life! Well I couldn't let her. I wouldn't leave her…I could never leave her!

"Ari no! Please! Oh god please, come on!"

"Go! Go now!" Ari said again and I cried harder, bawling in sight of my outstretched hand, one she refused to take.

"I'm not leaving you!" I tried one last time but then they came. The shadows were running straight at her and she just stood there and waited for them like this was her only purpose.

"I love you my sister." That was the last thing I heard before she jumped off the car and started running the other way so that they would follow her.

"ARIANNA !" I screamed her name alerting a few of them to run at me. They moved like nothing I had seen before, looking more like animals than humans.

"Ahhh!" I shouted my fright as I tried to find footing on the other side as I could only assume it was the same height down.

My foot slipped and my head disappeared just as one of the Fathers leapt onto the roof of the car like a giant cat. He even hissed at me, showing me his deadly fangs in threat. I fell, still taking with me that sight of evil but thankfully I hit the ground a lot sooner than I would have thought. I hurt my knee but at least nothing felt broken.

"You won't get far without your sister and we have her now!" I looked up to see that same foul face smiling down at me from the top of the wall. I knew I needed to run so I grabbed the stone wall to heave myself up only something unexpected happened. My touch seemed to trigger something within the stone because a bright white light suddenly burst from behind the stone, coming through the cracks. The Vampire screamed a high pitched wail as if the wall itself was burning hot. His hands lost their hold and he flung himself backwards from the stone until his body disappeared on the other side.

I stumbled backwards down the grass banking that obviously saved me from greater injury.

"What's happening?" I asked myself out loud as I moved back even further. The bright light had dimmed to a soft glow and I could now see what it really was. It was as if someone had painted invisible symbols that only showed under a certain light. I had no clue what they were, all these lines and shapes that made no sense but it seemed whatever they were, my touch had flipped the switch and turned them on. I looked around in desperation and then screamed when lightening hit the sky and thunder quickly followed. The rain started to pour down hard around me and I started to look for ways that I could get back in there.

"Ari." I had to save my sister. I had to get back to her! I walked back up to the wall and started to feel for any grooves that would aid my climbing but it was useless. The rain had made the stone slick and I just slipped and fell time and time again. I started to walk further down, hoping that maybe the wall didn't go on for as long I as originally thought but one more flash of lightening told me otherwise.

The wall was endless.

"NO! No this can't be happening! ARI!" I screamed her name again and fell to my knees. I hit the muddy wet ground over and over until my hands felt numb to the pain.

"Why! Why did you do that! Why would you leave me... why?" My question went unanswered and I let my head fall hopelessly into my hands as I wept for my loss.

"I can't do this...I can't do this without you...I can't Ari... come back to me, please just come back..." I whispered this hopeless plea into the ground before I got up and began to run. I ran and ran until I thought my legs would give out but when that didn't happen, I just ran some more...until I just stopped and my anger finally died. I knew why she had done it. She thought she was saving me but we could have made it. I knew we could have if she had just trusted me. But now what...I just didn't know.

It took me until now to realise that once I stopped running I could see that all this time I had been doing so along an empty road. At least it was a real road this time, which meant that it was used often. So when I saw the blinding headlights I wasn't surprised. I held up my hand to shield myself against the light and when the car stopped, I didn't have anything left in me to worry enough who was in that car.

"Hey, are you alright?" The question made me laugh and when I heard the unnatural sound coming from me I knew I was close to losing it.

"Oh dear, Denis look, she's soaked to the bone." I heard a woman call out to who I assumed was her husband, who was walking towards me.

"You stay in the car, Lucy." The man warned probably

worried I was some crazy person. Well if they heard any of what I had been through in the past forty-eight hours then they would be driving me to the nearest nut house.

"Oh Jesus, you're only a young girl." The man said and the name Jesus was one I hadn't heard in a very long time. It at least told me one thing and that was they had nothing to do with the Colony. He took a few steps closer to me and I found that I had finally hit my limit...or at least my body had, because he caught me just in time for me to collapse.

My world turned black.

'Bring them here Kay, bring them and save us all... He's looking for you Kay...Let him find you'
"...Who?"
'Your Demon.'

I woke with the whispers still dancing along the edges of my mind but I instantly knew there was something else wrong. For a start the bed I was lay in was the most comfortable I ever remember sleeping in and waking up warm and cosy was definitely a new experience. This was when the horror of last night started to creep its way back in. Suddenly I bolted upright and called out for the only person in this world I wished was by my side.

"Ari!"

"Oh lovey, you're awake." A lady's voice spoke and my mind had to focus on getting my eyes to work. I started to push myself up and this was when the lady started fussing.

"Be careful now, your fever only just broke and you need lots of rest after what you just went through."

"Wh..." I had to clear my throat and drink some of the water she held out for me before continuing my question.

"What I just went through?" I had to be sure I hadn't said

anything last night or this comfy bed might actually be the property of a mental ward.

"Yes, getting stuck in that storm like that and walking all that way…we looked for your broken down car for a bit but you must have walked miles! My husband thinks you must have gotten lost in the woods or something as he looked the next day for your car and still couldn't find it." Unbeknown to her generous heart, she had just offered me the perfect excuse.

"It was stolen." I said lying and no longer worried too much about the fire and brimstone we had always been threatened with growing up.

"Oh gosh no! How terrible." She said shaking her head and I felt guilty but to be honest if she knew what I had really been through, then I think I would have received a little bit more than an 'oh Gosh', so I felt better knowing I was sparing her the truth.

"That's just terrible, you poor dear." She said patting my hand and giving me a warm smile. She was a middle-aged woman with kind eyes and a pretty face. Her hair was cut into a cute bob and I could tell that only one side wanted to do as it was told, as it flicked out against the other side that curled under. I bet it drove her nuts like it did my own mother…but wait, where had that thought just come from? My mother didn't have hair like that.

"You must be starving!" She said shocking me with her enthusiasm. She got up and said, "I bet you could do with some nice warm soup and crusty bread…that always sorts me out when I am poorly…I will be right back." Then she left but before closing the door all the way, she popped her head back in and said,

"Silly me, I never asked your name?" I smiled at her and said,

"It's Katie."

"Well Katie, it's nice to meet you. I'm Lucy, my mom was addicted to 'I Love Lucy' reruns…" She laughed once and then said,

"Anyway, my husband is called Denis and he and I both welcome you to our home."

"I don't know how to thank you…" I started to say but she laughed again,

"Oh now, it's no bother. I am just glad we found you when we did…now I will just go and get that soup, you rest up honey." After she left was the time I finally broke down. I just couldn't help it or the soundless sobs of helplessness that bubbled over. I covered my face from the shame I felt at leaving my sister.

I just couldn't understand why she didn't grab my hand when she had the chance. None of it made any sense, especially everything she had said before we got separated.

Thinking back to it all made my head spin and the same words of despair played back over and over…

'Our whole lives Kay…it was never real…we were never real!'

It was chilling the way she had said it, like she truly believed this was the case. But how could she think this? After a lifetime of memories together, after everything we had been through, how could she think none of it was real?

Nothing made any sense anymore. It was as though all her words were jumbling themselves up in my head and only ones like…*Lies… save the world… they won't kill me…not yet…*were lighting up as though this was the key to it all.

"Here we are all nice and …oh dear! Your nose…here let me help you." Lucy placed down her tray and rushed to my side handing me tissues from the bedside. I looked down to see blood on my chest and realised I was having a nose bleed. I took the tissues and placed them under my nose to soak up the blood.

"Bath…room?" I asked with a muffled voice. She pointed through a door and as I stood I would have fallen if Lucy hadn't been there to steady me.

"Oh dear, here let me help you." I let her lead me into the bathroom, grateful for her help as I had never felt so weak. It made me wonder how long I had been out there in the storm, wandering the road in search of my sister. I reached the sink and moved the tissue to assess if it was still bleeding or not. Thankfully it looked to have stopped, so I placed the used tissue on the side of the sink and then washed away the dried blood on my chin.

"Now don't overdo it but if you feel like a shower then please help yourself. I will find you something better than one of Denis' old T-shirts to wear. I am sure my daughter Kelly is the same size as you…"

"Oh but I couldn't take…" I started to protest by saying she had done so much for me already when she interrupted me in the kindest way possible.

"It's no bother, if anything you are doing me a favour."

"I am?" I asked surprised how it was possible I could be doing her a favour when all she had done was help me.

"Sure. Kelly left all these clothes, half of them still have the tags on I think…a bit of a shopaholic my Kelly, but anyway, she went off to college and left me with a few bags in the attic that I never got round to taking to the thrift store." By the time she turned around to hand me the towels she found me sobbing again.

"Oh no honey, what's wrong?" She dumped the towels on the toilet seat and rushed to hug me from behind.

"I'm sorry, it's just that you're so kind and…and…" I think she got what I was trying to say as she pulled me in for a proper hug and for the first time in forever I cried in the arms of someone other than Ari.

"It's alright…that's it, you get it all out… its okay." She cooed whispering softly and rubbing my back in soothing circles. I pulled back to look at her and said,

"You are the kindest woman I have ever met." To which she blushed and hugged me again.

"Well aren't you a sweet child. Right time to get yourself washed up. I will grab those clothes for you and you can choose what you like, heck you could have the whole lot if want…now tut, tut, like I said you would be doing me a favour." She said stopping me again from protesting.

"Thank you Lucy." She gave me a warm smile and then left me to have a shower. I shook my head at how lucky I had been to have such loving people find me. I knew they had most likely saved my life as I don't know how much longer I would have lasted out in that storm.

I pulled back the shower curtain wondering when the last time was I had experienced a *real* shower. In most aspects living at the Colony had been like travelling back in time and being forced to live in poverty. I knew the house had bathrooms but it was rare we were allowed to use them other than to go to the toilet.

Washing ourselves had become something we *had* to do, not something we ever took pleasure in. Especially in winter when sometimes you would first have to break the ice that had formed on the top of the water bowl before washing yourself. Summers were something to look forward to in more ways than one, as it also meant not shivering in your bed until you finally fell asleep from the day's exhaustion.

So stepping into the shower now was like basking under the hot rays of sunlight only Heaven provided. I think I could have stayed there all day, with the hot water pouring down on my skin. Even using the shower gel felt like a new experience, especially having one that smelled so nice. Harsh and clinical smelling soap was the only thing we were granted when washing, so this almost had me salivating for the taste of fruit. To the point I had to resist from licking the bubbles off my skin.

Again, washing my hair with shampoo *and* conditioner was something I only remembered from when I was a kid. All the things the outside world must take for granted, because let's face it, unless it is taken away from you, then you rarely have the chance to miss it.

I was just rinsing the last of the soap from my skin after wanting to wash myself for the second time when I heard a noise. At first I thought it must be Lucy, maybe wondering why I was taking so long. So I turned off the water and stepped out of the bath the shower head was over. I grabbed a towel to wrap around myself and did the same with my hair. I then opened the door a crack and frowned when I found it empty.

"Strange." I muttered turning back to the mirror over sink. It was all foggy from the steam so I raised my hand to wipe it clear…

And screamed.

CHAPTER 8
ALL HAIL THE MODERN AGE

L ooking at my reflection in the mirror should never have to be shocking. Yes, there were a few times I had been hit across the face when living at the Colony and looking at the proof of how much you hated your life was never a pretty sight.

But this was something else.

Blood once again poured from my nose but this time when I looked down there was nothing to show for it.

"What the hell?" I asked aloud and then looked back up to my reflection thinking maybe I had simply imagined it all. But looking back only confirmed my fears and blood was everywhere. It ran down the mirror in streams and everything I moved to the side it would flow all over again from the same place my nose was. I couldn't understand what was happening, or more like why for that matter.

A sudden knock on the door had me squeaking in fright.

"Sorry Katie, did I scare you? I just wanted to let you know I found those clothes and put them on the bed for you. I was also going to reheat your soup for when you got out, so take your time." The whole time Lucy spoke I frantically tried to rub the one way blood from the mirror in case she came in.

"Umm…thanks, that sounds great." I said trying to sound normal whilst getting nowhere with the phantom blood that refused to go away.

"No bother Honey." She said before I heard the bedroom door close and I turned back to the mirror. I grabbed a flannel off the side and turned on the taps in my next desperate attempt to be rid of the sight. I was just lifting it to the glass when freaky turned into freakier. My reflection was the first to change and my other self started to shake her head making me drop the wet cloth back into the sink with a splat.

My nose still poured with blood but my reflection didn't seem to mind. She simply raised up her hand and tapped on the side of her nose before looking down at the blood. The crimson streams started to waver before joining the multiple lines together and then flowing down the mirror further to form words.

No, not words, just one word…

'AFTERLIFE'

"Afterlife? What's that supposed to mean?" I asked frowning as the red letters spelled out something I only knew as life after death. What was it trying to tell me exactly?

"What do you want from me?" I whispered feeling myself shaking with fear at seeing myself this way, so I gripped onto the sides of the sink as I waited for my answer. I followed the rivers down the mirror until finally they formed another message,

'FIND IT'

"Find it? Find what…death?" I asked now feeling even more confused. It wanted me to find death? I looked back up when the girl in the mirror that was me started shaking her head to indicate 'no'. Then the blood spelled out one last word until it was all lost…

'HOME'

"Home?"

After my strange encounter with myself in the bathroom I was left even more confused than last night. What were these visions trying to tell me? The only Afterlife I knew was what we learned of Heaven and Hell, and considering our teachers turned out to be monsters, I didn't think that was going to be much help. And how much could I really trust in something that was suggesting I needed to first die in order to get my answers, unless…

'Afterlife' was the name of a place?

As soon as the thought entered my head the light literally went on above my head as Lucy had just flicked the switch upon entering. I would have laughed under different circumstances, however seeing Lucy struggling with her tray had me rushing over to help. I took it off her and the delicious smell coming from the bowl had me salivating. My stomach must have sensed food was near as the rumble that erupted even Lucy heard as she started laughing.

"I guess someone is hungry." She said nodding towards the small table that was over by the window bay. I placed it down and pulled up the chair ready to dive in but out of habit waited until I was given the blessing to do so. Lucy frowned at me as if confused and then gave an odd look to the Colony's clothes I had been wearing that were now hung over the back of a chair. It was as if something clicked so she said,

"Oh please, go ahead and eat child, don't wait around on my account." My stomach sang up its Halleluiahs and I dived in. After only a few silent minutes watching me eat Lucy started laughing.

"My word Child, but I don't think I have ever seen someone enjoy my food as much…that's not to say I am a bad cook mind you, but well, I guess you must have been starving, when was the last time you had a good meal?" I gave her a small embarrassed smile before swallowing my mouthful of fresh bread and answering her.

"I'm not sure but I can't ever remember tasting soup so nice and bread so fresh." Lucy gave me a sad smile back and after a deep sigh got up.

"Then let me get you some seconds." She came over and once again waved off my polite objections. Whilst she was gone I looked out of the window and onto a cute decking area that had two wooden chairs with a small table between. The view when sat there would have looked out to a well maintained garden, with a sweet little pond surrounded by mature trees. There was even a BBQ under cover and I could actually picture the life Lucy must have. Her and her husband, Denis sat there on hot summer days watching the sun go down with a glass of wine.

I turned back to the room and finally started to take in the details. A cute patchwork comforter lay on the bed using the colours of the American flag which followed through in the whitewashed pine furniture and the red and blue rag rugs that lay on the wooden floor. Pictures of boats on the harbor and trees in fall told me someone was a keen photographer in the house and I wondered if it was Lucy's husband Denis.

As a whole it was so warm and welcoming that it put Mrs Collingwood's 'homely feeling' rooms to shame. It felt safe and secure in a way I had never known and I found myself wishing I never had to leave. Even looking down at myself now and seeing how different I looked had me feeling a sense of belonging in this new world that I never thought I could have. But the guilt that went with any of these feelings had tears burning to break free. It wasn't fair to feel this way when I knew Ari was still out there somewhere, or even worse, a prisoner to those monsters of nature.

All of these new things I had only ever dreamt of experiencing them with Ari, so walking out of the bathroom to find all of these clothes to choose from was conflicting. I had felt my heart leap at seeing all the colours and soft comfy materials but then the pang of regret would hit and all I could see was a pile of clothes that would look great on my sister.

In the end I had pulled on a pair of jeans that despite the dire circumstances still had me smiling at the feel of denim once again. I then picked up a T-shirt that still had the tags on as Lucy had said. It had Route 66 written on the front which I covered up with a soft grey knitted sweater that had a big rolling neck and long wide sleeves. Looking at myself in the mirror for the first time dressed like this had me staring open mouthed in utter shock. For the first time in my adult life I looked …well…*normal.*

I had even plaited my hair to one side deciding I never again in my life was wearing it in a tight and uncomfortable bun at the base of my neck. Looking at me now no-one would have guessed the life I had run away from but one look at that dress Lucy had washed and she knew. Her face said as much, so when she brought me back seconds I wasn't surprised when she started asking questions.

"Your car wasn't stolen was it?" I almost choked on my food at this point.

"It's okay, I understand why you would lie about it, after all I can imagine that the Amish lifestyle isn't for everyone." My first thought was the guilt I felt in lying to someone who had helped me but then confusion took over and I had to ask,

"Amish? What's that?" After this question it was now Lucy's turn to frown.

"You mean you weren't in an Amish community?" My face must have said it all.

"But your dress and…" I decided it was time that I confided in her.

"I escaped from a deeply religious Colony that me and my sister Ari were forced to go to when our father died in a car accident." Lucy gasped in shock and this is where my story began. I told her everything I could remember, sparing her the gruesome details when I could. I ate my food as she asked questions and left out anything unworldly as I didn't think she would believe me if I started accusing the Fathers of being Vampires. The only reason we knew what they could be in the first place was thanks to some monster cartoons we used to watch as kids before life at the Colony began.

I told her about only being able to leave once we had hit the right age, shocking her when I told her mine as she must have thought me much younger. I decided to warp the truth and said that my sister and I had this choice taken away from us so we knew the only hope we had was to leave. When she asked about my sister was when I found myself breaking down and admitting she had been recaptured just after I had made it over the wall.

Lucy talked about going to the authorities with this information but after I explained that everyone is controlled under fear and that they were unlikely to find any proof of my allegations, she agreed it wasn't such a good idea after all.

"So what are you going to do?" She asked once I had finished the last of my meal. I put down my spoon and looked out the window before answering with the only plan I had.

"Ari was in contact with someone from the outside. I know if I can find him then he will know people that can help us." Lucy gave me a nod and then said,

"I know what you need."

"What's that?" I asked smiling when she took my tray. She stopped just before leaving and said,

"Dessert…oh, and the Internet." She then winked at me and left me wondering what was an 'Internet'?

Lucy spent the rest of the day teaching me a crash course on the computer, eating lemon meringue pie and being introduced to the marvel that was Google. I couldn't believe you now had a library at your fingertips and could learn about everything at the touch of a button! I wanted to go crazy on it and I would have if Lucy hadn't been there. She thought it best if I go slow and first start to learn more about 'her' world as I kept putting it.

Being born in the early 90's meant I still knew about the existence of computers but by the time we were forced into the Colony having personal computers in your home meant having a TV with a keyboard, mouse and a computer tower plugged into it.

Our father had one in his office at home for work and he allowed me and Ari to play games on it every so often, which was probably why it felt so natural to me after being on it after only a few hours. Even if this was the case, I still couldn't get over how small and compact they now were. Lucy told me that since laptops came down in price hardly anyone these days bothered with 'Desktops' which I gathered meant the one like my father had.

I just remember Ari playing a game called Lemmings and getting angry when all her little men went splat off a cliff.

"Ari would have loved this." I told Lucy when she showed me a few of her favorite sites. She loved one called Pinterest where she got most of her recipes and craft ideas from. She also talked me through 'Social Media' and explained sites like Facebook and Twitter. She told me this was how she stayed in contact with her daughter Kelly and also one called Skype where they could actually see each other through 'Video Calling'. It was all amazing to learn about and I was in awe at how far the world of technology had come. But then there was the other side to it all, the one I chose not to speak to Lucy about as I didn't quite understand it myself.

It was the strange feeling that as soon as I was shown something new it felt more like I had just been reminded instead of seeing it for the first time. Almost what I can imagine waking from a coma was like and being reminded of the life you had been sleeping through. I tried to ignore it but the more she showed me the harder that became.

"I must say, you pick things up really quick." Lucy had commented proving to me that it wasn't just all in my head. I guess if I was to really think about it then a lot of things didn't seem that lost to me but more like simply forgotten. Even the clothes I was wearing felt more natural to me than if I had been wearing that horrid dress for the last eighteen years. The food, the smells, even the shower had all felt like life had at last found me again and I wondered if there was more to these feelings than I allowed myself to believe.

Using the laptop now was no different than Ari suddenly being able to drive the way she did last night. How was that possible after a lifetime of living together and never once seeing her in the driver's seat of a car or me with a laptop on my knee, yet we had both taken to it like old times? None of it made any sense and it wasn't long before I was given the time alone to think about this.

Lucy had left the room to make dinner for tonight and no doubt in time for when her husband Denis returned home from work. She had left me with the laptop to continue exploring and given me enough tips about looking for someone on the Internet. She had tried asking me questions about this 'friend' of Ari's but when I couldn't answer any she just patted me on the knee and said,

"I am sure it will come to you."

After that the answer had been clear and was exactly what Ari had tried to tell me. I needed to let my dreams and visions guide me and pick up on the clues they were trying to tell me. I needed to recap and think back to everything that had happened in them. If only I had paid more attention to the smaller details. However, that had been hard because as soon as a certain male figure had stepped into the room all thought process had been solely focused on him. Every single thought dominated by a man whose name I didn't even know and someone I believed evil enough to kidnap the other side of me in my dreams. The whole thing was as crazy as it got but unfortunately the reality of the matter was, it was simply all I had to go on.

So I thought back to my most recent vision and after a nervous shudder, typed in Google the only words I had to go by…

'What is Afterlife?'

CHAPTER 9
THE LONELY ROAD

How had this happened? How had I messed up so badly to find myself back here again. I couldn't remember what it had been that I had done wrong but if I was back here then it must have been something unforgivable.

Once again I found myself walking down an empty road to nowhere feeling as though the weight of the world lay on my shoulders. Well at least this time there was no storm to soak me to the bone and I looked down to realise that they thankfully let me keep the clothes. How could I not remember? Had I upset Lucy, my new friend...*my only friend?*

I looked straight ahead to see the endless road that held no answers but only more questions. Ones like 'Where was I going?' and 'How would I get there?' I knew I needed to be somewhere, I could feel it as though it was connected with my soul. As though something was calling me home. I wanted to believe I could get there, I really did, but the uncertainty was overwhelming my belief.

It was because of what Ari had said to me in the car. That

haunting sentence that warned me of things I knew were to come.

A truth I knew I didn't want to face.

'Our whole lives Kay…it was never real…we were never real!'

How could she say we were never real? How could she do that to me?!

"WHY?!" I screamed at the road in anger only hoping she would be there at the end of it to answer me. Because that's what I needed, answers not more questions. But more importantly this was the time I most needed to believe in myself and how could I do that if Ari didn't? It was infuriating and made no sense why she said any of what she did that night. I was caught between two frustrations of both wanting to grab her and hold her close when I saw her again and the other was to shake her so hard she would realise her mistake.

If only she had grabbed my hand. If only she had trusted me to take care of her. If only…

Wait, what was that?

I squinted against the fading light as night was quickly seeping in ready to take the place of the sun. It looked like a figure walking towards me in the distance and getting closer. Where all the cars were on this road I didn't know but like me the person was mirroring me by walking dead centre at the same pace.

I wanted to run to the person, knowing somewhere deep inside they were here because of me. I wanted to run as fast as I could thinking that on some small prayer that it could have been Ari but then logic started to seep in and I started to ask myself how she would know that I was here. So I continued to walk as the other person did. It felt like some act of rebellion that neither of us wanted to back down from. Two lone people out meeting each other in this deserted part of the world. The closer we got to one another the more the light died and night was all that was left to greet us.

So with the details lost I had no choice but to wait until the bitter end to see who I would come face to face with. They walked with purpose the same as I and I wondered which one of us would break first. In the end we both did and we starting running at each other at the same time. I felt my pulse beating against my skin as I strained to make it to the figure quicker. I ran and I ran, over and over just like I had done that night but the closer we got to each other the less and less it made sense. Because just before I could stop myself and before that point where I could comprehend what I was seeing I ran straight through the mirror before me.

Glass exploded all around me just like it did that day in the car, only this time I could see my own terrified expression reflecting back at me printed on all the tiny shards. I had run straight into the mirror that divided our worlds and as I burst through to the other side I stumbled onto the floor. I looked down at myself feeling no injury but still needing to check. I was amazed to find not one scratch on me and I looked back to find the locked doorway between our worlds had finally been destroyed.

"I did it." I said out loud speaking for the first time in my dream world but the most important question remained…had I been heard this time? I got up from the floor and looked around the room I knew well. It was the same one I had been living most of my nights locked on the other side and trying to find my way into for the last eight months. This was the room I had witnessed what loving someone could make you do.

It was the room *he* had locked her in and stolen from her soul time and time again. It was her prison and his hands had been the shackles that tied her to the bed. Her Demon jailor that…that…

"No, that doesn't feel right." I said aloud when my thoughts started to trip up on themselves. Suddenly thinking that way no longer felt right. Why was that? What had changed that meant bathing him in that light just felt like painting the truth with lies. I looked to the bed and saw my naked body spread out shuddering in rapture. I blinked back the vision and felt like something was crumbling away in my mind. It was as if I was stood on the edge of a canyon and had to keep walking backwards as the floor cracked beneath me.

Suddenly my small world started to open up around me and it felt as if I had finally started to open my eyes to *her world*. I turned as though that world was pulling me to do so and I walked towards the glass doors that led outside. I touched the glass not ever expecting them to push open as you would have thought. Nor was I surprised when they simply disappeared into the stone wall either side.

The cold wind testing my skin only made this world feel even more real and I sucked in a quick breath in shock. Not shock at feeling the air blowing through my hair or the even the smell of being surround by nature. Not the shock that it felt like I was actually here for the first time since the obsession began. But shock at seeing the beautiful sight before me that felt like it had been lost long ago.

"I have seen this." I said knowing it was true. This sight that felt like I had once fell in love enough to paint it and I didn't even know how to paint…did I? It was a stunning vista of oceans of green. Rolling mountains and sweeping valleys that looked touched by the Gods. But which Gods were those I wondered and why when thinking about them did I no longer feel any fear.

I stepped up to the railings and instead of looking down at

the immense drop I knew was there I understood that's not what I was here for. I had never known where this place was in the world or if it even really existed but none of that mattered. Because something pulled me to look to the sides and see what the building looked like and it looked like a castle. I frowned as soon as the thought entered my mind as though it knew the assumption was wrong.

"No, not a castle...*home.*" This is where she wanted me to go. This is what Ari was desperately trying to tell me. I had to find this place, I knew that now. I had to do everything in my power to try. Because I was no longer scared. I couldn't be because Ari couldn't afford me to be. I didn't know who these people were or what I might find when I finally knocked on their door but I knew one thing, if Ari believed they were the ones who could help me save her, then that was what I would do.

I just wish it had been as easy as seeing the address written down or why a vision couldn't tell me as much?

"But you know why, don't you?" The sound of his voice caused my breathing to hitch. I felt his presence right behind me but knowing he was there didn't prevent me from flinching when I felt his touch for the first time.

"Easy." He warned softly placing his hands on my shoulders and the weight of them scared me, knowing the power he held within. The touch of his fingers when they found the bare skin beneath the sweater I wore caused me to moan and the shock of it prevented my head from falling backwards against him. All I wanted to do was sink back into him and let him finally hold me the way I had always craved. To be the one to feel his touch now was...well, this was what breathing for the first time felt like. Breathing free and safe was the only way to explain it.

"Where did you go, Vixen?" He asked hypnotising me with

his commanding voice that at the moment was velvet smooth hiding the rawness that I knew lived there within him. I had seen it, the beast with wings he kept controlled and buried until the time came to release them upon the world. Was that what he needed me for, or did he believe I was *her* again?

"I know you." He told me, whispering his promise near my ear and I felt his lips form the words against my skin. His hands squeezed my shoulders before releasing his hold enough to caress up my neck, holding me still firmly in his control.

"You left me...*why?"* He hissed out the accusation as his grip tightened around the column of my neck. I thought this was it, my moment in this hidden world was coming to an end and I would take my last breath in it by his hands. But his grip simply became a constant reminder that he could apply pressure at any moment and end it all.

"I...I...never left you." I said this knowing it was true as I knew I never could. How I knew this I didn't know but it still didn't take away the truth behind every word.

"Are you coming home?" He asked and this time I let my emotions win. My head fell back into his chest and I felt the tears flow up and over. Because my next words were too much for me to bear, they escaped on a whisper that broke me...

"I'm trying."

"Good girl." A sob escaped when he said this as it felt as though I had heard it so many times before and not once when doing so had it not felt like it came from the deepest levels of love. This was the moment. This was what it felt like to be loved. Loved so much it made you do crazy things. Incredible things. It made you do the impossible but above all...

It made you survive.

~

Unsurprisingly I woke up to find it had all been another dream. But boy, what a dream! Not only had I finally broken through the mirror but I had also had my first encounter with him in a way that I never knew was possible. Yes, he scared me but when he touched me the way he had done it made me yearn for that fear in ways I could barely comprehend let alone explain.

This time it had all felt different, unlike before when I had received his anger at him finding the wrong version of me in his room. It was as if the last barrier between me and that world was as simple as opening my eyes to the truth of where I truly belonged. Before, looking in was like watching a secret life of my fantasies play out like an opera. What once felt like a sinful act of imagining the impossible or improbable world in which she lived was now becoming a sinful act in ignoring it. Because what if Ari was right, what if she had been hit with the proof we both needed but was robbed of the time to explain it to me?

What if this was the improbable world we lived in? The world created behind the walls keeping us locked in a prison, one we didn't even know about. What if all this time my other self had been trying to get *me* out, what if I had been the prisoner...*could that be possible?*

I sat up shaking my head wondering if thinking this wasn't just torturing myself further. I didn't know where that place was and you would have thought that if that was my goal then I would have received more clues up until now. But other than that one word 'Afterlife' I had nothing to go on.

Needless to say the genius search of putting 'Afterlife' in Google awarded me with thousands of theories on what happened after death. So I wasn't all that surprised when it didn't offer up any solutions. That night I joined Lucy and her husband for dinner and I didn't miss Denis' smirks when seeing how much I obviously enjoyed Lucy's home cooking. In fact it felt like eating real food for the first time and I quickly realised one of my new favourite things in life was spicy food. I don't ever remember feeling so full before and in the end Lucy had to cut me off before I made myself sick, besides she said, "There is dessert".

When this turned out to contain chocolate, to my shame I actually moaned out loud. Denis burst out laughing and Lucy scowled at him but it wasn't long before I too was laughing. I explained how it had been a long time since my chocolate days and this turned out to be a good thing as I was given the biggest piece of brownie.

"Ha, not laughing now are you!" Lucy said to Denis making us all burst out laughing again.

Having dinner with the both of them felt so at ease I was quickly getting to a point where I never wanted to leave. It gave me a taste of the good life and I envied Kelly, Lucy's daughter, for having the upbringing I always dreamed of. If only Ari could have been here, then I think my world would have been complete. It was obvious that Lucy was in no hurry to see me out the door and kept saying I was welcome to stay as long as I wanted.

At first I had been worried that her husband might not have the same feelings as Lucy but after dinner it was clear my fears were for nothing. After I thanked him for letting me stay he leant over and whispered to me once Lucy was clearing the table,

"I learnt a long time ago, that a happy wife equals a happy life." I gave him a beaming grin before standing to help Lucy in the kitchen. Yes, I liked Denis and I adored Lucy. To be honest I think since Kelly had left for College that Lucy didn't know what to do with herself and me being here was offering up a nice little distraction. Well if I could help in any way, as I knew repaying them back for the kindness they had shown was something I could only wish to do one day.

Lucy talked about them always wanting to go abroad and seeing Europe but money had been tight since paying for their daughter's college, so their plan was to go when she had finished her last year. I went to bed that night thinking about once all this was done and Ari and I were finally making it in the world then maybe I could do something.

This fantasy popped in my head of surprising them both one day with tickets to France or maybe Spain. Saving up my tips and paying for that trip sooner than they expected. Yes, that was what I was going to try and do. Maybe it wouldn't be soon but one day. I would do it even if I had to work as many shifts as a waitress or every hour at the supermarket that I could, I was going to get them their dream. Because I knew how important dreams were to people and I knew what it was like to hope for something in your life and even if they knew it or not, they had helped me with my dream, so it was only fair that I help them with theirs.

But first thing was first and that was...

"What on earth was Afterlife?"

I grabbed the laptop that Lucy had left in the room with me in case I couldn't sleep and wouldn't you know, she was right. I opened it back up, squinted against the bright screen and after finding my new best friend 'Google' I typed in the same thing I had fifty times before.

The first searches were all the same. There were films, TV series, even books and that was before all the hundreds of pages all relating to what happened after death. So this was when I thought it was time to get a little creative. First I typed in 'Afterlife people' but this only got me a list of Spiritual guidance and foundations and also links to articles titled 'My glimpses of the afterlife mean I no longer fear death'.

I even started to research dreams and visions but this only got me even more frustrated. But then an idea formed, what if some spiritual guidance was what I needed? So then I changed my search yet again, only this time I was looking for anything from palm readers, fortune tellers, tarot readers, mystics and clairvoyants, anyone who might be able to give me insight to what was obviously locked away inside my mind. I didn't care who and at this rate I was even willing to be hypnotised as long as it meant finding something useful in there.

But this again posed my next problem as I didn't have any money and these types of people usually asked for a fee. Not that I could blame them I guess as everyone needed to live and buy food and at the moment I could do neither. I would have to ask Lucy in morning if she knew of anywhere I could get a job, if only for a short time as that was the one thing not on my side at the moment...

Time.

One month.

That's all I had. Because playing back Ari's words and her saying they wouldn't kill her yet was what she must have meant. I also surmised that the reason a girl was allowed to leave, which was actually code for being brutally murdered, was so they could continue with whatever their plans were. Ari had mentioned something about shields, so this could have been it. Either way I believed deep in my soul that Ari was still alive and would at least remain this way until the next full moon.

This then had me wondering if that Righteous Blood in the barn had actually been acting out against orders or if he wasn't going to kill her, just meant to punish her for sneaking me out. No matter what the answer to that was, I couldn't find myself regretting what I had done. However, my regrets did include what happened next and that was escaping without my sister with me.

I shook away these thoughts knowing they wouldn't get me anywhere. I now had to focus on doing what she told me and that was to listen to my dreams and find the people she believed could help me. I had to wonder if I wasn't just wasting time by chasing visions of people that might not even be real. It was a wild goose chase without even seeing a goose before or knowing if one even exists for that matter. Because the heart of it all was that I had no proof that they, or more like *he*, was even real. That was a terrifying thought in itself and a crushing one at that.

No, I had to believe he was real and I had to believe that he was out there somewhere because if he wasn't then it wasn't just me and my sister that was lost but according to Ari...

It was the world.

CHAPTER 10

THE PERFECT ANSWER

The next day was like having half of my prayers answered. Lucy came into my room and asked if I would like to help her in the kitchen as she was making cakes to sell for a bake stall at the county fair. It was to help raise money for a new roof for her local chapel and I was more than happy to help. To be honest anything that got me away from my new obsession with a search engine was going to be a bonus. Besides any way I could finally show my gratitude wasn't something I was going to pass up on.

Baking with Lucy was fun and I found myself wishing more and more that I could have had a mother like her. But no amount of wishing it was going to change things so it was better to focus on the now, and now was filled with laughing and giggling over cake batter. She asked if I wanted to come along later and help her out, which I was only too happy to do. She told me about the fair they had every year in town and how Denis had come so close to being crowned the 'Veggie King'.

She started laughing so hard when she saw my utter look of confusion and whilst pointing her gooey wooden spoon at me she said,

"You should see your face...such a picture." Then she started spooning her mixture into tins as she started to explain.

"The contestants all have to see who can throw a vegetable the furthest starting with...I don't know, let's say a carrot...then as each person who comes last gets knocked out of the contest, the next round starts again only the vegetable gets bigger. I think that last round is a pumpkin. It's a lot of fun." Lucy assured me and I was giggling just thinking about it.

"I'm looking forward to it." I told her honestly making her smile.

"It will be nice having another person cheering for my Denis, who knows, maybe it's finally his year to win." Lucy said, smiling to herself. After that all I could think was how much I hoped it was his year too.

"That looks lovely." Lucy said and I looked down at the cake I had just made. It was as if I had been on autopilot and making something I had made hundreds of times before, only strangely, this was my first time. It was a chocolate cake with cream and fresh strawberries in the middle and I had just finished pouring on the melted chocolate for the top.

"Thanks, Lucy." I said trying not to let on that I had no clue how I had made it without a recipe to follow, it had all just come naturally to me. It gave me a deep sense that my sister loved it when I made this cake, which was even stranger when I had never made it for Ari before.

"I think you should make a few more like that, as they are going to sell like hot cakes!" I smiled at her kind words and just hoped I wouldn't disappoint when I forgot how I even made the first one. But just like last time my mind took over and before I knew it I had four more on the go.

The next thing I knew Lucy's friends started pouring in and placing cakes and pies down wherever there was space. The place looked like a bakery and the smell, wow...all I knew was that if there was a heaven and there was a distinct smell about it, then it would be this one. Who knew I had such a sweet tooth!

"And who is this fine lady?" One of Lucy's friends asked who smirked and looked as if she was out to cause mischief.

"Ah, well this is one of my cousin's daughters, Katie… she's from up state." Lucy said not even breaking into a sweat.

"Pleased to meet you, Ma'am." I said after first wiping my hand and then offering it to her.

"Oh my Dex is just going to love you. Isn't she a dear?" The older woman said taking my hand in hers and talking about me as though I couldn't hear.

"Jennifer! Behave…honestly she will do anything to set her son Dex up." I laughed blushing at the idea.

"Oh Honey Jesus, she even blushes!" Jennifer said to Lucy who just waved her off with a tea towel.

"Yep and she makes chocolate strawberry cake from scratch as well…this looks delicious, Katie." Another one of Lucy's friends said getting in on the action.

"Thank you." I said getting shy from receiving so much attention.

"Oh Mercy be! She can cook as well, upon my word Lucy, where do you find them! In fact, I will buy this one right now. My Dex just loves chocolate cake and I want to get in there before these puppies are snatched up." Jennifer said hurrying over to one that had already been wrapped up.

"Well that's not fair, if you're buying one then I want one too!" The other friend said picking up one of the others and I thought I was close to seeing war of the cakes. Lucy came over to me and whispered,

"Cake, gossip and marrying off sons can get brutal… welcome to suburbia Katie." I giggled and then asked,

"Should I make some more?"

"I think that's a good idea." Lucy replied winking at me just after Denis had walked in and asked,

"Is that a chocolate cake with strawberries?"

After many more chocolates cakes later we were at the fair and selling most of our stock in the first hour. It was lovely to see Lucy interacting with everyone as it was clear she was well loved within her community. She seemed proud when introducing me to everyone as her cousin's daughter and as a result everyone was more than welcoming. It was strange but it gave me a sense of belonging, one I hadn't felt since...well, since forever.

Once all the baked goods had been sold we packed up our stall and walked around the rest of the fair arm in arm.

"The day has been amazing, thank you so much for including me."

"Are you kidding, with all the help you gave me and not to mention the fact that I was getting double the price I would normally ask thanks to those amazing chocolate cakes of yours ...I don't know where you get it from but you definitely have skills in the kitchen...in fact I don't know how I ever did it without you." I smiled and then asked,

"Did Kelly ever help you out?" At this she laughed.

"Kelly enjoyed eating them more than she would ever have done baking them...besides that girl could burn ice cream given half the chance." I laughed alongside her but my mind flashed to burnt pizzas and a beautiful redhead trying to wave the smoke away with a tea towel. Who was that and where had that memory suddenly sprung from?

"Hey, you okay?" Lucy asked jarring me back into this world and I looked around to realise I had stopped dead at the vision.

"Yeah, sorry, I'm good."

"Oh, that's the bell, we'd better go or we will be late."

"For what?" I asked looking around and seeing everyone had started moving off in the same direction.

"The Veggie King Competition of course."

When we got there people made room for Lucy and I to get to the front and I gathered this was because her husband was competing.

"Oh Lord, but I am nervous for him." She said grabbing my hand once and giving it a squeeze. 'The Arena' consisted of an open field with white lines spray painted in arches to show the distances they had to try and throw. The first round was called 'Catapult the Carrot' and I had to laugh when a woman dressed as a farmer came out and held up boards with the name of the first round, just like you would get at a boxing match. I only remembered this from another of my father's favourite movies which was Rocky.

"He's got this." Lucy said leaning into me and nudging me on my arm. It was so sweet when she started yelling his name when it was his turn to throw. The love simply oozed out of her and the sight had me smiling. It was so beautiful to witness a woman so focused on her husband and cheering him on like no one else mattered. It made me long to find that type of love for myself one day and I knew I would treasure every second of it.

"GO DENIS! THROW THAT CARROT! WHOOOOHOOO!" She shouted when he stepped up to the line and threw the carrot the furthest. I screamed and cheered right alongside with her and Denis turned round and bowed to the crowd making them cheer louder.

I looked over to another part of the field when hearing more people cheering and realised that they had the similar thing on for the younger kids, only with fruit. I looked around at all these people smiling and chatting, cheering and shouting together and realised this was what a community was all about. Supporting each other and no doubt banding together when in times of struggle. Having that shoulder to cry on when experiencing a loss or that kind neighbour you know would help you out if you ever got a flat tyre.

The sense that you were never alone when walking that lonely road that life can sometimes offer. Because friends were important and could love you like family. Or in my case love you *more* if I had to compare Lucy to my own wicked mother.

"He did it again! He won the 'Toss the Turnip' round!" Lucy said clapping in excitement.

"That's great!" I said clapping with her as he once again bowed to the crowd.

"He's such a show off!" Lucy said shaking her head, smirking.

"Oh dear, he always struggles with this one, its 'Lob the Lettice' time." Lucy held up her crossed fingers and went back to screaming her husband's name when his turn was next.

"Don't forget to stretch…STRETCH!" She shouted putting her hands around her mouth like a megaphone. He waved her off and then started to do as he was told anyway, stretch his arms from side to side. I couldn't help but giggle watching five middle aged men all dressed as farmers getting ready as if they were at the gym.

"YES! You did it! He did it! GO DENIS!" Lucy was again screaming when he only just managed to throw his lettuce a fraction closer to the white line.

"Okay so there are only two rounds left, 'Hurl the Horseradish' and 'Pitch the Pumpkin' and he's done it!"

"He can do it." I said patting her on the shoulder and offering my support. Then I linked arms with her and we both watched the next two rounds play out. The 'Hurl the Horseradish' turned out as an equal tie and Lucy leaned over and whispered,

"That's Jennifer's husband and Denis' best friend. They

have a bet on every year that the loser between the two has to play host whenever there is a game on throughout the year and provide the beer!"

"Really?" I asked making Lucy nod.

"I am telling you that if I have to make one more hotdog and buy one more bag of chips, I am going to quit being a housewife...although Jennifer and Alan have no idea that Denis has been cutting Carbs and practicing every weekend since I made the threat...and it shows as look at the leader board, he's winning!" I looked to where Lucy pointed to and sure enough there was his name on the top and winning by 3 points. Lucy also told me that the last round was where the contestants had to kick a pumpkin like a football across the field and into the goal at the end. The first one to get their pumpkin in the net would get ten points added to their score. So it all came down to the hardest round.

"GO ON! YOU CAN DO IT! KICK IT, KICK IT!" Lucy screamed as soon as the whistle was blown and I did the same. All five of the farmers kicked the pumpkin but each having to fight the odd shapes, meaning they never went where the farmers intended. It was so funny to watch that everyone was trying to cheer through their laughter. Even Lucy was in a bulk and needed to bend at the waist to control herself. It was only when it got between the two friends that the cheering got more serious and Jennifer started screaming frantically when it looked like her husband Alan would lose.

"Ha, look at her, she's panicking now! GO ON, YOU CAN DO IT!" And Denis did just that and was first in getting his pumpkin in the net just before Alan.

"HE DID IT!" Lucy went crazy jumping up and down before turning to me and forcing me to do the same and join in. The crowd also went wild and Denis was clearly lapping up the attention and basking in the fact that he was finally the new

'Veggie King'. I had to laugh when he got presented with a crown made from carrots and peapods. But it was the trophy he really cared about and as soon as he received it he held it up and shouted,

"I did it, Lucy!" Her beaming smile told everyone how proud of him she was and after this he took the massive scissors that were handed to him and as the new king got to cut the ribbon to open the fairground. Everyone cheered once more before swarming towards the fair's rides and sweet stalls. For me it felt like Christmas again as I couldn't remember the last time I had seen anything like it. The flashing fairy lights, the delicious smells, the joyous screaming coming from the rides and children and families all laughing and having a good time. It was amazing to me and I tried not to let the sadness creep in that Ari and I were denied this.

"Ari would have loved this." I told Lucy who turned to me and gave me what I needed most right then…a big hug.

"Oh honey, one day." Was all she said and the thought filled me with hope.

"Right, time to have some fun!" She said and pulled me towards the fairground. Denis was there waiting for her along with their friends Jennifer and Alan.

"Ah, here she is!" Jennifer said coming towards me instead of Lucy.

"This is who I was telling you about…Dex…Dex!" Jennifer shouted to a man whose back was to us and who was wearing navy blue trousers and shirt, which I quickly discovered was a cop's uniform, when a handsome man turned round.

"Ma'am." He said giving me a head tilt and a knowing smile. I don't know why but along with feeling my cheeks go pink, I also bit my bottom lip which I never do. The action drew his eyes to my lips and this was enough to kick the habit, well for the time being anyway.

"Hi…I'm…"

"This is Katie." Jennifer jumped in and said before I had chance to finish. Dex rolled his eyes and mouthed the word 'sorry' before turning to his mother and holding her by the shoulders.

"I think we got this Mom…wait, isn't that Mrs Peterson waving you over?" I turned my face down and to the side to hide my smile at his tactics.

"Oh so it is…" She said turning to look and Lucy quickly took in the situation and decided to intervene.

"Let's go and say hi Jen, I think her son is getting out of Juvie this month." And like a meerkat, her head was up at the sound of gossip and she was off.

"I'm Dex and that there was the only woman in this town who doesn't ever listen to the sheriff." I smiled and took note of the star pinned to his shirt.

"I'm Katie, the very law abiding newbie to this town." I said not knowing where this new me was coming from. Where was my usual shy response to anyone with authority?

"That's good to know, Katie." He said and the smile he gave me made cute little creases appear around his eyes. He had a kind face with a ruggedness to him that screamed he was in charge and answered to no one…well apart from his mother maybe.

"So how are you finding our little town?" He asked turning and holding out his arm in a silent request that we walk around the fair together. I thought about that question for a moment and found that from the conclusion I made earlier there was only one word to answer that question.

"Enchanting."

"Enchanting…um, I like that. Come on Beautiful, let's see the big bright lights of our small town." He said walking ahead but I had stopped dead. Where had I heard that from before? It was like some crazy version of déjà vu I was experiencing. Had someone from the Colony said this to me before? It only took less than a second to realise how ridiculous that question was in itself but when I saw the face that went with those words it didn't belong to the sheriff who stood looking at me now. An easy going smile, a mischievous wink and kind eyes were the vision I was assaulted with and suddenly I wished to see that face more than ever before.

But who was he?

"Hey, space cadet, you good?" Dex said and after another lip bite I was back by his side and trying to ignore what just happened. Why did that keep happening? It was as though there was something at every turn trying to make me remember something that had never actually happened. Were they visions of what was to come? Was I becoming a bit psychic?

"So what do you say?" Dex asked and I realised I hadn't heard a word he had said.

"Sorry I…"

"Hey Sheriff." A woman in a tight dress thankfully interrupted me and I watched as she first gave me the once over and then flicked her hair back before smiling at Dex.

"Hello Shelly, how's Henry?" At this she laughed and smacked him on the arm saying,

"Oh you know him, probably asleep watching the game but forget about him, when are you going to take me up on that dinner, you have yet to taste my fried chicken, its finger lickin'…"

"Yeah you said. But you know I've been pretty busy lately." He said and even for me who didn't really know the ways of the world, I could tell it was him blowing her off.

"Babysitting the new locals I see." She said faking a smile my way and Dex rolled his eyes before she saw.

"Actually I am babysitting him, you wouldn't believe how

many married woman just throw themselves at him… *or so his mother tells me."* I couldn't believe the words had come from my mouth until seeing Shelly's mouth drop open in shock confirmed it. Dex burst out laughing before the obvious cheating wife stormed off in a huff.

"I am so sorry. I don't know what came over me." I said apologising.

"Oh don't be, that was the funniest thing I've seen this month! The truth is she had it coming to her, trust me. Her husband Henry is a good guy and hell, half my precinct go drinking at his house on Game day!"

"A good day to rob a bank then." I joked and seriously, once again I don't know where it came from. Dex started laughing again and nudged me on the shoulder and said,

"You know, you're pretty funny."

"Thanks." I said blushing at the look he was giving me. He had warm brown eyes that lit up when he smiled that were undeniably infectious. He was tall or seemed so next to me, which wasn't hard. He was obviously fit given his profession and looked smart, being clean shaven with short crew cut hair. Actually if I was to venture a guess I would say he walked straight out of the military into this job.

"So back to my question before we were rudely interrupted."

"Oh…OH." I said finally getting what he was asking when he thumbed the big wheel ride behind him. My eyes widened once again making him laugh before he grabbed my hand and said,

"Come on, you'll be fine giggles." I wasn't so sure about that but I let myself be led anyway. If it had been Ari then she would have been the one dragging him on there. In fact, I couldn't understand it when it seemed I had quickly developed a fear of heights in a matter of seconds.

"Well I don't want to keep you from your duty now." At this he laughed, shook his head and lifted the bar on the carriage that came down for us to sit in.

"Not at all, like you said, you are babysitting me against all the married women that continually throw themselves at me, you're not going back out of your duty are you?"

"Ha, I see what you did there." He gave me a wink in answer, a little push and then took the seat next to me before securing the bar. We were just about to swing up when a ruckus on one of the stalls started and it seemed a fight was about to kick off. Dex quickly turned professional and lifted the bar.

"Save me this one for later Sweetheart, I will be right back." He said after helping me off the chair. I stepped aside gladly letting another couple take my place and I moved away from the queue. I watched as Dex pushed his way through the crowd that had gathered to watch and he reached for his radio as he went, obviously calling for backup. I decided to stand way back on the side lines and wait to make sure he was okay when something caught my eye.

My eyes focused in just as another pair of eyes was doing the same back. It was like have an ocean of people all busy enjoying themselves so no one noticed the two people that stood frozen, opposite each other from across the fair. It was a woman, that much I was sure but the who or why was lost on me. Abruptly she turned and started walking the other way so I decided to follow her.

I know it was stupid and I am sure that if I had stopped and thought about it sensibly then I wouldn't have moved. But this wasn't the case and I wasn't being sensible. Making my way through the crowd was a lot harder when a large group of people were all getting off one of the big rides at the same time.

"Excuse me, pardon me…Ooops, sorry." I pushed my way through the mass of excited teens all talking about the loops and speed and I didn't understand how you could get excited about almost throwing up but either way, I left them to it and pushed on. I had just excused myself for the millionth time when I almost fell into the empty space where it was clear the fair ended.

I walked on, looking left and right trying to find the woman that I had been following. It was creepy out here away from the crowds and suddenly I wasn't feeling so brave about this decision. I was just about to turn back, thinking the daylight wasn't going to last much longer and being out here in the dark would be a stupid idea, when I caught a flash of colour. There off to one side was a small maroon coloured tent that looked as if it had been piled high with rug after rug thrown over the frame. It became like a beacon, drawing me in and I found myself stood outside it before I knew I had moved.

"You may enter." A voice from within spoke and after an unsure breath, I ducked my head and walked inside, where the same voice welcomed me...

"We meet again, young Electus."

CHAPTER 11
GYPSIES AND VOIDS

H earing that voice again was like bringing back a pain that had haunted me for eighteen years. I couldn't understand why it evoked feelings like this as I had never seen this woman in my life.

"Welcome to my home, I recall we never got this far last time." I frowned at the woman who was sat in the shadows cross-legged on the floor.

"What do you mean...I don't know you." I stated as firmly as I could which merely caused her to start laughing. It was more of an old woman's cackle you would have expected from someone who smoked their body weight in cigarettes a day.

"Oh the fools have you masked to yourself, that is to be sure, but the real you would have remembered me, of that I have no doubt. Now come here and let me see what I am working with." She ordered but instead I took a step back.

"What are you saying? I...I am me...you must have me mixed up with someone else." I said walking backwards and trying to escaped from the tent.

"You will find no exit there, my dear." I sucked in a sharp breath when looking round to find she was right. The opening had gone and when I frantically started searching for the opening all I found was a brick wall.

"But that's impossible!" I shouted making her laugh once more and it was an evil sound.

"Coming from you Electus, that is highly entertaining."

"I don't understand what you're saying and stop calling me that, I don't even know what it means!"

"Sit down, Keira before you do yourself damage." She said now sounding unimpressed. I turned slowly to face her as I felt the icy chill invade my senses.

"Wait...how...how do you know that name?" I said only ever hearing it being said in my dreams before.

"How do you think...we have met before, you and I."

"But...no, you lie, I have never met you before...I would remember." I said all this in a panic, only half believing in what I was telling her.

"It doesn't sound like it's me you're trying to convince." I shook my head but it felt as if it was the rest of the world that was spinning out of control. I stumbled over to where she was sat knowing this was my one and only opportunity to get the answers I needed.

"Finally you start making the right choices." She said cryptically and I frowned down at her before lowering myself into sitting opposite her.

"It's not like I have any other option, you turned the exit into a brick wall." I informed her dryly making her fully aware of my feelings about being trapped.

"Ah yes, but of course...you have felt locked up against your will on many occasions throughout your life...even the one stolen from you."

"I don't understand anything you say, so seeing as you are keeping me here then I suggest you start making sense." I threatened making her laugh again.

"Or what? Who would you call for help this time because according to you, *there is no-one.*" She whispered this last part at the same time leaning forward making me jump.

"I…but…?"

"What's the matter young Electus, do you recognise me?" Her voice was so smooth and alluring that it started to drag me under into an unconscious world of remembering.

"There was a little girl, I can see her. She's crying…she's crying for her sister." I said seeing it playing out in front of me.

"That's right little girl. Now what else can you see?" I listened to her words as if floating in a trance and the sound of her voice was only reaching me over the waves she created. I felt my body swaying and I couldn't stop it. I squinted trying to focus on bringing back the vision.

"You're there! You…you start walking closer, oh God don't hurt her!" I shouted fearing for the little girl.

"Are you lost, young lady?" I nod my head at the question at the same time hearing the little girl say,

"Yes, I can't find my sister, she was taking me for some sweets." This was when the vision suddenly changed. And adult version of myself felt trapped again, in a dark room but I wasn't alone not when a voice told me so.

"You shouldn't be *here.*" A deep voice growled from the shadows and I jumped at the words. It was *him.*

"I…I'm lost" I stammered for what felt like the second time.

"Oh no, you're not lost…you've been found." He growled at my neck before yanking my head to one side and biting down. I screamed out at the pain I felt but soon realised that the pain I was experiencing wasn't coming from my neck but my hand. Eyes that I didn't even realise were shut snapped open and the sight they met made me scream again.

A pair of cloudy white eyes stared back at me before blood seeped into them filling them from the corners. They started to flicker back and to as if reading some hidden page as quickly as she could. I looked down to where the pain came from to see a small silver dragon from the end of her finger, biting down into my flesh as if needing to taste my blood.

"Did I not say to you child... *'until next time'?"* Those same words spoken were heard for a second time and I was sure the first had been when I was but a child. I looked up to find her back to herself and looking at me with her head slightly tilted. It was the first time she wasn't hiding herself in shadows and I could now see a small red star close to her right eye. I wondered what it meant.

"It is you, yet it is not. I guess in order to hide you they must first hide you from yourself...very clever indeed."

"What do you mean?"

"What is it you believe your name to be I wonder." I laughed once without humour and said,

"Shouldn't you know, after all I thought you were the mystic." This made her mad and she snarled at me like a raging dog would. I fell backwards as she stood to loom over me. The shadows behind her started to grow taller and come alive behind her as though she had a small army at her back. I scrambled backwards even more in hopes of getting away from her.

"Yes and this mystic once gave you a gift! I wonder if you would like it back again seeing as you obviously lost it!" I started shaking my head frantically, saying over and over,

"No, no, please don't." I had no idea what she was planning on doing or what gift she spoke about but I definitely didn't want to find out any time soon.

"No, you didn't lose it...it was taken from you! My gift was stolen. AND I WANT IT BACK!" She suddenly screamed looking up to the highest point in her tent and her shadows all did the same. Then she opened her mouth and an almighty screeching sound came from deep within her followed then by a demonic voice of the likes I had never known. I screamed putting my hands over the sides of my head as the pain shot through my ears.

"The Rogues" She hissed as if it was a dirty word and then she was gone and all she left behind was me sat in an empty void. It was a massive space filled with miles and miles of nothingness. I slowly got to my feet and looked around for anything but it was like standing on the edge of the world and expecting to fall off at any moment.

"Oh great! Just great!" I said feeling the anger instead of the panic that I knew was lurking just around the corner.

"And she didn't even have a crystal ball!" I said sarcastically but then I heard a voice in my head say,

"Do you want one? Here…is this one to your liking?" And then just as if she had clicked her fingers a strange glowing orb appeared from behind me. I turned slowly and as I did I noticed that the nothingness around me became a dark and looming forest. The sound of a bird calling out to me made me jump in fright. Looking back at the orb I could see a figure standing on the other side of it. What was that?

I sidestepped the orb but like a mirror the image on the other side only moved with me.

"I want to go home" I heard a girl whisper in fear and I suddenly wanted to reach out to her. As if absorbing my emotions, the purple orb started to glow brighter and pulsate as if trying to grow bigger. Then only on the girl's side I saw demons start to crowd around her before I screamed at them,

"GET AWAY FROM HER!" I never expected for one second they would listen to me but that's what they did. It was as if I had commanded them and they had listened. As soon as the last one was out of sight and crawled back to the hellish night they had come from the figure got up off the floor. She started to come closer and her blurred figure got closer to the light between us.

"Come to me." I said trying to coax her nearer but as soon as she heard me she stopped. I wanted to try again but was scared I would frighten her but in the end it was me that froze in fear. I felt first the breath hit the back of my neck and then the large presence of someone big standing behind me.

"Yes, come to me...you belong to me." He said humming the words like chanting a spell and it worked. She started to come closer again only this time reaching out with her fingers. She was so close I had to warn her.

"N..." Before I could get it out I felt a hand clamp over my mouth preventing me from warning her. I could feel the tingle of my blood beneath the hand that covered my lips and she too could feel it on her skin.

"Yes...be mine... Electus..... The chosen girl... My Chosen One," Said my demon before he lunged forward and reaching around me he grabbed the girl's hand. As soon as he touched her and pulled her forward the last thing I saw was her falling into the orb before everything changed. The mirror image was destroyed and I became the girl on the other side falling into his arms.

I passed through the bright light emerging from a purple mist and felt a secure embrace hold me tight.

"It's time to wake up, My Chosen One." I looked up at him in wonder and couldn't stop myself from reaching up to try and become level with his face. Just one kiss. That was all I wished for. All I could hope for and crave. I needed just that one and I was sure I would wake.

One lover's kiss.

"Time." He said again and I felt my thoughts pull at me from another direction.

"To." I frowned and started to look around to see this

nothing world crumble away showing me what really lay beneath.

"Be." Another word and another piece shattered showing colour behind in large chunks like pieces of a jigsaw. Then my chin was grabbed and my face turned to face his as he growled the last word down at me.

"Mine!" On hearing this, the last of the void fell away just as my legs crumbled beneath me. I fell to the ground and just as I opened my eyes to see the full picture, a voice pulled me back.

"Time to wake up, my Keira."

"Time to wake up, my Keira girl."

"Time to wake up... Katie?"

"Time to wake up."

"Wake up…Katie."

And suddenly I woke up. I shot up and was panting as if I had been running.

"Hey, there she is…she's okay…everyone get back, that's it, give us some room now." I recognised Dex's voice speaking to people around me.

"Oh Katie! Katie...? Is she alright? Get a doctor!" I could hear Lucy's panicked voice and I rubbed my eyes as the flashing lights were blurred into one.

"Easy now, don't get up too fast. Whoa, I've got you."

"Where am I?" I asked getting confused with the lights and seeing the glowing orb again.

"You're still at the fair. Do you remember what happened?" I took a moment before answering this to focus on my surroundings. The last thing I wanted was to sound like a crazy person and start talking about Gypsies and Voids. Looking up first, all I saw was the night sky filled with stars, this at least told me that I had been gone a while. Then after finding myself in just an open field with little else, I decided against talking about the gypsy tent that led me here in the first place.

"I don't know. One minute I was walking and the next... well, I guess I must have passed out or something." I said thinking this was the most believable reason I could give. As soon as I said it the next thing I knew I was in Dex's arms being carried off down the field, with people following behind.

"It's okay, I can walk." Once again it felt like I had said this before, only it definitely wasn't Dex's arms that were around me. This Déjà vu stuff was getting more intense by the minute and pretty soon I wasn't going to know which world I was living in!

Dex was a fit guy, that was obvious but even I could tell he was glad when he could put me down in the back of his patrol car.

"How come all those people were out there?" I asked feeling utterly embarrassed by the whole thing.

"Ah, that. Well when Lucy knew I couldn't find you she kind of rallied together a search party and had pretty much the whole fair looking for you."

"Oh God." I muttered covering my face in shame. Dex laughed and pulled my hands away from my face.

"Hey, don't worry about it. That's what happens when you have people that care for you...panic comes with the territory." He winked and then stood up just in time to say,

"And speaking of the panic queen."

"How is she...does she need to go to the ER?" Lucy said talking to Dex but coming round him to see me. She started feeling my forehead and added,

"I knew you hadn't eaten enough today...she never eats enough you know." This last part was directed at Dex who frowned.

"Lucy, it's okay, it just happens sometimes." If I thought this was supposed to help the situation I was wrong.

"What! This has happened before?!" Lucy shrieked in

despair. Now what was I going to tell her, not to worry as it was because I had been worked to exhaustion without being given food as punishment for my supposed sins? Nope, I don't think this would have helped matters at the moment.

"Dex, can you drive her to the hospital?" Lucy asked and this was when I knew I had to intervene further.

"Please Lucy, it's okay and probably like you said, I just need something to eat and then some rest." Thankfully Dex seeing how uncomfortable I was at the thought of going to a hospital came to my aid.

"Right, drive through and then home. You guys go on ahead and I will make sure she gets back after she has been fed." He then nodded for me to get in the front of his car and I did but not until after I gave Lucy a big hug. Because no matter how much I didn't want to go to hospital her concern had meant the world to me and I wanted her to know it.

"Thank you for caring Lucy." At first she seemed shocked by my response to her fussing but after I said this she understood it. Other than Ari, there had been no motherly caring before and it was moments like this that hit you the hardest at what we were denied. Lucy was a good person and I would never forget that as long I remained on this earth and if the Hexad had their way, it wouldn't be for much longer.

Dex gave me a look I couldn't decipher, I only knew it was soft and with feeling. He held open the door for me and shut it after I was in the seat. Being in a car again was strange after so long without it and considering one of the last times was the most terrifying experience I had ever known, it had been hard the first time when Lucy was driving. Of course she understood after she knew what I had been through and I had felt better for it. But now I was in the car with Dex and he didn't know my past or why I would seem so nervous in the car.

"Hey, my driving's not that bad is it?" He asked laughing when I jumped again after we pulled away from a stop sign.

"I'm sorry Dex, I'm just not good in cars." I said feeling embarrassed about having to tell him.

"Ah, I see."

"So whereabouts in England are you from?" He asked changing the subject and for one a lot more confusing.

"England?" I asked, shaking my head but then the bright lights of a fast food restaurant came into view and his attention shifted elsewhere.

"I hope you like burgers." He said as he pulled the car into a spot so we could read the glowing menu.

"I did, I mean, I do…well, let's just say it's been a long time." When he frowned at me I guess he got the wrong impression as he must have thought I had been on an extensive diet most of my life…if only he knew I thought dryly.

"So what's good?" I asked trying to change the subject…*again.*

Eating a fast food burger again was like being transported into junk food heaven after being in boring food hell for over a decade! Dex laughed at me when I couldn't stop moaning in taste bud bliss. So much so that he had to try and compose himself as he ordered me another one from the lady in the window. Even the fries and coke had me making shameful noises.

"If you think that's good then I will have to take you to get some cherry pie and ice cream from the diner in town." I blushed when he said this outside Lucy's house as I didn't know if he was asking me out on a date or something. I had never been asked out before and couldn't tell if he was just being friendly or if he liked me. I actually felt like I was falling back into my missed teenage years by asking myself this question.

"Thanks for tonight, Dex." I said pushing a strand of loose hair behind my ear nervously.

"You're welcome Katie." I gave him a smile and was just about to open the door when I stopped as a question from before was still playing on my mind.

"Can I ask you something?"

"Yeah, go for it." He said seeming happy that I was still in the car.

"Why did you think I was from England?" His reaction looked shocked and he jerked his head back as if he couldn't tell if I was joking or not.

"Are you serious?" He asked and this time it was my turn to frown.

"Yeah."

"Because you have an English accent." At hearing this I was shocked.

"No I don't!" I said getting defensive.

"Look honey, I may not be some big city detective but I think I can at least detect an English accent like yours when I hear one."

"But…but…" I didn't know what to say other than,

"But I'm from Minnesota!" At this he laughed and then shrugged his shoulders.

"Well Honey, I don't know what to tell ya. I only call 'em as I see 'em."

After this I said goodnight and walked back into Lucy's house even more confused than when I walked out of it this afternoon. I didn't know what to think, especially after I asked Lucy where in the world she thought I was from and she gave me the same answer as Dex had.

What was I to think? I had never been told that before and

was sure I sounded exactly like the rest of the Colony had. Was it all a trick? I just couldn't understand any of it and thinking back to what had happened in the gypsy's tent had my head reeling even more. I lay back on the bed fully clothed and I curled myself up into a ball trying not to cry. I needed to focus on everything I knew so far if I was ever going to find this place…

"Place…place! That's it!" I suddenly shot up as the answer came to me. I thought back to the dream and focused in on the last thing I saw before I woke. It wasn't a person. It was a building! A very old building from the looks of it.

I grabbed the laptop and flipped it open before I had even sat back down. Then I impatiently drummed my fingers next to the mouse pad as I waited for it to boot up. As soon as it was up and running I did the single most important thing yet in trying to find any answers.

I typed in Google search…

'Places called Afterlife.'

CHAPTER 12
REMEMBERING THE MONSTERS

I didn't even remember falling asleep but when a noise heard from the ensuite bathroom woke me up, I knew I must have hit my limit. I had been researching for hours but found nothing. It was disheartening to say the least but I knew I couldn't give up, not when Ari was counting on me.

"What was that?" I asked myself when I heard the noise again. The bathroom door was slightly ajar and I couldn't remember if I had left it like that earlier. The noise started again as a scratching sound and then a tapping as if there was a pair of long nails clicking against the old enamel sink. I sat up further and I couldn't stop myself from asking,

"Who's there?" There was no answer but the tapping sound stopped at the sound of my voice. The room was too dark to see much but at least the moonlight was filtering through the window where I had forgotten to close the curtains. This created shadows that played on my mind and all I could hope for was that it had been a branch hitting the bathroom window in the wind.

After a few more moments of silence I took a premature breath in relief that it had been nothing.

But nothing it was not.

I sucked in a sharp breath in fright this time as I first saw a long black hand fold its fingers around the door from behind…*Someone was in my room.* This time I found myself holding my breath and too scared to move. The fingers seemed elongated and stretched as well as its nails that were more like talons belonging to a bird of prey. I winced as its razor tipped fingers scraped back grooves in the wood that curled and landed on the floor in ribbons.

I was frozen and completely dominated by my fear. I wanted to move. To bolt up from the bed and dive for the door into the hallway. This feeling increased tenfold when the door started to open and more and more of a shadowed figure emerged from within.

"You fear me…I can feel it." The croaky voice said once the open door revealed all of the shadow of a person. I didn't answer as I didn't need to. It knew the truth. It knew the power of fear it held over me but then what it said next shocked me.

"Which is surprising in my world…" I didn't understand so this promoted me to speak as my curious nature got the better of me.

"Why?"

"Because most in my world fear *you.*"

"What?!" I hissed finding this impossible.

"It is true young Electus, after all, our fate is in your mortal hands." Hearing this had me ignoring the cryptic part and focusing on where I had heard that name before.

"Who are you and why are you here?" I asked trying to sound stern and playing on the fact they told me most of their kind feared *me.*

"What child, have you forgotten our chance meeting so soon?" Just as the words were spoken the figure stepped out

146

into what little light the moon did offer and I jolted back at the sight.

"The Gypsy!"

"But of course. You say that like I have a reputation." She said sounding affronted by the thought and walked over to the window to take a seat as if getting settled.

"Like I said, what are you doing here?" I asked sternly then folding my arms for good measure. This was in vain because with a flick of her wrist the fireplace erupted into a roaring fire and candles appeared out of nowhere.

"Ah, that's better, less dreary…don't you think?" I didn't answer her but merely found myself staring. She was no longer the old crone I had seen before full of wrinkles and weathered skin. She was now a striking beauty no older than twenty, with thick ebony hair that looked like liquid gloss. Her clothes were no longer big and baggy garments worn by a larger lady trying to cover the body beneath. She now wore a tight corset over a white frilly shirt and the top part of her reminded me of a pirate costume. But then she wore layers upon layers of red material all wrapped up around her and pinned up in various places giving it body around her slim waist.

I looked down at her hands and saw even they were normal feminine hands…but if this was the case, where did those scary black clawed hands go?

"But you…you…?"

"Yes, less dreary also I think. Besides I feel it is time we both show each other our real sides. So let me introduce myself, my name is Nesteemia, but as I told you once before, call me Ness." I shook my head knowing that this 'being' was one I would have remembered and I was quickly back to wondering what she wanted with me. Again she answered me without hearing my question.

"I felt that our earlier meeting was far too brief and if I am to report back to my master, then I would rather not anger him with wasteful snippets of pointless information." Hearing this scared me, exactly which side was she on?

"Ah, fear not Electus, if I were ever to meet the ones that stole my gift to you then all they would receive is my wrath, not my compliance. I am loyal to but one Being this Earth plays host to." She said reading my mind again, which seemed to be the theme of the night. But the important question to ask was if she wasn't working for the Hexad, then who was she working for?

Who was this *master* she spoke of?

"What gift? Are you sure you have the right girl? After all I think I would remember meeting you before...*both of you"* This made her laugh.

"Child you don't even remember your own name or birthright! I doubt very much you would remember the day I changed your life and gave you the 'sight'."

"The sight?" At this she rolled her eyes as if dealing with a dumb wit.

"Well I will say this much they certainly knew what they were doing. Not even I have that level of power and as a Shtriga, that is unusual, trust me."

"What is a Shr..."

"Sht...ri...ga." She said it again, only slower this time. I nodded to which I received an unnerving grin in return.

"Why don't you google it when I am gone, I see that's where you have been getting most of your information these days." She commented dryly, nodding at the open laptop I had obviously fallen asleep next to which now only held a black screen.

"So what is your plan, to stay with these humans until the end of days?" She said gesturing towards the door where Lucy and Denis no doubt still slept. I frowned at the way she said

148

this, not appreciating the way she obviously looked down at me. I mean what did she expect of me anyway?

"I am going to save my sister." I stated sternly.

"Right, your sister…I am going to take a wild stab in the dark here and guess you're not talking about a redhead are you?" I gave her an odd look to match her odd question.

"No, why would you ask that?"

"No reason." She said sounding bored and looked up to the ceiling as if looking for divine intervention.

"So this sister of yours, what is her name?"

"And if I tell you, does that mean you will help me?" I asked already knowing the answer, so it wasn't a big shocker when she said,

"Oh Hell no, what in Lucifer's name would make you ask that?" She said laughing which very nearly managed to grate on my last nerve and make me snap. It was funny now that her image had changed so had her attitude, as if the two sides of her went hand in hand against the other.

"Then why should I tell you?" I snapped. She merely shrugged her shoulder as though she didn't give a damn but to me she played it too cool in this game she was trying to draw me into. Oh she wanted to know all right, that I would bet money on…that was if I had any.

"No reason really, just that I know my master would have been interested."

"And who is this master you keep referring to?" I asked, knowing any name she gave me would do little good, seeing as everyone I knew outside of the Colony I could count on one hand and still have fingers left over.

"Oh that's right, you won't remember him either. Such a shame, considering the history I hear you two share together." This time I was the one to roll my eyes.

"I told you, I am not the girl you think I am!" I said only getting further irritated with this pointless conversation.

"No, *you're* not the girl *you* think you are." She corrected making me sigh in frustration.

"Alright, so what's his name then, if you think I knew him as well as you say I did then surely I would recognise the name." At this she smirked like this was what she wanted all along. She tapped her long red nail to her lips for a few annoying seconds before she clicked her fingers like an idea she'd had all along only just came to her. She must have thought me to be an idiot if she believed I would fall for this flavour of BS.

"I will make you a deal…"

"Of course you will." I interrupted sarcastically making her smile.

"Is that a taste of the old you making a sneak appearance… I hear she was known for her wit and sarcasm, or so my master tells me." For some reason this made me angry as she hit a sore nerve. The truth was that some repressed part of me did keep making an appearance and the creepiest thing about it was that I was confusing the two sides of me until they merged into one. Was there any truth in what she was trying to tell me? After all, everyone else seemed to believe I wasn't being true to myself and thought of me as someone else.

"Let me guess, you want to know my sister's name, in exchange for your master's?" I said knowing I was giving her my best unimpressed face, that I could only hope looked as good as it felt.

"Bingo!"

"Fine, her name is Arianna …now it's your turn." Now if I thought this was going to be a complete waste of her time in knowing this I was very wrong. I knew that when her eyes got wide and her mouth opened slightly before she said two words I never expected.

"Holy shit." Then she got up and started to pace the room making her full skirt swish around her legs and the longest bits sweep along the floor.

"Why? What is it?" I asked after she started muttering to herself.

"I could never…By the Gods, its genius really. And in your memories, this sister of yours, she has always been with you at this place you escaped from?" With this question my unease doubled. For a start she knew far more than she should but I answered her all the same, if only so I could gauge her reaction.

"Yes, we are twins and went into the Colony when we were seven." Hearing this she clapped her hands, making her many rings clash together.

"It's brilliant! Flawless really but the question still remains and that is why?"

"I have no idea what you're talking about, so I'm afraid I won't be much help with that question." I said not caring how sarcastic it sounded this time.

"I gather since you're twins and all, that you remained inseparable during your incarceration."

"That's an odd question, why would you even ask that?"

"Well you did consider it a prison, am I correct?" I had no idea where she was going with this line of questioning so I refused to answer her.

"I will take your silence as a yes and considering her now obvious part in your little 'disappearing act'…" She made little quotation marks with her fingers and this was when I hit my limit.

"Now listen here you! I have no idea why you are here because it certainly isn't to make any sense or offer any help. If anything it seems like your sole reason is just to taunt me with more cryptic shit I really don't have the time for, so if you're not going to offer me anything useful then can you please just leave me the *Hell alone!"* Now at this she really did smile, which I found even more infuriating.

"Alright young Electus, I see you have found your edge and rightly so but I never said I couldn't help you."

"But you said…" She held up her hand to stop me and clarified,

"I said I *wouldn't* help you, not that I couldn't but that is beside the point because what I am blood bound to do next *will* help you, whether I like it or not."

"Okay, so now I am really confused." I said rubbing my forehead in frustration and for a moment the act seemed a very familiar one to me but for what reason I couldn't say.

"All in good time Electus, all in good time. But speaking of time, mine here is at an end and yours is just beginning, so stay here and start…"

"What! That's your plan, for me to just stay here and start living my life and all the time my sister is…" This time she interrupted me to continue,

"…start living the quiet life and in time help will come to you."

"Oh no. Not going to happen. I mean, why should I trust you, so far all you have done is try to scare the shit out of me and given me more questions to ask than answers."

"I am afraid that in this case knowledge is not power, it will only be a hindrance if what you truly want to do is save this sister of yours, trust me on that alone. My master will come." For some reason this last bit sent shivers down my spine and I didn't even know his name yet.

"And he will help me?"

"He has done so in the past, so I can't see why not." She said pulling her lips together and shrugging her shoulders and I can't say the look instilled me with confidence. Besides, the idea that her 'Master' would come here to maybe help me wasn't making me feel all warm and fuzzy inside.

"And so I leave you, until no doubt the next time I am summoned to finding you."

"Oh, so I disappear a lot then do I?" The question wasn't serious however a serious answer was what I received.

"Oh Electus, you have no idea." Then she started to walk back into the bathroom of all places.

"Wait, you didn't keep your end of the bargain!" She stopped in the doorway with her back to me. I think I could hear her smiling before she simply turned her head and proved me right.

"Ah yes, you're right, how silly of me...I owe you a name." At this point I really could have done with her saying something safe...like Eric or maybe Frank, or even Jack? Why was it those names sounded so safe to me? I held my breath and waited, which she seemed to enjoy and just before I snapped again she said,

"My master's name is... *Lucius.*"

Of course it was I thought getting quite used to this new sarcastic side to me. I guess names like 'Jeff' or 'Roger' just didn't have the right scary, bad ass vibe that bad guys were looking for these days. But then replaying that name back and I couldn't help but hear myself speaking it. It was strange but it also felt like a part of me had once mourned the loss of this Lucius.

"There it is." Ness said smirking at me from the doorway. She knew in the one look I had given her that I had heard it before and my quick frown now meant nothing to her.

"And my job is now complete...well, *almost.*" She added and then her face began to change. It was as though something was travelling under her skin from the back of her head, as if her veins were close to bursting if she didn't get it out of her as it fought its way to the surface. It quickly made its way to the front and she raised her head up as if relishing the feeling it produced. At one point her head snapped back so far it looked like she was going to howl up at the moon.

"Ness?" I braved whispering her name and her reaction to it was as if I had screamed it. Her head cracked back to looking at me but it was almost like her neck was now broken. It was to the side and moved around as if she had turned into some ancient mechanical toy doll. The whites of her eyes started to disappear, being overtaken by black shadows that spread out like an infection, spreading under her skin. I looked to her hands that had also started to disappear into the wide sleeves of her shirt.

What the hell was going on?!

Fangs began to grow from behind her closed lips, forcing her to spread her mouth to accommodate them. They grew and grew until they passed her lips and started to curl down over her chin and around the shape of her face. She was becoming a monster!

My fear had me lost in making the right decisions on how to save myself from this. I knew I should be running. I knew I should be screaming but it was like being trapped by the shackles of my own mind. Then her body seemed to contort back on itself and I half expected something to burst from the centre of her chest like I had seen on a movie once. It was utterly terrifying and I was once again frozen because of that fear.

"Ahh!" I screamed this time as she bent over and started to gag violently on something. She looked like she was choking and any minute looked as though she would find death because of it. I was just about to move towards her as my first instinct kicked in, even if it was the wrong one, I didn't wish her to die.

But just before I could make it off the bed her head once more snapped up and what I now saw made me start to gag! Her mouth was stretched wider than I thought possible as long black, talon tipped fingers emerged from within.

They grew in size as it seemed to drag itself from inside using its nails on her skin. Her face tore as it clawed its way out using her chin, until the whole hand was out, only stopping at the wrist. Then the hand turned around until the curled nails could rip down her face all the way from her forehead until it made a fist.

I screamed again as a demon within tore itself up and out of her body, drawing in the body that remained and spinning round and round into a blur. She turned into some sort of shadowed ink banshee and then flew at me full speed until I fell backwards off the bed. I felt a pair of fangs pierce my neck for a few seconds and heard her voice in my head as my mouth opened to release a silent scream.

"I bestow my gift of sight back to you Electus, ready for your master once more...save us all."

And then she was gone.

My hand flew to my neck in panic but only the slight pinch of pain told me it was nothing life threatening. She had pricked the skin enough to draw blood as I pulled back my hand back to see the evidence there. I jumped up ready to bolt for the bathroom to see for myself when I tripped and knocked the computer to the floor.

It beeped into life and as the screen illuminated I gasped at what it was showing me. There in what looked like a newspaper article was a picture of a huge old manor house, half covered in ivy.

"That's...that's it..." I said in awe, long forgetting the blood dripping from my neck or what the Gypsy Ness had just done to me. The fear, the confusion, had all just disappeared in that one moment as I finally saw the last scene gifted to me in my vision. The whole thing hit me again as I fell to the floor and before my eyes opened from the dream, there it was, the house I saw. I blinked back the memory of waking up in the field and simply stared at the screen almost too scared that if I blinked I would lose it.

I couldn't believe it was real! I knew without a doubt that this was where I needed to go. This was what I needed to find as this place held the key to not only my questions but helping me get Ari out. It had to be, Ari had told me to follow my visions, to find the Demon in my dreams. And this was where he was.

I read the text below it and gasped again before reading the words aloud...

"Club Afterlife."

CHAPTER 13
TIME FOR GOODBYES

The next morning, I finally had a plan.

Of course this helped now that I actually had an address to go by. Once more I had fallen asleep whilst trying to burn the midnight oil in my quest for research. Thankfully I had learnt most of what I needed to know about 'Club Afterlife' before my mind had given up the fight.

I don't know what had happened when the laptop had crashed to the floor but whatever it was I was more than thankful for it. The site it took me to was some Gothic blog where people were talking about where they had been over the weekend and posting pictures of their night. This had led me to the first picture I had seen on there, which also happened to have been the exact picture I had seen of the place in my vision. It was as if the locked part of my mind was trying to guide me with some strange power of foresight, which led me on to even more questions.

Mainly these were of what happened last night. I thankfully found out that Lucy and Denis hadn't heard anything of last night's screaming and when she asked me why, I just told her I woke after a nightmare…which didn't particularly feel like lying at the moment as that was precisely what it had felt like.

It had been after this conversation at breakfast that I decided I couldn't put it off any longer.

"Lucy, Denis, I would like to thank you both for everything you have done for me. Without you guys I don't think I would have made it off that road alive…you saved my life and I don't know how I will ever repay you but one day…"

"Oh hush now…you know kindness isn't driven by reward and…" Lucy said taking my hand but as she had interrupted me, it was Denis who interrupted her.

"You're planning on leaving aren't you?" The sound of Lucy's gasp was like an arrow to the heart.

"No! You can't leave, not yet and not after last night. You're not strong enough and still getting over your ordeal…Denis tell her." But Denis wasn't listening to his wife. No, he was smiling at me and then nodded his head like his mind had been made up.

"Where is it you need to get to, Honey?"

"Denis!" Lucy shouted frowning but he didn't react to being told off in the way you would have expected because he not only knew his wife, but his next actions only spoke of love. He got to his feet, stepped around the table and leant down to kiss his wife on the top of her head and said,

"Our help doesn't end here, Sweetheart but she needs our support and this is important to her. Where do you need to get to Katie?" Denis asked repeating his last question, as Lucy sniffed back her tears and leant her head on the hand he had placed on her shoulder.

"Portland, New England." He nodded again and then grabbed his jacket as he walked out the back door without another word.

"Lucy, I…" I started to explain when she got up out of her chair and pulled me up into a hug.

"You don't need to explain Honey, Denis is right, our help doesn't stop here and I want you to know that we are here for you. So if where you're going doesn't give you all the answers you're looking for or if you get in any trouble, then you come back here…you hear me?" This time I was the one sniffing back the tears as her kindness nearly bowled me over.

"You're good people and I feel blessed to have you both come into my life." I told her before pulling her in for another hug, one we both shed our tears over.

After the hardest part was over and done it was time to get ready for my journey. I had no idea where Denis had driven off to but Lucy had been determined to see me fully loaded and prepared for anything. She had packed a bag for me with the rest of her daughter's discarded clothes, which I was more than thankful for. She had also packed some bathroom essentials and as much food as I could carry. I could imagine it was this type of love one would feel towards a parent sending them away to camp for the summer.

"Now I want you to have this…just in case."

"Oh no, I couldn't, honestly it's too much." I tried to say as she made me take the small phone from her.

"It's fine. Look, it's one we don't use anymore since Denis got a new contract one from work. It still works and has some credit left on there from when we took it on our last trip to Wyoming to see Denis' family last spring." She said turning it on and showing me how it worked informing me it was already charged and ready to go. I smiled, thinking she had certainly been busy since I told her it was my time to leave. I knew Lucy and her husband were good people but the level of concern they had for me was nothing short of a gift.

"I have programmed all our numbers in here, along with the Sheriff's just in case you find yourself unable to get through and it's an emergency." It was clear Lucy was a natural born mother and if she ever felt the need or want to adopt me at this point I think I would have cried with joy! It felt so good to have people care for you that I knew the next hardest part wouldn't be the journey itself but leaving Lucy and Denis.

I had been here almost two weeks, which had been no time at all with regards to developing a bond between Lucy and myself. But I knew that with time passing I had even more pressure to find someone that could help me get Ari out and considering what I was dealing with, I knew that no human on the planet could help.

I don't know exactly when it had become so acceptable to me when finding about this other world that seemed to co-exist with our own but it was almost as if I had always known. There had been no real freak out or denial when finding out that the Hexad Fathers had been Vampires all along. But then I had to ask myself, had this been thanks to what my visions had often shown me. Had some subconscious part of me always known that what I saw had some truth to it? I couldn't give myself an answer to any of these questions but the one thing I did now know for certain and that was 'Afterlife' was real.

The rest of the day Lucy fussed around trying to think of anything else I could possibly need and I think if I could have carried a contortionist doctor folded up in my bag she would have stuffed one in there. She even decided on a massive hearty meal for tonight just in case the larder she packed me wouldn't last me the eight-hour trip. I had to smile and Denis, it seemed, had to roll his eyes.

But even though he poked fun at his wife it was clear he

was just as proud of her as she was of him. And if the trophy and Veggie crown she displayed on the mantelpiece wasn't proof enough, then the huge Superman card that said 'I knew you could do it, you're my HERO!' on there was.

When Denis had got back home he produced a folded wallet from his jacket pocket and handed it over to me. I asked what it was and received only a nod for me to open it and find out. Inside I found two tickets, one was for Lancaster, Pennsylvania to Portland, New England and the other was an open return ticket to Lancaster. I didn't say a word but simply got out of my seat and hugged him, showing him my thanks.

He hugged me back in one of those awkward man hugs men often give when they don't know what to do. Then he slapped me on the back and said,

"Let's eat, I'm starving!"

My tickets were for the next morning and seeing as Denis would be in work, he had arranged for Dex to give me a ride to the bus station as it was his day off. I was left just hoping that one day I could repay all these people back tenfold for the kindness and generosity they had shown me. The tickets had cost over two hundred dollars and God only knew how much a mobile phone and all those clothes had cost but to Lucy and Denis that wasn't the point. What was the point in their eyes was that by taking me in that night, they had chosen to take on the responsibility of me and they felt it was their duty to do so until the end.

So no matter what I said, they felt they were only doing what most good folk would do in their situation and all I could think was how much better the world would be if this were true. As far as I was concerned everyone needed a Lucy and Denis in their lives and that wasn't just for personal gain. They were two good and pure souls that I was happy had found each other in life and knowing I had them as friends made walking out the next day easier.

Before this happened though there was another number I added to my new phone that night and that was the number of the bar at club Afterlife. After so much internet hunting I felt I had learnt two things from all of this, one was finally I had an address for Club Afterlife and two, once this was all over maybe I could ask Dex for a job as a detective because my research skills were second to none.

Although I would have thought for being a nightclub it would have been easier to find a lot more information on the place. However, most of my finds came from Gothic blogs based around the Portland area. The only reason I had found the number was thanks to someone chatting on one of the sites about the chance of a job and which number to call if anyone was interested. Of course from the masses of replies to that particular feed, then there was no doubt they had received hundreds of applicants as it seemed everyone and their mother wanted a job there.

I had even rung up the number just to check I had the right place and someone hadn't been trying their hand at pranking on the internet. Someone called Jerry answered the phone and quickly informed me the position had been filled before I even had chance to speak.

I can't say I was surprised with the amount of conversation the question brought up. It seemed only two things that were spoken about the club and that was the mysterious VIP and the sexy club's owner, a man called,

Dominic Draven.

Reading this name certainly had an effect on me and that was nothing to do with that fact that along with half the population of Portland in agreement that the sexy man, also had a sexy name to match.

"Dominic Draven." I tried the name out for myself and doing so only invoked even deeper feelings within me. I said it again but it was only when I got to his last name that a thrill shot through me like never before.

"Draven."

"Did you say something, Honey?" Lucy asked walking into my room and surprising me into slamming the top down on the laptop. But more shocking than this was where I found my hand had crept to and thankfully the snap of the laptop hid the snap of my underwear as my hand shot back over the covers.

I couldn't believe what simply saying that name did to me... or more like what it made me want to do to myself! It seemed almost as familiar as my own name, in some ways even more in fact. As though I had said that name in a hundred ways before, both in anger and in ecstasy. I couldn't help it but I couldn't seem to take my mind off it and this mystery man that I then spent nearly the whole night trying to find a picture of.

I found it incredible then that with so many people talking about him, there wasn't a single photograph proving his existence. There wasn't even one when he would donate large sums of money to the various charities in the world or when he became benefactor for the college near Evergreen Falls.

There was nothing. And that in itself was both worrying and intriguing at the same time. I wanted to know more and was scared that since hearing that name I had become obsessed overnight. I had to wonder if he knew of the man I dreamed of or even the one Ari dreamed of for that matter, as either was needed at this point. Or could they both work for this man Draven? That was another question I asked myself. Either way it was off to Portland in the hope I would have all my questions answered and be that step closer to saving Ari.

The next day started with an emotional morning when it came to my goodbyes with Lucy. Denis merely wished me luck and acted as if he would be seeing me again soon. Lucy on the other hand acted as though she would never be seeing me again and that I might die in some terrible bus accident whilst being mugged by thugs and being forced to enter into prostitution by being doped up on drugs. Even for me that was a lot to go through in eight hours!

"I packed all those cereal bars you like, the ones with the chocolate chips and toffee drizzled on top." She reminded me making Dex cough to hide his laugh. I gave her a genuine smile and hugged her one last time in an attempt to hide the tears in my eyes.

"Thank you Lucy, for everything…but most of all for being my friend when I had none and being a mother when I never had one." After I said this there was no holding back, we were both crying into each other's arms. The last thing I said to her was,

"Ari is going to love you guys!" And then I waved goodbye from inside Dex's truck. They had both made me promise that when I managed to get my sister out of the Colony that I was to come back and introduce them to Ari. And this was one promise I made gladly as I wasn't lying, Ari was going to adore them.

Dex was quiet for the first five minutes of the drive as I think he knew I needed it. Of course he thought that I was simply saying goodbye to a dear family member as that was what I had been introduced as but something told me he wasn't completely buying it.

"There's something I don't know in all this…isn't there?" With this question it pretty much confirmed what I had only moments ago been thinking. I didn't know what to say and he knew this when it started with,

"I…um.." He held up his hand to stop me and said,

"Unless you're in trouble or about to break the law, then I don't need to know, but just promise me two things…"

"Okay."

"Promise me that you will be safe and if you get yourself into a situation and need help, then you will call me…I told Lucy to give you my number, have you got it?" Hearing this made me smile back at him as I first thought it had been Lucy forcing the Sheriff's services on me just as a precaution. So it was nice to know it had been done due to his concern as well.

"I will and I have. The second?" I asked causing his behaviour to change. The first promise had been full of authority and said with the confidence that I would listen to a man in uniform. But this next bit was obviously something more personal if his uncomfortable shifting was anything to go by. He ran a hand on the top of his head and sighed,

"Ah hell, it feels like high school all over again."

"Well if it makes you feel any better I never went, so I won't judge." He looked shocked but then his eyes grew soft as if things were fitting into place with his suspicions.

"I'm not sure if I should be sorry to hear that, school can be a nightmare." He laughed once but in my head I was thinking I would take nightmare school days over living in Hell any day of the week…thankfully I didn't say this.

"Anyway, what I was trying to say, in what could be the worst way possible…"

"Dex?"

"The second promise is to come back here so I can ask you out on a date…there whoa, that wasn't so hard, now are you hungry, 'cause I know how much you enjoyed those burgers and I could…" I placed my hand on his to calm his nervous rambling that I found endearing and said,

"Dex, I would love to."

"You would?!" He said sounding shocked and I laughed,

"Yes of course I would but there's stuff I need to do first and I promise it's nothing law breaking but it's some personal stuff I need to put behind me before I can move on with my life."

"I understand and it's good to know you're law abiding, as that's kinda important considering what I do." He joked and we both laughed although my thoughts instantly went back to what happened in the barn and how I didn't think it a good time to mention that in the eyes of the law, I might be classed as a murderer…no, dating a cop might not be a good idea after all I thought looking out the window. Although technically speaking he could have been a Vampire too and in that case would killing a Demon from Hell be classed as murder or doing the world a favour?

Although based on that same logic I had to ask myself, were all demons bad? I thought back to the one I was obsessed with in my dreams and the idea of hurting him had me soon realising that I never could…so what did that make me. Obviously not a very good Demon hunter, that's what.

"I would love to know what's going on in that head of yours." Dex said snapping me out of my disturbing thoughts. This time I was the one laughing nervously and quickly changed the subject asking how long had he known Lucy and Denis.

We made small talk all the way to town until he pulled up outside the bus station. I felt like I had learned a lot about Dex in that short time and my overall conclusion was that he was a good man. And most important to this was that he obviously cared, not only about his town but about Lucy and Denis. He respected them and the way they handled their daughter Kelly, as she had gotten in with the wrong crowd a few times but due to a lot of help and support they had got her through it and now couldn't be prouder that she had made it into a good college.

"So I guess this is it." He said switching off the engine.

"Yep, but hopefully not for long." I added unbuckling my seatbelt and also praying this was the case.

"So what are you a fish or meat kinda girl?" He asked making me laugh and frown at the same time.

"I'm sorry, if you can believe, that sounded so much smoother in my head." This had me biting my lip before reaching across and saying,

"Thanks for everything Dex…" I then kissed him on the cheek and got out of the car. Then before I shut the door I turned and said,

"Oh, and meat every time." Then I winked and slammed the door. But then I quickly replayed how that sounded and then opened the door quickly to say,

"That's not what I meant…I mean, I like meat but fish is good…oh never mind…bye." Then I shut the door hoping he would take the whole thing in good flirty fun. As I reached in the pickup to grab my bag I could still hear him laughing at my saucy parting line, one that was a first for me.

I never knew I could flirt or be funny before so achieving both was a new high for me. I walked away almost wishing I was wearing a sexy dress and heels just so I could achieve the sexy walk to go with the teasing. Thankfully though I was just wearing old sneakers so there was no possibility of humiliating myself by trying it. Because me in heels for the first time and sexy would be the last word that would be used when seeing it.

Instead I waved over my shoulder when I heard him beep and that was it, I was back to where I started…alone. And to be honest, I thought this was a good thing as the last thing I wanted was to drag more good people into this trouble. No, this next bit I had no choice but to do on my own.

So I hitched up the strap on the holdall Lucy had packed for me and walked over to the gate number it said on my ticket. There wasn't many people waiting but I was a bit early so I dumped my bag on the floor and waited. I decided to get out the phone Lucy had given me to use and sign into the free Wi-Fi they had here to do some more research to pass the time. I had been amazed to find out you could do this on your phone but it had also been another one of those cases where I probably wasn't as shocked as I should have been.

I didn't understand it but then again that was the same feeling I had with most things these days. I think in the short time since I had escaped the Colony it was obvious that the chains they wrapped around my mind were slowly breaking away one by one. I felt stronger, braver and even smarter every day I was away but more than anything I felt like...well, more like *me*.

I decided there was one search I had been putting off and that was finding out about my crazy Gypsy stalker, Nesteemia. She told me she was what they called a Shtriga, although who she meant by 'they' I had no clue...was she in a club? Somehow I couldn't see her having many friends but then after what the search came back with, I couldn't see her having any!

"She's a Vampire Witch that sucks the blood of children!"

CHAPTER 14

BUSES AND BAD ASSES

Needless to say that after blurting this out in public, it granted me with a few odd looks.

"Sorry, book I'm reading." I said hoping this explained my crazy behaviour. This got me mixed reactions, with one smirk from a younger, hippy looking girl and a grunt from an older man who only had three teeth max. I couldn't stop staring because the lone top one looked big enough to pierce tin cans, which was the only use I could see for it. I quickly looked away when he sneered my way.

"Well this is a good start." I muttered to myself and then heard a woman who was breast feeding next to me huff.

"Oh no, I didn't mean...*anything by it."* I finished the sentence to myself as she promptly took her baby, changing bag and exposed boob with her to the empty seat next to smiley Mc'Grunts a lot over there. Geez it must have been bad if I was getting traded in for a man who had obviously never got his head around the technical marvel that was the toothbrush.

Thankfully I didn't have to wait around too much longer before my Greyhound coach was pulling into its designated spot. I can't say I was disappointed when Mr Hygiene and Mrs

Hormonal didn't stand up for this one. I decided to keep my bag with me as Lucy had set me up with enough food to feed everyone on the bus, should terrorists attack and we were stuck for a while whilst the terms were being negotiated with the President.

Bless Lucy but why she thought something bad was going to happen was beyond me. I think in my situation the worse type of thing to go wrong would be if Dracula himself were to step on the…uh…what was I saying?

All my thoughts left me because just before the doors could close the sexiest sight I had ever seen in the flesh just stepped on to the bus.

"Do you have a ticket, Sir?" The lady driver asked and I couldn't help but lean around my seat just to catch better sight of him. I saw him bend slightly and whisper something in her ear. I didn't know if he had a ticket and from the looks of it neither did she. He straightened up and left a dreamy eyed driver behind him as he scanned all the empty seats.

At first I had been happy that the bus had been over half empty but now, I was thinking differently, wishing next to me was the only space left. He was tall, that much was clear and his stonewash jeans fit him like he was born to wear them. A worn brown leather belt matched his worn leather boots, giving him a cool edge that said, 'I don't care, I don't dress for you', kind of vibe. With this he wore an open black shirt on top of a tight black t-shirt that I wished was just that little bit tighter so I could see more.

God what was wrong with me? I was never like this before, it was as if I was finally catching up on the horny teenage years I had missed. On top of all this though it was the black leather jacket he wore that had me near salivating. It was like some vintage speed racer jacket that was tight around the elbows and had zips up the forearms. The high collar sat over the messy honey coloured hair that had been styled back in a way that looked like it only stayed there because he ran his hand through it a few times. I don't know how I knew but its name was the controlled bedhead look.

But all of this was nothing when finally getting a chance look at his eyes. They were almond shaped giving him an exotic look that seemed to mix well with the dark shadows around them. This just made the stunning pair of steel grey eyes scream out at you even more and I bet if I ever got close enough I would be able to spot specks of blue in there also.

He was utterly breathtaking and I think the whole bus did a collective sigh at just the sight of him...or was that just me? Either way, I must have done something as his eyes found me and no one else. The smile he gave me must have come straight as a blessing from the Gods, as it was nothing short of heavenly. But through all this something nagged at me and I couldn't put my finger on it.

"I take it this seat is spare?" When he spoke I did a double take. Was he really talking to me? I frowned and looked to my right to see row after row of empty seats.

"Uh..." This was the only noise I managed to make and if I thought his smile was sexy, then his smirk was the stuff of legends.

"It's not a trick question, Kitten." He whispered down to me behind his hand and I swallowed hard before giving him a very shameful snorted laugh...wait...did I just really snort! Oh God no! I quickly decided that biting my lip was definitely a better idea than making piggy noises, so I just nodded to indicate for him to take a seat...that was if he still wanted to after the farmyard impersonation.

"Yep, definitely you." He muttered and I frowned...had I heard him right? I didn't question this for much longer as he nodded to the bag I had sat on the seat next to me.

"Allow me." He said grabbing my bag before I had chance to protest and once more I was rendered speechless. The bus jerked forward yet he seemed unaffected. Instead he just reached up above us and I was rewarded with a full frontal few of tight jeans and a line of pale skin that definitely answered the six pack question.

"Oh my" I uttered with an exhale of much need air.

"Sorry, I didn't catch that?" I turned my head and muttered,

"Thank God." ...to the window before turning back to him, shaking my head, with my lips firmly closed. His lips twitched once as if he was trying not to grin at my odd behaviour. I on the other hand just wanted to slap myself on the forehead and start over.

He sat his big body down and suddenly I felt like he had trapped me in. I moved closer to the window to give him more room but he took this as more reason to spread out, so I decided the best thing to do was to offer him my seat.

"You can take the window seat if you like."

"I'm not a fan of the glaring sun, but thanks for offering." He said giving me a cryptic reason that had me frowning back at the window. For a start it was cloudy and looked like rain but in the end I mentally shrugged my shoulders and decided to introduce myself.

"I'm Katie by the way." I said holding out my hand.

"Katie, did you say?" He asked making me nod.

"Funny, I wouldn't have had you down for a Katie." I laughed once and asked,

"Why, what name would you have said I look like?" This had him smirking again and then tapping his lips with two fingers.

"Umm, I don't know, maybe...*Catherine.*" The seductive way he said the name wasn't the only reason it affected me. It was once again one of those times that had me wondering why hearing it made me feel an emotion that felt denied to me. As if a feeling I could barely touch upon was just out of reach from grasping hold of. The only word to describe it was…*Haunting*.

"Are you alright? Do you not like that name?" He questioned in a way as though he had known what it would do to me. But no, that was silly, I had only just met this man and couldn't take a simple comment as something more.

"It's a lovely name but it's just plain old Katie I am afraid."

"Oh I very much doubt there is anything plain or old about you, Sweetheart." The way he said it made my heart flutter or skip a beat, either way I struggled to breathe normally for a few breaths.

"Thank you." I said blushing and again biting my lip. We had a moment of silence before I realised he hadn't yet given me his name.

"You never told me your name." I said turning back to face him to find him staring at me intensely.

"Forgive me, my name is Luc."

"Luc…um, well I am happy to report it suits you, no other name needed."

"I'm glad you think so." He said smiling in a way that made handsome little lines appeared at the corners of his eyes. I don't know why but every look he gave me was like he knew me and this was just one big tease to him.

"Have we ever met before?" I asked thinking it best to just get it out there and I was intrigued to see what he would say considering the impossibility that we had ever met before but he didn't know that.

"In another life perhaps." He replied looking past me at the world that flew by. I turned my head to see what he saw and for the moment it was the simple sight of life living in an ignorant bliss of the horrors that shared their world.

"Why, do I seem familiar to you?" He asked drawing my

gaze back to him. One honey coloured eyebrow was raised waiting for my answer. I thought about his question for a moment and then gave him the wrong answer,

"Not particularly."

"You were always a shitty liar." He commented more to himself and this had me frowning at him as I snapped,

"Excuse me?"

"I am merely making an observation that you can't lie." I crossed my arms and said,

"And you're an expert at this, I take it?" At this he laughed and then said,

"I have had my fair share of occasions where the talent comes in handy, yes… but I never lie to myself."

"And you think I do?" I asked getting annoyed at how handsome he still looked when acting smug.

"I believe you lied when saying that I don't seem familiar to you and giving me the wide eyed beautiful look only increases that belief." He said making me blush again…he thought I was beautiful? Wait, no I was angry but was that because I had been busted? Because in truth I did feel like we had met before but because I knew there was no possible way for that to have happened I felt confident giving him my answer.

"Okay look, the truth is I do feel like I know you from somewhere but I know that would be impossible, so I didn't lie." I said all this and couldn't believe we were having such a heavy discussion after only just meeting one another. He looked thoughtful for a moment and then leaned into me, pushed my hair behind my ear and whispered,

"Nothing is impossible, my little Katie Girl." Then he pulled back giving me the space I needed to have my internal meltdown. Holy shit but there was that sharp jolt to the heart again. Hearing him call me this was the same as hearing myself say the name *'Draven'.* It almost caused me pain and I couldn't

understand why? It felt like trying to breathe under water, knowing you couldn't do it but it was try or drown anyway... *and everyone had to try, didn't they?*

So was that what I needed to do now? Did I need to try and listen to what everyone seemed to think about my life? Everyone was telling me I was someone else or implying as much, so why did I continue to hold back? But even as I asked myself this question I already knew the reasons why...*Ari.* She was my anchor to it all. Because if I wasn't who I thought I was then that would mean Ari wasn't either and this I wasn't willing to accept, not yet and not without proof. Because she was my sister and every memory I had of us together taught me about love. And if I didn't have that, then I was left with nothing.

Everyone needed at least one person in this world to love them and *Ari was mine.*

"So where are you heading?" I asked Luc trying to get past the awkward beginning.

"Same place you are." This made me laugh because it was either the worst pick up line ever or it bordered on creepy stalker and I so badly wanted to believe the first.

"And how do you know where I am going?" I asked feeling cocky which lasted about all of three seconds when he nodded down to my hand and said,

"Because that ticket you're still gripping onto for dear life tells me where." I looked down to see he was right and I hadn't even realised it. But I guess he was also right because at this moment it did feel like my last lifeline.

"So what's in Portland, if you don't mind me asking?" Why did it feel like he was prying for information, or was I just being paranoid? I didn't actually know what answer to give and seeing as I'd learnt my lesson before with lying I decided being vague was the way to go.

"I'm on a research trip." Again I don't know why but this

made him laugh…damn him even more for having a sexy laugh! I thought bitterly because even though he was the most handsome man I had ever met he was also slightly infuriating.

"How about you, what takes you to Portland." He gave me a sideways glance and again that half knowing smile was back.

"I'm meeting an old friend of mine."

"That's nice." I replied trying to carry on the conversation.

"Not really, he's a big pain in the ass." I seriously wanted to roll my eyes at this point. Jeez it was like pulling teeth with this guy!

"Then why are you meeting him?"

"Like I said, he's an old friend and besides, he's having a few problems with his wife."

"Oh no! That's terrible." I said now seeing Luc in a different light. I mean he couldn't be all bad if he was travelling all this way to help his friend through tough times.

"Yes it is and so, although he may not be my favourite person this world has to offer, I do like his wife." Ah…so this was what was really going on.

"What?" He asked when he saw my disapproving frown and crossed arms.

"Nothing, it's none of my business." I said and for some reason again he found this funny.

"I highly doubt that but please continue." He said confusing me further.

"What, you think it is my business?" I asked shaking my head at him and raising an eyebrow.

"Never mind what I said, tell me why you disapprove of me liking his wife?"

"Because it's wrong." I whispered like we were being watched.

"And why is that?" He whispered back mocking me.

"Because he's an old friend of yours."

"Yesss…and?" He rolled his hand motioning me to carry on after dragging out the word yes.

"And you're in love with her." I hissed. He sat up straighter and pulled back giving me a shocked look.

"I didn't say that!"

"You didn't need to, it's written all over your face when you said you liked her but what you really meant to say is that you liked her, *liked her."* I said thinking that by bobbing my head at this last part would somehow emphasise my point.

"So I meant to repeat myself?" He asked making fun of me and I don't know where it came from but I smacked him on the arm and said,

"You know what I meant!" He rolled his eyes and sighed.

"See! I knew it!" I said this time being smug myself.

"I care for her." He admitted softly.

"Do you love her?" I asked wondering why I was pressing for this so hard. At this he closed his eyes and held the bridge of his nose with his fingers for a moment before dragging his hand down his face. It was only when he did this that I noticed he barely used one hand and when I looked I saw it was gloved in black leather.

"Jesus, I can't believe I am having this conversation." He muttered and suddenly I felt bad for pushing. After all, you couldn't help who you fell in love with.

"I'm sorry, I didn't mean to push and it's really none of my business. I don't know what came over me." I said placing my hand on his forearm. He looked down at my hand and then back up at me. The emotion I saw there nearly had me forming tears. It was like looking directly into someone's soul and finding nothing but a raw, untamed steel coloured beauty.

"Forgive me but it seems I am having my first surreal moment." I didn't understand what he meant by that but I just nodded deciding to give him a break…after all, the word surreal didn't even cut it in regards to what I had been through that last few weeks.

"It's okay and hey, at least you're being a good friend because despite how you feel about his wife, at least you're still there for him...that counts for a lot in my book." I said hoping this would make him feel better.

"And it gets stranger still." He muttered again under his breath and I barely caught it.

"Sorry?"

"Nothing. So when you get to Portland, what then?" He asked obviously needing the subject change.

"I'm not sure to be honest, I guess I am going to try and make my way to these people that are supposed to help me out." I replied not wanting to give too much away, like where I was actually going.

"How about you?"

"My friend has a place by the mountains." I nodded thinking it sounded nice.

"So some quality guy time eh?" I don't know why I said this and bit my lip as he described how I'd made it sound,

"Oh yeah, lots of hugging, drinking wine by the fire, we may even mix it up a bit and play some Michel Bolton...oh and don't forget crying, there will be lots of manly crying." He said teasing me.

"Ha, ha...I just meant that with him having problems with his wife that..."

"I know what you meant Pet, but to be honest, I have a feeling she will be making a surprise appearance." This confused me even more, how would he know that? My face obviously said it all.

"Trust me, I have a nose for these things." He said tapping his nose and I rolled my eyes trying not to laugh. He certainly had flirting down as an art form if my racing heart beat was anything to go by.

"So they have split up then?" I asked wondering why I was so interested. However, he continued to answer me so he obviously didn't find it odd.

"His wife left him, quite suddenly in fact."

"That's terrible and even worse if he didn't know anything was wrong." I added feeling sorry for the poor guy. His eyes went soft again and he gave me a small smile as though what I just said meant something to him.

"Very true, I believe the act left him broken hearted. So he enlisted my help in trying to get her back."

"So he doesn't know about your feelings for her?" I asked thinking as soon as I said it that this might have been a question too far. He looked thoughtful towards the window again and then spoke without looking at me...

"He knows."

CHAPTER 15

FIST FIGHTS AND FIRST KISSES

"**O**h." I said after he dropped that bombshell as I didn't know what else *to* say, so I remained quiet until he spoke again.

"You have to understand, although I have certain… attachments should we say, I still know what is best for her. I believe that somewhere buried deep that she loves him and always will. And because I know that will never change, that is why I am helping him find her." I nodded understanding that there was much more to this man than I first thought. One word that stuck with me when wanting to describe him was honourable. He obviously knew how to put others before himself and even though he may not like his friend, he clearly loved his friend's wife enough to do right by her.

"Then that makes you a good friend, even if he isn't." He surprised me by bursting out with laughter.

"What? What did I say?" I asked waiting for him to calm enough to tell me but enjoying the sound as I did.

"Private joke, Sweetheart." He said patting me on the leg.

We continued to make small talk for the next few hours and I learnt he usually lived in Germany. I had asked why he didn't fly direct into Portland as I saw from the website that they had an international airport. He told me he had business to deal with around this area first and I had to wonder why he chose to take the coach and not hire a car himself or take the easier option of an internal flight. Gosh when did I get so nosy?!

He asked about my life and I was as vague as possible but instead told him about Lucy and Denis, calling them family I had stayed with. They had certainly felt like that which was probably why he didn't call it out as a lie.

We passed through New York and he found it amusing the way I acted like a child seeing it for the first time.

"Have you been before?" I asked him and this was when he leaned in close right against me and we looked out the window together. I felt the heat rise and my skin became super sensitive every time he accidently brushed against me. He blocked me in as he flattened his hand again the window and suddenly the amazing view of New York skyline was lost with me trying to concentrate how to breathe without panting.

He would whisper in that seductive voice all the places he loved to go and most of them sounded like private clubs. It felt as if I was being lured into a magic spell and if he had tried selling me a timeshare there right now I would have agreed. Hell, I think he had the power to get me naked with just a thought. Luckily he finally let me breathe once we were through the city and I swear I could hear him chuckling to himself at my behaviour.

We were about half way there in Hertford when the bus had to refuel and also pick up some more passengers as it had been doing all the way to this point. I was surprised how the bus never got full or maybe I just never noticed as being sat next to Luc seemed to sap all of my attention.

The driver informed us that we should take this chance to stretch our legs and maybe get something to eat as we would be there for the next thirty minutes. I decided now would be a good time to use the toilet and get some breathing space between me and Mr sexy and intense here. But before I excused myself Luc said,

"I could do with a coffee." Then he shifted to stand up after letting the people behind us off first. I was shifting myself across to his seat when he held out his gloved hand. I nodded to it, first making sure that I wouldn't hurt it.

"Accident at work." He informed me abruptly.

"It's fine, it won't bite." He added when I hesitated too long. I reached out and took his hand. He curled his fingers tighter before he gave me a little tug and I was quickly falling into his arms. I had to say there were worst places in the world to be. So with my forehead landing in his hard chest and my hair scattered around me I looked up at him as if I was about to be ravished…well a girl could hope, I thought wickedly.

"You keep giving me that cheeky smile Kitten and I won't be held accountable for what I do next." He promised in a throaty voice. At this I bit my lip and lowered my gaze in what I can only assume appeared as submissive as I felt. I heard him groan, one that sounded a lot like a growl… What was he, part beast?

"Oh fuck it! I'm not that good a friend anyway." He said sternly before leaning down and before I could begin to understand what he meant, his hands were at my face. With little force my head fell back and he crushed his lips to mine. I gasped, opening up to him and he took this as his opportunity to taste me. His intoxicating flavour burst across my tongue as we fell into a blissful rhythm. It felt like a dance I was born knowing the steps to.

This time I knew it was a growl coming from him and he felt my fright nearly pull us apart. He refused me this by entwining his fist in my hair and banding an arm around my waist, simultaneously pulling me tighter to his tall frame. His possessive actions told me he wouldn't have allowed it any other way. I wasn't sure how long we kissed for, as it was without a doubt the most incredible moment of my life so far and because of this, it wasn't one I wanted to end.

I thought he would pull away but he surprised me when he held me to him and then rested his forehead to mine. It seemed I wasn't the only one affected by our kiss.

"That was…was…"

"My Salvation." This confession took my breath away and I was just about to speak when he shook his head softly and placed a finger across my lips.

"You were perfect." He whispered and it was the most beautiful, shocking thing anyone had ever said to me.

"I was?" I asked against his fingers. He smiled before nodding once and added to the beauty with even more confusing words,

"Because finally, *you were mine.*"

"What about the 'Wife'?" I had to ask and ruin the moment. He released a heavy sigh, closing his eyes in what looked like a moment of pain.

"Keir…Katie, we have to talk…there are things you need to know about me and…"

"And?" I asked when he stopped thanks to something that caught his attention outside.

"Stay here, do you understand?" He said sternly and clearly giving me an order.

"Luc?"

"Do as I say Katie, stay on this bus." And then before I could get any more from him he left.

"What the Hell was that all about?" I asked myself. I reached up and grabbed my bag. I knew he told me to stay on the bus but I don't think he realised how much I needed the toilet. And what had he seen anyway? Well I had spent eighteen years being told what to do and look where that had gotten me!

"You might be sexy but no man rules over me." I said aloud lifting the strap of my duffle bag over my shoulder and then walked down the aisle. I nodded to the driver who was reading a folded book that looked like it had taken a beating over the years.

"Be back in twenty, just to be sure okay?" I nodded after she checked her watch and then stepped down onto the wet tarmac. I looked around as if expecting someone to jump out at me any second and then shook my head at how silly I was being. Luc had freaked me out but he knew nothing of my past so it meant that whatever he had seen was to do with him not me.

After all it wasn't like anyone had come looking for me from the Colony. I had spent the first week with Lucy and Denis looking over my shoulder, expecting to see faces I recognised. But deep down I knew it was Ari they wanted, which meant it was left up to me to save her and to do that, there was nowhere and nothing I wasn't willing to go or do.

I walked into the building at the rest stop and was hit by the smell of cooked food and coffee. I was sure this was where I would find Luc but first I wanted to see to business. I found the sign that guided me to the lady's restroom and nodded to another girl I knew was on the bus with us as she held open the door for me. The toilets were empty so I picked a middle cubicle, locked the door and dumped my bag on the floor.

I decided to check the phone to see if there was any free Wi-Fi here when I noticed there was a message from Lucy. I smiled and not wanting to waste time I read it whilst I used the toilet. I heard the door swing open and watched under my cubicle as footsteps walked the length but strangely stopped at my door. Were they blind, there were four other doors open?

"There's someone in here." I shouted when they tried my

locked door. I frowned when there was no apology and the shadows of feet moved away and picked the free cubicle next to me. I shrugged my shoulders and went back to reading my message.

"Oh Lucy." I whispered when I read how she and Denis had put some money tucked in the zipped pocket of my bag. 'Just in case' she had said and I let my head fall back to the wall behind in wonder. It felt as though they had been sent to me straight from Heaven as Guardian Angels, because I certainly felt blessed having them both in my life and looking out for me.

I finished using the toilet and after putting my phone back in my bag, I replaced the strap around me before opening the door. I walked to the sink to wash my hands and noticed in the mirror the two doors either side were now occupied. I looked back to my reflection and nearly screamed when I saw myself with my wrist slit and I had written on the other side of the mirror in blood. It said one word...

Run.

I didn't need to be told twice! I ran to the door, flung it open and only just managed to get out a small scream before a hand slapped over my mouth and pushed hard enough that I fell back into the bathroom. I landed hard on my backside and scrabbled backwards as the suited man walked through the door and closed it, cutting off my exit.

I quickly got to my feet and my head snapped to the cubicles as two more men in suits stepped from behind the doors. Okay so now I was totally screwed! I recognised two of the faces as Righteous Bloods and knew they had found me but how...?

"What, you think we would just let you go? Your Uncle had us watching all the public transport just waiting for you to make your move." I thought on this for a second and that would have been impossible as he didn't have that many men...unless of course they could narrow it down by knowing where I was headed...holy shit, they knew about Afterlife!

"You knew where I was going?" I asked with my mind turning a million miles an hour. The two that came from the cubicles started laughing at my question and I continued to back up until my lower back hit the sinks.

"Of course we knew, you stupid whore! We know everything!" The one by the door said sneering and then my panic turned into overload when he smiled and showed me his fangs.

"You're...you're..."

"That's right Bitch, *Vampires.*" One of the others hissed showing me his own set of fangs. The two closest to me started to walk towards me and I knew the time had come to make a choice. I could just let them take me back there and face my fate, or I could fight and make my own...okay so I could die quicker with the second one, but I decided to take a gamble on the stupid shit road.

"Your Uncle has missed you Katie, although I hear he has had fun playing with your sister." Oh yeah, it was stupid shit time alright!

"Yeah?" I said making him frown with the reaction he wasn't expecting. Then I lunged! I ran at him and kicked out aiming straight for his man jollies! I hit my mark and relished hearing him wailing like a baby. The other two ran at me and I flung my bag into one and kneed the other, unfortunately missing his package. He grabbed me by the back of the neck and hit the side of my face into the mirror making me cry out in pain.

"Try that the fuck again and I will kill you!" He said into my cheek and then punched me in the kidneys causing me to fall to my knees. I felt the blood from my nose trickling down into my mouth so I spat it out making sure it hit one of their shoes. I looked up laughing like some crazy person and rolled just at the right second before his kick connected with my face.

"We need to leave, just grab the Bitch and get your revenge in the van!" The one by the door ordered. I felt the hand at my shoulder ready to pick me up and I took the opportunity once more to fight. I whipped my head to the side and sank my teeth into the hand until I taste metallic in my mouth.

"Fucker!" He shouted pulling his hand away and cradling it to his chest. I got to my feet and placed myself in the corner like some wild cat ready to strike from all angles.

"Did you see that? She fucking bit me!" He whined and I thought that for a bunch of Vampires they were pretty shit if they couldn't handle one small human woman. My thoughts were interrupted when suddenly the door burst open hurling the Righteous Blood standing guard there into the other two.

"Luc?" I said praying I wasn't imagining the sight in front of me. He had kicked the door so hard that it too was flung forward after it came crashing off its hinges! What was he, a kick boxing champion or something? Christ I bloody hoped so!

Luc found me and after first scanning my body for injury I saw a muscle in his jaw twitch when he saw the blood dripping from my nose.

"Of course you didn't wait on the fucking bus." Luc said looking away from me, shaking his head and rolling his eyes.

"What do we have here then, ladies?" Luc asked and I couldn't help but feel from his confidence that he thought he could take these guys.

"Look Dickhead, you don't want to mess with us!" Luc looked around at the mess he made of the door and with one raised eyebrow said sarcastically,

"Clearly."

"Fucker, you just walked into the wrong bathroom!" The

guy in the middle said nodding to the lackey to his left and Luc laughed which sounded pure evil,

"Is that right?" He said as the man approached him pulling a large knife from behind his back.

"Yeah!" And then he lunged for Luc. What happened next I could barely keep up with. Luc simply sidestepped dodging the blow with ease but catching his attacker's arm in the process. He bent it up further than it should go making him scream in agony and drop the knife. Luc caught the blade and at the same time pushed him backwards up against a middle section between the cubicles. Then in a speed I have never seen before buried the knife in his hand, fusing him to the wooden panel.

"And clearly you just fucked with the wrong fucker!" He said before silencing the screaming man by knocking him out when connecting his forearm to his face, cracking it back against the wood. His body slumped to the ground leaving only his hand suspended in the air where the knife refused to let it fall. This all happened in three seconds flat.

"Close your mouth Love, you're getting blood in it." Luc said turning to me and my mouth snapped shut.

"Good girl…right who's next?" He said pulling one of his leather sleeves down like nearly killing a guy had caused him only mild irritation in wrinkling his jacket.

"Leave now before we release the wrath of God upon you." Luc chuckled and said,

"The wrath of God, umm interesting, so beating on a defenceless woman is God's work is it?"

"Why we need the girl is none of your concern, mortal. We are the Righteous Bloods and have been chosen to do God's work." He said and I could tell he was trying to mask the fear in sight of what Luc could do.

"Funny, I never knew God was employing assholes this year, I do hope I don't lose half of my staff." He replied looking at his nails like this was all very boring to him. Jesus…but who was this guy!?

"Luc, they're Vampires." I decided now would be a good time to warn him in case one of them tried to bite him or something.

"Oh really?" He said dragging out the word as if this new information amused him greatly. He turned back to look at them and they hissed showing him their fangs. I couldn't believe it when he started laughing again.

"Let me guess, Twilight fans? Tell me…*do you sparkle?"* He said whispering this last part behind his hand in a comical way. The guy on the right bellowed in anger and ran at him. Luc looked like he wasn't even going to react at first but just waited for him to get within arm's length and then his hand whipped out like a snake striking. His hand circled the man's throat as he held him in choke hold.

"Now do you want to see what a real Vampire looks like?" He said and my heart stopped. Oh God no! But there it was, the proof literally growing in front of me. He opened his mouth slightly to allow for his fangs to lengthen past his lips and I gasped at seeing him look so deadly.

"Oh fuck!" The other guy said, for the one being choked that was close to turning blue.

"Oh fuck is right. I only came in here for a coffee but…*it looks like you'll do."* Luc said in what can only be described as a demonic voice. Then wasting no time in taking his meal he yanked the swaying body to his lips and bit down into the guy's throat like…well like a wild beast.

"Jesus Christ! St…stop…stop that! Put him down or I will shoot you, Demon!" I watched as Luc smiled around the bloody meat in his mouth before he threw his meal away and I jumped when he smashed into the mirrors shattering the glass on impact. He too slumped to the floor in obvious defeat. Hell, he could have been dead for all I knew, but who was I to judge as I guess our death count on Righteous Bloods was now even.

Meanwhile the only guy left held out a gun in an unsteady hand pointing directly at Luc. Watching Luc's bloody smile form was one of the most unnerving sights I had ever witnessed and one I can't say I ever wanted to see again.

"DIE FUCKER!" The guy shouted and I screamed when the gun went off. I couldn't keep my eyes off Luc waiting to see the impact and waiting for him to fall. I was surprised considering what I now knew about him how much the thought of him getting hit disturbed me. I didn't want him to get hurt, let alone die so what happened next I was both in awe and thankful for.

Luc was looking at me when the gun fired and when he caught the bullet in his hand he was still looking at me.

"Time to go Kitten, you don't want to see this bit." He said softly nodding to the open door behind him. Then he dropped the bullet and his voice swapped back to something truly terrifying.

"Wrath of God did you say… well here's some *Venom of God for you to try!*" Then just as he lunged for his next victim, I ran out the door leaving behind the sounds of gunfire and the terrified screams of death. I tripped over a folded sign on the floor that said,

'Toilets closed for Maintenance'

This at least explained why no one had come back here but now that gunfire could be heard there was panic! People were running for the exits all around me, having no clue the reason why. I looked back as I saw two men wearing leather jackets this time trying to push their way through. They may have looked different from the other three in the bathroom but when they spotted me I knew they were Righteous Bloods. They were trying everything to get to me and on this occasion being big and muscular didn't help them. I pulled the bag I still had around me closer to my body and slipped in and out of the crowd.

I couldn't let them get to me but I also knew that I would have to lose them before I got back on the bus or they could end up trapping me on there. So I ducked and spun through a tiny space, pushing one lady out the way by accident.

"Sorry!" I shouted before running for the open door and passed some tourists that were gathered around taking pictures with their phones. I hid around the side of the building and waited for them to emerge hoping they would go running off in the wrong direction. But this never happened, they reached the door yes but only walked as far as the covered entrance before they stopped. They looked up as if trying to judge something, which was when it clicked...

The sun.

The sun had come out momentarily from behind all the clouds and this they didn't like. They looked around and I ducked back out of sight before they spotted me. So *who* were these guys if the ones in the bathroom had been fake Vampires?

"Holy shit...Luc?" I muttered knowing the truth. Luc had been the only real Vampire in the room.

I shook that from my mind putting it back in the 'crazy shit to deal with later' pile. I looked towards where the bus was parked and this time saw two guys in black suits walking around it when one walked off the bus itself shaking his head at the others. I frowned wondering what the hell was going on.

If I had to guess, it looked like there were two different gangs after me, ones were fake Vampires and the others...well looking at them now and they certainly looked like the real deal to me. These guys looked like they ate gym weights for breakfast!

Well either way, I wasn't waiting around to find out. I needed to get the Hell out of here that was for sure, now of course I just needed a do-able plan to achieve that.

"Think Katie, think!"

"You there!"

"Shut up dickhead, they will hear!" Oh shit, another man ran out of the door joining the other two who were trapped near the entrance.

"Where is she?!" The new guy demanded and he looked like a freakin' biker giant! He had a long wiry grey beard and piercings all over his face. He was terrifyingly huge and if I thought the other two ate weights for breakfast then this guy could eat the weight machines!

They pointed to me and he looked up at the sun that still caused them problems.

"Fuck!" He snapped. One of the men next to him hit him on the shoulder to get his attention to the fact that the suited men by the bus had now also spotted me, quickly doubling the amount of shit I was now in!

"Run to us!" The giant shouted to me and I gave him a look of shock! Did he really think I was going to freely go to someone like him!

"For fuck sake girl, you know me, now fucking RUN!" The utter disbelief on my face made him scream in anger but with the others getting closer I did at least listen to half of what he was telling me to do.

"She's going to bolt!" I heard one of them say and the big guy's response was,

"Of course she is! I knew she was fucking trouble! Get them on the phone!" He snapped, obviously being the one in charge.

This was when I finally could make my move as the cops turned up obviously responding to the reported gunshots. I started running along with some other panicked travellers to the end of the parking lot but then veered off when I saw they had me surrounded. I turned around and saw the ones who had been checking the bus were closing in so I was trapped. Then out of nowhere a beeping horn sounded over and over like the person behind the wheel had the worst case of road rage. I saw a flash of yellow driving straight at us and three of the suits had to dive out of the way.

"Is that...*a school bus?*" I said squinting as the small bus came at me and turned with perfect timing to skid to the side right in front of me. It was a 70's VW bus customised in a way to make it look like an American school bus, complete with flashing lights above the windscreen. Painted flames along the side merged into letters that read...'Too Cool for School' with the words, 'This Shit's Real!' in smaller lettering like smoke below.

I jumped when the passenger's side opened like the double doors being pulled on a real school bus. There it revealed a green haired girl putting on an Arnold Schwarzenegger voice and shouting from the driver's seat ...

"Come with me if you want to live!"

CHAPTER 16

PALLADIO HAUNTING AFTERLIFE

"Hold onto your asses my lovers as I hightail it outta Dodge!" The strange girl said as she turned the wheel as if she was on a ship fighting a storm. The small VW bus skidded around and then as she pulled it full circle two wheels started to lift off the floor.

"Pipper." A man's voice warned softly from behind us and I would have looked if I hadn't been pinned to my seat with the force of the car turning.

"My bad but no biggy big daddy, I totally got this!" She said righting the bus and thankfully banging all wheels down and back where they were meant to be. As this happened a song came on the stereo and she shouted in excitement,

"Oh I love this song! Gotta love a bit of Motley Crue, eh Toots!" Then she turned it right up to blaring and started singing,

"Smoking in the boy's room, Smoking in the boy's room, now teacher don't you fill me up with your rule, 'cause everybody knows that smoking ain't allowed in school...oh yeah!" All the time she was driving around the parking lot trying to dodge cars and what I could only assume was trying to find the exit.

"I think it's that way." I said in a stunned voice that only occurred when you had too many emotions to deal with all at once. Fear, surprise, confusion, panic...I think even a bit of silent hysterics were in there as well.

"Ah, so it is. I see we have an A star student here enrolling in the School of Rockin' Pip!"

"Sweetheart, please focus." The man behind us spoke again in that calm voice, one that told me he must have simply been used to this girl's brand of crazy.

"Sure, sure...*jeez and they call wives for nagging.*" She whispered to me even though I was pretty sure he could hear every word she said as the heavy sigh behind us was a dead giveaway. Finally, after her crazed bit of driving she found the exit saying,

"Wow, they didn't make that easy did they? What if I had been visually impaired, see, they just don't think about these things...*see* what I did there." She started laughing to herself and my eyes widened at the thought.

"Who are you guys, if you don't mind me asking?" My heart rate had finally slowed enough to ask.

"We're the Carvery!"

"Cavalry Honey, you mean Cavalry." The man corrected and she laughed again.

"You know I always get those two mixed up...and in this case the last thing you need is a butchering right....am I right?" She repeated and I realised she was waiting for my answer.

"Oh...yeah, you're right." I said feeling as though I had stepped into an alternative reality. Thankfully the driving continued at a less death defying rate and I felt my pulse calm with every mile put between me and that rest stop.

"Hey are you okay...is she supposed to looked this pale?" The girl asked the man in the back seat.

"I don't think so." I said honestly holding a hand to my forehead.

"Oh shit a brick...you're not gonna hurl are you, I just had this baby detailed and re-fringed." I frowned wondering if I was now hearing things...did she say re-fringed?

"Yep, that's right...did it myself and all." She said answering what I had obviously asked out loud without realising it. I looked sideways to see her nodding to the door panel and yep, there it was, bright pink ribbon with dangling fringe glued to the frame.

"Smokin', right?" I bit my lip to stop from laughing at the madness and turned to quite possibly the cutest person I had ever encountered to say honestly,

"I think it's perfect." And then I must have hit my limit as the world of crazy went black and the last sound I heard was...

"At least she didn't hurl."

I opened my eyes to the world outside and it was burning.

I looked out to a rolling valley that looked as though a piece of the sun had fallen and crashed into this part of the Earth. Thousands of trees became torches swaying in violent winds and what once looked like rivers became passageways for molten magma to travel.

It was horrifying. It was petrifying...

It was Hell on Earth.

But most startling of all it was a view I had seen before and knew it was one I loved dearly. This place meant something to me although trying to find the reasons why was just as hard as trying to find the memory of when I first saw it. I felt the tears fall just as the beauty before me fell into the abyss of Hell, lost to a place that was taking a piece of my world that didn't belong to fire and brimstone. And then the emotions hit new levels as I quickly realised why it affected me so deeply. Because it wasn't just seeing the world we lived in come to an end, it was more about watching my home consumed by the flames.

"NO, NO, NO!" I screamed closing my eyes once more against the sight of my world dying. Why had this happened? Was this the end that Ari spoke of? I was forced back to that damned painting in my room at the Colony and suddenly I knew I didn't want to be that lone girl awaiting death.

No! I wanted to live damn it! I could feel the anger building up inside at the injustice of it all. I was free, finally free and now this! It wasn't going to happen and I don't know how I was going to stop it I just knew that I had to try. It was silly really, thinking about how one girl lost in her own mind could ever have the power to stop something like this.

But as silly as that seemed it was equally so in believing that I could. So with my fury bubbling to the surface and getting hotter the closer it came to erupting, I began to feel my body starting to change. I could feel the tingling in my fingertips and it was as though all my blood started to fuse with this new energy, this new power that coursed through me centred at my core...the core of my soul.

It was like waiting for someone to shout go, as if my body needed the sign and when I felt it hit its crescendo I screamed. My body had dropped to bent knees and my arms covered my head in utter anguish. I panted into the cocoon of flesh and bone I had created around myself, holding myself as secure as I could until I felt my body start to calm.

Only when I started to feel the cool wind did I raise my head and braved the sight I might have to endure.

And there I found beauty.

I found my home.

My Salvation…I found my,

"Persian Sun?" I said aloud and heard the sound of stone grating against stone behind me. I turned away from the sight of now perfect rolling mountains of green and faced an opened passageway in the immense stone wall. I frowned as I tried to get my brain to engage the situation and the only answer was that I was obviously dreaming. Although seeing the view all around me fall to damnation was more like a nightmare and felt like an arrow to the heart, with little reason behind such feelings. Or at least reasons that would make sense right now.

I looked back at nature's playground one last time and hoped to find answers in my memory bank as to why the sight invoked such emotion from me. But coming up empty wasn't the most frustrating part, it was when I realised this wasn't the first time I had seen it in flames that things became really confusing.

I wanted to scream at myself and I think if hitting myself on the head would have helped then I would be black and blue right now. But I was merely left feeling like I was the enemy and I was clearly losing the battle with myself.

So I took control of what little I had left, which seemed to be the decisions I made in this dream. Turning back to face the open door I took a step back to look up at the building I seemed to be stood against. It was a huge structure, like some sort of castle but looking up and across, I quickly found a bigger balcony than the one I was stood on. It was higher than me and I couldn't understand why looking at it created a barrage of emotions. I was almost as though I had once stood there feeling shy, scared, hurt, confused, hatred, desire but strongest of all was the love that overruled any before it.

"That's…what the…?" I whispered asking myself when

seeing the faded silhouette of a man carrying a woman and stepping off the wall that surrounded the balcony. I couldn't make out the details of either of them but he looked very similar to my Demon. He started falling this way and then suddenly disappeared mid-air like a pair of ghosts that had never crossed over to the…

"Afterlife." I uttered the name and that's when I knew what this place was. I reached out and touched the cold stone like it could communicate with me if only I let it. Well I didn't hear anything back but it gave me the comfort I needed in walking into the dark passageway with my head held high and my fear firmly in check.

The floor was slick and I held onto the wall to hold myself steady only to find it too was wet. I had no clue where this would take me but I could only hope it wasn't into the belly of the beast that would consume me. I needed answers and that was my driving force in all of this. I had one single goal in mind and that was Ari. I needed to get her out of that place at all costs…even my own life.

Thinking of Ari and seeing her in my mind's eye seemed to guide me along the passageway enough that when I came to a door at the end I walked through it knowing where I was going. It was almost as if I was following her voice and I felt safer when walking into the main part of the house. I must have been in a secret passageway I thought when taking in my new surroundings. The slate tiled floor went well with the bare stone walls and my first thought of this being a castle was looking more and more probable. Even the paintings that were dotted here and there looked as if painted by the Masters of Art, no matter how grim most of the images were.

"Well whoever lives here sure likes his battles." I said aloud after walking past the fourth one of a bloody battle field. They also must have liked their mythology as Godly figures also fought their bloody wars against Hellish monsters.

Thankfully I didn't come across a single person as I wasn't sure what would have happened if they had appeared. It was confusing enough being in this dream world and the longer I stayed the more lost I got holding on to that thought. It was like staring at a word long enough that it no longer made sense. Well that's how I thought when being here. As if thinking about the real world long enough in this place and that became the one that no longer made sense to me.

So it still begged the question that if I came across anyone else, would they be real or just as trapped in my own mind as I often felt?

I cast these crazy and maddening thoughts from my mind and focused on the aura that Ari was giving out, like a beacon to the truth. I continued on as though I had a map in my hand and ignored the feeling that I knew this place as if I had walked these corridors daily.

I even had to place a hand to the back of my neck as a mark I had there tingled and I scratched at it to get it to go away. I had never felt so embedded in a dream before and if I didn't watch myself I could quite easily be led down the road of insanity. Hell, I felt like I was half way there already!

"Is that…*a piano?*" I asked myself hearing a song being played in the distance.

"Ari?" I said her name the closer I got to the sound, knowing that Ari loved playing the piano or at least she had done before…but wait, that's not right. She never played at home…we didn't even have a piano. Then why do I see her playing one?

"Ari?!" I shouted before breaking out into a run. She was here, I knew she was! Could it be possible? Could we have crossed over our dreams and be sharing them right now? This thought made me run even faster and the rest of the house went past in a blur. I ran so fast it almost looked like the paintings stopped fighting to look at me shooting past and I could hear the rustling of the leaves in the painted trees. I could hear the whispers all around me like unseen souls hiding in the walls waiting for someone to free them. But I was not their girl…

Not today.

I came to a door and sucked in a sharp breath as it felt like two of me suddenly merged to open it. The strange feeling left me as soon as it was open and I was left gaping at the sight before me.

"This place isn't real!" I said wondering how my mind had conjured up such wild and exotic things. The massive golden dome looked like some ancient temple roof shining under the sunlight and for a moment I could believe I was in…

"Persia…*Persian Sun.*" As soon as I said it the sun went behind a cloud as though someone had cut the lights and dulled the gold. I put my hands on the stone wall that ran all around the huge square that looked to be cut out of the building. Looking up and around at the arches I realised that they ran the full length of each of the four sides and when I heard the piano, I knew which way I needed to go.

"I'm coming Ari, hold on…just hold on." I said running the full length and skidding around an arched doorway at the end. I continued to follow the sound only praying on finding my sister when I got there. It was getting louder now and behind what I knew was the last set of doors I would find my answer.

"Please…please God, let it be her." I said laying my forehead to the wooden panel and letting my heart catch a beat. Then I opened the door and muttered a sigh…

"Ari." There she was. I wanted to run over to her and pull her into my arms telling her how sorry I was for leaving her. I wanted to cry into her shoulder like I had done so many times

before. But most of all I wanted her to tell me it was going to be okay because we were now free.

I stepped forward more than ready to do all of these things but a shadow watching her in the background stopped me. The room looked like it was inside a giant turret as it was a vast circular space and at its centre was a huge, round bed, very low to the floor. Stark white sheets covered the sleeping island complete with a wall of pillar church candles surrounding the space.

A grand arched window stood from floor to ceiling directly behind the bed flooding the room with light. Soft floating white material hung down from elaborate wrought iron rods that were curled at the ends. The whole room looked like one you would have found in Heaven and I don't know why but I automatically thought of Zeus atop of Mount Olympus.

Grand marble pillars framed the room all around and it was behind one of these that the shadow stood hidden from Ari's sight. She was sat, as I'd expected, at a grand piano. Only this one was made from what looked like etched glass, adorned with stunning delicate flowers and vines creeping up from the black glass clawed feet.

Ari started to play a different song and I stopped breathing at the sound. Where had I heard this song before?

"I know you're watching." Ari said after a time of playing and for a moment I almost thought she was speaking to me. I don't know why I remained hidden but it was as if I knew that I had to if I was going to make any sense of what was happening now. I needed to know who was in the shadows stalking her and who it was she now spoke too.

"I know you do." Said a soft male voice that held an underlying power to it.

"You play it beautifully." He said stepping away from the shadows after the song had finished and there was a stretched moment of silence between them. The closer he came the more of him I could see and shock quickly replaced my confusion. He was breath-taking! Actually he looked like an Archangel just stepped from behind the pearly gates.

Tight golden curls were cut close to his head and startling crystal blue eyes were easy to see, even from where I remained hidden. But none of these features detracted from the masculine body of strength or the strong jawline that told me this was a man in charge of a great deal of power. He looked like someone very used to being in control and maintaining that control at all times. He didn't need to be wearing a suit or a uniform to tell me of his ranking in life because even in the well-worn jeans and T-shirt he wore now I knew. As would everyone else around him.

"In this place you hear it playing enough." Ari said lowering her head in sorrow. The man released a deep sigh before looking to the window above what I assumed was his bed.

"Yes and I am only left to hope that one day Palladio will no longer be heard amongst these walls." He said still looking out to the view beyond the glass, one that not so long ago I saw consumed by the flames of Hell.

"You think she will make it home?" Ari asked turning to face him and he looked back at her over his shoulder and said,

"I think she is unstoppable." Hearing this Ari allowed her tears to fall. The man watched as only one fell to the white marble floor before striding with purpose over to her. He took her face in both hands, tilted it up for his view and said,

"No tears…*I command it.*" This last part was exactly what he said it was and the power behind it came across in his stern voice. She looked up at him with wide, frightened eyes that also held something deeper than fear, something more powerful…*Lust.* He growled down at her then used a hand in her hair to pull her lips to his own before devouring her in a primal kiss. She moaned in his mouth causing him to pull her even closer, banding arms around her so she couldn't escape.

I knew I shouldn't be watching this. I knew I should be running back to my own fantasy man, looking for him wherever he could be in this stone maze. But shamefully I knew I couldn't look away. I was suspended between what was right and wrong, between sin and seclusion and my sinful decision was winning.

So I stayed hidden and allowed myself to dream within a dream of what it would feel like to have a man overpower my senses that way. I was transported back to my first kiss on the bus with Luc and I felt myself getting wet at the junction of my thighs. Again I knew this was wrong on so many levels but I seemed frozen by my own desperate need to be touched.

The man I suspected was Ari's Angel pulled away from her mid kiss as if frustrated with himself for losing a shred of control. He frowned down at her and then commanded once more,

"Turn around and place your palms on the top of the piano." She looked hesitant at first and he became impatient for her submission.

"Now Arianna." He ordered in a tone not to be defied. She lowered her head and turned around to do as he instructed placing her hands on top of the glass. He leaned into her and whispered,

"That's my girl." Then he ran a hand down her spine across the silk strappy dress she wore and she arched her back into his touch. I knew in that moment that she wanted this and her submission was all part of the dance they equally stepped into.

He moved from her back to grasp her waist and yank her bottom further down into a position he wanted her in. She yelped in surprised to feel him step into her as he did this, forcing her back against the desire he still kept hidden in his jeans. The outline of such was easy to see as his length strained against the zipper, needing to be freed into her body.

I was no stranger to watching two people make love, not considering how many times I had seen the image of myself being taken time and time again by my Demon. But this was different as it felt like a violation. I turned away from my sister and knew I had to get out of here before it was too late and I had stepped too far.

"Are you ready for your punishment?" My head snapped back round when I heard him ask this. He was going to punish her?! No, this wasn't the way it was supposed to go. He couldn't hurt her, not him, not the man I knew my sister had quickly fallen in love with. Not the man of her dreams.

"Yes my...*My Master.*" Her reply was even more shocking and I closed my eyes against the confusion. Why after so long and so many years of being punished would she want this? I couldn't understand it and I certainly couldn't watch it. I felt disgusted, I felt ashamed...I felt, oh God no...but I felt *aroused.*

I turned back just in time to see him raising her dress, taking a stance to the side and administering the first swing. The slap of skin against skin echoed along with the sound of the random keys on the piano sounding out her pain along with her.

"Do you know why you are getting punished this time?" He asked her in perfect calm. She nodded her head and received another hard slap to her buttocks for it.

"You know it gives me pleasure upon hearing my beautiful girl's voice when answering me."

"Yes." She moaned arching back again as if waiting for his next hard touch.

"Yes?" He asked and then delivered three more slaps in quick succession. She cried out and I saw what she did not. It seemed the sound of her crying out in both pain and desire did great things to him. He had closed his eyes and looked up at the arched ceiling as if drawing in every ounce of pleasure the sound of her moans provided.

"Yes Master, I know why." She corrected herself and this time received a comforting stroke to her red and heated skin. It was nothing short of a loving touch, no matter the reasons for giving it.

"Tell me why." His smooth voice asked but I could see from behind her that he was bracing himself for her answer, one he knew he wouldn't like.

"Because I left you." She whispered sounding ashamed by the confession.

"Then you shall know the same pain that my brother and I are forced to endure as our punishment." He said like it actually gave him pain to even speak the words.

"No! Please, you can't...please, not this time...don't leave me, anything but that." She pleaded, getting up and throwing her arms around his torso in desperation. She held on tight as if clinging on to him for dear life would change his mind. He didn't give it long before he wrapped his arms around her and held her head to his shoulder but the pain in his eyes never left him.

Because he knew it would end. It always did. And because of this the bitterness wouldn't leave him.

"She will find a way, I know she will...like you said, she is unstoppable." Ari begged crying into his body as though he was all that mattered right now. Then suddenly the great windows blew open and a gust of wind blew out all the candles just at the same time Ari's Angel looked directly at me, like he had known I had been there all along.

"Keira was unstoppable." He said to me and I felt my tears fall at the failure I felt. That name was back and it meant so much to me at the same time as it meant nothing. On hearing

this, Ari looked up with tear filled eyes, grabbed his face as he had once done to her and made him look at her.

Then she spoke for me,

"Then so can Katie. Have faith Angel..."

"...Palladio won't play for much longer."

CHAPTER 17
CANDY, SODAS AND BLOOD

"Okay, time to wake up Honey Sue!" The combined voice and small tapping against my cheek started to bring me around.

"Where am I?" I asked opening my eyes only to shut them quickly against the blaring light.

"Alright Doc, I think she's good now." A man's voice said and I felt the bright light disappear from behind my closed lids. I braved opening my eyes to find grinning pink and purple glossy lips along with a tiny skeleton hand curled round one side.

"Is that a lip ring?" I have no idea why I found this on my list of priorities to know, but I asked it all the same.

"It sure is Tootsie Pop a Doodle, awesomeness isn't it!" I pushed myself into an upright position and tried to make sense of what she just said. Opening my eyes, I saw what looked like a dog's squeaky toy in the shape of a police officer with a light coming out of his little bum.

"Who are you guys?" I asked looking from the strangest girl I had ever seen to the librarian that was now up front driving.

"Remember what we spoke about sweetheart, don't get upset." I shot the man driving a confused look before I realised he was talking to the colourful girl sat next to me on the back seat of the bus. She looked ready to burst into tears at the sight of me and I felt so bad for her but I didn't know what I could do to make it better. For a start I didn't know why she looked so upset and her cute round baby features stood out even more. Her big bright green eyes were watery with unshed tears and I couldn't help but place a hand on top of hers and say,

"Hey, what do you call a teacher that's always late?" I asked doing anything to wipe that look of devastation from her face. I saw a little dimple appear and knew it was working.

"I don't know, what do you call a teacher that's always late?"

"Mr Bus." I told her making her burst out laughing.

"Missed the Bus! That's a good one!" She said and then retold the joke to the man driving. I took this opportunity to look around and see that there was a definite Beano/school theme going on in the back and I gathered it went well with the bus they owned. Glued staplers acted as cupboard handles, kid's comics were pasted on the doors and hundreds of post it note pads made up the roof. Even the material on the seat was a rainbow of colour with its colouring pencil print. And even more randomly a little Elvis was hanging from a sucker on the side window, looking like he was giving us the pelvic thrust as we drove along.

But stranger than all this was reading the black t-shirt she wore that said, 'My cats ate a crazy cat lady' on the front. On the back there were bloody paw prints as if one of the murdering kitties had walked the evidence of their crime right across her back. This was paired with a pair of leggings with a pattern that looked like a Unicorn on one leg, fighting a Robot under a rainbow on the other. On her feet I wasn't surprised to see white skeleton's feet painted on her black boots.

"Who's Adam?" I asked referring to the tattoo of the name ADAM written across her knuckles, with hearts and flowers around the swirly writing in reds and pinks. Of course this wasn't the only tattoo she had as you could see all the bright colours flowing down one arm. She smirked at me and then nodded up front to the man driving.

"That's Adam, my Hubby Boo Bot." She said proudly and I coughed, choking on a swallow.

"Husband!?" I couldn't help my reaction as I would never have put these two together in a million years.

"I know right, I am so out of his league but I thought, what the Hell, give the geek a chance." She said winking at me.

"I could pull over little one." He threatened softly and she started bouncing in her seat, saying,

"Please do." I blushed thinking about my last dream and realising it obviously wasn't only my sister that enjoyed a bit of male domination and punishment.

"Behave dumpling." He warned and I giggled along with her.

"Nah I am only joking... it was totally love at first sight." She said behind her hand in the same tone as she had been speaking, so confusingly I wondered why considering he could hear her.

"For me too, Love." I thought it was cute seeing how these two were with each other, even with an obvious stranger hitching a ride. Which brought me back to more important questions.

"So I hate to ask again but...who are you guys?" Thankfully this time my question didn't upset the girl like it had before.

"Okay, so you know that my Hubba Bubba there is Adam." I smiled at him when he looked back and gave me a nod.

"Well you can call me your BFF or Pip, either one is true."

"BFF?" I asked never hearing the term before. She bounced again in her seat and quickly enlightened me,

"Best Friends Forever." I gave her a smirk and held out my hand for her to shake. I found her one of the most endearing people I had ever met and couldn't help but fall in love with her instantly.

"BFF it is." I said taking her dainty hand in mine and shaking on it. Her smile developed into a beaming one hearing this but disappeared just as quick when I introduced myself.

"I'm Katie by the way."

"I think I will just call you Toots if you don't mind." She said folding her arms and Adam laughed from the front. She shot him an evil glare and I was left feeling confused once more.

"I don't mind, it's a fun nickname." I said hoping this would diffuse whatever situation hearing my name had caused.

"Magic, that's it then! You know my other BFF loved it also." She told me and I heard Adam sigh in exasperation.

"What! I am allowed to talk about her."

"Pipper, this is not wise." He warned making her sulk.

"Did you guys have a falling out?" I asked curious to know why Adam didn't think it wise.

"Not exactly but more like forced time apart… I miss my friend." She added in a dejected tone that spoke of mourning.

"I'm sorry. But if it helps I know how it feels." I said and her eyes got wide, making the little cat ears she had painted over her lids crack a bit.

"You do?"

"Sure." She seemed very happy to hear this and stuck her tongue out at her husband when he looked in the mirror at her in warning. They were adorable.

"I bet your wondering Ke…Katie where we are going."

Adam said almost forgetting my name. Well, he had a good point but why had the important questions left me all of a sudden?

"Yeah, kind of. I'm sorry, it was great of you to pick me up when you did, it was as if you knew...*I was in trouble...*" I trailed off as I thought about it all. Who were they really but more importantly who sent them?

"Don't worry Toots, it's all in hand now."

"What do you mean? Where are we going?" I asked now not feeling so sure about these two. As soon as the thought entered my head I heard the automatic locks click into place. I can't say this gave me the warm and fuzzies knowing these two thought I might jump out of a moving vehicle. But the main question was what did they think would warrant such an action on my part...? That was the most worrying question of all.

"Do you think we should give her alcohol?" Pip asked her husband and I shook my head the same time Adam said,

"I don't think that's a good idea, Sweetheart."

"I second that, but hey, what would be a good idea is if you guys tell me what's going on here?" I said losing my patience real quick. Adam took a deep breath after shaking his head at Pip, probably thinking it best coming from him.

"A friend of ours saw that you were in trouble and called us as we were close by." I frowned back at him and then at Pip, who just gave me a flat smile and shrugged her shoulders like someone getting busted.

"And this friend of yours, do I know their name?" I asked having a bad feeling about this. Neither of them would answer me, they just kept looking at each other, so I said the name I suspected,

"It was Luc, wasn't it?"

"Okay, this is going to get confusing real soon." Pip said to Adam and I asked why.

"Have you ever caught the end of a movie and then spend the whole time asking yourself what the Hell pants is going on?" She asked me and I thought about it for a second.

"No, I'm afraid I haven't."

"Well that's my example up the shitter, your turn handsome." She said throwing her hands up in the air.

"I think what my beautiful wife is trying to say, is that without knowing the whole story first you won't understand the answers to your questions."

"Alright, so in that case what is this story I need to hear?" I asked folding my arms and getting impatient with all the cryptic replies.

"I am afraid that isn't our story to tell."

"Then whose is it for crying out loud!?" I said snapping.

"It's yours." Pip said softly placing a kind hand over mine and sapping all the frustration right out of me.

"I just don't understand." I muttered honestly as I deflated back against my seat.

"I know you don't but you are going to have to trust me when I say, you soon will." Adam said in that placating tone that you give someone who's clearly on the edge.

"Can I at least know where we are going?" I asked half expecting them not to answer this question either. So I was shocked for both reasons when Pip shouted out,

"Afterlife, of course!"

As we reached Portland I had a few hours of quiet time to myself which I suspected I wouldn't have had if Pip hadn't fallen asleep back near Boston. We had driven through a place called Worcester and Pip had said something odd before falling asleep,

"I bet this one is a little different than the last one you saw."
I was just asking her what she meant when her snoring filled the
silence.

"It's the excitement, she often crashes like that." Adam
told me before looking back at the road. I grabbed a blanket I
could see folded over the back and covered her up with it
smiling at the picture of sheep counting humans jumping over
a fence.

"Will whoever you're taking me to help me?" I asked Adam
cautiously as I scooted forward in my seat. I was almost afraid
to hear the answer…well, if I got one that was.

"I know you must be so confused right now but would you
believe me if I told you I was once in a similar position as you
are now." My face said it all and he laughed softly. His
handsome face certainly was made to smile I thought secretly.

"It's true. The people that you find bombarding into your
life now did the very same thing to mine. And with them they
brought along more strange and unbelievable questions for me
to ask than answers."

"So how did you cope with it all?" I asked trying to figure
out if what he was saying was the truth and with one loving
look toward Pip, I knew that he was.

"I met the love of my life. After that nothing else mattered.
It was all simple formalities left for me to cast aside." I looked
at the beautiful picture of a green haired girl sleeping soundly
knowing she had her man safely by her side and I knew nothing
else mattered to her either.

"That's what love does you know." He added making me
look back at him.

"What's that?"

"It makes you do the uncontrollable, the unthinkable and in
all these things it makes you unstoppable." When hearing that
last word spoken, I then heard it repeated by the Angel in Ari's

life. But where Ari had been referring to me he had been referring to this *'Keira'*.

After this I sat back, looked out the window and thought about everything that had happened. I wanted to ask so many things but where did I start? They knew who Luc was but if that was true then did they also know *what* Luc was? And more importantly to add to my list of worries was, if he was who I thought he was, then who were these two...*truly?*

Could they have been the same...Vampires? One look at the cute bundle of colour that was Pip and I didn't think so. Also I had to ask myself how they knew I wanted to get to Afterlife as I was pretty sure I hadn't mentioned anything to Luc on our bus journey together.

Either way I had to trust them because let's face it, what choice did I really have? It wasn't like they had hurt me and other than locking the door for fear of my take flight instincts to kick in, they had been friendly and loving towards me. Especially Pip. In fact, it felt like I had known her most of my life we got on that well. She even broke out the board games shortly after I found out where we were going.

She was so much fun to be around it almost felt like a road trip with friends rather than running from Colony goons that could be chasing us. We stopped for gas a few times and I was looking cautiously over my shoulder half expecting to see them, as I had the strongest feeling that someone was watching us. Pip then drew my attention away from my paranoia by asking me a strange question,

"What do you call gas in England again?"

"Just petrol or diesel if...uh, wait I..." She gave me a cheeky wink like she had just caught me out and then to change the subject she asked,

"Do you want any candy or a soda...? I'm gonna get a Mountain Dew, I love the stuff only Adam says it makes me hyper, ha what does he know…! Did you know it was first invented for whiskey…? True story that!" She carried on like this as she entered the store and came back out buying what looked like one of everything. We then stuffed ourselves over a game of Kerplunk, which I had to say wasn't easy in a moving vehicle and then a game of Operation which was near impossible. During both Pip never got hyper and I was left agreeing with her… what did Adam know?

Now however, I was left wondering who would be meeting me on the other side and if I would finally meet this Draven character. I knew he owned Afterlife so the chances were good but then the chilling thought came and I wondered if I would also see anyone from my dreams there…*like my Demon.*

But I tried not to focus on that right now. No I had to lay my trust on Pip and Adam that they weren't leading me into danger. I had to believe this Dominic Draven could help me save my sister…that was all that mattered to me now.

"Is everything alright?" I asked when I noticed Adam had been eyeing the road behind in the mirror ever since we passed a sign for Evergreen Falls.

"I think we are being followed. Can you wake Pip up, please?" I nodded after looking back myself and seeing what Adam was seeing, which was a black van following us close behind.

"Oh no, it looks like…"

"I know Katie, but you need to do as I say and wake up Pip, I will need her." He said losing his cool persona for a moment as if he was desperate for his wife. I shifted over closer to Pip and started to gently pat her, becoming more forceful when she wouldn't wake up.

"Uhh Adam?" I called his name, afraid that by doing so I would be taking his mind away from the speedy driving he was now doing.

"Yeah, is she awake yet?" He asked and I looked down at her, gave her a nudge and said.

"I think we have a problem." He whipped his head back frantically to find his still unconscious wife.

"What's wrong with her?!" He shouted definitely now losing his cool completely.

"She's out cold, ever since she…" I started to think back and before long I was acting frantic too by searching for what I thought was the cause.

"Ever since what?!" Adam demanded and just before I managed to say what, I was thrown forward crashing into the seats in front as the van behind rammed us. Thankfully with the position I found myself in it stopped Pip from rolling right off the seat.

"Hang on!" Adam yelled and swerved around oncoming traffic and overtook the car in front to put space between us and the van.

"I think she's been drugged! She was fine before she drank this." I said holding up the empty bottle.

"It shouldn't have affected her…*unless*…hold on, they're having another go!" He never finished telling me why it shouldn't have affected Pip as the Van behind had caught up by overtaking the same car.

"Damn it Pip, why didn't you listen to me, I knew we should have taken the Lamborghini Estoque!" He said talking to himself as he swerved a little too hard and only just made it when trying to right the bus again before it tipped up.

"They're trying to ram us off the road!" I looked back and shouted,

"Here they come!" Then they hit us a second later but this time I grabbed onto Pip's body to hold her in place. I felt my neck jar painfully at the impact. I heard the crunch of metal behind and knew it wouldn't be long before they won the fight.

"What are we going to do?!"

"We can't take another hit like that so you have to listen to me. If we crash, then I want you to run…"

"I can't leave you both!" I said interrupting him but he shook his head and said more forcefully,

"Yes you can! I can protect my wife but not if you're there as well…do you understand what I am saying…? I need you to run, get to Afterlife!" I started to shake my head when Adam pulled on the steering wheel and fought against it skidding after barely making it away from another hit.

"Promise me you will run, no matter what you hear, no matter what you see! Promise…" He never got chance to finish as we were hit for the last time. The VW bus spun around on the road before tipping up on two wheels. The force took us over onto its side and the glass smashed all around us as the van still travelled off the side of the road into the trees. It was only Adam that barely moved thanks to his seatbelt but Pip and I weren't so lucky. We were both bashed around inside the bus and I hit my head against the window, feeling pain explode from my temple.

It finally came to a stop when the front of the bus crumpled around a tree and the memory of having another car accident flashed before my eyes. I couldn't hear anything but a high pitch that was constant for a moment and I opened my eyes when I felt a trickle of water dripping down. My vision was blurry at first and I tried to wipe the water off my face, only my hand came back crimson.

"Blood?" I muttered still trying to get my bearings when I remembered I hadn't been alone in the back.

"Pip!" I shouted lifting my head and feeling the world spin.

"Ahhh!" I shouted in pain as I moved my legs knowing I must have done some damage. I wiggled my toes and was relieved when I could feel them moving.

"Get the girls, I will deal with the guy!" I heard voices speaking around the bus and knew that I had to do as Adam had told me. I had to get up and I had to run! I looked around and found Pip's leg hanging over part of the seat as she must have fallen closer to the back as we flipped.

"Adam?" I hissed and I looked back to the front to find that Adam too was also unconscious. Like me, blood poured from his head as he must have hit it on the wheel when we crashed. That's when I first caught sight of them coming round the bus, the men wearing black suits...the Righteous Bloods.

"What do you want me to do with this one?" A man's voice said after they pried open the driver's door and held up Adam's unconscious head by his bloody hair.

"And what about this little freak, we could have fun with this one." The other one said at the back when looking in at Pip. My blood ran cold at the thought of them violating Pip and I wanted to scream not to touch her. But I decided my best chance at helping them was like Adam had said, getting to Afterlife and telling whoever was in charge there. So I remained still so they would believe I was still knocked out like the rest but my hand searched beneath me for anything I could use as a weapon.

"Let's take them with us, the Fathers will know what to do and who knows, they might even come in useful for something."

"I know this one will, nice and small just as I like 'em!" The vulgar one said and I knew if given the chance the shard of glass I just found was going straight through this one's skull!

I gripped it tightly to my chest as I heard them trying to find a way to get me out. I heard more glass smash and tried not to jump when I felt hands grab me under the arms.

"She's out cold." The man behind me said and I almost

smiled at the grave mistake he was making. They had to haul me out backwards and it was difficult letting my body go as limp as possible so they would believe the act. I hung my head down, thankful that my long hair had come loose and was hiding my face tightening in pain. Thankfully it didn't take long but it was hard not to call out when it felt like they would wrench my arm out of its socket as they dragged me from the bus.

Thankfully the guy tasked with the job had obviously had enough as well giving the fact that he dropped me to the ground the first moment he got.

"Fuck that was hard!" He grumbled.

"Here you pussy, let me get her! I wanna see what else we have to play with on the long journey home." Said the disgusting raping parasite that needed this deadly shard more than most. He yanked me up painfully and I knew this was my opportunity, so I took it!

"Surprise asshole!" I shouted thrusting my hanging arm upwards with such force it stabbed him right in between his legs, causing him both to drop me and start howling in agony. The blood spurted out of the tear in his trousers and dripped down my hand, mixing with my own until I let go. Then I turned and ran into the tree line as fast as I could, knowing I had to be quick as they would follow.

"Go and get her!" One of them shouted over the bellowing of pain I had inflicted on the other one. I looked around frantically searching where I should run to when I froze on the spot.

"What the...?" I muttered to myself when I heard the sounds of men screaming as though they were being ripped apart. I looked back and at first I thought he was running to try and catch me but then I saw the terrified look in his eyes and knew differently. He wasn't running to me, he was running to get away from something and from the sounds of the crashing metal...

It was something big.

I saw the man running faster towards me looking behind him so much that he tripped up a few times. I knew I too should be running but something had me rooted to the spot. I squinted when I saw the trees start to sway behind him until they moved so violently I half expected a tank to come rolling through. But I saw no tank, however what I heard would have given Hell's Demons nightmares!

The loudest roar shook the trees as if an orchestra of bears and lions had all thundered at the same time. The man screamed again and I looked back just in time to see him disappearing backwards as if something had grabbed hold of him. Another scream followed by a gurgling sound was all I heard before a deathly silence.

I panted almost gasping for breath as I waited for it to come back but there was nothing but a distressed sound like a huge animal was whining in pain. I looked back at the vast woods in front of me and then back to the road. I knew the right thing to do could get me killed but I couldn't just leave them there. I had to know, one of them might need my help, they might need me to help get them to a hospital.

"I'm sorry Adam." I said as I started running back to the road knowing I would be breaking a promise I had intended to keep. I just couldn't do it. The thought of Pip lay on the road bleeding or Adam still unconscious from his head wound, just left there to die wasn't an option.

So I ran as fast as I could until there were some trees I could hide behind to see what I was up against. I closed my eyes and took a deep breath as I took my first step. The crunch of branches beneath my feet was all I heard and I decided it was a good enough sign that it was time to step up to being brave and open my eyes to what lay ahead.

That eerie silence was soon shattered with the sound of my screams as I looked upon the massacre at my feet...

Everyone was dead.

CHAPTER 18
FINDING MY WAY

For what felt like a long time I walked, trying to stay parallel with the road but keeping well out of sight. Ever since seeing the unthinkable carnage I had found spread across the road like human roadkill, I had continued to throw up and heave every time the horror re-entered my troubled mind.

I had held it together enough to look for both Adam and Pip only I hadn't found a single trace of them. I had even braved looking in the black van the goons had been traveling it but it was hard to get to seeing as it had been flipped on its side like the VW. I looked through the windows to see it was empty and I was left hoping that Adam had woken up and managed to get both himself and Pip out of there.

I had no idea what that thing had been but I made sure to hurry up before it decided to come back. One thing was clear enough for sure and that was all the Righteous Bloods had found their end in the most horrific of ways…if all the severed limbs and scattered flesh and organs were anything to go by. I saw a car coming in the distance knowing that I needed to get out of there before I became classed as a witness. For a start what on Earth would I ever tell the cops about this one?

So I ran back to the trees, after grabbing my bag from behind the broken glass at the back of the VW. I ducked out of sight just as a car came to a screeching halt only to find what I had. I couldn't help but feel sorry for whoever it had been in the car and only hoped there were no kids in the back seat and that they had a strong stomach, as they were going to need it!

Time was getting on and I knew it would be dark soon. I had stopped to dig out a few breakfast bars from my bag and the bottle of water I had there thanks to Lucy. I also found the money I had stashed and knew I would have to do something if I was ever going to make it to Afterlife before the night was over.

So I decided to walk alongside the road, knowing by now I was far enough from the crash/murder site to make anyone seeing me suspicious. I had used the top I was wearing to clean myself up as it was now torn beyond repair. I changed into one of the others I had in the bag that was black with a huge pale grey flower on the side that looked as though it had been x-rayed. It had quite a low neck line but right now I didn't care if my cleavage was on show. Instead I concentrated on getting myself looking as though I hadn't been in an accident.

I used the old t-shirt to clean up the cut on the side of my head with some of my water, along with the cut on my palm from the glass I had used as a weapon. I had done the same with the cuts on my leg, tearing it into strips to use as a makeshift bandage on the deeper wound there and I used the last strip for my hand. I then changed into a pair of black trousers hoping if any blood seeped through it wouldn't be seen.

Walking along the side of the road turned out to be a good thing or I might have missed the motel and roadside café that advertised the best pies in town along with rooms available. I almost jumped for joy at the sight, or would have if I hadn't been limping slightly.

I decided now was a good time to pull on the lightweight jacket I had rolled up in my bag that was thin but at least it was rain proof if the heavens opened.

I crossed over the road after a truck went whizzing past and lifted up the hood on the jacket I now wore to hide my face. I felt exposed out in the open but I knew I had no choice. I needed to find a number for a taxi and get myself to that club before anything else happened!

I opened the door to the diner and the smell of fried food, cherry pies and coffee hit me making my stomach groan. I had eaten some bars but they had made another appearance when I shamefully went through a mentally weak patch and threw them up when thinking about that road.

"Don't think about it, Katie." I muttered to myself as I took an empty seat at the counter.

"Coffee?" A lady asked me after popping her gum and I looked up to see her holding out a coffee pot ready to pour into the cup that had appeared from nowhere. Wow, she was good!

"Uh…just tap water please." I said thinking I really needed to conserve my money, just in case.

"Ah, you're one of them are ya, well I guess I will just skip the specials then." I felt embarrassed so before she left to serve someone else and thinking that I was just a low life bum, I said,

"Cherry pie please." My hood slipped a bit and she got more of a look at my face and her features changed. Pity wasn't something anyone enjoyed seeing when being looked at but considering how sore I was on the side of my face, I knew what it must have looked like. Then a little smile appeared as she must have read my face and she gave me an understanding nod before she whispered,

"You're lucky, today's special is a drink on the house with

every slice." Then she winked at me and I think if she had been on my side I would have hugged her for her kindness. Thankfully though there was a counter between us and therefore I was saved from looking like Queen of the nut jobs!

"Thank you." I decided this was the safer option and then ordered the iced tea. When she came over with the pie I stopped her to ask about taxis.

"I could call you a cab, sure thing...where are you headed?"

"Uh, a club called Afterlife...do you know it?" At this she laughed.

"Honey, in a town this small, everyone knows about that place. *And you seemed like such a sweet girl.*" I wanted to ask her what she meant by that muttered comment but she was already walking away. I saw her fish out her mobile and scroll through some numbers before she hit ring on one. She flashed me a curious look whilst speaking on the phone and I looked down to concentrate my attentions back on my pie.

"That cab should be with you soon, meantime you enjoy that pie." I did just that, enjoying every mouthful. Then when my plate was empty I got up to use the bathroom to assess the damage. This time I was thankful to see it was a single room that I could lock, so I wouldn't be caught out again like last time. I used the toilet and was washing the dried blood from my hands when I braved a look in the mirror.

"Oh Katie." I whispered chastising myself at the mess staring back at me. I dumped my bag on the toilet lid and rooted out the hair brush I knew was packed in there. I gingerly brushed through the knots being careful where the cut on my head had started to crust over. My blonde hair was stained crimson on one side, so I tried to wash it off as much as I could in the sink.

Then when I was satisfied I plaited it to one side and tucked it into my jacket. I washed my face but there was nothing to be done about the bruising that had had plenty of time to turn purple and snake around the side of my face and one eye. I must have taken the brunt of the damage to my head and one side of my body when the VW smashed on to its side. I closed my eyes against the throbbing pain in my head and the sting where my flesh was cut. What I wouldn't have done right now for some painkillers as it was obvious the adrenaline was long gone and I was now running on empty.

But there was nothing to be done...I couldn't stop now, not when I was so close. After deciding I had spent way too much time in the bathroom I walked back into the diner and heaved my stiff body back up on to my seat. Not long later I heard the beep outside that was my cue to leave and I got up from the stool, pushing the empty plate the waitress's way.

"The sign was right, best pies around." I told her after putting a few bills down for the pie, including a good tip for her kindness. She laughed as I walked through the door and when seeing the taxi, I knew that by getting in it I was one step closer to my goal.

"Not long now." I said to myself pulling my jacket around me to shelter me from the cold seeping in. In the time that I had been in the diner the last of the daylight had gone being replaced by night. Getting in the taxi the first thing I noticed was the time and was surprised to see it was gone nine in the evening. Well at least the club would be in full swing and easier to go unseen amongst the crowds.

"You wanna go to Afterlife, am I right?" She sounded a bit abrupt, so I gathered it wasn't one of her favourite places to visit.

"Yes please." I said ignoring her look of distaste and wondering what it was about the club she disliked so much. We started driving in the same direction that I had walked to get here and I realised I had been holding my breath in case we needed to go back the other way. Right now I don't think my fragile nerves could have coped with even getting close to it. By now at least the cops should be all over it and I would have been surprised if the road wasn't closed because of it.

"Is it far?" I asked after a few minutes of the tension building.

"Not far enough in my opinion." She replied curtly.

"I take it you're not a fan?" I said pointing out the obvious. She tutted and said,

"Most definitely not."

"Can I ask why?"

"Only if I can ask why you would want to go there?" She replied throwing my question back at me.

"I am meeting someone there, so didn't have much choice in the matter." Upon hearing this she seemed to lose the attitude towards me, at least for now.

"So you've never been there?" I nodded confirming what she said.

"Oh, well I guess you will find out what it's like soon enough. The turning will be coming up in five minutes." Those five minutes turned into twenty, as I thought it must have been that long since she had agreed to take anyone this way, she had forgotten how far it was. In fact, the further we travelled, the more my confusion increased. It seemed we were heading way out of town and started to think maybe we were lost because it made little sense why a club would be in the middle of nowhere like this. I was just about to ask the awkward 'Did you get us lost' question that no taxi driver likes to hear when she spoke, surprising me,

"Here we are." Then she turned down a dark track that was tunnelled by the trees overhead. The whole thing had my nerves pulled tight like strings on a violin. I was desperate to get there as much as I was silently dreading it. What if it looked exactly like it had in my dream...*what if it didn't?*

What if *he* was there? No! I couldn't think about that now. I had to focus on the job at hand and that was finding this Draven character and then trying to convince him to help me. So far everyone that seemed to know him told me he would and why would my dreams bring me this far if only to fail. Well I was left with no other options at this point, I needed to go through with this whether I wanted to or not.

"Holy shit..." I said on a gasp as Afterlife finally came into view.

"That's one way to describe it." The taxi driver said bitterly but I was no longer listening. I just found myself getting out of the car in a daze, not being able to tear myself away from the sight.

"It's beautiful." I whispered in awe. The sound of the window going down and someone clearing their throat barely meant a thing and wasn't enough to drag me away.

"I think you're forgetting something." She snapped and without looking at her I fished out some dollars from my bag and handed them through the window, again without being able to look away. It was as if I was afraid if I did it would disappear into the abyss that was my dream world.

"Thanks." I muttered.

"Crazy Goths!" She said to herself before she drove off leaving me standing in the middle of the car park staring at perfect dark beauty, lit by a soft warm glow of a few old fashioned street lamps. I thought I would have been surprised seeing that it wasn't a castle but looking at the large stone blocks that made up the structure, I understood how my mind had easily made the mistake in my dreams.

So it wasn't a castle but instead it was an enormous manor

house that looked as though it was hundreds of years old. I wondered how far it went back considering most of it was hidden by the surrounding forest. Even the thick ivy that grew all over one side was trying to take over the building and I had to wonder how much longer it would take to be completely taken over by nature.

Looking at the imposing grand entrance I didn't know how I was going to make my legs work. But it wasn't just the stone archway or the thick black gates either side that caused me to worry but the two over built security guards who stood either side of the gates. What if they wouldn't let me in?

Well there was only one way to find out. So I pulled my hood further down, hiding my face and shifted the strap of my bag over my shoulder.

"Here goes nothing." I said looking down so no one would see me talking to myself. I walked to the entrance just as another group of people had been dropped off closer to the doors and they must have been regulars as the security guards nodded in acknowledgement. I used this as my opportunity to worm my way in so it seemed like I was part of the group.

Luckily I had thought to change into black trousers back in the woods because combined with the black jacket I at least looked the part. The group of regulars laughed around me and I excused myself as I was pushed to one side in their hurry to get inside. I landed against one side of the enormous wooden doors that seemed impenetrable. With my hands flat against the iron studded oak I was surprised to find it felt warm. It was so strange but the feelings of security that seeped in felt connected to my soul. It felt like…

Home.

My fingers automatically went to the symbol carved in the middle and just as my fingers ran along the curve of what looked like a family crest a voice shouted at me from behind.

"You there, move it!" I looked back for a split second and

when I saw one of the security guards coming at me I ran inside before he could get to me.

"Hey, I know you! Come back here!" I shook my head against where I had seen the face before and pushed my way through the mass of bodies, hoping to get lost in the sea of black. I looked back to see him scanning the crowd trying to find me and I felt better knowing he had little chance now I was in. I ducked and pushed my way further into the centre and just as I thought he might see me again, the band started playing the chorus. Everyone around me went crazy and started jumping around me doing a perfect job of hiding me.

In the end I saw him throw his hands in the air in a gesture that told me he was giving up and this was confirmed when he started to push his way back to the entrance. I took a minute to calm my racing heart and bent over in the small space I had. Then the band began a new song that started off strange before everyone around me started singing in sync… 'Freedom, la, la, la, Freedom, follow me' before the main singer started the song. That's when I started to take in my surroundings.

"Amazing." I whispered to myself looking up at what could have been the inside of a forgotten cathedral. The ceiling was a series of stone arches interlocked with medieval wrought iron chandeliers hanging down at the central points. It reminded me a little of some modern day throne room and I half expected to see the King seated at the end. I looked that way and saw no king, however what I did see was two grand staircases that mirrored each other, curving around the stage until they met the top of the mezzanine level.

I don't know why I was so drawn to the upstairs but when I saw them I gasped, knowing this was where I needed to go. However, one look at the giants standing guard at the base of both staircases and I knew I would have no chance! No, I needed to find someone who worked here that could take me to the owner or I would no doubt be thrown out on my sore behind.

I scanned the vast space that was separated into different levels with seating all around in hopes of seeing someone that obviously worked here but one look told me I doubted it was the uniform type of place. Finally, through all my searching I found the two largest groups of people were either by the band on the dance floor or by the bar. So even though I couldn't see it for people, I took a chance and squeezed my way through to the other side.

The closer I got, the tighter the queue for drinks got and at this rate I knew it would take me half the night! I umm'd and ahhh'd for a minute and then said,

"Oh sod it!" Then I pushed my way around the mass of people and approached it from the far end.

"Hey!"

"You pushed in, she pushed in!"

"Oi! Get back!" The chorus of angry Goths made me wish I had rethought this plan of mine.

"Sorry, I just need to ask a question, I'm not ordering anything." I said to one girl with black lines down her face like she had smudged her make up on purpose.

"Oh well that's alright then!" She said sarcastically. Then she turned back to her friend and continued to moan,

"Can you believe this Bitch?" I decided to ignore them and try and grab the girl's attention who was serving.

"Excuse me!"

"Back of the queue, Blondie." She said without looking at me and I looked down to see my plait was on show.

"But I just need to ask you a question...I..."

"I don't do chicks, happy now?" She replied dryly and I was getting frustrated and angry.

"That's not what I..."

"Look you heard her!" The irate clubber barked and I rolled my eyes, which turned out to be an even bigger mistake.

"Did you just roll your eyes at me?!"

"Wow observant much." I muttered.

"What did you say to me Bitch!?" She snapped and I was finding my patience was unravelling and quickly.

"Jerry, we have a situation here." The barmaid said just as I turned my back to the girl, which turned out to be my third mistake since entering this giant hub of negativity.

"I am just looking for someone and he…" I was cut short when I was pushed from behind, hence me falling forward and slamming into the bar. Oh yeah, now I was pissed! I didn't come all this way to deal with this shit! Oh Hell no!

"That's it! You got a problem Shithead!?" I shouted turning around and pushing her back. She fell backwards into the crowd of people and was unable to right herself due to her hooker heels. I could feel that similar tingling in my fingertips that I had done back in the barn that day, so I took a deep breath to calm myself. But doing this gave the crazy Goth time to get up and the next thing I knew I was being punched in the face.

"This. Is. Not. Happening!" I shouted in disbelief as I dodged another blow. She powered forward with her fist out and after I ducked it was her turn to fall into the bar. She turned round with murder in her eyes and grabbed a bottle from the bar. The beer poured out of it as she raised it up ready to hit me with it like a woman possessed! I decided I didn't want to get hit again so I side stepped as she swung it down aiming for my head. As I did this I brought my fist up into her stomach, hoping to get her hard enough to wind her.

Thankfully it worked. The bottle fell from her hand and smashed as she sacked it to the floor gasping for breath. I looked down at her panting, with my fists still tight and ready to go. When I knew she wasn't going to get back up for round two

I tried to calm my body down from the adrenaline rush. I looked up and noticed everyone had suddenly given me a wide berth. I took another deep breath for good measure and simply stepped over the girl I had knocked to the floor.

"Now, let's try this again. Where is Dominic Draven?" I asked the barmaid who looked terrified of me. Her eyes shot behind me and I knew what I would find there if I looked.

"Come with us." The stern voice said behind me and there was only one thing left to say,

"Ah shit...would you believe me if I told you this wasn't my fault?" I asked without looking at the security guards I knew were there.

"Now!" They snapped and I eyed the glass of clear liquid on the counter and thought, what the Hell, I am in enough trouble anyway. I grabbed the glass, held it up and said,

"Here's to Afterlife!" Then I shot it back in one, trying not to kill the cool and cough after swallowing what felt like battery acid! I let it fall into my other hand and before I knew what I was doing I dropped it back on the bar after doing a neat little trick with it...where did I learn that from?

I turned around to face my judgement and saw it wasn't the guys from outside like I thought it would have been but more like the giants from the stairs. These guys were scary but I put on a brave face, raised my head high and let them lead me out of the club.

"You know that's unnecessary, I'm going to leave without making a fuss, so if you wouldn't mind." I said nodding to the grip they both had on the top of my arms. They didn't answer me and I became even more confused when they started to walk me to the back of the club instead of the front.

"Where are we going...? Is there another exit back here?" I asked but again wasn't surprised when all I received was the silent treatment. What was surprising however was when they led me directly to the stairs and started marching me up them. Suddenly I wasn't so sure this was where I wanted to be and I wondered exactly how many mistakes I could make in only an hour.

"Look guys, let's talk about this!" I said losing my bravery with every step I took up the stairs. We were nearly at the top and I started to squirm around but it was no use. They held on tight enough that I was going nowhere. Well at least they weren't hurting me I thought finding it my only silver lining.

Once we reached the top there were two more mammoth guys standing guard and I had to wonder who was up here, the Sultan of Brunei! I scanned the room finding a small bar to one side and tables full of characters of the likes I had never seen before. My dread doubled as all eyes watched me in shock, probably wondering what on earth I was doing being dragged up here.

They continued to storm me to the centre and I looked behind me and over the edge of the balcony longingly at all the free people below. In front of me I could make out a large table that was slightly raised than all the rest with people all sat around. There was a bigger seat in the middle and it didn't take a genius to guess that whoever was sat in it was who I would have to deal with. I couldn't make out the details yet as my eyes quickly found a sight that had my bravery quivering in its boots before it hitch hiked right outta here!

"Whoa." I said as the guys let me go right in front of the real giant! Jesus this guy made the other two look normal sized. I stumbled a step in front of the Goliath who had his tree trunk arms folded and I giggled in a nervous habit as I looked up and up and up some more before finally reaching his head.

"Okay, come on home bravery." I muttered to myself and righted my jacket, taking my hood down. As soon as I did this a whispered wave shuddered through the upstairs area.

"Little Apple?" I thought I heard the big guy in front of me whisper but ignored it and I decided to get out what I wanted to say first before I was in even more shit than I was right now.

"Okay, so what happened down there…I can explain…" I started to say when I heard a deep delicious voice speak,

"Ragnar." It was a warning so he stepped aside and I was hit with another memory I couldn't touch. I mentally shook the feeling aside, readying myself for what was to come. I took in all the people sat around a huge table all staring at me like I was some kind of freak…that or some holy messiah!

"I think I should say now, that girl was crazy and tried to smash a bottle over my head…so you see…" I stopped when the man in the middle seat leant forward so his features came into view and my heart stopped.

"It…it can't be…" I stuttered my disbelief at the sight of him. What the Hell was going on…was I dreaming this as well! I kept taking steps backwards but I had no clue where I expected I would get to.

"Hello, Keira" His gorgeous voice spoke someone else's name which was like a bullet to my heart.

Because of the pain the only thing I could think to say slipped from my lips before I hit my limit for the second time today…

"Hello, My Demon."

Then I fainted.

CHAPTER 19
'I DO' NOT WANT TO
BELIEVE

Waking up this time I wasn't sure where I was expecting to find myself but I would say the very last place in my mind was where I ended up. Opening my eyes to a very familiar sight was both shocking and exhilarating. Of course my first thought had instantly been, 'am I dreaming' again but then as soon as I lifted my head and felt the pain, I knew this wasn't a dream.

No, this time it was real. But most importantly of all, now I knew that *he* was real. I didn't know what to do next as I think I was in a state of shock. As I lay there too afraid to move just yet I started to notice the small differences to the bedroom I always saw when looking through that barrier of glass.

For one there wasn't a mirror above the bed as I had often seen. The second was that there were quite a few picture frames around the room that strangely had all been turned down. This intrigued me the most and just as I reached out to grab the one closest to me on the side table, I heard voices.

I didn't know what to do. Should I hide, should I pretend to be asleep, should I run or find a weapon? In the end I completely panicked. And because of this I ended up rolling backwards off the side of the bed furthest from the door and getting tangled up in the covers as I went. I landed on the floor with an undignified 'Umpf!'

"She's as graceful as ever I see." I heard a woman's voice say in amusement that lacked any malice. I popped my head over the bed considering there was very little point to me hiding…if you could even call it that. There I found myself staring at two of the most beautiful people I had ever seen and one of them I had been dreaming about for what seemed like forever.

The small beauty queen next to him was so utterly striking you couldn't help but be drawn to her. She had doll like features with silky dark curls and flawless skin, I almost wanted to go up to her and poke her just to check that she was real.

And then there was *him*…

My Demon.

This thought brought me back to the idiotic thing I had said to him before my re-enactment of the perfect wimpy freak out. I noticed the girl was smirking at me and for some reason looked as pleased as Punch. So I decided this was the point I really needed to stop staring at them and say something.

"I uh…panicked." As soon as I said it I had to squash down the urge to smack myself on the side of the head…and for some reason this thought didn't seem like a foreign one to me.

"So I see." He said and I then found myself having to now squash down the urge to sigh at just the sound of his voice. He was breathtakingly handsome, even more so in real life. And I don't think I had ever seen anyone who looked as if they held so much authority it just oozed from them like a dark aura.

I could feel myself biting my lip as my eyes drank in the sight of long legs encased in suit trousers of a colour very similar to my own eyes. The white shirt he wore matched the dark blue/grey colour but was worn as if ready for action, with his sleeves rolled half way up his forearms and the first two buttons undone with no tie in sight. Even the belt he wore looked expensive, like the black leather men's dress shoes on his feet. But this handsome attire would mean nothing if it wasn't for the man wearing it. And boy, what a man!

Black raven hair was pushed back in one of those smart casual ways that seemed effortless to achieve. This matched the rough stubble a few days without shaving produced and it gave him a raw beauty against his flawless olive skin. However, the real striking feature he held above all others was his incredibly powerful eyes. They were like pools of heated dark emotion that looked to be barely kept in check. They made me want to cower in both fear and quake in desire all at the same time.

I realised I had once again just been staring at him when the girl cleared her throat, thankfully letting me know that I was still slumped in this ridiculous position and of course looking like a love sick teenager.

"Oh…uh yeah…*Jesus Katie, get a grip girl.*" I whispered, chastising myself for my embarrassing behaviour and I could have sworn I heard the girl giggle but then quickly try and hide it with a cough. Happily, I hadn't lost all my functions and made quick work getting untangled from the web of luxury fabric I was wrapped in. I almost felt like jumping up and saying 'Tada' but thankfully found the power to squash down yet another ridiculous urge. However, my next foolish act came from stepping out of the mound on the floor and catching my foot, stumbling forward.

"Whoa, it's okay, I'm okay." I said as I righted myself just in time. Mr tall, dark and sex on a stick looked like he was about to lunge forward to catch me but luckily didn't have to. I saw him release a sigh as if he didn't know what to make of my clumsiness. Well given the ballerina next to him, I doubted he was used to it, I thought with a bitter edge. And this was when a heart breaking thought entered my mind…

Were they a couple?

This was when the girl burst out laughing and then said,

"Oh shit no...! Don't worry, I'm just the big guy's sister." She waved her thumb to her side at him and on hearing this I felt as though I could breathe again. But wait, had I said the question out loud? Oh God I hoped not…but how else had she…?

I never got to finish that thought as I felt eyes were burning into me. He was staring straight at me with an intensity of the likes I had never known and I felt trapped. That was until he demanded something of me, something that I just didn't want to give,

"Leave us." His stern voice cut through me like a blade and I swallowed hard before lowering my head in what oddly felt like defeat.

"Oh…right, of course." I said and walked past him towards the door, muttering to myself,

"I will just find my own way…Ahh!" I soon found myself shouting out as solid arms circled me from behind, stopping me from going any further. As soon as I felt the first touch from him I knew I was lost and all my fears of his ability of mind control came flooding back if only to be ignored swiftly after.

"Oh no, you're not going anywhere, Sweetheart." He said in my ear making me shiver against him and suddenly feeling trapped by him felt like the best thing in the world.

"Leave us, Sophia." He commanded and now I knew that he had meant for his sister to leave us alone. All the while his hands never left me and I could feel his breath against my neck. Once more he had me swallowing hard and I had to concentrate on keeping my legs from collapsing at just the simple fact of having my dream man at my back.

"I think that would be best." His sister said smirking and with just that one look of approval, I liked her already. I barely heard the door close when I felt his hand snake up my side and come to rest at my neck. Quickly I was transported to one of my dreams of him in this exact same position and I couldn't help but feel like it had been some sort of premonition of fate. It was the one where he was trying to get me to come home and I had to admit that now I was here part of me couldn't help but feel that way. But it was also as though something was holding me back and tied to another place and I found myself once more battling with myself on what felt right and wrong. Almost as if somewhere along the line my life was being...

Re-written.

But no matter what I was feeling it didn't detract from what was happening now. Because no doubt about it, this was a very trustworthy position I was allowing him to have with me considering his hand was firmly around my neck and I had to wonder if it wasn't a test. I didn't know what to say or do, but when he bent his head and inhaled deeply, I sighed back against him from the sweet gesture. This too reminded me of the dream as I had done the same thing in sinking back into his hold. But unfortunately, as I had learned so often in this life, nothing this sweet lasted forever, because then he quickly ruined it.

"My Keira's finally home." At the sound of her name I wanted to crumble to the floor in heartbreak. He still thought I was this other girl and it wasn't *me* he wanted in his arms...*it was her.*

I jerked free from his hold and put the much needed space between us. I heard his primal growl coming behind me and jumped at the sound turning round to face him in case he pounced. This was the reminder I needed. After all he was the Demon I had also seen in my dreams and…

My Demon was back.

"Come here." I could tell that demand came from forced control and even though I was terrified I stood my ground. So okay merely shaking my head like a defiant child wasn't going to win any bravery awards any time soon. I knew that but it wasn't just about being stubborn, it was more importantly about being hurt.

"Now is not a time to test me Keira, not after all this time apart." He grated out warning me how much my behaviour was costing him. But hearing her name again was when I snapped.

"MY NAME IS KATIE!" I shouted back at him holding myself tense in my anger. I could even feel my nails digging into my palms from tight fists I held at my sides. His eyes widened in surprise for a moment before he closed them in what seemed like pain. He took a shuddering deep breath and swallowed hard as if needing to take this moment to comprehend what I was telling him. Finally, he opened his eyes to look at me and the breath I was holding was freed from my chest. Jesus, he looked like he was in agony and I had caused it all. In fact, he looked as if I had just destroyed his entire world, crushing everything he had ever known under my foot.

"I…" I had to clear my throat before continuing as the emotions he drew out of me were almost choking.

"I'm sorry…I…I shouldn't have…" He raised a hand to stop me from saying anymore and I bit my lip to physically prevent myself from doing so. I saw him take a deep breath and I braced myself for what he obviously wanted to say next.

"Only my Keira would have come home." He said and again it sounded like each word had been dragged from deep within him, it had been that hard to say. I slowly shook my head wishing I could have given him what he wanted right at that moment but the truth of it was as simple as I couldn't, for it would have been a lie.

I would have been a lie.

"All I can say is that I am sorry I'm not the girl you wished would turn up here." I replied softly knowing I had no power to offer him anything more.

"That's where you're wrong." He informed me sternly and I raised my eyes to find he was serious as my heart skipped a beat.

"But you just…"

"You're her, you just don't realise it yet…*but you will.*" He said interrupting me and this last part sounded like a threat. And given the intensity of the look he was giving me I would say it looked like one as well. I imagined right now would have made a comedy moment as I gulped down a frightened lump but given the severity of the conversation I could only take a step back in fear and laughter was the last thing on my mind.

He raised an eyebrow at my actions and then did something I didn't expect when he started smirking.

"You know this reminds me of when we first met." I frowned in confusion having no clue as to what was coming next.

"You were just as you are now."

"How so?" I asked letting curiosity replace the confusion.

"Skittish and afraid of me, yet you were also intrigued which is why you didn't run."

"I'm not afraid." I said frowning at him and his smile told me he easily detected my lie.

"No?" He said stepping forward and my natural instinct kicked in making me take a step back. I was angry at myself for letting him prove my lie by reacting the way he knew I would.

"There's no need for you to fear me."

"No?" I asked throwing his question back at him and crossing my arms across my chest to show my disbelief.

"Not ever." The way he said this gave me little doubt to the depth of his sincerity but I found myself asking what I knew I had no choice but to ask,

"Alright, so you say that you know me...yes?" This question made him smile and the sight was nothing short of glorious to witness. Bloody hell but if I thought him handsome before then when he smiled it was something else!

"Yes little Dove, I know you." Hearing the sweet endearment was almost as sweet as feeling his gentle touch.

"And you know me well?" I asked continuing down along this line of questioning.

"Intimately." He whispered stepping forward and I shuddered. A series of memories flooded my mind of him taking my other self over and over again.

"Then tell me...have you ever hurt me before?" He looked affronted by the idea but then something flickered in his eyes before he answered,

"Never. I have never physically hurt you." I knew his answer wasn't a lie but he was a fool if he thought I hadn't picked up on what that flicker in his eyes had meant.

"But you have lied." I said seeing the truth in his face. He sighed and rubbed his jaw with a hand before speaking,

"Keira I..."

"Katie." I corrected him and there was that quick, brief flash of pain again that caused me the same pain to witness.

"I cannot tell you that I haven't lied to you as that in itself would be a lie...but, I can honestly say that I have only ever done so to keep you safe and for your own wellbeing." He told me and I couldn't help the sting delivered when he wouldn't repeat my actual name.

"So are you telling me that when you lied to me it didn't

hurt?" Now this question really affected him and after a desolate moment of staring at me in regret he turned away in anger. It didn't matter, in that look alone I had my answer.

"I see little on why this matters to you if you don't even remember the past we shared!" He snapped. I decided to enlighten him on exactly why it did matter, very much so in fact.

"Because if you lied to me as this Keira you believe me to be, then what's stopping you from lying to me now?"

"You think I would lie to you about something as important as this?!" He said whipping back round to face me and I could see that my questions were testing his obvious temper.

"That depends…"

"On what?!" His frustrated question made me rethink for a moment on whether I really wanted to go down this sensitive road.

"On what you lied to me about before." I finally answered him knowing that if he ever wanted me to trust in what he was telling me then I needed some foundations on which to stand. After all, I didn't know him and just because he said otherwise it didn't mean I could believe him. But one look at him now told me that I couldn't. Because he hadn't just lied to protect me as he said, he had lied enough to hurt me and there was a big difference in my world.

"Like I said, that was in the past and for what I believed at the time was for the right reasons." His excuse didn't work for me so I pushed for more,

"What did you lie about?"

"Enough! It is in the past and where it shall remain!" He shouted getting even angrier but I knew it wasn't with me, it was with himself.

"Then you give me no reason to trust you." I informed him sadly and he looked mortally wounded from it.

"Very well." He said after releasing a sigh in frustration.

"You have to see this from my side. I have been lied to all my life, by everyone I thought I knew and the only one left I trust…well I am afraid to say isn't in this room with me." I hated saying this and the anger he once had for himself was now directed at someone else and thankfully they also weren't in this room.

"I will make them pay…I promise you that when I find them I will make them pay for everything they have done to us, everything they have taken, I will get it back… if it's the last thing I ever do Keira, I will get it back…*I promise you.*" His stern promise almost broke my heart as hearing that name once more did. His belief that I was her was crushing my strength, one that I needed to keep hold onto my own beliefs.

"So you need to trust in what I am telling you when I say you are not Katie!" He said cutting the distance between us and I backed up to the wall behind me but it was no use. He stood before me, locking me there before taking my face in his hands and placing his forehead to mine.

"You are Keira…. *my Keira.*" He said pleading with me like a desperate man and again my heart broke but this time it wasn't because of a name… it was for him. I closed my eyes and shook my head softly but he held me still.

"No, no…Ssshh now, don't…don't say anything, we will figure this out." He told me and it sounded like his voice was close to breaking.

"I'm sorry but I can't do this if you think I am her…I'm not her." I whispered back feeling my tears finally fall at the same time his hands did. I sucked in a sharp breath as my emotions got too much and I started to cry. He took a step back and his face told me it was more than just a rejection of the truth he believed in, it was a rejection of the love he trusted in. That's

when I saw his own tears fall and in that moment I had never hated myself more.

For long moments we just looked at each other, witnessing the misery we both created in what we each believed. I knew I couldn't break away from him so was glad when he turned from me first. I wiped away my tears while I had the chance but then I jumped when he snapped back at me,

"Why?!"

"Why?" I asked wincing at his hurt, angry tone,

"Yes, why? Why do you refuse to believe what I suspect you already know to be the truth?!" Oh yes, he was angry and it only acted to fuel my own anger when I shouted,

"Because I am afraid!"

"What are you afraid of…tell me?" I knew this was it. My time had come to admit my biggest fears,

"I am afraid that if I'm not Katie then who am I, because all I am then left with is a name I don't know. I am left with no past that I recognise and if that is the case then what is to be of my future? What would be left for me to live for if the one person I have loved in the world isn't real? I would be completely alone in a world I didn't know. In a world that would never be mine." I shook my head feeling my tears drip from my chin, hitting the slate floor beneath my bare feet. I turned away from him to hide my shame, to hide the depth of my fears like I always tried to do at the Colony.

I hated this. I hated not knowing as much as I feared discovery. I hated feeling weak and vulnerable and I was tired of it all. The pain, the suffering, the fear and the longing. I hated it! But now most of all I hated the self-loathing I felt every time I thought back to leaving Ari. I was tired of feeling weak and helpless and most of all feeling scared but deep down I simply couldn't help it. I was all of those things. So all that was left was to apologise for it all when he said,

"Please, you have to trust me."

"I'm sorry, but how can I trust someone I don't even know when they tell me that I am someone else?"

"Because..." He took a breath and then said something that would blow apart both the world I knew and the world I didn't...

"You're my wife."

CHAPTER 20

HERE WE GO AGAIN

"Seriously Dom, I thought the plan was not to scare her!"

"Not now Sophia." The sound of a man's voice filled the dark void and it was one I vaguely recognised but couldn't remember exactly where from.

"No I think now is the perfect time considering she keeps passing out on us! Did you not listen to anything he told us?" The girl's voice I recognised and I now had a name to go with it. It was strange but I couldn't have chosen a better name for her. It was as if every Sophia I had ever known had been a lovely and warm natured person and this was the reason it fit so well. Of course the only problem with this logic was that I didn't know any other Sophia.

"I suggest you heed our brother's warning sister, as I am close to the edge as it is." Now this was a male voice I recognised and I felt myself shift uncomfortably knowing *he* was close. I felt a reassuring squeeze at my side and a cooing 'Ssshh' before his sister, Sophia snapped back,

"Then maybe you should have thought twice about bombarding the poor girl with a past she can't remember and a name she doesn't know!" I then heard the quick tapping of heels against stone and then a loud slam of a heavy door.

"I know she isn't helping but she's just upset." The other male voice said softly and his first reply was a gruff grunt before the words,

"Aren't we all?"

"I will go and talk to her." The man said and this time when he left he closed the door with a little less emotion.

"You can open your eyes now Sweetheart, it is just you and I." I did as I was told, surprised to find him looking down at me at a sideways angle. I frowned for a moment as I waited for my mind to kick back into gear and when it did I realised I was lay with my head in his lap.

Knowing that my head was close to that part of his anatomy I tried to think of anything else than just that. Of course when that failed I decided the only way forward was to get up and try and regain some dignity. Because from that knowing grin I was now getting, I was pretty sure he knew where my thoughts had been.

"Easy now. You must have received quite a knock to the head in that accident." He said helping me up until I was sitting upright next to him on a big luxurious sofa."

"You know about that?" Something passed in his eyes before he gritted out,

"Yes."

"How, was it on the news or the police…? Oh God the police haven't come looking for me have they, because you know it was none of my fault, these guys…?"

"Calm yourself. Nobody is going to come here and take you from me…*ever again.*" He swore this last part under his breath to himself and I inwardly shivered at the stern promise he obviously just made with himself.

"So I guess I did another fainting act then uh?" His answer

came in the form of a smile and him running the back of two fingers down my cheek. When his actions made me bite my lip his smile got bigger and I saw the quickest flash of purple in his eyes.

"Hey, your eyes must have a hint of purple in them." I couldn't help say after what I just saw there.

"It happens a lot where you are concerned." I frowned not really understanding what he meant by that but I decided to move on before he confused me even more.

"I wonder why I keep fainting. Honestly I am not normally like that." I said thinking it best if I didn't mention the times that I was half starved at the Colony.

"You needn't worry, the reasons I suspect are nothing harmful, merely side effects." The way he spoke was so precise and to the point it made me wonder what his background was. He seemed a lot older than he looked, in fact it was as if he had come from a completely different era all together.

"Side effects?" I asked getting back to more important questions than how old he was.

"I think it's best not to go down that difficult road again, at least for the time being. It's like my sister said, best not to bombard you with things you don't yet understand." The way he said this was as if I would break if he pushed too much and now I found I was no longer wishing to be kept in the dark. I wanted to know what they thought…or more to the point, what he thought. But I also knew I couldn't have it both ways and until I was willing to accept what they were all telling me was true, then there was little point me asking questions if I wasn't going to trust in the answers given.

"Alright. But I have to ask, where does that leave us?" He gave me a gentle smile and looked as though he wanted to say something other than what he did.

"I would like to ask you some questions if I may?" I was

unsure how this was going to go but by the soft way in which he asked me I knew I couldn't refuse.

"I can't see why not." I said and no doubt he could hear how sceptical I was.

"I promised I wouldn't make it difficult for you but I am curious as you can imagine." Yeah I bet he was I thought sarcastically considering he thought I was his long lost wife from another life. Oh God...wife! That little doozy of a factor had only just come back to me.

"Because you...you think I am your wife?" I struggled asking him this and for a minute thought I might chicken out.

"You are my wife and you always will be." He said without a hint of hesitation and because there was a side of me that longed for that type of love and devotion, it felt painfully beautiful when hearing it.

"You seem so sure." I commented shaking my head slightly at the thought.

"And you seem so sure that you're not. So let's just say we both must have our reasons in what we choose to believe." Well I had to give him that one.

"Okay, but just so you know, yours is a lot nicer belief than mine is." I don't know where that came from but as soon as I said it I felt my face start to get hot from blushing. However, the grin he gave me was more than worth the embarrassment my confession caused.

"You know not the joy hearing that brought me, so thank you...*Katie.*" Hearing him finally say my name for the first time brought me a type of joy that he would never know but at the same time, it did feel strange hearing it. I almost wanted to tell him that he could call me Keira if he really wanted to but I knew that would also have been strange. Either way, I knew from just one look what it had cost him in saying a name he didn't believe was mine, so I was touched at his kindness shown.

This suddenly reminded me that I still had no clue to what his name was! It felt like a sin not knowing but how could I ask him his name when he thought he was my husband?!

At first I thought I might have been talking aloud as he was frowning at me as if he heard every thought I just had.

"I would like to start with my questions now, if you don't mind?" He asked and I kind of wished that had been his only one. I wondered then if I told him no would that have been the end of it? One look told me I didn't think so, not with him looking so determined. In the end I just nodded for him to start.

"Last night you entered the club in search of someone…who was it you were looking for exactly?" He asked folding a leg over the other and picking a piece of lint from his trousers. The action shouldn't have made me nervous but combined with the question I felt more like I was being interrogated by a mob boss or something.

"Uhh…well, I was umm…looking for…" I was still stalling for time trying to decide very quickly whether or not I should tell him. I don't know why but for some reason this question felt like being led into a trap.

"Looking for?" He said prompting me further by rolling his hand.

"Dominic Draven." I said his name and again a deep purple flickered in his eyes. What the hell was that?!

"I see."

"You see?" I mimicked trying to decipher his code.

"And tell me, for I am curious, did you find him?" Again, why did I feel like a small animal being led into a lion's cage?

"No, I was about to ask after him before that girl launched herself at me…although I guess after that the owner of the club wouldn't have wanted to meet with me anyway." I could just see the small smirk appear before he hid the lower half of his face behind a hand he held across his lips as his elbow rested against the back of the seat.

"I didn't cause that fight you know." I said defending myself against what I believed he was smirking at.

"Oh I have no doubt." He said moving his hand back to emphasise his point. I frowned at him when I suddenly realised something,

"You're teasing me!" At this he laughed and if I thought his smile was a beautiful sight, then his laughter was the beautiful sound to match.

"I wouldn't dare, not after seeing you throw a gut punch."

"You saw it?!" I shouted in mortified shock.

"You can see a lot from up in the VIP area." He said, informing me of this fact about twelve hours too late.

"The VIP, is that what it was called?"

"Yes Sweetheart, it is." I couldn't help but bite my lip when hearing him call me this again and I was quickly becoming addicted to the tingles his presence constantly gave me.

"Well in that case we both know what happened next." I said rolling my eyes and he laughed again causing the tingles to intensify.

"Yes… you found me." He said as this had somehow been his intention all along.

"Wait a minute, how did you know about the accident?" I asked going back to one of my original questions.

"Let's just call it convenient connections and leave it at that."

"Oh no, I don't think so!" I said forgetting myself for a moment and he raised an eyebrow as if questioning my bravery.

"I mean…uh…well, that's not very fair." Okay, so saying this did make me sound like a whiny teenager but thankfully he quickly looked amused by my outburst.

"No? How so?" He asked and when I frowned his laughter told me he was teasing me again.

"You do like teasing me don't you."

"Don't worry, there used to be a time where you teased me equally so." He told me and I didn't know what to say to that at first but when his smile faded as an obvious memory seeped in I knew I had to make light of it somehow.

"Then I will just have to find a way to put up with you again." I said nudging him and I don't know who was more surprised by my flirting, me or him. I blushed again and lowered my head to hide my pink cheeks from view. I was startled when I felt his fingers under my chin and I had no choice to lift my head when he applied pressure.

"You are free to tease me whenever you want little one." I started to slip into the annoying urge of biting my lip again when his thumb pressed against them, preventing me from doing so. Then he leaned in close and I quickly held my breath, thinking that he was going to kiss me. He was…he must be…is he, was he? I asked myself with every inch he eliminated between us with the closer he got. Then he stopped and just before I was stupid enough to close my eyes and wait for something that might never come, he spoke…

"I once told you a long time ago about that lip of yours and what a shame it would be if there was nothing left for me to kiss." He uttered the words in such a way it almost felt like that kiss I craved and I think using that voice I would have done anything he commanded.

"Don't make promises you wouldn't be able to keep." He said cryptically as that sentence would have only made sense if he could read my thoughts. That in itself was a horrifying thought considering all I wanted to do was throw myself at him and beg him to make me a woman, ripping away the last shreds of innocence my virginity held on to.

I don't know why but directly after having these carnal thoughts he was gone. He had moved away from me so fast you would have thought someone had held a gun to his head. He had his back to me and even through his shirt I could see all his muscles tensed as if something internal was causing him great pain.

"Are you alright?" I asked him, suddenly worried I had said something to offend him.

"I am fine." He grated it out in such a way even the dumbest of people would have known he was lying.

"Did I...?" I didn't get to finish.

"It isn't you, but please, just excuse me a moment." And after this he quickly left through the other door which I was currently facing.

"Something I said?" I asked myself out loud, knowing that I must have had something to do with it. I thought back to my behaviour and instantly started chastising myself. The way I flirted with him was shocking but on the other hand, it simply felt so natural, almost as if I didn't know any other way to be around him. He hadn't seemed offended at first and even looked like he was enjoying our banter but then what had that all been about at the end?

What was I doing?! I needed to get a grip, I didn't even know him and what I did know was pure fantasy. What would he think I wondered if he knew that for the last eight months I had been dreaming of him almost every night and in these dreams he had been so many things...Lover, punisher, Demon and Captor and at the centre of all those things was the exact image of myself trapped there by his hand.

What did any of that really say about me? After all, he had done nothing to hurt me and had taken me into his home. So alright, he did all of these things thinking that I was his long lost wife but still, I was more than thankful for his kindness.

I thought back to when he asked me who I had been searching for and he didn't seem surprised when I gave him Mr Draven's name. I took this as a good sign that he knew him and might be able to find him for me. Because as much as being in his presence was like finally living my dreams, I had to remember why I was here. My first priority was saving Ari and nothing could get in my way of that, not even my dream man. But what if when everything was over…no, I couldn't think that way! Those were dangerous enough thoughts to even dream of but to actually make them a reality, well in truth I would be falling for a man who was already in love with someone else… it just so happened that she looked like me.

No, I was making the decision now to back off and keep my dream man at arm's length, which reminded me, I still didn't know his name. As I thought on this, two things happened simultaneously and that was one my stomach growled and two my bladder screamed out at me to be emptied. I stood up feeling the slight twinge from the cuts on my leg and decided to take a look once I found the bathroom.

"It must be here somewhere?" I said as I scanned the room. Actually to call it a room was a bit of a joke considering it was more like a suite. It had its obvious sleeping area in the biggest bed I had ever seen and I knew now from experience that it was the comfiest bed I had ever been in.

Then there were the glass doors that led onto a massive balcony at least that was if my dream had been correct. I couldn't see why not considering everything I had seen so far had been pretty spot on. I ran my eyes along the same wall as the glass doors and found a huge, solid wooden desk pushed up against the wall that looked to be a carved antique.

Then there was the area I was sat in that seemed to be a sitting area full of comfy plush chairs and sofas. Small highly polished wooden tables were dotted here and there, holding candles and some with beautiful tiffany lamps. There was also a carved grandfather clock with what could have been a battle scene up the sides. Tapestries and paintings broke up the bare stone walls and it was behind one of the biggest ones in the corner that I seemed to be drawn. I knew surely in a room such as this one there must have been an en-suite bathroom somewhere and unless my mystery man found solace by taking a leak, I knew it wasn't through the door he had just used. That only left one option.

The tall tapestry was embroidered on the front with a magnificent goddess that looked to be half turned to stone. I don't know why but it felt like I had studied this once before in my life and with frustration I whipped it back, sick of continuously feeling as though I was living a double life.

I knew on so many levels it made sense what people were trying to tell me but it was also like my brain just wouldn't let me find the answers or even admit them when presented with what people believed was the truth. It was almost like my brain had been programmed to deny everything and it continued to do so even if I didn't like it.

I shook my head at myself, ridding these disturbing thoughts from my mind and looked up, unsurprisingly to find a door. I hung the tapestry over the wrought iron holder that I found sticking out from the stone so that I wouldn't be walking back into it when coming out of the bathroom.

I couldn't help but look over my shoulder before stepping cautiously inside as if I was doing something wrong. But hey, when a girl needed to go then a girl needed to go! By the time I got inside I was close to walking with my legs closed to stop any pee coming out so I didn't take anything in around the room until I was in a safe position. So it was only when I was sat down did I realise I was in the most luxurious bathroom I had ever seen.

"Crikey, what does this guy do for a living?!" I asked myself looking around and finding something that could have been a bath or a small swimming pool!

I finished doing what I needed to do and before I pulled up my trousers I checked my bandage was still in place. It really needed replacing so I decided when the guy came back to ask him if he had a first aid kit as it could do with a good clean before it got infected. I gingerly pulled my trousers back over the damaged area and zipped up before checking out my face in the mirror.

Unfortunately, the reflection didn't match the beautiful gilded frame the glass sat in. I winced at the mess of my hair and tried the best I could to contain the knots, folding them into another plait. Then I washed my face and was surprised to see there were no bruises around my eye or forehead from where I had hit my head on the side window of the bus. I also washed my hands and remembered the cut I had there from the glass I used as a weapon but where was it now?

It made me wonder how long I had been asleep because no one could heal like that overnight! I left the bathroom wondering what the hell was going on and because I wasn't concentrating on where I was going I walked straight into one of the side tables.

"Arghh! Oww, oww, oww!" I said holding on to the top of my leg where the table had hit my bandaged area.

"Are you alright?" I jumped at the sound of his voice coming back into the room and finding me on one leg hopping around with the table on its side and smashed glass all around me from the now broken lamp. After seeing all the damage, I had caused I looked back up at him in horror.

"Oh shit! I am so, so sorry, I will pay for it…*somehow.*" I muttered knowing I would probably have to work for half a year to pay for it. I bent down and started picking up the pieces of broken glass when I felt his hands come to mind. I yelped in shock, as once again he had shifted across the room insanely fast.

"Don't... you might hurt yourself on the glass." He removed the coloured glass I held and dropped it back to the floor. I was about to take a step back when suddenly I was up in his arms like some damsel in distress. The way he held me was as though I weighed nothing at all and I was quickly reminded of the extreme differences between Dex and this man. When Dex had carried me you could see it hadn't looked like an easy feat but when my dream man did it the only word to describe it was...*effortless.*

"Whoa! What are you doing?" I asked as he crunched the rest of the glass under his heavy foot, as he carried me round the other side and set me down gently on the sofa like I was something utterly precious to him. Then before moving back he leaned further into me and spoke,

"I care little for the lamp... I do however care about your bare feet getting glass in them." He said and I couldn't help but sigh, taking in his scent, something that only made me want to sigh again. He smelt like...well like I imagined a real man should. He lingered a moment too long which told me he didn't want to move away when he did. I lowered my head and allowed myself a small smile at the thought of him needing to be close to me.

"Have you cut yourself?" His question caught me off guard and I looked at my feet to see I was fine.

"No, why?" I looked up at him to see he was frowning down at me and it was a sight I was quickly becoming used to...but that was a strange thought, had I really seen him frown at me that often?

"I smell blood on you."

"Uhh...okay." I said finding that an odd talent indeed.

"Well I'm fi…"

"Your leg." He said interrupting me nodding down at where I had hit it and I saw that he was right, there was a wet patch which was most likely blood.

"Oh that."

"Yes, *that.*" He said folding his arms as if I had done something wrong.

"It's nothing really, but I was going to ask you if you had first aid kit or something I could use?" This was when he sat down beside me and pinched the bridge of his nose between his thumb and forefinger.

"Do you have a headache or something?" I asked leaning forward to look at him.

"I'm getting there." He replied dryly and then before I could comment on his sarcasm he asked,

"I gather my table didn't do all that damage?" This time I let him see my small smile and then shook my head.

"No, your table didn't attack me. I got this from the…"

"Accident, yes I thought so. I must have missed it." He said to himself cryptically, looking down at my leg but then it clicked, so I asked,

"Oh, did you give me first aid when I was passed out?" He raised an eyebrow up at me and said,

"You could call it that."

"Would you call it that?" I asked back folding my arms at the way he kept avoiding my questions by giving me half answers.

"I would call it healing you. Now take off your trousers." At this I jolted back and coughed out an,

"Excuse me?!"

"You heard me little dove." Okay so the endearment did make me melt a little but not enough to strip off in front of him. For a start I hadn't had chance to change my underwear since setting off on this trip! Which reminded me, I really needed to ask him where my bag had gone and if I could use his awesome shower.

"All in good time pet, now take them off."

"Seriously am I saying these things out loud without knowing?" I asked the room.

"Yes, now do as you're told."

"Excuse me! I am not a child and will not... Ahhh!" I screamed when he muttered,

"Very well' before grabbing my trouser's leg and tearing it right down the centre to the very top of my thigh.

"What are you...?"

"This is a mess...your handy work I take it." He sounded pissed off but then again so did I.

"Look, Mr Grabby, you can't just..."

"Did you seriously just call me 'Mr Grabby'?" He asked looking up from my leg and interrupting me yet again.

"Well if the shoes fits." I snapped back and tried to pull my leg back. He grabbed out at me and pulled it back, straightening it and then holding it down.

"Hold still." He demanded and this time I did as I was told thanks to his stern voice, one I knew not to mess with. He started to unwrap my makeshift bandage and I saw him frown when part of the material was stuck to the cut thanks to dried blood. I knew this had happened when checking it out back in the bathroom but I would have thought the new blood dripping from it would have helped when trying to peal it off. Obviously no such luck, I thought bitterly.

"I need to clean the wound. I will be back with a first aid kit." He got up off the sofa and told me not to move. I thought this might be a perfect opportunity to ask him to tell Mr Draven I was here, in case he bumped into him.

"Uh...Can I just ask...?"

"Go ahead and ask Katie." He said and the sound of my name coming from his lips once again did strange things to my girly bits.

"I was just wondering if you happen to see this Mr Draven, will you tell him I'm here?" I asked in a hopeful tone.

"He already knows." He answered with a slight grin, surprising me.

"He does? But how? Did you already speak to him?" His answer surprised me even further,

"No but you did."

"I did? I'm sorry I don't remember, who was he?" Was I that out of it when I first arrived? I think I would surely have remembered something like that!

And then before he left he ended up giving me the most shocking answer so far…

"He's your husband."

CHAPTER 21
HIDDEN BEAUTY, EXPOSED FEARS

"Holy shit!" I said letting my head fall back onto the sofa and looking up at the ceiling thinking how the hell had I missed that! Once again I was left feeling dumbfounded but at least I could say I hadn't fainted like I had last time. But seriously, how did I miss it as now he had said it everything seemed so obvious. I even now recalled his sister calling him Dom when I was coming round earlier,

"Duh Katie, Dom is short for Dominic." I said this time freely smacking my forehead with how idiotic I felt. And why didn't he tell me when I had been asking about him? I would have thought that would have been the perfect opportunity to introduce himself as the man I had been looking for.

It was only when I heard the man himself clear his throat that I knew he had been witnessing this little meltdown of mine. I whipped my head back down to see him stood casually, leaning against the door frame with his legs crossed at the ankle.

"You could have told me." I accused making him merely shrug his shoulders before saying,

"I could have."

"But?" I snapped crossing my arms and giving him a glare.

"But, I first wanted to know where I stood."

"I don't understand." I told him and watched as he pushed himself from the frame and came over to sit next to me. I hadn't realised until now he carried with him a green box with First Aid written in white lettering across it.

"I wanted to know if you knew who I was and if it was actually me you were looking for." He stated and I instantly felt guilty that the answer to both of those questions was a no...and worse yet, was that he knew it.

"Ah."

"Yes, Ah indeed." He repeated making my guilt double. He didn't look pleased at all so I let him focus on sorting out my leg thinking this would give me some time to think of how to explain. What exactly I was supposed to explain I didn't yet know considering the only way I had recognised him was that I had been dreaming of him for the last eight months...now how the hell I was going to tell him that without sounding bat shit crazy, I had no clue!

"So if you don't remember me from our past together then pray tell, how did you recognise me?" He asked this like he knew I was struggling with trying to find a viable reason to give him. Damn him but pretty soon I was going to believe he had the power to read minds after all. He looked up at me, giving me a bad boy grin and a wink before continuing with his medical work.

"You look as though you know what you're doing." I said trying to bypass the question. One raised eyebrow and an order of,

"Answer the question, Katie," and I had no choice but to come clean.

"I see you in my dreams, okay?" I snapped and then jumped when he opened a packet. He looked at me and said,

"See, that wasn't so hard was it. Hold very still…okay?" He said gently and something inside me was quickly getting lost. It felt like I had a line to say in this drama we were acting out so I went with it and asked,

"Will this hurt?"

"Do you really want to know that?" He asked me back and then he too seemed to realise what I was doing and he had automatically done the same by saying the next line.

"What did you say?" I whispered stunned by the impact that sentence had on me. I had been hit by abnormal amounts of Déjà vu ever since leaving the Colony but this was something else.

"Easy now, just breathe." He said forgetting about my leg for the moment. He placed both hands on the side of my head and forced me to look at him. I could feel my eyes darting around as if searching for something more. I needed to grasp it back, I needed for him to say the next line.

"What's happening?" I asked him feeling as though I was going to lose consciousness any time soon.

"No, no! Katie, listen to me, you're having a flashback. Just stop reaching for it and come back to me. Listen to my voice Katie."

"That's not my name Draven." I felt my lips moving but had no control of the sound they made. I heard his sharp intake of breath before he uttered a different name,

"Keira?" And once more on hearing that name spoken something snapped! Like my reaching arms touched the flames and recoiled back from the pain of getting burned. But I could see her through the window now, no, not a window but a two-way mirror. Yes, I could see her there lay on the sofa I lay on now. She was bleeding from her side and I felt my hand go to the same place and when I looked down at my hand it was sticky and wet with my blood.

"Why is she bleeding?" I asked the void and heard his voice in the distance,

"Come back!" I winced at the sound of being told off for just looking at her. But then a figure turned around and was placing a glass to her lips for her to drink.

"It's you Draven. I can see you now." I told him and I heard the pain in his voice when he spoke,

"I was there with you as I am now but you have to let it go."

"I don't want to. I want to know who she is, Draven." I told him as a tear fell down in frustration.

"She's you sweetheart and she is perfect...*she always will be.*" Hearing him telling me this made me cry out a sob and that's when I started to turn away from the sight and run back into the darkness where I knew he waited for me. I ran and I ran until I couldn't breathe. Then I jumped when I knew the end was near and gasped rising up from where I landed.

"You're okay, I've got you...I've got you now." Draven's voice soothed me like I had never known before. His arms held me in an embrace and I had never felt so safe. His lips kissed my forehead and I had never felt so loved. It was in this moment that I knew he was my never-ending story and one day I would get it back. I would find my way home.

"Ssshh, easy now. That's it, just breathe... deep breaths with me, that's it." I finally calmed enough to pull back and look at him. He used both his thumbs to clear my cheeks from tears and I saw the same emotion staring back at me in his eyes.

"Now let's sort out this leg of yours." I nodded thankful he wasn't bringing up what had just happened. We were both quiet for a moment and I watched him work as if he had been a paramedic in a past life.

"You look like you have done this before."

"Easy now, best not to let your thoughts drift down that road again." I guessed he was right and besides, hearing his answer was confirmation he had definitely done this before and if my flashback was anything to go by, then it had been with me.

"Do you think these visions are tied to why I pass out?" He gave me a cautious look and I said,

"I think I'm good." And then I laughed trying to at least make light of the situation.

"Yes, I think that whenever you are faced with something your mind doesn't want to accept, it simply shuts down." I thought about that for a moment and well, it kind of made perfect sense.

"I didn't pass out when you finally told me who you are."

"You mean your husband?" He said and this time instead of teasing me he was *testing* me. I could see what it meant to him in his eyes and he could see what it meant to me by my blush.

"I think it means on some level you are starting to trust me." I didn't want to argue with him for reasons that were both to do with what it obviously meant to him and that I couldn't actually be sure he wasn't right. *I was starting to trust him.*

"Oww! Well that was until you did that!" I shouted as a stinging pain burned my flesh.

"Baby." He said, affectionately teasing me.

"I had to clean the wound and then use antiseptic to prevent any infection. Although I will have to keep my eye on it given the appalling job you did in bandaging it."

"What! I cleaned it!" I shouted defending myself.

"With what, *dirt?"* He asked scoffing at my survival skills.

"Well excuse me Bear Grylls, but I didn't exactly have time to build a camp, set up a triage tent and get into a nurse Betty outfit as I had more important things to think about, like the police finding me and charging me as the only survivor in a roadside massacre!"

"And there's my girl." He muttered sucking the wind from my sails purely because of how good him saying that sounded.

"I take it your wife has a sarcastic streak?" I asked as he continued to swipe a piece of soaked cotton across the surrounding area. God, but why did it feel so damn good having his hands on my bare skin.

"Just a tad, yes." He said winking at me and I had to clear my throat just to hide a moan. Seriously did everything this man did turn me on?!

"Did it not get annoying?" I asked honestly curious. He raised his eyes at my question and then took a moment as if giving it deeper thought before answering me.

"I think before I answer that question you must first understand that I am not a man to be challenged...*by anyone.*" He added this last part after snapping the box shut when he had finished the job. I was about to speak but he beat me to it.

"That was until I met *her.* She changed my life and every change she made was for the better. I found I liked to be challenged by her and even more so when learning quickly of her weaknesses." I frowned when he said this.

"You took advantage of her weaknesses?" I asked in a horrified tone, one that made him smirk.

"Most certainly, especially when I learned her main weakness was my lips upon her body and my hand firmly embedded in her hair so she was going nowhere...oh yes, I found this worked perfectly to my advantage considering I benefited from the act in all aspects." I swallowed down the hard wet lump that was clearly labelled...

LUST.

The picture he painted was one I just wanted to jump straight into and immerse myself into each stroke.

"You're...you're teasing me." I said stuttering as I tried to regain my composure.

"That depends."

"On what?" I definitely made the mistake of asking.

"On if you are up for the challenge?" Oh Holy Mother of God at the Disco! Why, oh why, did he have to paint that erotic picture in my mind.

"Don't look so worried Sweetheart, I can be gentle…there, all finished. Now time for a bath I think."

"Uh…sorry?" I muttered as if I had heard him wrong. Because in one minute he had me almost begging him to be whatever he wanted to be with me, gentle, rough, soft, hard, generous or just damn well take whatever he wanted! I didn't care, I only wanted the picture he painted but then he wanted to dump water all over that dream…literally!

I heard him chuckle after he got up and I wondered if my face had said as much because he seemed to be reacting to what I was thinking.

"All in good time sweetness, now time to get you clean little bird." He said coming back to me and taking both my hands to pull me up. I shrieked when he kept pulling my arms straight and then placed his shoulder into my belly to heave me up over his shoulder.

"What are you doing!?"

"There is still glass on the floor." He stated and as he walked around the sofa I looked down to where the smashed lamp should have been to see nothing there.

"But wait a minu…Umpf!" I was cut off when I got pulled upright and was now sliding down the length of him.

"I uh…" I didn't know what to say when he kept me to the height of his face, with his arm firmly wrapped around my waist.

"You are so beautiful." He told me softly and he pushed a stray bit of hair back behind my ear. I didn't know what to say but I know my mouth opened a little as if trying to find a way to thank him.

"No…nobody has ever told me that before." I admitted to

him shyly. My eyes were drawn to the corner of his mouth when he gave me a half grin. Then he tightened his hold and bent his head to whisper in my ear,

"Trust me beautiful, *they have.*" Then he let me slide the rest of the way down and I bit my lip all the way. He stepped away from me and held out an arm towards the bath that I was amazed to see was now full of steamy water.

"But I was just in here and…"

"Here, let me help you." As soon as his hands framed the bare skin at my belly I forgot any coherent thought.

"Uh…I don't…oh but I…" I tried to say, what I don't really know, but before I discovered what he pulled my t-shirt above my head, leaving me in just a borrowed bra that was clearly a size too small for me, if the bursting cleavage was to go by. Remembering this made me react and I hugged myself over my chest, hiding myself from view.

"Turn around." He ordered in that authoritative voice of his and suddenly Dominic Draven's teasing tone was long gone. My heart beat wildly in my chest and I could feel myself shaking from the inside out. I started to chant my doubt in my mind, saying over and over, I couldn't do this…I couldn't do this…I couldn't do…

"Ssshh, easy now. *You* need not do anything but let go." He said tilting my chin up so he could see the fear in my eyes.

"I will take care of you… *all you have to do is let me.*" And with those words said I knew what he was really asking of me.

To trust him.

For I knew this time *was a test.* So I took a shuddering breath and nodded, turning round, facing the mirror and putting my back to him as he wanted me. I shivered at his touch when his hand came to my neck to sweep my stray hair back to one side.

"Good girl." His whispered praise lingered on my skin like

his fingertips did even though he was no longer touching me on my exposed neck. No, instead he had moved both hands to my shoulders and started running them down along my arms that I still held crossed over myself. He continued down to my wrists, leaving trails of goosebumps where he made contact. I held my breath and soon became dizzy with the need for air.

"Breathe for me." He demanded softly, looking at me in the mirror, his intense gaze still burning into me. I did as I was told and inhaled at the same time he gripped my wrists in a tight hold. He tried to pull my arms outwards, which would mean exposing me to him from all sides thanks to seeing my shy reflection in the mirror. I fought him for a moment until he spoke again, this time with a hard edge that told me who was in charge in the room.

"Let go." I did instantly and let him move my arms until they came to rest at my sides.

"That's it, you're doing well." He cooed, stroking back my hair and again never taking his eyes from mine. Then I felt his hands at my hips and they followed the contours of my torso up and around to my back until they met in the middle of my shoulder blades.

I sucked in a quick breath when I realised he had unhooked my bra and the flimsy black lace started to slip from my breasts. The straps fell down my arms and the sensual act continued at such a slow pace, it was maddening. I could literally feel every nerve bursting with anticipation at being discovered by this man's hands.

I could barely believe I was here half naked in front of him, exposed for his pleasure to take and for the first time in real life, I actually felt like his willing captive. All of this and we hadn't even kissed yet.

I felt the last of the thin strips of satin leave my skin and land at my feet with a soft thud. He didn't say anything more or give me warning when he lowered himself on one knee. I wanted to move, I wanted to speak, to question what he was doing but I was too scared to move. Too scared that it would end. The greatest experience of my life... No, it was too precious for it to end now and never by my doing, I wouldn't allow it!

So when his fingers ran along the inside of my waistline I remained as still as I could, burying the urge to pull away from his touch thanks to troubled feelings of not being good enough. All the time he watched me as if reading every fear, every sensation and every need I had just from the reactions I was trying not to make.

But whatever I gave away he knew he had me under his spell with the way he held his fingers hooked, not only in the waistline of my trousers but also under the elastic of my underwear. So at the slightest caress to a place that was so close to where I felt myself needing it the most, it quickly became delicious torture and I wanted to scream and cry and moan all at the same time.

"Enough teasing now." He told me as I was on the cusp of begging and I almost praised the Gods for the end to my mental suffering. Putting me out of my beautiful misery wasn't how I thought it would be because he deliberately started to drag my trousers down my legs at a painfully slow rate.

Damn him but I closed my eyes as every move he made was done so with what seemed like the sole purpose to touch every inch of me and to torture me further whilst doing it. Even the trouser leg that was ripped up near to the waistline and had been flapping around was taken off as if it had been skin tight. In fact, it was becoming difficult to keep my legs strong and not crumble from the intensity of it all.

It was only when I opened my eyes once more that I realised he had taken everything from me and now I stood in front of him with nothing left to hide behind. He rose from one knee and his large frame loomed behind me, reminding me what he could now see.

I looked down feeling ashamed of what he saw and how disappointed he must be, for what did I have to offer this God of a man? I felt so exposed it was as if he could see more than bare skin over flesh and bone, but more like the flesh and bones of my soul.

He didn't like my shame. He didn't like my lack of self-confidence or insecurity. I knew this when I felt him raise my chin once more from behind me and issue me with my next order,

"Look at yourself. Look at what I see when I am gifted with your magnificence." I did as I was told having no other choice and for the first time saw myself as he did.

"Do you know how much I have missed gazing upon the beauty I own. I am a lucky man indeed, for with you back in my life, back in my arms again, I am both blessed and envied by the Gods themselves. Do you know that…? Tell me that you do… tell me now."

"I wish I could." I admitted in a small voice and instead of the stern, hard look of disappointment I was expecting I got something unexpected in his smile.

"Why are you smiling?" I asked softly being curious.

"Because I am happy to see my girl hasn't changed, even if her beauty warrants an ego. It still pleases me she hasn't found one in my absence, for if my words could never make you see what I see, then no other's should accomplish such a feat in my place. I would not have liked that…as such it remains my battle, one I will happily fight for you." This, along with everything else coming from his lips, was one of the most perfect things anyone had ever said to me. So it was no wonder when I blushed.

"Exquisite." He said before picking me up into his arms and carrying me over to his bath. Then before I felt the water caress my skin, he lifted me higher so he could kiss me. It was the lightest touch on my lips and just before I could do what I craved to do, which would have been to deepen the kiss, he lowered me into the water.

I couldn't take my eyes off him but in the end I had no choice as he silently broke my heart and walked away...

And left me.

CHAPTER 22
BAPTIZED

After he left the bathroom I was left feeling cold in this steamy water and I couldn't get warm no matter how much I wished for it. I pulled my legs up against my body and held them there as if this would shield me against the feelings that assaulted me. I was so confused why he would leave after something so intimate passed between us, something I was reminded that he instigated in the first place.

I was surprised at how hurt I felt and couldn't help but see it as how it looked…like a rejection. Was he playing some kind of game with me or was this all just another test of his, to see how long I could go without admitting something I was still unsure about. I knew he wanted the Keira he knew but I was far from it, even if he didn't think so.

Was it crazy to want him to want me as…well, *as me?* When he touched me, I needed it to be *me* he touched, not the thought of me as someone else. I wanted it so badly I almost tasted a bitterness on my tongue that wouldn't go away. And then inevitably the guilt would follow and I would be left feeling unworthy either way as I knew what *she* must have meant to him.

On one hand it was probably best he had left the room or these poisonous thoughts might have ruined my one chance at that perfect moment I would wish to carry with me forever. But then again thinking about how he made me feel with his arms around me… the way his eyes drank in my naked body with nothing but lust and desire reflected back in them, then how could I think such things in sight of it all.

"I can assure you, there is nothing in that bath with you that bites…*at least not yet.*" As soon as I heard his voice I spun around in surprise. I found him leaning against one of the marble pillars with his back to it and he nodded towards me drawing attention to my protective position. He was right, I looked as though something could be lurking beneath the water, ready to strike.

I looked back to him and seeing him there, stood the way he was I knew I had seen the sight before. I must have given away the look of recollection as he pushed away from the pillar and commanded in a serious tone,

"Don't chase it, Katie." I did as I was told, knowing it was for the best and let go of the memory that was trying to invade the here and now I was living in.

"Good. Now tell me, what's with the sad face and protective position?" He asked taking a seat at the lowest step that surrounded the raised bath.

"I thought you'd left." I told him honestly knowing there was little point in trying to save face and lie.

"I did."

"But why?" I tried to keep the whining sound from my voice, I really did but from the looks of his satisfied smirk I knew I hadn't accomplished it the way I would have liked.

"Because your grumbling stomach told me you were hungry. You may have not heard it but I did. I will not have you underfed and from the looks of things, it has been a regular occurrence." He said looking angry, which was the complete opposite to the gentle touch he provided when running the back of his hand along my collarbone.

"What do you mean?" I asked feeling my insecurities seeping back in.

"What I mean is simple. I do not take pleasure in seeing someone I care for, *deeply,* come back to me half-starved! As such, I have ordered some of your favourite food to be served for when you are finished in here." I knew I should have been touched by how much he cared but I couldn't help my reaction. I sank further down into the water and hid what clearly upset him to see...*my body.* I jumped when he growled as he sounded more like a beast than a man. I was also startled when I saw that flicker of purple again, knowing now it obviously occurred when he was highly emotional.

"Don't do that." He growled again, only in words this time. I moved further away from him to the other side and only when there was distance between us did I turn back round to face him...and boy, he didn't look happy!

"I thought..." I swallowed hard, trying to control the urge to cry so I could continue.

"...I thought... you said I was...was *beautiful."* I uttered the last word like it was admitting a sin and I bit my lip so hard it hurt. I had wanted him to look at me as though I was a woman he wanted more than his next breath and for a foolish moment, I had believed that was what I had seen.

"And you think I lied?" He ground out, now clearly very angry but thankfully it looked to be more with himself than with me.

"I...just...I... *don't know."* I felt a tear bred from insecurity fall from my nose as I looked down at the water feeling ashamed for too many reasons to count.

"Look at me." It was clear this wasn't a request by the strain heard in his voice. He seemed as though he was only just holding his patience in check as it hung by a thin cord, twisting there until one of us snapped it free. This was until I did as I was asked and looked up at him. I don't know what he saw when he looked at me but whatever it was the cord definitely snapped. He got to his feet and still fully dressed he walked into the bath with all his focus centred on me.

"What are you...?" I started to speak as I was moving backwards only to find the edge of the bath at my back. He cut through the water with the sole intent of getting to me as he didn't stop until he was inches away. I had to arch my neck to look up at him he looked so tall.

"Sometimes words just aren't enough..." He said down at me and then he placed his hands on my face so intimately I stopped breathing for a time.

"...*So I will show you how beautiful you are to me.*" He whispered softly before finally marking me as his with his kiss. As soon as his lips touched mine I opened up to him without any hesitation, for I knew now that I belonged to him, not just in this moment but for all moments to come. I was his and in this second my own cord snapped for I wanted to make him...*mine.*

I wrapped my arms up around his neck and locked him to me. He growled in my mouth as the kiss deepened and burst into mind-numbing sensations that rendered me drugged from his taste, his touch and the feel of him straining against me to get to my core. So I wrapped my legs around his waist, trying desperately to get close enough to feel the tip rub against my clit.

Once that first contact was made I threw my head back, closed my eyes and moaned at my first experience of such pleasure. He placed a hand behind my head in worry that I would hit it against the stone.

"Easy." He whispered in my ear before kissing his way down my neck. I moaned again and rocked myself against him, quickening the pace as though I was chasing something I didn't yet know. No, that wasn't right, I knew what it was I running towards in my mind, I just didn't have a clue as to how it would feel once I finally reached far enough to grasp it. I craved it, I was desperate for it and I wasn't letting it go this time.

"Please...please..." I started pleading with him and then arched back again to press myself nearer to him. I wanted to feel him breaching my barrier and breaking through so I finally knew what it was like to be connected to the man of my dreams.

"Tell me, what do you beg of me, Vixen?" He growled the question against my skin before pulling me up to him and taking my protruding nipple into his mouth to feast upon. I cried out as the bite of pain connected straight to the junction of my thighs and I felt it getting closer. He rotated his hips against me and I wanted his clothes off, so we were skin on skin.

I found without knowing it I was clawing at his wet shirt over his back in desperation. I felt him smile around my breast and he nipped at me making me scream out before backing away. I let out a moan of protest but when I realised why, I decided to use this time to drink in the sight of him. It was my time now and I wanted to enjoy the show.

His white shirt clung to his muscles like a pale second skin and I could easily say it was the sexiest sight I had ever seen. The material clung to defined pecs and deep ridges of a six pack making me want to drool. I had never wanted to taste what a wet shirt over a body like his tasted like before but seeing it now I could think of nothing else.

He undid a few more buttons and then dragged it from his back and over his head. This is when my mouth went dry! Christ alive but if I thought the wet shirt had been sexy then this took things to a whole new level. He didn't need to ask my approval as my mouth hanging open was enough but this man didn't strike me as someone who needed to be told how incredible he looked. For a start he didn't seem vain enough to care and I guess when you had a body like that to match such a handsome face, then confidence just came natural.

"There is only one woman I want to please." He said reading my thoughts and unbuckling his belt. I thought I might choke as I swallowed the hard, lustful lump down, that or come at the sight. I certainly didn't think my heart was going to survive this man for much longer.

"Just wait sweetheart, we have only just begun…I have lots more in store for you." He said, his eyes once more flashing purple as he yanked on his button and his zipper travelled south.

"Oh God." I whispered on an exhale as I realised he was a fan of going commando. I had to lick my dry lips at the sight of the length of him coming up through the water. Well if I thought I wanted a taste before, then now I was definitely feeling starved. Which was why my own demand slipped from my lips,

"I want to taste you." His reaction made me feel powerful as this time when he growled I wasn't scared, I was turned on.

"Come here, pet." I bit my lip as I stood, rising from the water and baring all as I walked over to him. He wrapped an arm around me and pulled me closer to him before he kissed me once more. I wanted to wrap my arms around him but he was so tall he had to bend lower for me to do so. I could feel his naked length pressing against me and I wanted it in my mouth so badly, it felt I was ravenous for it.

"You want me that way?" He questioned, pulling back to gauge my expression and the lust he found there must have spoken volumes for all I did was nod, too shy to say the words.

"Very well sweetheart…*on your knees."* This last command was the most dominant I had heard him yet, as it felt like the demon I had seen in my dreams was breaking through. I sucked

284

in a sharp breath at what it did to me to feel myself submitting to this man, I couldn't help the tremor it sent through me.

He took my hand to help lower me to my knees before him and I was almost panting in anticipation of what I was about to do. But then his hard length was presented to me and my natural instincts took over. I looked up at him making sure to keep eye contact as I encountered my first taste. I licked up the steely length, marvelling at how soft the velvet skin felt, even against my tongue.

He threw his head back and groaned telling me what I was doing was affecting him in the best way. Then I took it a step further and took him into my mouth the best I could considering his size. There was no way I was making it all the way so I let him go and dragged my hands over his ass, yanking his trousers from him the rest of the way down. Then I placed both my hands around him and went back to tasting him. He moaned again and with each animalistic sound coming from him it simply spurred me on to suck him down harder and faster.

I felt powerful. I felt invincible. I felt as though finally he was locked to me under my spell...And I freakin' loved it! I used my tongue on the underside, pressing against him and trying to draw out what I wanted from him. He threw his head back again shouting,

"Yes! By the Gods, don't stop!" This time it was my turn to smile around a piece of him. So I sucked harder still, teasing him with tip of my tongue against the head and I was rewarded with my first real taste of his cream beading from the slit. I worked it out until there was nothing left of the salty flavour but I craved more...so I worked him faster. I felt his hand entangle in my hair and he gently tugged as he moaned.

"Enough...*enough*...enough I said or I will..." This is when he lost it as he was quickly catapulted past the point of no return and instead of trying to get me to leave his cock, he was holding me to him making sure I finished the job. I felt my body tingling and pulsating with a raw energy as I pumped him harder knowing what I wanted. I was getting closer to my own release the more of him I took and the bigger the kick I got out of this level of control and it was staggering.

"Yes! Yes...FUCK YES! Rarrhhh!" He roared to the ceiling as I felt his seed burst from him, bathing my tongue in his offering. I swallowed him down as much as I could but even the feel of him spilling from my mouth was beyond erotic. I looked up to see the veins corded around his muscles were pronounced from under his sun kissed skin and again I wanted to lick my way around them.

He was still panting as I licked him clean, not wasting a drop and I had to be physically removed from that part of him. His hands gripped under my arms and lifted me up for him to kiss me passionately, as if he was desperate to taste himself on me. It was above anything I could have ever imagined and it felt like being injected with an electricity that I couldn't control. I was buzzing, my whole body humming with a power I couldn't understand.

Suddenly he ripped his lips from mine and before I could protest he started walking me backwards.

"What are you doing?" I asked gripping on to his colossal shoulders even though I knew he wouldn't let me fall. Without answering me he bent his knees and first sat me on the stone edge of the bath. Then his strong hand was placed gently in between my heaving breasts, finding my pounding heart under his palm. He stayed there, simply feeling it beat beneath his hand for a moment as if finding great pleasure in doing so. He closed his eyes and took in a deep breath.

"Draven?" I said, speaking the name that felt right coming from my lips and his eyes snapped open. He grinned and there was nothing amusing about the sight. In fact, he looked like he was a predator about to pounce and eat me. So when he started to push me backwards until my back was flush against the stone that surrounded the bath, I knew he was about to do just that.

"My turn, Vixen." He told me flashing those purple eyes before he yanked my legs open, spreading me wide. Then he hooked each one over his shoulders until my heels were firmly against his back. There was nowhere I could move to. Not that I would want to but with his solid frame preventing me closing my legs, I felt trapped in the most perfect of ways.

"Mine." He growled before he dove straight in. I cried out on contact as his lips kissed and sucked at my most intimate parts. Perspiration formed as the intensity grew and beaded, dripping down in between my breasts as I arched into him, dripping then from where it pooled at my neck.

My feet ground down into his back and he groaned into my core, causing little vibrations to travel along the sensitive folds. His tongue worked its magic as he devoured every inch of me as if he was a man obsessed with my flavour. He would nip and bite at my tight bundle of nerves and I would cry out in pain only to be quickly soothed by him sucking away the pain, quickly reforming it back into pleasure.

I could feel myself building over and over but he wouldn't let me grasp on to my orgasm.

"Pleeease...oh God please!" I pleaded, begged and implored for him to let me find it.

"You're mine to play with. I will say when you can have it." He told me, snarling out the first part like a sexual fiend keeping me a slave to him. I started crying out and felt my legs shaking against him as I couldn't take much more. But more was exactly what he gave me and it almost felt like my punishment for when I punished him with my tongue.

I could feel myself dripping down the crevice of each cheek he held securely in his hands, as if anchoring me to him, locking me there and forcing my body to take more. Every muscle in me was tensed but it was my stomach muscles that were suffering the most as I seemed to keep my abs locked tight and aching for my release.

It was only when I could hear myself screaming 'no more', that I just couldn't take the way he would pull back when he knew I was so close. This was when he gave it to me...

"AAAAAHHHHH!" I roared my own release into this world and my whole body shuddered as I felt the orgasm rip through every part of me. It was unlike anything I had ever experienced and more amazing than I ever imagined it would. It was like lighting up every cell in my body and releasing a drug of euphoria straight into my veins for it to travel all around my body, feeding the same light.

My legs still shook as the feeling continued and my torso slapped on the wet stone as I fought my way through the sensitivity until I could take no more. I tried to squirm away but he wouldn't let me.

"Mine!" He snarled again, dragging me back to his eager mouth so he could lap up my juices and in this moment it was harder to see the human in him, reminding me of the demon I had seen in my dreams...

Could it be?

Only once he was finished with me did he gently lower my still shuddering body back into the water and I let it cool my overheated skin. He pulled me to him, holding me close and I wrapped my legs around his waist so there was no space between us. I placed my head at his shoulder and tried to catch my breath. I couldn't help but kiss the heated skin I found so close to my lips, tasting the salty beads of sweat, knowing that he too had worked his body up with the heat we had created together.

"I need you...I can't wait any longer, I need to take you, I need to make you mine once more." This was the only indication I got before he gripped my waist and thrust up inside me, impaling me on his solid length.

"Ohhh ahhh!" I cried out as the intensity hit me, one I wasn't expecting. He too cried out in pleasure as we became one and connected as lovers should. I had expected to feel pain when he penetrated my virginal barrier but was surprised to feel only extreme amounts of bliss that shamefully made me cry out over and over again in satisfaction.

I gripped onto his shoulders, holding on to what felt like the centre of my world as he took me on this journey of discovery with him. Every time he pulled in and out the dizzying feeling would take hold and I knew this time I wouldn't last long. The drag against all those freshly discovered nerves was sending me into a frenzy of need and I rocked against him as fast as I could, trying to keep up with his immense stamina.

The feeling that built felt different than before but no less wonderful. It felt as though he was fighting with himself for greater control and I wanted to break it, seeing what would happen. I don't know what came over me but I saw the pulse in his neck and I was gone. All reasoning left me and something purely primal took over. I lowered my lips to his neck and instead of kissing him there I opened my mouth and bit him.

He roared once, yanked me from his neck and for a split second I felt fear that I had gone too far. However, the feeling seemed to fuse with the pleasure, increasing it to maddening heights and I knew I was lost. He grabbed my hair and displayed my own neck for him and I had little time to do much else as I watched him descend as I had done to him. I felt his fangs break the skin and the pain bloomed quickly into an exhilarating eruption sending me down a path straight to my own personal nirvana.

He quickly followed my release with his own and as my

walls pulsated around him, he ejaculated more of his seed deep inside me, roaring out like he had done last time. We continued to hold each other as if waiting for the storm to pass that our raging hearts had fought against. I felt myself coming down slowly from my high and something unexpected came with it.

Feeling such tenderness was definitely what I knew I needed right now as I felt strangely vulnerable after experiencing my first sexual encounter, along with my first ever orgasms. He obviously knew what I needed as he pulled me closer still and cradled me against him as I silently wept at the overwhelming beauty of it all. I don't quite know what had come over me but I was just grateful that he seemed to understand it perfectly.

"Ssshh, now, I have got you...you're safe with me." He whispered softly against my hairline. I gripped onto him as if I never wanted to let go, knowing what such a thing would do to me. I couldn't leave him... *ever!*

For I knew it would feel like the death of me and I would choose that over living in a world without him from now on. He had shown me a beauty and love of the kind I had not only ever known, but of the likes I never believed could exist.

I felt reborn.

Almost like discovering a new religion that was solely based on what I felt in my heart and because of it,

I felt as though I had been...

Baptized by Love.

CHAPTER 23
TIME FOR SOME Q AND A

I must have fallen asleep in his arms briefly because I only woke when I felt myself being placed down on something soft. This must have happened shortly after my emotional outburst. I internally winced at how silly I felt before opening my eyes and bracing myself for his reaction. I found him lay next to me with his elbow to the bed and his head propped up against his hand. He was looking down at me and playing with a piece of my wet hair, wrapping it around his finger and then letting it go again.

He seemed fascinated, so when he spoke without looking at me I was startled.

"I am surprised they didn't force you to cut all this off." He said making me frown in confusion.

"I think if they had done that I would have killed them all for that offense alone but their list for their death sentence is great enough …So tell me, where are they, Katie?" I pulled back from him as I think in this moment I had never been so frightened of him. He grabbed me, pulling me back to him, cooing in my ear,

"Ssshh now, calm yourself and don't fight me, little dove." I realised I was trying to squirm free and his simple talk about murdering people had scared me enough into needing space between us. However, he refused to give me the space and placed his hand at the back of my head, forcing me to accept his embrace. It was only when I stopped struggling against him that he trusted me enough to let me go.

"You know about the Colony?" I said for some reason feeling ashamed it had taken me until now for us to speak about it. I saw something in his jaw twitch and his eyes again changed for half a second.

"I know enough to decree their death sentence, that I can promise you."

"But you don't have the authority to do something like that!" I said assuming this was true.

"I may lack the details on what you have had to endure for the last eight months you have been gone, but make no mistake, I have more than enough authority to make those who took you from me suffer the consequences for such an act." I jerked at this last bit of information but not because he was once again talking about murdering people but because he mentioned the eight months I had been gone.

"Say that again?" I muttered trying to get my head around it and make sure I was clear on what I had heard.

"Katie, I understand this may be difficult for you to hear but you don't fully grasp the severity of the crimes committed by taking you from me."

"No, not that bit…I'm mean when you said how long ago it was that your wife was taken?" I asked quickly noting the soft look of regret he gave me and I knew this was because I had referred to her as someone else.

"*You* were taken from me over eight months ago." He said correcting me firmly.

"*Oh God.*" I whispered as the horrifying timeline started to fit into place. It was over eight months ago that I started dreaming of him and Ari and I had started rebelling more and more against the Colony.

"Tell me." He demanded, knowing there was something important I wasn't telling him.

"I need to get dressed, there's something I have to do." I said getting up from the bed and only now realising I was in nothing but a towel.

"Katie." He reached across and grabbed my arm, gently tugging me back to him.

"Please, I will tell you everything you wish to know but only if you help me first." He eyed me suspiciously before nodding.

"Alright, let's get you dressed. We have lots to discuss, you and I." He let go and got up off the bed. At the sight of him wearing only a towel wrapped around and hanging low on his hips I wanted to cry in frustration at how much I wanted him to take me again. I even felt my sore, beautifully abused parts weep for more and instantly the dampness I felt down there told me I was more than ready.

Draven was walking towards another long tapestry, this time closer to the bed when he stopped and sniffed the air. A growl came from him and he turned slowly to look at me. The heat rose from within me at the intense look of desire he gave me. His lustful gaze travelled the length of me and only stopped when it came to the place that was causing all the fuss. The thought that he could actually smell my desire was both mortifying and strangely erotic.

The next thing I knew I was in his arms again and I shrieked out as I hadn't even seen him move. He tore the towel from me spinning me round and pushing me up against one of the tree sized posts that held up the roof of his enormous bed. In one small move his towel was gone and he entered me in one swift thrust after dragging one of my legs over his naked behind. I threw my head back and shouted in exhilaration at getting what I wanted...what I seemed to now constantly crave.

He pounded into me with a ferocity that seemed to come from his anger at having time stolen from us. He growled and sucked and kissed my neck and breasts until they became so sensitive that I felt like my skin was on fire. Each thrust was done with the sole purpose of finding my G spot and I cried out over and over each time he rubbed against it with his cock.

It didn't take long before I came screaming around him and I bit into his shoulder to try and control myself. This only managed to excite him further as he grabbed my other leg, hitching me up over him and dropping me down hard on his erection. I cried out again as the pain once again morphed into pleasure and before I knew what hit me my inner walls were once again quaking around him buried deep inside me.

This set him off and after driving deep into me one last time he threw his head back as I had done and shouted out his unrestrained sexual gratification to the world. This time the rawness of it left us both panting and this time without my girly meltdown. Instead I let him simply hold me close until we came down from our drugged euphoria together, then I pulled back my head and said,

"I'm really sorry, I don't know why I keep biting you." At this he burst out laughing and I could feel the effects of it from not just the way he shook my body but also where he was still buried firmly inside of me. It was the first time I had heard him let go and fully laugh and I was amazed how much even that turned me on.

"By the Gods sweetheart, you can bite me as much as you wish." He said leaning his forehead to mine as he caught his breath. I couldn't help but rejoice in the knowledge that I could make him lose control the way he had done. In fact, my legs were still wrapped firmly around him, making it obvious that I didn't want to let go.

He took a step back and before I could unlock my legs he held them in place so that he could lower me to the bed. Then he pushed his hands through my hair and kissed his way along my collarbone before finishing his kiss at my lips. I knew I could easily get lost once more in this embrace, so when he pulled away I knew it wasn't because he wanted to but because if we didn't then we would never leave this bed.

"You're killing me here." He whispered against my cheek and then held it with his teeth playfully without hurting me. I giggled against him, which quickly turned into a moan of protest when he pulled himself from me. I definitely felt the loss and had to stop myself from reaching out for him. Of course when he grabbed the towel from the floor and came towards me I reached out to take it from him.

He shook his head and smirked.

"It's my mess to clean and it just so happens to be my favourite chore." He winked at me when I frowned and then chuckled when I shrieked in protest when he pried my legs open, letting me know exactly what he meant by favourite chore!

He laughed when I hid my face in embarrassment. I only braved a look through my fingers when I felt the towel had been removed and with it, all evidence of him being there. I actually felt saddened by the idea but then turned my head and took a sneaky smell of my skin. I was smirking myself when I smelled his scent there and was happy that there was still some proof of our time together. I know it was silly but after I had dreamt about him for so long, I needed that physical evidence like a comfort blanket.

"You are such a sweet girl." His voice startled me and I looked up to see him giving me a warm smile. I didn't know why he said this and I never got chance to ask as he leant down and gave me a swift kiss, that in my opinion was far too brief. I also noticed he was fully dressed and I was not.

"I left the door to the dressing room open for you, after first checking it this time of course. I will leave you to dress in peace, for I fear if I have to lay witness to your beautiful body any longer then I will never let you out of our bed." I loved the way he called it 'our' bed and I was still smiling to myself long after he left.

It was only when I was up and had wrapped the comforter from the bed around myself that I started to wonder what he had meant when talking about the dressing room? Why had he needed to check it before I went in there? Also I hoped that he meant for me to go in there to get my bag because I very much doubted that he had anything that would fit, unless I could wear one of his shirts as a dress.

I circled the bed, kicking the covers so I could actually walk until I saw the dressing room he spoke of. I approached the open doorway and got no further. I don't know what was wrong with me but I couldn't physically step in there and when I tried I ended up staggering back against the bed. What the hell was going on!? I got up angrily and tried again, ready to storm right in there but that's when it hit me…

This time I was terrified.

"Katie?" I heard him approach from behind as he said my name gently, probably wondering what I was doing just standing in a sheet and staring into that room like it held all the answers. But that was it wasn't it? That was the reason for him checking it.

"This is where it happened…wasn't it?" I asked him quietly.

"Yes, it was." The pain in which he said this was heart wrenching.

"I don't remember." I told him letting a single tear fall. He didn't say anything but he put his arms on the top of my shoulder as though knowing I needed the comfort only his touch could give me.

"I don't remember anything and I don't know how to get it back or if I ever will. I don't even know what they took from me…what they took from you, I know none of it! And yet when I look at this room now I find myself terrified that they will take it all away from me again and I don't even know what they took! I don't fucking know! Why don't I know…WHY!?" I shouted the last part getting so angry that I let him turn me around, putting my back to the room. He then took me in his arms and I cried for what I hoped was the last time.

"Ssshh, it will be alright. We are together now and that is all that matters. We will fight this as one, we will get your memories back…you are not alone anymore." I suddenly pulled myself from his arms and walked away for a moment before telling him the root of my fears.

"But what if I never get them back?! What if it's impossible and they are lost forever!?" He folded his arms, took a deep breath and said,

"Then I don't care."

"You don't care?" I questioned, I had to because deep down I knew what it meant to him. I knew what it meant to get his wife back.

"No. I don't care because we can make new memories, we have all our lives to do that."

"But…"

"All I care about is you. All I care about is that I've got you back and I am never letting you go again." He said interrupting me and I knew this was the point where I had to tell him my greatest fear before I fell too hard and I knew I would never return. Hell, who was I kidding, I was already there! But I had to do this…I had no choice. So I told him the truth.

"But what if it's not real?" He frowned not understanding where I was going with this.

"I don't…"

"What if I am not her? What if I am not your wife!?" I snapped knowing my emotions were feeding my fear. He shook his head and said,

"You are."

"But you don't know that…not for certain." I argued.

"Yes, *I do.*" He seemed so sure and it was such a beautiful thing to witness. I was half tempted to agree and spend the rest of my life wishing for that very thing. But what if I wasn't and what if there was a girl lost out there who just happened to look exactly like me. No, I couldn't do it. I had to tell him the truth…I had to make him understand once and for all.

"But you don't know me. My name is Katie…Katie O'Brian. I have a Mother called Cynthia O'Brian who doesn't give a shit about me ever since my Father, Matthew O'Brian died in a car crash when I was seven. The only person who loves me in this whole world is my twin sister Ari and what did I do…? I fucking left her! I left her to those bastards at the Colony!"

"Sweetheart…" I turned away in shame and angrily wiped the tears from my face that now ran freely.

"I left the only person I had in the world and I don't even know if she is still alive! And what am I doing, having the time of my life with a man I have been dreaming about since the day you said I was taken. But what type of person does that make me…what type of person does that make your wife, Draven?!" I snapped again and instead of getting angry as I would have expected him to be when facing an angry woman, he softly said,

"It simply makes you human."

"And you…what does it make you if I have been seeing you as a demon in my dreams?" I asked throwing the question at him like some cruel bitch that had lost my mind. I saw him wince and struggle to answer making me feel even worse for being so mean.

"I'm sorry, I shouldn't have said that."

"But it's true isn't it? That's why you called me 'Your Demon' when you first saw me…right?" I nodded not able to speak the shameful words.

"Do you often see demons, Katie?" The question caught me so off guard I faltered when trying to find my answer. I instantly thought back to that night when seeing all the Fathers drinking the blood of that poor girl. I had been convinced in what I had seen, what both Ari and I had seen. And then in Lucy's house and that day at the fair, that gypsy hadn't been human…but had it all been in my head? I just didn't know any more so I gave him the answer I believed.

"Only when I am asleep."

"Tell me then, why did you come here?" He asked and I so wanted to tell him what he wanted to hear. I wanted to say that I was his wife and I escaped that terrible place with the sole purpose of us being together again but I couldn't.

Because it was a lie.

"I came here to find Dominic Draven to ask him to help me save my sister. I didn't know it was you as I never heard her speak your name before and when one of my dreams led me to the name Afterlife all I could find out was…"

"That I owned the place." He finished off for me.

"Yes and the last thing Ari told me was to listen to what my dreams were trying to tell me. She said it was the only way to save her and to save…" I stopped myself before I sounded even crazier than what he must already be thinking of me.

"Continue, what did she say?"

"Uh, and that was it." I said turning away so he wouldn't see the lie but he was too smart for that. He was at me in a heartbeat and now stood in front of me demanding what he wanted to know.

"Katie." All he needed to say was my name in that warning tone and I caved.

"She must have been confused because she told me it was the only way to save the world." He took a step back in shock and that's when I knew that I had blown it! I started to think of any way I could pull it back or any second now he would be throwing me out of here and calling the men in white coats!

"Look she was upset, confused, I don't know she just was acting…"

"I need to know exactly what she said to you word for word." He said surprising me with how serious he looked. Okay, so much for thinking I was crazy!

"Well I don't remember it all…Why?" I asked warily.

"Then, I'm afraid that I have no choice." This scared me as I didn't know what it meant but it sounded way too much like a threat for my liking.

"I don't understand what all this is about and what do you mean 'you don't have a choice' a choice in what?" I asked looking up into his stern face and trying to find my answers there as well. He didn't look happy but surprisingly it had been what I had said about Ari that had disturbed him the most.

He didn't answer me, instead he disappeared into the dressing room only to reappear a moment later with some clothes in his hand. He threw them on the bed and instructed,

"Get dressed."

"Why, where are we going?" I asked in a small worried voice, one that seemed to finally get his attention. He released a sigh before walking over to me and enveloping me in his arms.

"It will be alright but you have to trust me." I nodded knowing that now I did trust him and not because I had little option to do much else but because I wanted too.

300

"Good girl." Whenever I heard him calling me this I couldn't help but dig deep and find what felt like the last shreds of my bravery.

"Now get dressed as I must leave you a moment. I will have someone come to get you and bring you to me. Have no fear Katie as everyone you're about to meet knows you well but more importantly they care for you deeply and...you care equally for them." I knew why he had paused before saying this last part and I bit my lip against the pain it brought me. What he was saying was that in my old life, the one he was convinced was mine, I had once loved these people. People I could no longer remember.

"I don't know if I can do this, Draven." I admitted looking up at him with wide eyes that clearly displayed my distress.

"They understand the situation, no one will push themselves on you and as long as you are yourself around them then everything else will slot into place." He seemed so sure, which is what I told him.

"Of course I am sure." He told me confidently.

"Why?" I asked wondering how he could be so sure. A cocky grin appeared before he said,

"Because it's you." And with that he kissed me softly and left.

I slumped down on the bed and threw myself back dramatically.

"What have you gotten yourself into this time Kay bear?" Hearing my sister's nickname for me aloud again brought me the comfort I needed to do this, even if it had come from my own lips.

This was enough to get my behind in gear, so I dropped the comforter back on the bed and started to get dressed. I couldn't help but go red when I picked up the matching underwear set that was a deep purple colour and it reminded me of Draven's eyes. I still couldn't understand how they changed colour like that and had wanted to ask a few times but it was never really the right opportunity.

After putting these on and being surprised that he knew my bra size I picked up a soft pair of indigo coloured jeans. They were tight and stretchy on the leg but still incredibly comfy to wear. The last items of clothing were a black strappy vest and a light grey sweater that had faded black wings on the back. It was cute and I loved it. But I had to wonder how he had picked the exact same thing that I would have picked if given the option.

I had to ask myself if this had been one of his wife's favourite things to wear but then if that was the case then why were the tags still on the clothes? I gave up wondering and went into the bathroom to see what I could do with my hair. Most of it was dry now and I quickly realised after brushing the knots out that it was clean. I bit my lip, smiling in the knowledge that he must have washed it for me before carrying me out of the bath. I was so astounded at the kindness of this man that no wonder this Keira had fallen so in love with him, I was beginning to think I was already there myself!

I looked around but I couldn't find anything to tie my hair back with so decided to do something I never did and that was leave it loose. I would have been shunned in the Colony for this, which is why the threat of having it shaved off in a public display was enough for me to hide it away at all times.

I walked back into the bedroom and the instant my eyes spotted the food spread out on the tables my stomach sounded its approval. There was everything there, from a selection of sandwiches, cheese burgers and fries, chocolate muffins, croissants and Danish pastries, even…was that Chilli Con Carne and rice? I think everything and anything I would have picked off a menu if I had the choice was here!

I actually didn't know what to pick, so was completely greedy and had a bit of everything. I washed it all down with diet soda and was pulling at the waistband of my jeans laughing to see there wasn't much room there anymore. I knew there would come a point where I would regret eating that much as I felt stuffed to the brim but boy had it all felt good! I was still giggling to myself when the door suddenly opened. I quickly shot out of the chair, as the last thing I wanted was someone to walk in on me and see me poking at my full belly that now folded over my waistline.

"Hello Katie." I heard that same voice I thought I recognised earlier and pushed all my hair back to see who it was. I gasped at the sight and as I had done with Draven, said the first thing that popped into my head without thinking…

"Ari's Angel!"

CHAPTER 24
OKAY, SO THIS IS AWKWARD!

"Excuse me?" He asked in one of the calmest voices I had ever heard spoken. In fact, I found the only reaction to this was to repeat my obvious blunder,

"You're Ari's Angel." As soon as I said it I wanted to smack myself. He gave me a confused look, which I had to admit wasn't as frowny as it could have been considering what I had just blurted out at him for the second time.

"Am I?" He asked obviously trying to contain the smirk that we both knew was lingering there on the surface.

"I'm sorry, let me try that again…I'm Katie." I said after shaking my head and walking over to him to shake his hand.

"I know who you are, darling." He said taking my hand in his and this time letting that smirk show. Once again the urge to smack myself reared its punishing head. Of course he knew who I was, for a start he had already said my name and after all he was here right now no doubt sent by Draven to fetch me.

"Of course you do." I rolled my eyes at myself and he laughed.

"It's good to see you again." I knew he said this only because he felt like he needed to say it for his own benefit, as he must have known I had no memory of him. Well of course apart from dreaming of him in that shameful way with Ari that one time, but I definitely think that was better left unsaid...*for like all of eternity!*

He raised an eyebrow at me as if he was trying to figure something out and I realised it was probably why I was just stood here not saying anything.

"So I take it Draven is ready for me?" I said trying to prompt something from him as the way he looked at me now was starting to freak me out.

"Yes, my brother is waiting for us." He informed me after coming out of his dazed state...but wait, did he just say what I think he did?

"Your brother!? Draven's your brother?" I asked again in obvious surprise.

"Dominic is my brother, yes. I am Vincent Draven and I believe you have met our sister Sophia." He told me smiling and I don't know what it was about it but there was something so calming about him. The soft way he spoke and the reassuring way in which he said everything was so bewitching. He drew you in to feeling safe and trusting.

"But you don't look anything alike!" I found once again my brain and mouth weren't working together as I blurted this out. Thankfully he just chuckled and said,

"Yes, we are different in many ways. I have been told that I favour my mother's side of the family."

"Ah, like me and Ari, we take after our dad...thankfully." I added thinking back bitterly to the wicked witch of the Colony!

"And this Ari...she is your sister?" He asked and I couldn't help blush knowing what I had shouted out when he first entered the room. Of course this wasn't the only reason I blushed as I really didn't need to think of these two being in the same room as each other, not considering what my dreams had

306

shown me. No wonder Ari hadn't gone into detail when telling me about him, not if that was what she dreamed of!

"Are you okay?" I asked because he got that confused look again and I couldn't understand why...unless I was talking out loud again, but no, then surely he would have asked me about it.

"If you are finished here, then should we go?" He asked me, looking to the mass of food I had barely made a dent in.

"Oh yeah, I am stuffed! That chilli was amazing." I said and the smile he gave me was one of the things I could relate him to his brother for. He was so handsome but in a different way to Draven, which reminded me, why I had got into the habit of calling him by his last name I didn't know. Looking at Vincent in the flesh, it was strange how I could actually picture him and Ari together. He was gentle and serene which would calm Ari's wild streak. Although thinking how gentle he looked I had to try hard not to think how he had been in the dream and nothing about what he had done to her looked gentle.

Vincent coughed once as if needing to suddenly clear his throat and then said,

"I am happy to hear that." He said referring back to me enjoying the food. I smiled back at him and managed to take in more of his appearance without openly staring, which is really what I wanted to do. I couldn't help it, a man that handsome and Angelic looking just needed to be stared at by any girl with a pulse. He had a halo of tight golden curls and a pair of the most striking, crystal blue eyes I had ever seen. Actually I think I had only ever come across one other man, other than Vincent, that I would have classed as being 'beautiful' and that was his brother. I looked sideways to catch another smirk and decided now would be a good time to say something before I did blurt out how attractive he was.

"Did you know that in Latin your name means 'To Conquer'" I told him remembering this from my tedious lessons at the Colony and one of the Fathers being a fan of the writer Vincent O'Sullivan.

"I did and I believe it was the very reason I was granted the name." He answered me, this time seeming surprised for the right reasons.

"I wonder what Dominic means." I asked myself out loud.

"Of the Lord."

"Sorry?"

"Dominicus, which is Dominic in late Latin, means 'Of the Lord' and quite fitting I think." Well I couldn't argue with him there as he did seem to fit the 'Lord of the Manor' title quite well.

"So how about your sister Sophia?" I asked as I let him lead me down the grand looking hallway.

"Ah, now that's where I think our parents must have got it wrong as her name means 'Holy Wisdom' in Ancient Greek but don't tell her I said that." I laughed at his teasing and could tell from the way he said it that he and his brother obviously adored their sister.

I followed him down the endless corridors, quickly realising this place was huge! I knew that if I ever had to walk this mansion alone that I would easily get lost in its maze of stone walls.

"It's not as daunting after you have done it a few times." Vincent said as if reading my thoughts.

"Seriously, do you guys have like mad observation skills or something, or do I just have one of the most expressive faces this side of the US?" I said not adding on the part where I thought they might all be physic.

"Just blessed I guess." He said grinning and if he hadn't have been looking I would have rolled my eyes as I thought 'yeah, they were certainly blessed alright!' I quickly felt colour invade my cheeks as I then thought back to what his brother had done to me only moments before he'd left and had to agree that *he* was most certainly blessed in the downstairs department.

"Are you alright?" I asked Vincent as once again he started coughing.

"Yeah, it's just the dry air." He said and with where my naughty thoughts were I knew I had the opposite problem in between my thighs.

"Oh, by the Gods, woman." I heard him mutter something under his breath but I could barely make out what.

"Excuse me, did you say something?"

"I said that I think we should hurry, don't you? Dom will be waiting." He ground this out and it was the first time since meeting him that he seemed to have lost some of his steely calm.

"Yes and no wonder." He walked ahead muttering something more and I had to jog to catch up.

"Something I said?" I muttered back before we approached the door at the end.

"Is he in there?" I asked almost panting with the speed he had been walking.

"Yes he is….*thank the Gods."*

"Sorry, I didn't catch that last…part…*oh my."* I said as he opened the door to a magnificent, long room that was surrounded by marble. Table tops and plinths that held carved marble figures I couldn't quite make out framed the room along the walls and a grand fireplace I could have lived in was at the centre of the room. Multiple chairs and sofas were situated around the fireplace, where most of the heat could be appreciated and rich reds and golds stood out against all the pale stone coming from the soft furnishings.

But this wasn't the most striking feature in the room, or the most terrifying for me right now, it was the biggest wooden table I had ever seen. But, it wasn't the fact that it seemed like the focal point of the room or the fact that it was big enough to hold forty people around it… it was however, the twelve people it did hold around it that I found most terrifying and they were all currently staring at me in awe. Every single person stood up at the same time, creating an echo in the vast room of the sound of wooden chairs being pushed against the stone floor.

"Uh…I don't think I can do this." I whispered to Vincent, feeling that same strange sense of déjà vu creep over me again.

"You will be fine." Vincent said closing the door behind me and standing at my only exit, no doubt in case I decided to bolt.

"Come to me, Sweetheart." I looked to the top of the table and I released a pent up breath of anxiety when I saw Draven stood there waiting for me. I did as I was told and walked slowly past everyone sitting around, watching me as if they too had been waiting for me.

"Uh…sorry if we are late." I said nervously, as if I needed to make my apologies. Most of them gave me warm looks and respectful head nods but looking at them all, one by one and I don't think I had ever seen so many diverse people all in one place in my entire life, which, I grant you wasn't hard considering I grew up at the Colony.

When I finally made it round to Draven I felt instantly better when he wrapped an arm around my waist and pulled me to him. I was surprised he was displaying such affection in front of what must have been all of his employees or something. I gathered as much considering he had been sat at the top of the grand table in what was an even grander chair.

Actually from where I now stood I looked down to see it was in fact a solid stone throne made from pure white marble that had blood red veins branching out all around it. It was an incredible work of art in its own right, including the tall arched back that held a fiery coloured glass, featuring a strange symbol at its centre.

"Be seated." Draven commanded the room and I looked around to find enough spare chairs, so I took a step away from him and said,

"I will just grab a..." I was quickly cut off as Draven's hands gripped my waist, pulled me back and sat down. I had nowhere else to go other than to follow him down, which meant his lap became my seat.

"You will stay right where you should always be." Draven said running his hand down my loose hair in affection. Vincent then walked over to the empty chair on his brother's right and before sitting down he informed him,

"Never again, Brother." Draven placed a hand on Vincent's shoulder and after a moment of what seemed like great concentration Draven burst out laughing.

"Don't worry, I will send Sophia next time." He replied and I frowned, hoping this 'never again' wasn't referring to me. I thought back to everything that was said since Vincent walked through Draven's door up until this point and I knew I was just being paranoid. It wasn't like I had dropped my foot in it at any point or made the brief journey unpleasant for him.

"Miss me, did you?" Draven whispered in my ear and I blushed when his hand squeezed the top of my thigh, making it obvious what he meant with that question. I was shocked at his behaviour in front of everyone, wondering what type of business he was into anyway, as this didn't look like your typical boardroom meeting.

Or maybe I had got it all wrong and he was part of some elite, special forces group that helped get out and save hostages or prevent world domination from terrorist groups with bombs. Thinking about it now with the easy way he had talked about murdering those responsible, it would make sense if that was the type of thing he was used to. It was this or he was some billionaire Bruce Wayne type that had one, two, three...*a lot* of sidekicks.

"See what I mean." Vincent muttered to Draven and I heard him chuckle behind me as he pulled me closer to him.

"I think it's cool and I am half tempted to set it up." Sophia said who was sat on Draven's left and I had no clue as to what any of them were talking about...had I missed half of the conversation?

"Katie, I would like to introduce you to my council." Draven said ignoring his sister and starting the meeting. I looked around to each chair and tried not to react badly at how much they intimidated me. I think it was only Sophia, the oriental dude and one other woman with lovely but mad orange hair, that didn't frighten me. The rest of them I could split between two groups and that was either biker bad boy scary and just plain wet my pants scary!

I heard Draven sigh at my back and say,

"Please, if everyone could introduce yourselves, then I think that may help."

"Well you know by now I am Sophia, and this hunk on my left is my husband Zagan but don't let his pale complexion fool you, he's actually blushing right now." She said mischievously. I looked to the man that was clearly an Albino and was surprised to find this was her husband. Although she was right, his ghostly skin didn't detract from his handsome features and the tattoo that snaked through the scar on his face only gave him a sexy edge.

"Moving on." Draven said curtly, sounding strangely unhappy and there were a few sniggers in the room. Zagan gave me a kind smile and nodded in what looked like appreciation and it was almost as though I had voiced my compliments to him aloud.

"Takeshi, My Qu...Dear." The oriental one said graciously

and as he bowed his head in respect I wondered what he had almost called me. Moving on to the next person and I would have said I was back at the fair as the only way to describe him was as a jester that was trying not to be one.

"Hello Cookie." He said waving his hand and he was wearing red leather, fingerless gloves, so I could see that his nails were painted black. He also had long blood red hair that was slicked back and tied at the base of his neck, where his high collared, black tight top curled up. The outfit matched the strange, thin black lines painted through his eyes and also down the centre of his chin and neck. He looked like some attractive clown that held an air of arrogance about him, one you wouldn't expect to find in someone whose sole purpose was to entertain.

"She's got a point dickhead." A massive black guy said and there was nothing funny about the way he looked.

"I'm Orthrus by the way…and pencil dick over there is Marcus." The Jester, who I now knew was named Marcus merely flipped him the bird and said,

"And we all know how the real pencil dick belongs to Mr Walking Steroid."

"What did you say to me?!" The black guy roared banging his fist on the table.

"Fuckin idiots!" Muttered one of the biggest guys in the room as there was only one man bigger than him and he was most definitely the scariest of them all.

"Sucks to be you, old man." He added chuckling after I thought this and meanwhile the other two were still bickering. I was left bewildered at half of this bunch that were actually acting like unruly teenagers.

"Well thought, Lille øjesten" The big guy said nodding making his hood move back slightly.

"She means you too, Snake Ass!" The black guy name

Orthrus said and with that type of name I had to wonder where he was from.

"Ha, wouldn't that be an interesting conversation between the two of you." Marcus said laughing and I was quickly losing the plot.

"Cerberus, if you will please control your men." I heard Draven say from behind me as if he was close to losing his temper.

"Gladly." The man Draven had aimed this at growled the word and it was a sound that really did terrify me. He was, like most sat around the table, a very handsome man but this being said, it was in a different way entirely. If there was one word I would use to describe this man, it would be...*raw.* Hard lines, and rough edges through and through and when he spoke, he was definitely used to being obeyed for it was clear he was in charge of the rowdy bunch.

"Speak your fucking names and be done with it!" He snapped and his silver eyes seemed to flash with something darker lurking behind them. I couldn't help but shift closer to Draven at my back, needing to feel safe.

"Marcus."

"Orthrus."

"Hi I'm Smidge." The girl with orange hair was the only one who didn't snap this out like the other two.

"Chase...howdy" Said the stocky one with a nice smile.

"Otto." The one sat next to him said.

"And I am Jared Cerberus. It's good to see you, Kitten." He said winking and making Draven growl low at my back. I whipped my head round and whispered,

"Did she know all of these people?" He knew what I was asking him and after another sigh he said,

"Unfortunately, yes."

314

"I thought Bill was to remain in your Council, Cerberus?" Draven said, once more back to his commanding tone.

"He is on a mission but will join us in a few days." I looked back to Draven who had one eyebrow raised but whatever he wanted to say, another voice spoke.

"Can we move this shit along before I grow even older... Hey øjesten, I'm Sigurd, that big scarred guy over there is Leivic and this scary guy sat right next to me is Ragnar...good, now we all know each other again." He said sarcastically making the 'Scary guy' next to him snarl.

"Show some respect boy! My Lord I apologise once more for my son's lack of respect."

"Seriously old man, doesn't that ever get *old?*" The hooded one said and I was still stuck on all I was learning. Like for one, Draven was a Lord!?

"Well I knew it would be entertaining." Sophia said wryly and Vincent responded with,

"Not now Sister." Making her laugh.

"Silence!" Draven shouted, finding he had hit the end of his patience. Just then the door opened and I couldn't believe there were even more people here ready to join...whatever *this* was.

At the first sight of them I shouted,

"Pip, Adam! You're alive, oh thank God!" I was so happy to see them and just before I could turn around and tell Draven who they were someone else walked in behind them.

"Uh...Luc?"

"Hello Little Katie Girl." He said in that confident tone of his as he walked past Adam and his wife. It was at this moment that my mind started to go into overtime and as the pieces of the puzzle started to fit into place I knew this was going to get bad.

"Oh shit" I said, knowing I should have just kept my mouth shut. But as everything he told me about his friend's wife came slamming back to me, it became one of the puzzle pieces, including the fact that he had feelings for her. But this wasn't the worst part about any of it...or the fact that I now realised *I* was the bloody wife and Draven was his friend...

No, none of it was as bad as what had happened on the bus together. As bad as that amazing kiss we shared...

My first ever kiss.

Quickly Luc made a clicking noise with his tongue and said,

"Ah honey, you just had to do it, didn't you?" Then directly after this there was an almighty roar as Draven erupted behind me and my hands flew to my ears to help with the demonic bellow that came from somewhere hellish inside of him.

Suddenly I was plucked out of Draven's lap by Vincent and he spun me around, protecting me as I heard Draven's threat that was more than clear...

"I will fucking kill you this time, Lucius!"

CHAPTER 25
THE SCARY TRUTH

" *I will fucking kill you this time, Lucius!*" Draven's roar of fury was followed by Vincent picking me up from his lap and spinning me around, but something unexpected happened. The second he touched me light exploded around us and I slammed my eyes shut against the blinding light. I moaned in his arms that were wrapped around me and when I finally opened my eyes, expecting to see the chaos around me, all I saw were feathers.

"What's happening?" I whispered as I reached out a hand and ran my fingertips against the soft feel of pure white wings. Wings that were wrapped around me from behind and came straight from the Angel at my back. I could barely believe this was happening…had I passed out again and was now dreaming?

"Vincent?" I said his name and turned in his arms to stare at him. With one look at his face I knew,

"I'm not dreaming am I?"

"No darling, I am afraid you're not." He said gently as if breaking this news to me would cause me mental damage. And

317

I suppose he was right, considering what I decided to do next turned out to be a very stupid thing.

After this I can honestly say the next few moments were the scariest moments in my life so far. It wasn't because I was about to see two grown men fighting over a woman, that woman being me. No, it was because even though Vincent tried to hide me from the truth, with one single turn of my head I realised I had fallen in love with a *Demon*.

It started very quickly after Luc had entered the room and I had no clue how but Draven knew something had gone on between us and that was enough. All it took was for me to mutter an innocent 'Oh shit' and that was it. Draven had transformed into the demon I had seen from my dreams and he was at Luc in the time it took for me to gasp.

For Draven wasn't the only one who had changed. He picked Luc up off the floor after I had no idea how he got there in the first place. Then he threw his body across the table, causing him slide towards us and Vincent only just managed to push me out of the way before he slammed into him.

"Come on Lille øjesten, let's get you outta here." I looked up from where I had fallen to see the colossal figure stood over me and I screamed! A black, shadowed serpent seemed to be circling him and snapping out, hissing like it was angry. I scrambled backwards getting away from him and he stepped forward saying,

"Lille øjesten? What is wrong with you?"

"What's wrong with me!?" I shouted nodding to his body and he looked down and asked in a horrified tone,

"What can you see, girl?" I shook my head frantically trying to get away.

"What have you done to her Sigurd!?" The one that was his father came over to ask him and as soon as he came into view I screamed yet again! Jesus Christ, this guy was a monster!

"GET AWAY!" I shouted frantically but just as I made it to my feet ready to run, Luc was back on his feet and had snatched one of the marble plinths to use as a weapon against Draven. I had to duck out of the way and when I looked back up, Draven wasn't the only demon fighting. Luc too had grown wings that looked like he had ripped them straight from a mighty phoenix. His eyes looked as if they had been injected with blood and the length of his fangs was as I saw them when he was fighting the men in the bathroom.

Draven rolled, his own wings going with him as the plinth smashed into the floor, leaving destruction in its path. It was clear the two Demons were equally matched, either that or they could equally take a beating! Draven sprung back to his feet and kicked Luc squarely in his chest, sending him flying backwards. I sidestepped, yet again getting out the way.

"Let's get you out of here." Sophia said and I turned thinking this was a good plan that was until I saw her face.

"No! No, no, no…not you too!" I stammered at the terrifying sight that was cracked, caked skin and a mouth that had been slit up her cheeks. Black venom oozed from the cracks in her skin and around her eyes and mouth like blood overflowing.

"She can see you, Sophia!" Vincent shouted from across the room where he was now trying to contain his brother's rage.

"Oh by the Gods!" She uttered in horror, covering her mouth and taking a step back. Then her hand flew out as the one name Ragnar stepped forward. He was utterly monstrous to look at with his horned face and beast like eyes that seemed to want to draw out my nightmares so that he may feast upon them.

"Calm yourself Kitten, no one is going to hurt you here." The biker said trying to reach me slowly as I had started moving backwards trying to get away from them all! I looked to him and when I saw the face of many beasts trying to break free I shrieked in fear.

"Holy Shit! What the Hell are all you people?!" Luc was stood the other side of me and could see what was going on as everyone seemed to crowd around as if ready to pounce.

"Give her some fucking space!" He snarled out at them all before turning back to me,

"Listen to me Katie, you need to concentrate, you need to fight this…focus on the sound of my voice and this will all go away…trust me, I will take care of yo…" Suddenly Draven broke free from his brother's hold and charged.

"She's mine!" He roared at him before flying straight into him, knocking them both onto the floor and rolling in a heap. Draven came out on top and was currently pounding Luc's head into the floor. Luc didn't put up with this for long as he managed to crack a sideways punch across Draven's jaw and it was enough for Luc to gain the upper hand.

"She can fucking see us, you Asshole!" Luc shouted at him but Draven was far too lost in his rage to listen. He charged at him once more and took him off his feet until he ran straight into the table. There he body slammed him onto the solid wooden top, only for it to split straight down the middle. Then he ripped one of the winged statues from the fireplace and with crumbling stone raining from its base he held it high above Luc, ready to kill him.

"Oh God!" I said putting my hands to my mouth just as Sophia had done and it was only when I uttered the question,

"What in God's name are you?" that he finally stopped, realising for the first time that I had witnessed everything. He was stood there panting in his torn clothes, wings out and still holding his weapon above his head.

"Are you still my Draven?" I asked through the tears and this was enough to finally stop the madness. He lowered the

statue and dropped it beside him, cracking the stone slabs underneath. The whole terrifying room was silent and the only sound made was coming from his heavy breathing and me trying to keep it together.

For long moments everything stopped. I just stood there as he did as if we were both too afraid what the other one would do if we moved. Then Draven looked around the room at both the destruction he had caused and the room full of Demons he had allowed me to see. I saw the very moment he realised what his actions had caused as pain sliced through his features. His eyes that were once purple simmered back down to black and he folded his wings back in a subdued, more relaxed position.

Then he did something that surprised me. He reached his hand out to Luc and with no hesitation, like I would have expected to see, he grasped the offered hand and let Draven pull him from the splintered wreckage.

"You are in love with my wife?" Draven asked him and Luc quickly looked to me, when I inhaled sharply. He straightened his stance, looked me right in my tear filled eyes and said,

"Yes." I sucked in a shuddering breath and let even more tears fall, for somewhere deep inside of me knew what this meant. They knew the depth of this single word spoken and I cried for the loss of so many things.

Draven winced against the torrent of emotions hearing this must have flooded him with and instead of tearing into him again he seemed to just accept it.

"Yet you know she can never be yours." He stated and it wasn't done in an arrogant way but just in a way that told him I had sealed my fate long ago and there was no going back now...And not one single part of me would ever want to go back on that vow, not even after seeing him before me as he was now.

Luc turned to face Draven side on and said,

"I know, old friend." Draven closed his eyes for a second, no doubt because of the pain he heard in Luc's bitter acceptance and then after placing his hand on his shoulder he said,

"Then it is done." Luc nodded. The moment quickly passed for him and everyone else but there were still two people that had explaining to do, so I wasn't surprised when Luc, knowing this, shouted,

"Everyone out!"

Draven and I didn't watch as Hell's creatures walked from the room. All we saw was each other as the door closed and left behind the fractured mind of a terrified girl that was so close to breaking entirely.

"You didn't answer my question." I told him, finally finding my voice and I was shocked when it didn't waver like I thought it would. He looked down at the floor for a moment as if trying to decide what he should do. I found something shocking in myself as I waited for what my answer would be and that was the longer I waited the more I started to panic. Not about what you would have expected after witnessing everything that just happened or finding out the truth about what these people were. It wasn't what they could do to me, or what they would for that matter. No, it was nothing that questioned my survival or even my beliefs in this world. It was all centred around one thing…

Around one man.

Was he still *my Draven?*

His answer first came in the actions he took as in only five long strides he was in front of me. He put both his hands on my face and told me the only thing I needed to hear,

"I will always be your Draven." And then he wrapped me in his wings and kissed me.

. . .

After this emotional turn of events, Draven simply picked me up and carried me back to his bedchamber without either of us saying another word. Once there I quickly realised the food had been cleared away and the bed had been remade. He set me down on the couch taking a seat opposite me and ran a hand through his hair before saying,

"Okay, so let's start from the beginning."

This turned out to be a long beginning, and even longer middle and the end, well that was taking us into the night. But by the time we were done, we both knew a lot more than what we started with. So much so in fact Draven was ready to storm into the Colony right now and massacre the whole lot of them just to be sure he punished anyone that had ever hurt me.

But even as I stated that we both knew a lot more, which was true, there was a lot that Draven held back and I could tell it wasn't because he wanted to. There was still the issue of this other life of mine looming over us and a lifetime of history I didn't remember wasn't what I needed right now. Sure, I was buzzing with questions, but as much as I wanted to know there was an equal amount that I didn't.

So even though Draven explained it the best he could on how we met, this was a difficult task without delving too much into my past life. At one point he asked me how I got my scars and he seemed surprised when I simply held up my arms and said,

"What these? Oh they were from the car wreck when Ari pulled me out. She has some too on her back." He gave me a kind and tender look and then raised them both up to kiss all the way down the various lines. After this I knew there was definitely more to the scars than I first thought as he seemed both saddened and strangely pleased by my answer.

So I continued on freely with my side of the story and he continued on restricted by his side. I managed to tell him most things about how Ari and I grew up and for a lot of it I could tell he struggled to hear all the pain we had suffered. I had only got as far as to tell him about my time at the Colony, not about when I escaped, which brought us to now and what I had to explain next.

"I think they were Vampires, like Lucius." I said his full name and this hadn't been for the first time today, as during our talk, I had learnt all about the real 'Luc'. I knew of the rocky past he and my other self had been through together but more importantly, what we had overcome. And in the end, what he had done for me.

"You mean these men you call the 'Fathers'?" He asked pulling both my legs up and draping them over him when he saw me stretching them out from being sat so long. I smiled at how natural the act was, still not used to that type of caring attentiveness that came from a lover who cared deeply for you.

"Yes. I mentioned about what we discovered they were doing to the girls every month…" I made a disgusted face at just thinking about it again. He nodded so I continued,

"Well, when Ari and I found the cabin, we knew what they had in store for one of us and how walking away from the Colony was never going to happen, so we knew we had to get away."

"So that's when you ran."

"Yes but…" I didn't know how to finish as I had tried to block most of the details from my mind.

"It's okay, let's just take a minute and continue…"

"But that's just it. I can only remember bits of what she said to me. She started acting crazy, telling me things I didn't understand at the time but now looking back, I think she was trying to tell me something important, something that could have helped us." I said after interrupting him and feeling as

324

though by not remembering every word she had said, I was not only letting him down but I was letting Ari down as well.

"I may have a solution to that but again you would have to trust me."

"I do." I told him, squeezing his hand.

"You know not what it means to me to have your trust and I can only hope my brother is rewarded with the same." I gave him a confused look and asked,

"Your brother? But what has he…?"

"He is my solution."

"Oh" Was all I thought to say. Since the disastrous meeting I hadn't seen anyone else as Draven thought it best not to until everything had been explained. I couldn't say I was looking forward to seeing these people again but not for the reasons you would expect. It wasn't through fear but through the utter shame I felt in my first reactions to seeing them in their 'True form' as Draven had called it.

The very first thing Draven had done since entering the room was to explain about his world and the people in it, most of whom had been in that room. He also explained how, before I lost my memories, that I had been used to his world long before he had ever come into it.

Then he continued to explain about my gift at seeing Demons and Angels in their natural forms, one I had been dealing with since the age of seven. He also had a theory that when I experienced Vincent's touch when he was in 'Angel protection mode' which is what I named it, that this is what must have triggered it. I then in turn told him about the Gypsy and he in turn told me how she worked for Lucius.

It all quickly started to slot together and make sense, so the next job after that was to teach me how to control it. I was shocked to find out he wasn't really an expert on this and when I asked him who was he told me,

"Well…you are." When I questioned him he simply explained that I had learned how to control it by first drawing what I saw, which then managed to lock out the form until I chose to see it again. Then he told me how my gift continued to get stronger before pretty soon all I needed to do was,

"Well, switch it on or off." He grinned at me and it took me a moment to decipher what that look was, until I realised it was pride.

However, other times it would be the choice of the supernatural being I was encountering at the time. Or in some instances in which the power gets too great for the supernatural to control both elements of sorcery and hiding what those around them can see. Sometimes what happens or what you see can't be hidden from the world as it's too important and the Gods take over. Fate intervenes and decides for you. It's just the way of their world Draven told me.

If you asked me, it all sounded very hazy with the rules and confusing enough to make me realise that I just needed to focus first and then make sense of it later.

Either way, after about half an hour of trying various different tricks he advised, I found it was only when the clock struck the hour that Draven's form went back to the one I was most used to. I gathered it had something to do with when I listened carefully to the number of chimes as my back was to the clock and I wanted to know the time.

"I did it!" I had shouted like an excited child finally finding the right answer to an equation and the praise I received from him came in the form of a kiss.

"As I knew you would."

A little after midnight Vincent came in to find me yawning and half asleep on the couch. Draven had gone to fetch him and as soon as they both walked through the door I shot up.

"I'm awake!" I shouted automatically like I would

sometimes do at the Colony when hearing my mother/bane of my life, banging on my bedroom door.

"I'm glad to hear it." Vincent said chuckling. I sheepishly pushed my hair back behind my ears and said,

"I'm so sorry about what happened earlier, I told Draven to apologise to your sister for me and..." At this point Vincent raised up his hand to stop me and said,

"After what you have been through, your reactions were only natural. Everyone understands that there is a great difference between learning how to cope with a gift such as yours on a daily basis as opposed to having one thrust upon you in a room full of the world's most powerful beings...*fighting.*" Vincent added this last word in reprimand aimed solely at his brother as he looked off to the side to where Draven stood. Draven cleared his throat and said,

"Yes, well let's get on with it should we." Then he walked towards me putting his back to Vincent who then winked at me, making me giggle. Draven and I hadn't discussed what happened back there between him and Lucius and to be honest, I think it was obvious enough that we didn't need to. I had kissed Luc back in the bus before Draven and I had even met, so even though I felt some guilt, it wasn't solely for Draven. Lucius, as I needed to start calling him, was simply a man in love with another man's woman, and from what I gathered, had been for a long time. I had to ask myself then, what had gone on between him and my other self?

My musings were quickly interrupted when Vincent came to sit down next to me.

"Are you staying this time?" I was about to ask what Vincent meant when I realised he wasn't speaking to me.

"I will."

"Very well but Dom, please try and..."

"I will control myself, just be gentle with her." Draven replied and I shot him a quick look of panic.

"As always." His brother replied in a smooth, hypnotic voice that could have one believing you would sit back happy while he tortured you with a smile on his face and be asking you to do the same.

"What are you going to do?" I asked him tentatively.

"Don't worry, it won't hurt. I am just going to access your memories to see if I can piece things together." I nodded, thinking that didn't sound so bad, so I gave him my hand.

"Oh wait, umm…well you might see something that I had no choice but to do and it was to save my sister, so you will…"

"She killed one of the bastards that hurt them." Draven stated very matter of fact and I had to grant it to him, it sounded much better the way he said it. I looked up at him to see him standing next to me like a private guard with his arms crossed over his chest.

"Fair enough." Vincent said and I coughed in surprise,

"No offense, but that's not very holy of you." I commented in jest.

"What can I say? I must get it from my father's side." Then he winked at me again and I instantly relaxed, which is what I think he was aiming for.

"You have done this before…right?"

"Yes, Katie, we have danced this tango before." I laughed and said,

"Oh good, because for a second there I thought…" I never got to finish before he suddenly made the connection. At first it felt like being plunged into an icy lake and for some reason my memories started to show me just that. I was floating under water in the dead of night, trapped in an arctic cage. Then someone burst through the icy roof above me, shattering my prison and saving me from death…*it was Lucius.*

I could feel my mouth opening and see in a fogged gaze the frozen breath escaping before being plummeted back through a series of memories I didn't recognise. Flashes of ones appeared that I did know but they were few and far between the horrors my past life had been filled with. So many prisons, so many captors, so much blood lost. If I thought life at the Colony had been hard then this was something else. But amongst it all there was hope, there was strength and there was *love*. A tremendous amount of love that if I had been standing would have knocked me over.

Pretty soon all visions that were shared between us became about the Colony and how I escaped. I didn't hear what Ari was saying to me by the wall that night but I could see her lips moving. I cried out her name silently, mimicking what I had done that night before falling back onto the other side of the wall.

This was the point I'd had enough and tried to pull away from him, knowing what he could possibly see if he hung on much longer.

"Vincent?" I heard Draven's voice as it was clear he must have seen the start of my distress but Vincent wasn't ready to let me go. He held on through, skipping passed Lucy's house, the fair, the gypsy, all of it until he finally found what he needed to see. It was the memory of him and Ari together. It started with how it did in the dream, with me walking in on Ari playing a glass piano and Vincent watching from the shadows.

But then it suddenly changed.

"Vincent stop! What are you doing?!" Draven shouted as he took over my own memory and banned me from seeing it. He took my dream from me until all that was left was a blank void as I was left staring into an empty nothingness.

"I SAID STOP!" Draven's command cut through his power over me and suddenly I was free.

"By the Gods Vin, what were you…?"

"My beautiful soul…*at last.*" Vincent whispered breaking into Draven's outrage.

"Vince? What's wrong?" Draven asked now replacing his anger with concern for his brother. Abruptly Vincent stood up and was at the door in seconds.

"Vincent, speak to me!" Draven said after making it to him in time to slam the door closed, not letting him leave before he gave him answers. I didn't know Vincent very well but even I knew that this was not the man I had met earlier. All his muscles were tense and his black motorcycle t-shirt was tight to his body, as if he was ready to spring into action at any second. His face had become hard and his eyes were glowing with an unusual darkness. It was as though the Angel in him had been locked away for a short time and what he had seen in the vision had brought out the demon.

"I found her." Vincent said determinedly and Draven jolted in astonishment.

"You're sure she is the one…the one from your dreams?" He asked and Vincent nodded.

Then replied firmly with every emotion he had behind the next four words…

"She's my Chosen One."

CHAPTER 26

RAW BEAUTY

" I need time Dom…just give me time." This was the last thing Vincent said before he left the room.

"Fuck!" Draven swore and banged his fist into the stone, making me jump. Then I don't know what possessed me but I flew off the couch and stormed right up to him and snapped,

"Don't do that! You could bloody well hurt yourself, you big Moose!" I took his hand in mine and brushed off the debris from his knuckles.

"Uh…did I just hear that right, did you just call me a… *Moose?"* I smirked and looked up at him saying,

"Maybe." To which he burst out laughing. He then picked me up and kissed me as though this was what he needed most before dealing with the aftermath of what had just occurred.

"Are you alright?" He asked me, still holding me close with my feet dangling above the ground.

"Yeah. It was just intense." I said giving him a half smile, trying to show him that I was okay. His brother on the other hand, I wasn't so sure about. Draven's head turned back to the door as if his thoughts ran parallel with mine.

"I think you need to tell me everything there is to know about Ari." I nodded thinking this was a good idea. We sat back down and I told him everything I knew and loved about Ari, including the things that drove me nuts, as sisters often did. I also told him how we both seemed to start dreaming about them both around the same time and at this Draven raised an eyebrow.

"Not together! Geez, I would need therapy! Witnessing that one dream of her and Vincent together was enough, thank you very much."

"I am sure it was. But I have to wonder if she shared any of your own dreams, when thinking of me." I thought about it and blushed, which he took for another reason. It wasn't so much the idea of what she would have seen but it was how did I tell him that it wasn't really me I saw him with in my dreams...*it was her.*

"What aren't you telling me?" He asked obviously picking up the regret on my face.

"I think there is something you should know."

"From the look of things, I agree." He said and I knew it was now or never.

"When I started to dream of you, it was never with us..." I motioned between us with my hand,

"...together."

"What do you mean?"

"Okay, I am just going to say it and hope you don't hate me." At this he laughed and said,

"I could never hate you." I didn't know if I believed this or not but I was about to find out.

"The first time I saw you it wasn't with me, it was with her."

"I'm sorry but I'm not following...who did you see me with if it wasn't with you?" I really wished there was an easier way to put this so I didn't sound quite so crazy but considering the whole thing was crazy then what options did I have.

"My other self."

"Excuse me?" Okay so now he looked completely baffled. This is the point it all came spewing out,

"Whenever I saw you, I would be watching through glass. Like a two-way mirror or something. I would be stuck there, like she was and neither of us could break through. I couldn't hear anything and neither could she but she would seem desperate to get to me and at first I always thought it was to escape…uh…"

"Ah…I see. You thought she was trying to escape from me." He said finishing off what I hated saying.

"Yes. But I didn't know you then. And what I saw of you confused me."

"How so?" He asked frowning.

"It scared me but it also excited me in a way I have never known. You have to remember I was different then. I hadn't experienced…umm, well, you know…what we experienced in the bathroom." At this he chuckled and said,

"Katie, that wasn't our first time." I knew what he was saying and it hurt that I didn't remember our actual first time together.

"Yes but to me it was. So before that I didn't know what it could be like…what it *was* like being with you. I didn't know at the time if you were using mind control on her…"

"Mind control?" I ignored his question and carried on,

"I didn't know she was there by freewill and not because you weren't her Demon captor…"

"Demon captor…? By the Gods, woman!" Again I didn't give him chance to say more,

"And I didn't know that when you made love to her and

then bit into her neck you weren't just keeping her there to feed from."

"Ah, I think I am beginning to understand where this is going." He said, so I continued,

"So naturally because of this, I assumed she was trying to get me to help save her but now I know what she really wanted…"

"She wanted to be free of you." He finished sympathetically and I lowered my head in shame.

"I was her captor and I didn't even know it. It must have been the only way for my subconscious to communicate with me, playing it out in my head like one of us was locked in a prison. I just stupidly always assumed it was her that was the prisoner but all this time, it was me."

"Hey, come on now, you are not to be blamed in any of this. Listen…listen to me." Draven repeated himself, raising my chin up so I had no choice but to look at him.

"Someone took you from me. They hid you away and so that I could no longer feel you in my world, they played with your mind. They took away your memories and made you believe you were someone else so they could control you." I had no choice but to believe in him, but it was still so difficult and for one very important reason.

"But…" I tried to explain but he continued,

"I don't know why yet but I promise you this, they will pay for the time they stole from us, and after they do, I will do everything in my power to get those memories back, if it's the last thing I do."

"But you don't understand." I said getting up from the seat as my emotions were bubbling too close to the surface.

"I understand enough Katie, to know that those who wronged us must suffer." He said firmly.

"No and I get that, I really do but what I mean is you don't understand what you're asking of me…"

"What I am asking of you?" Once again he didn't see it and I can't say that I really blamed him, not considering he knew who I was and wanted that lost part of me back…no, I couldn't blame him for that.

"What you're asking me to give up!" I said throwing my arms up and this was when it finally clicked.

"You mean *who* I am asking you to give up." His soft words made me close my eyes against the pain I had been running from ever since people started telling me I wasn't me. If I was utterly alone in this world then I would have gladly thrown that life aside for this one that Draven offered me now, but the fact of the matter was…I wasn't alone.

"Ari is my sister. *My twin* sister. And if what you are telling me, if what you are *all* telling me is true, then by my admitting it is like admitting that my love for Ari was never real. That our past together didn't happen. *That she's not my sister.*" Draven released a big sigh in defeat. Now he understood my reluctance in accepting who I really was.

"Come here." He held out his two fingers and motioned for me to go to him. I felt the tingles zing in my belly at the sight as no matter what this man did, he did it looking sexy as Hell…no pun intended!

I went over to him and as soon as I was within reach he gripped me by the waist and shifted me in front of him. I didn't need to look down much, even though he was sitting down because there was a big difference in my five foot three and his six foot four. Either way, he still manoeuvred me so that I was straddling his lap with my knees either side of his thighs.

"At some point we will figure this out but for now, let's just concentrate on getting your sister back here safely…after all, if the looks of my brother are anything to go by, then pretty soon I am sure I will be calling her sister as well." On hearing this, my eyes got wide and the thought of us all being here together was one I couldn't wait to make a reality.

"Will he be alright?" I asked, concerned about the way he had run out of here and to be honest, he didn't look too much like a man ready to settle down.

"It's complicated." Draven said looking thoughtful, no doubt going back and trying to gauge his brother's reaction to the news as if it was a good thing or a bad thing, just as I was doing now.

"How so?"

"Well for one thing, other than her connection with you, we don't know much about her." Okay so I had to give him that because if it turned out she wasn't my sister after all and she had simply had the same done to her as had been done to me… then I didn't know her either.

"Did you know much about me before we got together?" I couldn't stop myself from asking, however his answered stunned me.

"I knew everything."

"What?! How is that possible?" I asked frowning at him in disbelief.

"Well, alright, I will rephrase that for you. I knew everything about you that a crazed, obsessed stalker could find out about a person." I laughed and shook my head at the thought of anyone being obsessed by someone like me, especially because the person saying these things was Dominic Draven, sexiest man alive.

"So I didn't have a chance then uh?" I asked teasing him.

"Nope, not one." He said teasing back.

"So tell me, what particular powers of yours seemed to work on me then?" This time I found myself easily getting into this teasing game and his bad boy grin told me he knew it too.

"Let me show you." His voice quickly turned very seductive and he hadn't even done anything yet and I could already see a glimpse of what I was up against.

"For example, if I do this…" He started running a hand very gently up my spine and the sensations tingled all the way up to the base of my neck. I tried not to shudder against him, not wanting to lose the game we were playing but when you were playing against a pro, then what chance did I have?

"Then I can hear your lovely heart beating faster…and if I do this…" Quickly he pulled my hair so my head went back and my neck arched, baring my throat to him. I sucked in a surprised breath and instantly felt myself getting wet from being on the receiving end of his dominance.

"Then this little pulsating vein here starts to beg me to kiss it…" He kissed it softly and then he continued to speak against my skin,

"To suck it…" Then he sucked on the same spot and I moaned, arching further into him. I could feel his length pressing into me and I felt suddenly empowered knowing that he wanted me too.

"…and to bite it!" He growled and then took a mouthful of my flesh and held it with his teeth. The fear of pain and the anticipation of wanting that pain was sending me into a senseless fog with needing him inside me. He never bit me but I felt his knowing smile against my neck and around his teeth that still held me firmly in their grip. When he released me I moaned again only in disappointment making him chuckle.

"I do love how you react to me, little dove…like this…" Then he grasped my breast through my top and found my nipple with ease. He applied enough pressure to make me cry out and arch my back this time, forcing myself further into his hand.

"Ahhh!" I shouted a little louder as he wanted yet more of a reaction when he pinched harder.

"Oh how I have missed playing with you, touching certain parts of your beautiful body and getting you to obey without even knowing it. Like playing the finest instrument and making the sweetest sounds known to man." As he said this he quickly tore my bra cup away on one side and bit at my nipple until this time I was screaming out and rolling my hips against his erection like a woman possessed.

"And now I think it's time for the sound of you screaming my name as your body's core quakes around my cock." He said this after releasing my abused breast long enough to spin me around so my forehead was to the seat and he mounted me from behind. After ripping down my jeans and unbuckling his trouser pants, he thrust up hard into me and I cried out at the sting of pain that quickly forged itself into pleasure.

Now in this position it felt like I was truly owned. In fact, it felt like I was his submissive slave, there solely to give him the pleasure he felt he deserved. The idea warped my already turbulent mind, sending it into a spiral of desire and because of it I found myself screaming his name, coming after only a few deep thrusts.

One of his hands ran flat down my spine, whilst he reached round underneath me so that he could find what he was looking for.

"No! Ahh, too sensitive!" I told him as he started to drum his fingertip against my clit and as I tried to shift from him he pinched it hard, making me scream.

"Stay still for me, or I will do that again." He said sternly, which again only added to the carnal aspect of it all. I did as I was told but as a result continue to moan against it.

"That's my good girl, see how much fun having me play with you can be…now release another one for me, so I may feel you shuddering around me once more." He said bending over me and dominating me with his intimidating size. It wasn't surprising after only a minute more I was doing as he commanded, coming around him and once more screaming his name. If I thought the first time was intense then this was something else again. He was forcing my orgasms from me, one after another and all the while ploughing into me with such force, I felt if he hadn't been holding me, I would have shot to the other side of the room!

He was endless and brutal and I loved every tortuous second of it!

"Please, oh god Draven please...I can't have another...I..." I heard my pleas and he growled in my ear the same time he yanked me hard back against him. I whimpered back when the tip of his cock reached its limit inside of me.

"I am addicted to you...do you hear me...*fucking addicted!*" He snarled the words again in my ear and the thrill I got was like no other.

"My need for you borders on insanity, that is what you do to me. I want to drown in your touch and take my last dying breath smelling your hair. I want to feel you coming around me every single day for the rest of our lives and I want to hold your body in my arms as you shudder through the euphoria..." He never stopped moving as he spoke, gently in and out, continuingly rocking into me from behind and I was quickly getting lost in not only what his body was doing to me but also his words.

"And do you know what I demand in return, little one?" He hummed the question in my ear and for a moment everything stopped. His movement, my breathing, our hearts and time all stood still, until he yanked my head to one side, and growled by my ear,

"To own you forever!" Then he bit into me and sucked deep at my essence, feeding the very need he spoke of. I came one last time relishing in the feel of him doing the same. He ripped his lips from my bloody neck and thundered up at the ceiling as he held me rooted to his body behind. I felt as though my body had fallen apart under the immensity of it all but then stitched back together again just as quick. I felt broken and reborn all at the same time and it was only the feel of him holding me tight that kept me in one piece.

"You leave me and I am a man without a soul, you come back to me and I want to imprint my soul to yours so that you can never leave me again. So never again…never will I let you go again." I took in his words through a haze of ecstasy and knew I wouldn't last long before giving into the fight of exhaustion.

I could feel myself falling backwards or sideways or simply moving without being in control. Either way I didn't have the energy left to care because all that mattered was him and me and the raw beauty we shared.

So when I felt him lay me down, there was only one thing left to tell him…

"I love you Draven."

CHAPTER 27
TIME FOR RUNNING SCARED

Waking up and finding Draven beside me was more like a perfect beginning rather than the perfect end that I never wanted it to be. But inevitably when meeting the man you fall in love with, one you know beyond all shadow of doubt is your soulmate, destined to be yours forever, well then you have fear looking over your shoulder laughing at you. Because no matter how much you try, you can't help but be terrified that someone or something is going to come and take it from you! And even though I had not yet experienced this and hoped I never would, it still felt as if I had…many times before.

Was this to be the price for being with a man like Draven? Was I always to watch my back or was that hurt going to come from somewhere closer to home? I hated that I had to ask myself these things and even more so wondering now if Draven himself hadn't at some point been the one that had kick started a series of events that had led to this point? Because for some reason now I couldn't help but think back to when he told me he had lied to her and what type of lie would break someone's heart or hurt them to their core?

But did any of this really matter unless I was going to let myself run scared. Because taking the risk was worth what the outcome could be every time I would ask myself that question and that outcome was a lifetime with Draven. And as much as I wanted to protect myself from getting hurt, as I felt in my bones I had been before, I knew what level of pain would be waiting for me if I ever decided to walk outside these Afterlife doors without him.

I slowly shifted under the heavy arm he had draped over me and took my time to look at him under the moonlight that came through the glass doors opposite. It was just enough to dance across his features, now softened by the serenity of sleep. I quietly reached out and brushed back some of his raven black hair, feeling the greatest urge to take care of this strong man any way I could, or more like any way that he would let me.

I had no idea what it meant to be Draven, holding the weight of the world on your shoulders and I wondered if I ever would. But that didn't mean I couldn't be the woman by his side that helped him through the difficult times. It didn't mean I couldn't be his Lucy to my Denis, his Sophia to my Zagan or even his Pip to my Adam. Because they were all the same…*we* were all the same if only we chose to be…if only we chose to embrace love with everything we had. No restraints, no what ifs, no what could have been. No, it was all or nothing and that was what Draven deserved…

My all and none of my nothing…And I knew right now I would rather die giving him that than live knowing that I hadn't.

I don't know the reason I awakened but decided to use the bathroom before trying to get back to sleep. I carefully wrestled myself free from Draven's arm and set it back down where I had been lay. Then I turned round and looked down to find my footing as I remembered the bed was surrounded by steps it was that high.

"What the...?" My muttered sentence trailed off as I saw long shadows start to grow and branch out around my side of the bed. It almost looked like some dark creature was under the bed trying to claw its way out. I looked back to Draven to see he hadn't moved but by the time I moved back to view the shadows once more, *they* had moved.

They started to elongate and join in certain places that started to form letters. It was just like the blood had been when it had poured from my nose in Lucy's house. I didn't understand what was going on and just before I turned to wake Draven up, the letters finally formed into words.

'*Take a step towards your destiny,*
Walk this line to find the key,
Answers await you beyond your sanity,
So take your freedom and follow me.'

I don't know why I did it but I just couldn't help myself. I was being lured into the unknown with the promise of answers something inside of me was desperate to find. Was it me...the other me that was controlling this now? I couldn't say for sure but I had to find out, which was why I placed one foot on the floor, reaching out my toes so that I could be ready to pull myself back at any minute.

But as soon as my big toe made contact the stone beneath it started to waver and the words started to blur. I know what I should have done at that point but I was too captivated by the unknown to stop now. So I took a deep shuddering breath and plunged straight in...

Literally.

My foot hit the ground and sunk through the stone floor as if it was water. Half my leg was missing as black shadows swirled around it like black ink. I looked back to Draven and reached out but he kept getting farther and farther away from me. The bed was growing and stretching, taking him with it and out of my grasp. I knew now there was no going back, I had to continue…

So I jumped.

And instead of falling through the air like I had expected I was back in the freezing lake Vincent had taken me to earlier. I had plunged into my own icy grave and this time there was no angel to keep me linked to the world and there was no demon to drag me out. I was simply suspended in the water like time had no meaning down here. I looked around with the last of my breath and saw there was a world beneath me. I squinted in the dark water to see fire burning on torches and men in cloaks walking past with staffs taller than they were.

I looked up one last time to see the distorted night sky through the ice and knew my only hope lay beneath me. So with the last of my air quickly running out I made the decision to let myself sink to the bottom. I saw the vision getting clearer the lower down I got and just before I opened my mouth to seal my death by swallowing down freezing water I felt air touch my big toe.

I looked down and astonishingly saw that the surface of the water was beneath me! I reached out my hand feeling the air also hit my fingertips, so I did the only thing I could…I swam to the surface below me. I was just crying out for more air as my head breached the core and suddenly I fell, landing on stone and gasping for air. My lungs burned at how close I had come to succumbing to the deep.

I looked up, pushing my soaking hair back so I could see where I had travelled to. I managed to stagger to my feet, still taking in my strange surroundings of what looked like underneath a castle but it was so dark down here. With only a single torch mounted on the wall I could only make out certain details. Like the cobbled stone that looked like wet chipped flint knitted together creating the uneven floor on which I now stood. I looked up to see the water waving softly above me and I reached up, touching it like you would the sea when on a small boat. Not one drip escaped and the sight quickly started to play havoc with my equilibrium.

I bent over and had to breathe through my nose, trying to quell the urge to be sick because the ceiling above me was moving when it shouldn't have been. The sound of a giant lever being moved made me look up quickly to find one of the robed figures I had seen when in the water. His black cloak hid most of him from sight and he reminded me of a demonic monk, with the large hood he wore being separate from the rest of the robe.

The lever protruded from the wall and the robed man needed two hands to push it down, causing the sound of grating metal to echo, bouncing around the bare stone walls. He didn't look at me and it wasn't like I was easy to miss. I was stood in a white floaty nightdress that clung to my skin as if someone had poured white paint all over me. Draven must have dressed me in it after I fell asleep in his arms.

"Hello?" I said, testing out my voice to see if he would respond. I can't say I was surprised when he didn't because if he wasn't going to notice a dripping wet girl in her nightie, then he wasn't going to hear one being polite.

"What is this place?" I murmured to myself, seeing as no one would be answering me anytime soon. It was still so dark in here and when the flaming torch began to flicker and crackle, I knew it wouldn't be lasting much longer. This was proven shortly after the thought and I froze as I was suddenly plunged into darkness.

"No!" I gasped the second it died. I held my hand up and dread quickly started to be replaced by cold hard fear as I could see nothing.

I spun around in the pitch black when I heard a crank turning, grinding against something that sounded like it was scorching stone, trying to ignite it. I followed the sounds around the room and screamed when flames travelled down the centre, making me jump out of the way, so that I wouldn't get burnt. I hadn't realised there was a long gully carved out of the centre that must have held something flammable for it catch fire like that. This lit up the room and I found that seeing where I was for the first time was no better than the dark.

"I'm in a prison!" I said looking down the long corridor at too many doors to count. Each crude iron door that I could see looked as if they had been hammered into shape by a giant with a mighty hammer. Dips, bumps and bowl shapes made all the doors uneven but the massive rivets kept everything in place. Each one had grated squares at head height and I could only hope none of them were occupied.

It was a medieval looking place, with chains and other devices I didn't want to think about hanging from the walls. I wanted to ask why I was here and what had brought me to this place but there was no one to ask. Even as the robed figure walked towards me now, there was no acknowledgement of my existence.

"The blind don't see and the deaf don't hear." Came a voice from farther down the row of doors. I had to take a minute to let my racing heart calm down from the fright...so I wasn't alone. I watched as one of the figures walked right past me and as it did, I gasped as I finally saw his face under the hood.

Blood soaked bandages covered eyes that were no longer there and looked like they had been gouged out long ago by his own blood stained fingertips. I also couldn't help but gag when seeing his ears had been sliced off and the hole that would have been left had been sewn shut, with the thick stitches in the shape of a star. Even what little I could see of his grey dead looking skin had symbols carved into it by what looked a thin blade.

I finally could breathe again once he had passed me and continued to walk the length of the prison like some mindless drone.

"Who's there?" I asked looking each way down the corridor, so nothing could creep up behind me.

"Many demons hide in plain view however it is the demons in your mind you should be afraid of." I glared into the endless space now knowing which side the voice had come from. I followed the robed figure from much further back and wondered what he was doing when he raised his arm out to one of the doors. Elongated, bloody fingers stretched out from beneath the lengthened sleeve like a spider coming from behind his chosen home. They extended out one by one and one by one they folded back into a fist. As soon as the last finger curled there was snapping sound that resembled someone breaking a stick and then a vicious howl of pain followed quickly after.

"Jesus!" I shouted in fright however the robed figure didn't even flinch as he continued down his path.

"He won't help you down here." The voice sniggered.

"Who are they?" I asked as I continued to follow the voice.

"Death Wardens." I don't know what surprised me more, the fact my question had been answered or the fact it had been answered by a girl.

"Why do they look like that?"

"They do it to themselves, it is part of a rite of passage if one wants to join the brotherhood." She told me.

"That's barbaric!" I said horrified that I had been right, he had gouged out his own eyes!

"It's what makes them such a good choice for death wardens. No sneaky little spells to be cast if one doesn't see it or hear it."

"So how do they do their job?" I asked wondering if I hadn't already witnessed it.

"They can only feel the presence of evil, the intent to do harm, escape or just a whole magnitude of unlawful things."

"But how would they stop such things?"

"Oh they have their powers and aren't called Death Wardens for nothing...you can't drown out your demons if they know how to swim." She added cryptically and this made me look up at the water ceiling, still floating gently above me. I nervously then looked to the doors as I passed them and for the most part I was happy when I wasn't tall enough to see inside...of course that was until the next door, when I realised I had spoken too soon.

As I approached the door I had seen the 'Death Warden' raise his hand to I tried to tell myself not to look and for the most part I achieved this. That was until I heard the voice...but surely it was a trick.

"Come here dearie...I have a treat for you, hold out your hand so I can give you some candy." I looked to the door as soon as I heard the sweet voice of an old lady and quickly thought it must be a trick. Why would she be down here locked up in this dreadful place?

"The only treat she has in store is for herself if she ever got hold of you. Now come to me, Katie." I was startled to hear the girl knew my name but for some reason I couldn't help trust in what she was telling me.

"Don't listen to her, she just wants your bones for herself... now come here and let me kiss you." The old lady said and I took a panicked step back only to take a quick one forward again, as I felt the heat at my back from the flames I had forgotten about. I stumbled forward because of it and put my hand out to stop myself from falling and landed against the door.

"That's it pretty girl, you will look nice bathed red like the wolf I ate." I looked up slowly and screamed! Because there lurking from the shadows was an old woman stepping forward with the most terrifying face a woman could hold. It was the ageing face of death in motion. A face so wrinkled and cracked it looked painful to move and that creepy smile slit the skin right in front of my eyes. Blackened, rotting teeth were filed into tiny points and peeling flesh curled away from the bone on her forehead. She looked half decayed but her forbidding eyes that lit up with anticipation spoke volumes to how alive she felt with the sight of her prey close to being in her grasp. Tiny black dots grew larger at the centre of white cloudy eyes, eyes that matched the hair that was pinned back like a respectable old woman ready to meet with company.

"Move away slowly, Katie." The girl warned me and when she did the old woman snarled like a cornered beast protecting its kill. I did as I was told and ended up falling backwards when panic took over. She had lunged for me though the low bars and she roared,

"LET ME PICK YOUR BONES, YOU WILL LIKE IT!" Down at me. I scrambled up and that's when I decided to run. I quickly wished I had never stepped off the bed into this nightmare world! I continued running too scared to find out what was in this place with me until pretty soon I had no choice but to stop. I had come to the end of not just the room but the end of everything!

I pushed open the single door at the end praying for an exit but not like the one I was offered. Because the world that I knew had reached its limit on living and now I stood at the brink of its end. As the wood swung back against itself I saw all that was left and like that damned picture in my room, the world was crumbling away into the bowels of Hell below. I stood at the cliffs edge clutching onto the wooden frame as if this would save me.

"It doesn't need to be like this." A voice said from behind me. I turned around still gripping onto the frame, not wanting to fall like the others.

"I don't understand, what does this all mean...? Why do I keep seeing the end of the world like this?" I asked, in a desperate plea for answers. The robed figure that was stood before me now was dressed all in white and the hood she wore reached down to her chest, hiding everything from view.

"Because you're the only one who can stop it from happening." She told me and I shook my head in denial.

"No, you've got it wrong! I can't stop this! I can't stop anything like this...I mean...how would I?! I'm just a girl...I just a normal girl!" I told her, crying out and trying to make her understand.

"Normal doesn't exist in any world, least of all yours. Remember these words...'Time. Time Keira, that's all our world is. 'Faith has its tight grip on our lost time like endless sands we cannot touch. Oceans of hopeful space between us mean nothing if the ship cannot sail and Courage is lost in the darkness without the stars to guide us. One by one the crimson moon will take our sisters of the earth on a never ending journey of stolen power. The cups will fill, blood will flow and nine by nine will fall to the Hexad. Time is power. Power leads to destruction. Destruction brings forth the end of Time...our time." She spoke these words as though everything was on the line and it was all up to me.

"What does that even mean?! What must I do?!" I asked needing her to tell me!

"Take away their time and you take away their power. They have taken eight...don't let them take nine. Find yourself and learn of the Prophecy's seven, find the key and you will find me next time in Heaven"

"But I don't know...wait! Don't go, what key...WHAT KEY?!" I shouted as she turned around and started walking the other way.

"I will be here waiting for the Electus to come home. Find the centreless key to unlock the door to your mind, as bartering for souls is what he must bind. In blood and in tears and flames will be the price but that will be nothing but a roll of the dice." She spoke the words as clear as if she had been stood next to me but hearing them meant nothing if I didn't understand them. I watched as her ghostly figure was disappearing from sight and I shouted one last time,

"But what does it mean!"

"To remember there is power in time and it is time for you to remember...

"To take time back."

CHAPTER 28
I KNOW YOU

"Eight Girls!" I shouted bolting upright in bed.

"Keira?" Draven called out the name he was most used to and being half asleep I can't say that I blamed him. Even the girl in my dream had called me it, so I just gathered I should get used to it, for a time anyway as I think if people were still calling me it in my eighties I might be a bit pissed off by then.

"It's okay, I'm okay." I told him as he reached for me as if quickly turning into protection mode.

"What is it...what's wrong?" It was sweet and heart wrenching at the same time when seeing how he feared for me. As if he kept expecting me to disappear at any moment and considering what had happened in the past, I couldn't say with certainty that it would never happen again. Which compelled me to ask him,

"Tell me about the mirror." He took a deep breath and rubbed his forehead as he thought about what I was asking him. I knew the basics, which considering my dreams it hadn't exactly come as a shock to me. But I had a feeling that we were missing something important…and that something I had a feeling he was keeping from me, but the question was…why?

"First tell me why you cried out 'eight girls'?" I don't know why but something told me not to tell him about the girl in my dream and what she had said…almost like some strange feeling came over me, whispering 'that would be cheating'. It was odd but no matter how I tried to fight it I couldn't, so instead I told him a warped version of the truth.

"I heard voices whispering to me about the Hexad and how to stop them." At this Draven seemed to breathe a little easier. He pulled me close and said,

"I wouldn't worry, soon we will be making plans to leave here and we will be dealing with them in our own way…you have nothing to fear in that." I smiled up from where he held my head to his shoulder, embracing me in no doubt an attempt to sooth my worries. But as much as I relished being in his arms, I knew I had been given that dream for a reason.

"Can I just ask though, has every one of your plans turned out the way you expected?"

"In regards to you?" I nodded and he huffed out a laugh before saying honestly,

"No, hardly ever in fact."

"Okay, then you won't be offended if I come up with a backup plan…just in case of course." I knew with the undemanding look he gave me that the next words out of his mouth would sound patronising but I didn't take offense, as I knew he hadn't seen what I had seen.

"If it makes you feel better, then I can see nothing wrong in doing so."

"So getting back to the mirror?" I asked and I think I could hear him groan in his mind.

"Do we have to discuss this…*again.*" I almost laughed at

what a whiny teenager he sounded but after all we had spoken about today, I knew he had a weakness.

"Alright, would you prefer to tell me how old you are?"

"Fine. I came back into the room thinking you were still getting dressed or struggling to decide what to wear, as was often the case…"

"Draven." I said his name in warning as I knew he was trying to brush over what I wanted to know.

"I walked in and as soon as my feet crunched on the mirrored shards, that's when I knew something had happened. I found the empty frame and after searching everywhere for you for weeks, you had simply vanished. It was the first time I couldn't feel you." His pain ridden expression made me feel guilty for asking these things but I needed to know. I don't know why but something kept nagging at the back of my mind.

"What do you mean you couldn't feel me?"

"Ever since you came into my life I have been able to sense you and the closer we became the stronger the bond grew. But when you disappeared it was as if someone had severed that bond, slicing through the tie that bound together our souls." The way he spoke about our destiny and fate bringing us together always sounded so magical and now was no different, which is why I hated asking,

"Did you not then…uh…how do I say this…?"

"Did I not think you were dead?" He finished for me and I winced at how gut wrenching it sounded for him.

"No." He answered sternly.

"Why not?"

"Because when I said I searched for you everywhere…I mean, *everywhere.*" I gasped as the penny dropped on what he was trying to tell me. He had gone to Heaven and Hell in search of me!

"Besides, the mirror told me enough to know witchcraft was involved."

"How so?" I asked knowing he had definitely missed this part out when explaining the first time.

"As soon as I picked up a piece of the glass it showed me only one vision and that was of you sleeping, calling out my name. I shouted for you and that was when all of the pieces of glass turned into dust. I tried to get it back but my powers were useless against it. In fact, it seemed the more we tried to find you with powers of our own, the stronger the resistance we were faced against. In the end it was surmised that we had unknowingly fed the contending force but of course by then it was too late, that damage had already been done." I can't imagine what it must have been like for him. To see the person, you love slip through your fingers and fade into nothing, knowing there wasn't a damn thing you could have done. For a powerful being like Draven I can imagine this hadn't been received well. No wonder he didn't like talking about it!

"So I left nothing behind?" He frowned, thinking a moment and then shook his head.

"Nothing, not even your wedding ring." He said lifting up my hand and kissing the finger it had been on for only a single night. This made me sad again thinking about it as I had shed few tears over hearing it the first time. How cruel was fate anyway, to give us only one night at being man and wife before ripping it away from us!

"I have never seen it." I told him wondering where in the world it was now. Yes, it was a sad thought indeed knowing the symbol of our love was stolen from me and the saddest part of it all was that I couldn't even remember what it looked like.

"Hey, don't do this to yourself." Draven said.

"Do what, there's not a lot I can do when I don't even remember saying my vows or even knowing what my first kiss as a married woman felt like." This was when he gripped my chin and lifted my face to his.

"It was beautiful, like every kiss we share." He said before placing his lips to mine and kissing me so softly, it alone made me want to cry for it felt so close...oh so close, I could almost touch the memory for myself when he kissed me this way. Then he deepened the kiss and I felt myself being pushed back against the bed, quickly losing myself in his gentle touch. He pulled the covers from my body, baring my insecurities to him and silencing them once and for all with the adoring way he admired my naked form. Then without saying a word to each other he simply looked into my eyes and gave me that piece of him I needed to feel.

I cried out silently as I felt his strength slip inside of me, touching that forbidden part of me that was only his to explore and conquer. He reached up, shackled my wrists and held them above my head as he took me to that secret place only two people in love can find together. Because up until now every time we had united our bodies this way I had been consumed by the intensity of it all but this...well, there was only one word to describe what this was, what this would *always* be was...

Love.

Later that day came the meeting take two, this time without me freaking out but this probably had something to do with the fact that I wasn't there. Draven had decided it best not to push me too far when it came to my newly mastered skills at controlling my 'gift'. He thought a more gradual intake of the world's most powerful beings would be a wiser route to go down, and I couldn't say I disagreed with him.

Let's just say that I hadn't been chomping at the bit to get back in that room and face them all again. But like I said before, this hadn't been because I was still scared of them all. No, it was because I was still ashamed of the way I had handled things and thinking back to how they were just trying to all help me at the time, didn't make it any easier. And poor Sophia, she had been nothing but nice to me and the way Draven described our relationship before my memory loss was as if we were sisters.

So this is why I told Draven to tell them how sorry I was until the time was right when I could say it myself. He told me in his 'I am a man and I know best' kind of way that this was not needed but I felt adamant that it was. Which was why I wouldn't let him leave before he promised me.

I also asked if it was possible for him to first get me some more clothes, as I still didn't want to face that dressing room. The second was if he could somehow get my bag to me. I hadn't seen it since I arrived and I was worried about Lucy as she hadn't heard from me in a few days. I just had visions of her forcing Dex to call the FBI to get them to do a worldwide manhunt in search of me.

Draven had given me a short kiss on the cheek after handing me another chosen outfit before leaving. He also told me that he would have someone fetch my bag for me and to expect it after I was finished in the bathroom. To be fair I don't think he was anticipating me being in the shower for at least ten minutes longer than usual as I couldn't fathom how you turned the bloody thing on! It was only when I fully walked in there and started patting the walls like I was Indiana Jones looking for some lost city, that the water scared possibly a little wee from me.

Luckily for me though I was in the right place for potential embarrassing accidents and thankfully had gone on my tap/lever finding mission in my birthday suit. So other than a high pitched girly scream, I had a very peaceful and more importantly, uneventful shower.

Once I was finished, I towel dried my hair as I was always used to doing and wiped the steam from the gilded mirror. I looked at my reflection and little by little I was starting to change. To begin with it had been slight when at Lucy's but now I was here you could really see how free I felt. The dark circles around my eyes had altogether disappeared and my hair now had more of a healthy golden colour to it. It was softer, along with my skin now that I was no longer forced to use that harsh soap on my face.

I think looking in the mirror now was actually the first time upon seeing my reflection that I felt like a woman. I let the towel slip off one shoulder and decided to attempt the sexy look. I even pouted my lips and looking to the side over my shoulder, tried my best to look seductive. In the end I just burst out laughing at myself.

"Ha! I think you need to work at playing the Sexy Vixen, Kay Bear!" I said out loud and walked back into the room in just my small towel, as I'd used the bigger one for my long hair.

"Ahhh! Holy shit! What are you doing in here?!" I shouted at the sight of Lucius stood in the door frame. I quickly tugged down at the bottom of the towel that barely covered what I considered south of the indecent border. I also tightened the top without flashing him my girls. And Jesus, did he have to look so bloody composed, cocky and freaking handsome! I mean he was King of the Vampires for sucking blood sake!

He held up a canvas bag hung from one finger and said,

"I got to play errand boy…*Vixen.*" He said smirking and flashing a bit of fang. I rolled my eyes and tried like holy hell to act like I was immune to his charms. Of course this was easier said than done, considering who was I kidding, was there a human on the planet immune?

"Well thanks for the bag…oh and please don't call me that." I said thinking it felt weird coming from him and not Draven. I mean ever since I had found out how he felt about Draven's wife Keira, not me because let's face it…he didn't know me… or thinking about it like that neither did Draven.

"That's some hard thinking you're doing over there, Kay Bear…do you need to take a seat?" He said and this time I went right in for scowling at him. No surprise when he started laughing, taking me about as serious as a papercut.

"Funny, isn't it time for you to turn into a bat or something?" I said trying to keep a straight face when teasing him. This time he was the one to roll his eyes.

"Yes, right after my fight with Van Helsing, I can pull the stake from my heart, pick my teeth with it and wash my mouth with holy water, before bedding down for the night in my coffin." He said in a serious tone that I suspected was him still teasing me. However, I was still suckered in enough to ask,

"You sleep in a coffin?"

"Fuck no! I sleep like a freakin' starfish!" I burst out laughing at this and nearly lost my towel.

"I think I should go change."

"Don't feel the need on my account sugar, I am quite enjoying the view." He said and I don't know why but his bad boy grin made me look down. I gasped at the distinct shape of a rather large erection pressing against the tight black leather pants he wore.

"Oh God!" I said hiding my eyes and I ran off into the bathroom after grabbing the clothes off the arm of the sofa.

"It's all the extra blood I suck, remember!" I heard him shout before I slammed the bathroom door shut. I could still hear him laughing as I was pulling up a pair of stone wash jeans. These were more of a boot cut and didn't fit so tight to my legs this time but like the other pair they were just as soft. I don't know if it was daft or not but I found myself wondering if I would be allowed to keep these clothes once everything was... well I don't know...said and done maybe?

It was strange even thinking about it really. Would Draven and I date? I mean I know we were married but did that still stand considering it hadn't been me that had said my vows? Where would I live? I know Draven had started to tell me about my other family but I had to stop him before he'd begun. Thankfully he had understood why quickly after explaining my fears about losing Ari. Of course that didn't mean I wasn't near bursting with curiosity and the idea of having another family was both an exciting and terrifying prospect.

But I told Draven that when I find out about them would be the day that I would want to meet them and to first do that I would have to relearn everything about them. This was obviously something that needed to wait until I saved my sister and for more good reasons than not. But it didn't mean I didn't wonder what it was going to be like.

"You still alive in there? By God's Asshole, you'd better not have been kidnapped again, because I swear to fucking..."

"Calm down. I'm a girl remember, we have more shit to do." I said after quickly pulling the burgundy long sleeved shirt over my head.

"Well you never know with you. Even mirrors are hazardous to your health." He said and this time when I frowned at him, I really frowned.

"That isn't funny."

"Oh trust me sweetheart, it is. Although looking for you for eight months wasn't, so my grave apologises, my fair maiden." He said bowing, making it hard to stay angry at him.

"You said grave on purpose didn't you?"

"You got me...oh but come on, believing all that TV shit

about Vampires and what did you expect." For some reason I had switched off and quickly blurted out,

"Can you swim?" He gave me one of those 'What now?' looks and said,

"Okay, I must have missed that movie. You're gonna have to help me out with this one pet, because I have no…"

"Did you ever save me from drowning in a frozen lake?" I said and for some reason I *needed* to know.

"Ah, so I guess this means that not all memories are lost to you?"

"So I guess that means a yes." I replied back, knowing I was fixating on that because of what the girl in my dreams was trying to tell me. That was why I fell through the water to get to her…she was drawing the memory out of me.

Lucius looked like he was trying to get a read on me and I felt a strange sensation, like something nagging and pulling at my mind. Long intruding fingers were trying to pick their way through the void and I frowned at him wondering if this was his doing.

"Sorry Love, it was worth a try." He said shrugging his shoulders like trying to pick through someone's brain was like forgetting to put sugar in their coffee!

"Yeah, well it doesn't work, trust me, we tried." He knew I was referring to Draven and I and I could also tell he hid a lot of reactions so that he wouldn't give away his feelings…feelings that had already been admitted in front of everyone. At some point we would need to talk about it but it didn't feel like my place to do so…*it was Keira's.*

"Alright sweetness, in answer to your question yes, I did save you that night but it was also through my mistakes that landed you there in the first place, so don't go making me out to be a hero here because I'm…"

"But you are!" I shouted interrupting him as I wasn't willing to listen to him say otherwise.

"Look, I know I may not have all my eggs in one basket here...I mean Christ, it's probably not even eggs I'm looking for..."

"Losing me here, love."

"The point is I may not remember everything between us Lucius but I know what you have done for me and...I. Know. You. Don't ask me how or why but that day on the bus I trusted you and in that bathroom you proved me right. You saved my life I don't know how many times but I have a feeling its becoming a habit...am I right?" I asked and he laughed before saying,

"Habit...Hell, with you girl, it's a fucking hobby!"

"Alright, no need to be dramatic it about it...*pussy.*" I muttered the insult so he could hear it and I couldn't believe it had come out of me. His wide eyes flickered brighter and this told me he thought the same. He took the few steps that were between us, coming so close I now had to look up.

"Now *there* was my Little Keira girl." He said fervently looking down at me. I couldn't help but blush as I felt the heat coming off him, knowing that right now he was looking at me the way he looked at her and I had to wonder...

What was it about this Keira?

"I uh..." I didn't know what to say but thankfully he took the lead, as most of these supernatural men seemed to do.

"Don't worry beautiful, I am learning swiftly on how to behave, but hey, if it slips and I feel like kicking ass again, then you know where I will be before it." He said winking.

"Kicking ass?" I said questioning him on who really kicked whose ass, teasing him once more.

"Hey what do you know, you missed most of my good hits

freaking out. And you call me a pussy!" I had to laugh as he had a point.

"Speaking of pussies, then I'd better get going before there's a dog fight." He said and I now knew from my conversation with Draven that he was talking about Jared and his crew.

"Well, you be careful if you have to break one up." I said and he scoffed before saying,

"Who said anything about breaking it up, I just said I wouldn't want to miss it...after all, it's been a few years now." Again around Lucius I couldn't help but roll my eyes, of course trying to fight a smile whilst doing it.

"And thanks for this..." I said pointing at my bag but then I quickly frowned down at it.

"Oh wait, but this isn't mine." I told him but when I looked back up I found he had already left.

"Okay, so not big on goodbyes then." I said to no one and then stared down at the canvas bag that still looked familiar. So I wondered, could it have belonged to me...*before?*

I plonked myself down next to it and for some reason poked at it. I don't know what this was supposed to have achieved exactly but neither did it explode or did anything gross pop out of it, so I took these both as good signs. I wanted to open it as much as I didn't. For a start it belonged to someone else's life and that was something I knew wasn't the time to be opening that can of discovery but what if it held something important in it. What if Draven had forgotten that this was something I left when they took me...what if it had the clue I felt as if I had been looking for?

So I looked

And what I found nearly killed me all over again...

"Holy Shit...we're in trouble now."

CHAPTER 29
OH YEAH, I KNOW THE BITCH!

I ran out of the door without shoes or socks on and my feet slapped against the stone floor but I didn't care. I had to get to Draven! I had to tell him what I found as it could change everything. He was there now in that meeting making plans against an enemy that he didn't know but I did.

What I had found was the last nail hammered into the box that contained everything I thought I knew. Well now it was confirmed, everything they told me was true and everything I *thought* I knew was lies. Draven had been right, it was all done to control me, my whole life and that's what Ari saw that night. She had tried to tell me our lives and everything we thought we knew about growing up was all…

One. Big. Lie.

"Lucius!" I shouted his name when I saw him round a corner and I thanked my lucky stars I found him in time before I got lost. I rounded the corner way too quickly not realising he would be stood there waiting for me. I ran straight into him and he caught me before I bowled him over.

"Whoa! Where's the fire?" He said and I shuddered at the

thought of it. The fire, the man I killed, my prison, never a home! Jesus, but I thought it had been there most of my life! And Ari...what about Ari and I? What about...no! No, I couldn't do this now, I had to focus!

"Katie? What's wrong?"

"I have to find Draven! That bag...you don't know what was in that bag!" Lucius frowned down at me and instead of coming up with a witty remark he grabbed my hand and we set off running together.

"Sorry Honey but your little legs just won't cut it! Hold on." He said swinging me up into his arms so he could run at his own great speed. Carrying me didn't seem to faze him or drain his stamina in any way. No, he simply ran at a dizzying speed and I was left with no other option than to do what he told me to, which was to hang on.

We quickly came to the door I recognised and when Lucius set me down and opened the door I half expected to walk in and see it the way I had last time. But it was back to being perfect and I knew if I didn't have this impending doom lurking over me then I would have asked how any of it was possible. But instead of running in there and enquiring about their quick decorating skills, I ran in there and blurted out,

"It's my mother!"

"Well at least it's not sperm this time." The one name Sigurd said dryly... and cryptically I might add.

"Katie?" Draven said, standing quickly at the sight of me. I ignored all the stares I got and walked down the length of the table passing everyone. It was as though I'd had something I should have done before being taken. Something important that might have changed everything if I had only chosen a different path. Was this part of me taking back time? Well there was only one way to find out and to do that I only needed to show

Draven one thing. So I pulled out the piece of paper I had stuffed into my back pocket as I felt like I had done once before.

Draven could see it was something serious as the worry was clear to see. But I continued to the top of the table as silence descended like a devastating wave. I felt my hands shaking as the anger of it all was bubbling over.

"Easy now." Draven said but I didn't understand why or how you could have heard a pin drop in the vast marble room. I could hear the sound of my own heart beating and pounding undiluted fury around my body until I felt like I was pulsating with power.

"Dom?"

"It's alright, I've got this...Katie, I don't know what's happened but you need to calm down." I frowned and felt a spark snap at my fingers in my frustration with him.

"Okay...okay, let's just take a breath." What was wrong with him, did he not understand how important this was?!

"Lucius...give me something here." Draven said without taking his eyes from mine.

"Hey, I've got nothing, she was fine getting here." What were they all talking about?! I had the proof in my hand, the proof that I had been lied to all this time! She wasn't my mother! She never had been and now the horrifying truth I had to face was that Ari wasn't...My Sister.

Oh God! I could feel something coming. I could feel something building and I didn't know what to do with it...what do I do with it?! I needed to do as Draven told me, I had to calm down. I had to but if Ari was here she would know...Ahhh! And there it was, the hate! The burning hate I had for the one responsible. *She* was to blame, for all of this! *She* put me through the pain!

She...she...

"She did this to me!" I shouted, slamming down the picture on the table and causing cracks to branch off all around my hand. I looked down at that face once again and that was it.

"SHE TOOK MY LIFE FROM ME!" This time I screamed and I heard someone shout before I erupted,

"HIT THE DECK EVERYONE!"

"I WILL KILL HER!" This time I roared out over the picture and before Draven could reach me I released all that rage and fury and power all at once, feeling it come straight from my hands like a storm building until it became uncontrollable!

Everything in the room was blown backwards with such a force that everything smashed into the stone walls like I was the bomb and I had just gone off. All that was left was a clear radius around me that I was stood in and I panted like a wild beast trying not to charge at any of the fearful beings around me.

I couldn't seem to get enough air and for the moment that's all I concentrated on. I was looking down at the dip in the stone I stood in with my hair as a curtain around me.

Then I started to remember what had just happened and horror started to replace the anger. And then quickly what followed was the sorrow as realisation seeped in at what I had not only done but what I had finally lost and looking around now at the faces I didn't recognise, it looked as though I had lost...

Everything.

"Draven?" I called out his name looking around and seeing the destruction I had astonishingly caused. There was Adam shielding Pip, Zagan shielding Sophia, another man I didn't know shielding someone I couldn't see, and then the jester, Marcus shielding the girl with orange hair.

The room was full of love and I let the proof of that destroy the last of my hate. Even the cocky one Sigurd looked to be trying to protect his father. It was everywhere to be seen as they helped each other up and stood together. They had all taken me into their lives and I was only now starting to realise what that meant. But through it all there stood Draven like a beacon in this dark time, waiting for the storm I had created to calm.

Waiting for me like he had done for the last eight months. He hadn't given up on me and looking around the room now, none of them had. So what did that tell me…? Had I really lost everything like I thought because looking at this unlikely family now, I didn't feel as if I had.

I felt like I had just gained everything.

"Oh God! What have I done? I'm so, so, so sorry!" I said, finally crumbling to the floor only finding myself in Draven's arms before I got there.

"It's okay, I've got you now…I've got you." Draven cooed in my ear, holding me close like he wasn't afraid of what I had just done.

"I don't understand…I…didn't want to do that…I don't even know how I did it…I…" I told him looking up at him and seeing nothing but loving concern looking back.

"It's okay Katie, we will figure it out." I could tell that Draven didn't really like calling me by the only name I knew but he did so now because he knew how much I needed it. I looked over his shoulder to see everyone was now on their feet and looking around at the destruction I had caused. I was just glad to see that everyone looked to have survived it in one piece.

"I could have hurt people…I could have…"

"Nah, we're a lot tougher than we look, Pet." Jared said giving the big black guy a hand up out of the stone wall that had crumbled around him.

"Speak for yourself Bro, I think I broke a nail." Jared rolled his eyes and said,

"Yeah well your pansy black ass will survive I think."

"Jesus, what is it about this room? If I were you lot, I would just give up and burn it. That or we start having our meetings in the training room." Sigurd said throwing back his hood to shake the debris from it and I finally got to see his face for the first time. His hair was thick waves the colour of sand, not quite blonde yet not quite auburn but somewhere in between. He raked a hand roughly through it, pushing it back as if it annoyed him.

I would have expected him to look...well not quite so handsome considering he hid his face most of the time. But with sculptured cheeks bones and a square jaw that was speckled with just enough tawny stubble that made his arrogant air seem sexy as he seemed to certainly have enough power behind him to back it up, well if the size of him was to go by anyway.

But as handsome as he was it was all insignificant in sight of his incredible eyes. They were like fire flickering behind amber walls and one had something different about it. Not only was it brighter but it had something moving around the iris...*It was a snake!*

As soon as he saw me looking he gave me a wink and I blushed, looking quickly away.

"Still got it I see, Son." The massive guy next to him said who I now knew was his father and also Draven's head of security.

"Yeah whatever, Pops." He replied replacing his hood and his father chuckled with his arms crossed. He was certainly a colossal sight to see and I was shocked when Draven told me that he'd once been charged with being my personal body guard. Apparently in my other life Ragnar and I had quite the bond and it started all over hot chocolate. Having such a sweet tooth this hadn't surprised me at all.

"Am I a danger to everyone?" I asked Draven who was lifting me off the floor and after kicking one of the heavy sofas upright with just his foot, he sat me down on it.

"No Love, you're not. We just need to find a way to control any anger you may be feeling in the future."

"Well that's one good reason not to piss her off!" Sophia said laughing as she came up next to me pulling plaster from her hair.

"Aww what, no fair! Why can't I have some of that, then you would let me do whatever I wanted in case I had a temper tantrum!" Pip said after showing us the less graceful way to get parts of the room out of her hair and that was bending over and shaking like a dog. Although I had to say, it was certainly effective. She did however have to side step before she walked over towards us as she lost her balance doing so.

"You get away with quite enough, my little wife." Adam said picking her up and swinging her round so she didn't have to walk through the rubble. She wore rainbow tie dye shorts that had ripped pockets and some nautical themed tights in black. All the anchors, twisted ropes and captain's wheels all looked to glow in the dark and this she matched with a T-shirt that had FBI written across her small breasts with smaller writing underneath that stated… 'Funny Bitch In da house'! I had to agree with it, she was definitely the funniest person I knew.

Adam set her down on her high heels that were designed to look like Nike running shoes, complete with laces and iconic tick up the side. She bounced her way over to the sofa and said,

"Man alive and desperate for a soda, you pack a vodka loaded punch Toots…put it there…no like this…" She said showing me how to give her what she promptly told me was a 'fist bump', which consisted of me knocking my fist into hers.

"So did we find out who was the cause of the…" Lucius was interrupted by Pip when he took a breath to try and find the right word on what to call what just happened.

"Temper tantrum." She said and I groaned making everyone laugh.

"Can we please find a new name for it?" I asked and Pip clapped her hands, jumping up and down and said,

"Oh I know…me, me, me, pick me!" I laughed and said,

"Oh no you've done it." Lucius moaned and Pip smacked him in the gut before saying,

"Hulking out? Oh no wait, I've got it…The ultimate freak out…so, what does everyone think, we could call it the 'TUFO' for short…hey, tufo sounds cool! We could even get t-shirts that say, 'It's TUFO Time!' I love it." I looked up at Draven to realise he had left to walk back to the table. He must have got curious when Lucius had mentioned the picture and Lucius decided to follow. Draven was bending down and shifting through the mess I had made, only straightening again once he had found what he had been looking for. I watched as he brushed off the dust and then he reacted.

"Tell me this person is not your mother…tell me now." Draven said and the tone of his voice filled me with dread at how angry it sounded. He looked at me over his shoulder side on and I swallowed hard wishing I could tell him something different but I couldn't.

"She looks a lot younger in that drawing but yes, without a doubt it's her…she did this to us." I told him sitting up straighter so that he knew how serious I was.

"No mistake?" I knew he felt he had to question it, not because he didn't trust me but because he must have needed my absolute assurance on this.

"I have never been more certain." I told him and he nodded in acceptance.

"Dom?" Sophia said and I only realised until now that Vincent had not said a word, which was unlike him. I looked to where he stood in the background and I nearly didn't recognise him. He looked hard, fierce and unyielding but most of all, he looked ready to kill someone.

"Katie was this the only picture you found?" He asked me ignoring his sister's question.

"No, I found loads of them, over a hundred at least." I told him and Lucius held his hand out to take the paper from him. Draven handed it over without looking at him and Lucius' eyes widened at the sight. It was beginning to look as if they all knew who my mother really was.

"And was this woman, the one you say is a younger version of your mother, was she in all of them?" I shook my head and answered,

"No but she was in a lot of them."

"How many is a lot?" He questioned further as these little facts seemed to be most important to him.

"I would say over half." As soon as I said it Draven growled in another language which I could only assume wasn't something very nice. Lucius walked over to Vincent and handed him the paper. He took one look at it and shocked us all by reacting the worst. He roared and powered his fist into the stone wall. Sophia gasped beside me and the others looked at each other in a questioning way, hoping no doubt someone held the answer. It became very obvious that nobody was used to seeing Vincent react this way, including Draven who looked shocked.

"Something must be done about this!" Vincent said storming up to his brother and Draven stated in a calmer tone,

"Something will be done."

"Now Dominic." Vincent growled at his brother and even I

could tell this wasn't the way things usually went between these two.

"I understand your torment at the moment brother, as it has been my own...*many times over.* But in light of this new information, now is the time for caution."

"No, now is that time for action. You heard it yourself, your Chosen One has been targeted ever since she was a child and by someone in your own council!" Vincent said getting angrier but with this new information Sophia stood up and demanded,

"Who is it damn it!?" Meanwhile Zagan had been handed the picture and came over to stand next to his wife to break the news.

"It's Celina, sweetheart."

"What!?" She screeched out in shock.

"Who is Celina?" I decided now was a good time to ask.

"She's a fucking traitor, that's who!" Sophia shouted and Pip who had joined me on the sofa whispered,

"She's a bit upset because they were kinda friends...not like BFFs like us three but still, bitch has gotta burn." I frowned not understanding the last bit but this seemed to be a common occurrence being around Pip, so I was quickly getting used to it.

"Oh." I said thinking my mother was sure pissing off the wrong people. But wait! Why did I still keep calling her mother? She was an imposter, plain and simple but most of all, she needed to be stopped.

"We need time to think about this." Draven said addressing the room but it was clear Vincent wasn't happy.

"No, what we need is to stop wasting time." Draven sighed and turned back to his brother,

"We don't know who she is working with, so we don't know what we are up against. We first thought this could be the work of one of our kind using the humans as pawns, but now we know that is not the case."

"And if it was Keira that was still in there, would you wait then!?" Vincent snapped, stepping up to him. I hated that he said her name but then what else could I expect. In the end I ignored it and could only hope there wasn't going to be another fight. Draven folded his arms and said sternly,

"You're crossing the line, Brother."

"And your Chosen One isn't the only one on that line anymore!" Vincent snarled back.

"Okay, am I the only one that fancies some popcorn?" Pip said nudging me and Sophia shot her a look that told her best not to go there. Pip just held up her hands and then made a zipping motion across her lips.

"I agree with Dom." Lucius said speaking up and Vincent shot him a look.

"Just hear me out. There was more than one reason none of us could find her until she left the Colony and now we know Celina is involved then it makes sense, as she would know the lengths we would go to and therefore know exactly what to do to stop us. This might be the case also if we just storm in there without a plan to guide us." I could see that Vincent was finally starting to see sense as his shoulders started to relax and his tense muscles didn't strain as much against the sleeves of his t shirt.

Draven nodded his thanks to Lucius behind his brother as this had been what Draven had been trying to say all along. He placed a hand on Vincent's shoulder and said,

"Have no fear brother, we will stop at nothing until she is safe. And understand, I didn't not just make this promise to you." Draven said then nodding towards me and it was true, he had also promised me that he would save my sister.

"Okay, so now is anyone going to tell me who by the Gods' names this person is and more importantly, what she means to my Brother?!" Sophia said losing her patience now the tense moment had passed.

Vincent looked slightly guilty and my guess was it was because he was only telling her this now. He turned to face her, walked straight up to her and put both hands to the top of her arms, before dropping the bombshell to everyone in the room…

"She's my Electus."

CHAPTER 30
DANGEROUS DECEIT

I found out very quickly that Draven had kept his cool because he was a King and that was what was needed of him at the time. But as soon as we were back in his room and I showed him all the pictures 'Keira' had drawn, he lost it.

"Fuck!" He shouted before picking up one of the side tables and throwing it across the room. It was destroyed on impact and I jumped as splintered wood littered the floor around where it landed.

"Better?" I asked and he shot me a look that said everything. I held up my hands and said,

"Hey, I'm not judging, as I think we know who wins the 'destroy the room when angry' contest here." Thankfully saying this helped diffuse his anger enough to stop scowling.

"Come here." He ordered in a gruff voice. I did as I was told and it was a bit like getting into a cage with a male lion that was slightly domesticated. You knew they were unlikely to attack you but Hell, it was still a lion!

"Now I feel better." He told me once I made it within reach and he pulled me into him. I turned my head and laid it against his chest, only to hear the quick beat of his heart pounding.

"Everything will be alright." I told him and he huffed,

"That's usually my line." I smiled against him and then looked up, putting my chin on his chest.

"Yeah well didn't you hear, I'm kick-ass now, so I think this means I have to take care of you from now on." Hearing this I finally had him laughing.

"So, what now?" I asked and he kissed me briefly on the top of my head before pulling back.

"Honestly I don't know, I just make most of this shit up as I go along." He replied shrugging his shoulders and I laughed saying,

"No you don't!"

"No I don't but it got you laughing."

"Now that's my line." I said repeating what he said.

"Do you think Vincent will be alright?" I asked and he turned from me, dragging a hand through his hair in that frustrated way he usually did.

"Based on how I was...then definitely no, he will not be alright." I gave him a small smile of understanding and sighed.

"To give him his due, he is holding up a lot better than I was or ever have done when it comes to you being taken from me."

"So it's happened a lot then?" I asked and he shot me a look that added to him saying,

"Let's not go there." In this I had my answer.

"Well they haven't met yet."

"No but he has been dreaming of her for a while now." Now hearing this surprised me. Had they both been sharing the same dreams? But then asking myself this question was quickly followed by another and this was one I asked out loud.

"So what about you?"

"You mean did I dream of you?" He asked clarifying things and all of a sudden I felt very vulnerable whilst waiting for his answer.

"Yeah."

"I have dreamed of you a lot since first meeting you and not once have you been from my thoughts." He said and although it was lovely to hear, it wasn't what I was asking and he knew it.

"Draven, please… you know what I am asking." I said softly, biting my lip and playing with the ends of my sleeve. He took a deep breath and said,

"I know what you're asking Katie but you have to know, that before you turned up that night I had only ever known you as Keira. So every night in the last eight months that's how I saw you…*as my wife.*" I swallowed hard against the lump in my throat. I mean what had I expected really?

"Do you think it will ever be the same again?" I asked sadly knowing that deep down, no matter what he told me, it must have been so difficult for him to see me as a different girl.

"Listen to me when I say that a name doesn't define you. You define you." Hearing this I remembered someone telling me something similar once only it wasn't about my name, it was about my scars.

"I'm sorry I can't remember for you." I told him and he stepped right up to me so I had to look up at him. He took my face in both hands and said,

"And I am sorry I can't help you remember *for you.*"

After telling Draven everything I could about my 'mother' he left to discuss all he had learned with the others. The difficulties they had were simple, most of whom they were up against were human and as Draven was King, he more than most had to abide by the law of the Gods. That law being that no harm should come to humans by a Supernatural's hands. Now there were grey areas to this rule, especially say if there were people

379

standing in the way of the Prophecy. Which let's face it, we were all pretty much dead anyway if the end of the world happened, so I could see their logic with the whole collateral damage side of things. But that didn't mean they could just go in there killing everyone and then saying 'oops' later.

Of course what now made it even more complicated was they doubted very much that this Celina could be working on her own, so I told them about my Uncle. Draven, after hearing all I had to tell him, could say there weren't any clues as to who he really was in his world but now at least they could start looking closer into Celina's past.

He told me briefly how they met and that Draven was actually supposed to punish her for her brief time with a human, one he said was unimportant to mention at this time. By saying this at all had me wondering who the human was because it wouldn't have been an issue otherwise. I had a feeling that the human had something to do with the Keira he knew, one I still needed to admit to being.

I know it was getting beyond irrational, considering all the mounting evidence there was to prove I was her but I don't know, it was like something in my mind had been programmed to never fully accept it. It had me worried that if this was the case and they had done something to my mind then I would never get over this. For obvious reasons I refrained from saying anything to Draven about this as I think we all had enough on our plate at the moment.

And speaking of plates being full, Vincent surprised me by knocking on the door briefly before walking in. I just had my mouth full of a toasted bagel loaded with cream cheese when he said,

"I hope I am not interrupting…" Then he laughed when he saw me with a mouth full.

"Nope, com' 'n in." I said with a mouth full and only getting half words out. He laughed again and came to sit opposite me, so I shifted my feet over giving him more room.

"Nice?" He asked, nodding as a mound of white spread fell off the doughy goodness and thankfully hit the plate not my knee.

"Oh my God! Its sooo good and it's been so long...or maybe it hasn't?" I added frowning as I thought back to all the things I didn't know about myself.

"Hey, it will be fine, we will figure it out." Now it was my turn to laugh, so he asked,

"What's so funny?"

"Oh nothing really, it's just you sound exactly like your brother sometimes. He also thinks everything will be fine and we will figure it out."

"Oh, then I guess there's no point with my next speech of, 'We've got you back, that's the main thing' then uh?" I smiled at him and said,

"It would be a good call to just ask me about the weather." I said nodding and he chuckled this time.

"So I take it you came to ask me about her." I decided not to beat around the bush and just get to what I knew his point was.

"Am I really that transparent?" I nudged him on the arm with my own and said,

"That depends, how were my observation skills?"

"Well you never really liked Aurora or Celina much." I frowned when hearing this new name and he picked up on it quickly,

"Ah that's right, you won't remember Aurora." I put down my plate and waited for him to elaborate.

"It's a long story and definitely not one for me to tell but I can tell you that she too was a member of my brother's council and well, let's just say she deceived us all." Okay so what was it about female council members in this place...other than Sophia obviously.

"Then I seriously think Draven needs to rethink inviting anymore women to the group because other than your sister, I really think it's men all the way."

"I am beginning to easily see your logic."

"Right well now that we have established the no girl rule, unless they pass the psycho test, which will of course include showing them a picture of me and if they snarl and spit, then I would say it's a, 'sorry but better luck next time' kinda gig." Again I had Vincent laughing, which was a nice sound and made me feel good considering how I had seen him acting earlier.

"What do you wanna know?" I asked over the rim of my cup that held amazing English tea in it, one that Draven told me was my favourite. He also told me something about which products were bought to impress your posh aunt and something about a monkey on the front of a box. He of course must have been teasing me or it was a joke I didn't get as he was smirking throughout the whole conversation. However, he had been right about one thing, English tea was awesome and I think I could quite easily become an addict!

"What's she like?" I could almost hear the vulnerability in his voice and I had to wonder if coming to talk to me now had been the first stage of him breaking. Because I got the impression with Vincent that he kept his feelings very close to his chest.

I told him what he wanted to know, or more like what I thought he would want to know. Things like how funny she was, how she could make me smile no matter what we were going through at the time. I told him about her kindness and the way she always took care of me. I even told him things like her love of adventure, something he found quite amusing indeed. I told him everything that, even though I knew now had never happened, I still thought knowing Ari that it would have happened if any of it had been real.

"I'm sorry, I never meant for this to upset you." Vincent said after I started to cry without any warning.

"It's okay, it's just hard you know…finding out that none of it was real, I guess I'm just in denial about the whole thing. Actually no, I'm not in denial, I'm just torn."

"Torn?"

"Yeah, because every time I look at your brother I realise how much I love him and I want to know about our history together so badly that I wish I could just remember it all but if I did that, then I would be afraid of what I would lose with the other person I loved in my life. Ari means the world to me and I would do anything to save her…even if means losing everything we had or everything we thought we knew…but you know what the worse thing would be?"

"What?" He asked tenderly and I had to hold it together just to put it into words for the first time.

"What if she had no one? Looking around that room earlier today all I saw was family. I saw a room full of people that all cared enough that even after what I did, not one person said a bad word to me. There was only concern and after living a real taste of life at the Colony, you can't know what that means to me." I shook my head as even now it astounded me.

"Because a single second before I jumped over that wall I only had one person in the whole world…but Vincent, when this is all said and done then what if I *am* her only one person left in this world. What if I am the only one who ever cared? I just don't know how I am going to break any of this to her." I said letting my head fall back against the couch and wiping angrily at the few tears that fell. I was so sick of crying that it was making me feel ashamed at myself.

"I may not know Ari yet but I know what I feel and I can honestly promise you that she will not face this new world of hers alone. And even though you see a room full of family then in you we not only see the same but we also see hope...you bring hope to everyone you meet and you don't even realise it." I let my head roll to the side to face him and gave him a confused look before I asked what he meant.

"I don't understand."

"Everything that happens in this life does so for a reason. We may not even realise it because without seeing the flip side of life, the 'what could have been', then how are we supposed to believe so unless we have faith in such things." I knew what he was saying but again I wasn't following as to what this had to do with me.

"It's no different for us and having all the facts doesn't help matters, if anything it simply complicates them further. What I am trying to say is that we have faith in you because my kind know you are here for a reason. You are different for a reason and it's only as time goes on that we learn what those reasons are. So when you look at us you see family, when we look at you we see the same but we also see that you are *our salvation.*" Okay so if I thought I wouldn't cry again then this blew that right out of the water!

"Come here." Vincent said, pulling me for a hug and it felt so good that I had to smile, knowing what Ari had in store for her if Vincent was the one for her.

"At the chance of sounding like a family broken record, everything will work out, you just have to have faith in yourself and your sister." I nodded into his shoulder and he held me there for as long as he knew I needed it.

"So tell me, did Draven send you to check on me...? He worries too much." I said rubbing my eyes as I sat back, making sure all evidence of my tears were gone. It was only when I was blinking away the blur when I noticed his face.

"Vincent? What is it?"

"Dom didn't send me." I know hearing this should have been one of those 'shrug of the shoulder' type moments but it was the seriousness of his facial expression that told me there was much more to why he was here than just to check on me.

"This might be my only chance to speak with you as he is busy with the Prophecy's council."

"Prophecy's council?" I asked wondering if this was a new thing.

"Each powerful Being in that room, each leader has their own council...well, with the exception of Sigurd but that is because he refuses to step up to his position."

"And what is his position exactly?" I asked knowing I was getting off track but I couldn't help myself as I was curious about them all.

"He is the King of the Ouroboros."

"The what now?" I asked jerking back in confusion.

"Just think of him as a sort of shadow King that doesn't want the title." I thought about this and saw exactly what Vincent was describing in him. He seemed almost arrogant with power but at the same time not. Almost as though he had lived with it for so long now, that he simply knew what he was but the cocky edge was there hiding the fact that he didn't want what he had. I could see him as a king though and I didn't know why, as he was so different from the rest.

"So getting back to the point, the councils have joined together for all things to do with the Prophecy and since they took our Electus, then let's just say we have had many a meeting and not all of them without bloodshed."

"Oh no." I muttered, hating the thought of everyone arguing and fighting because of me.

"Nothing less to be expected I am afraid, not when you put us all in the same room for the first time in history."

"You never all did things like this before...you know, like when there was some worldly disaster looming or something?" At this Vincent laughed.

"No, most certainly not. In fact, you may be surprised to know that you were the one who brought everyone together."

"Me?" He was right, this did surprise me.

"There is a lot you still don't know Katie, but give it time. You will soon know your true path and when you do, you will look behind you to see us all following, of this I have no doubt." This made me blush as I had no idea what to say. I mean, what was there for me to say, other than I was terrified I would let them all down, or worse, they would discover that they had the wrong girl!

"Don't look so worried, we won't make you sit an exam." He said laughing and it was probably at my horrified look of panic.

"But there is something more I need to discuss with you and this is something I unfortunately had to do in private for a reason." This I know was code for, don't tell anyone.

"You don't want me to tell Draven?" I guessed.

"Especially not my brother...do you think you can do that?" I could tell this was as hard for him to ask as it would be for me to agree to.

"That depends on what it is we are talking about and why we are keeping it from him." I told him honestly.

"Trust me, I don't enjoy this anymore than you do, but given what I saw, I know I have no choice...not if we are to save her."

"You mean Ari?" I asked sitting up straighter as it just got even more serious.

"When I looked into your memories, I saw something that

didn't mean much at the time because my mind was…well, it was elsewhere." Yes, I could imagine I thought but kept it to myself.

"But after thinking about what Lucius said about not knowing what we are up against, then I thought back to what I had seen and soon realised that whatever my brother plans it won't work."

"But why not?!" I said in alarm.

"Because they don't know about the Hexad wall."

"The what?"

"The wall you crossed over. It is protected against our kind. It lit with the symbols of the Hexad when you touched it, which is the only way I saw it through your memories."

"But wait, what are you saying…can you not cross it?" I bit my lip, needing the pain to stop me from screaming the question in blind panic.

"It can only be stopped from the inside. It keeps those who cast its spells safe as long as they continue to power it with a monthly sacrifice. The research I found tells of six masters that are needed for the ritual and the blood of an innocent soul must be consumed from…I don't know, some sort of engraved stone, something with the symbol of the Hexad that has travelled straight from place in Hell." I thought back rapidly and remembered what he was talking about.

"I know what it is! It was round and had the symbol of the Hexad carved into the stone. They killed that girl, they killed her and let her blood drain onto it before filling their cups from the six points. Then they drank it…oh God, eight girls for the eight months I was there." I said looking down in shame. All those girls gone and all to keep me hidden.

"You know where it is?"

"Yes, it was in a cabin in the woods not far from the wall." I told him remembering back to that short, manic drive we took until we reached the wall.

"That makes sense as it would have to be close enough to work." He said looking off to the side and more to himself as he no doubt started to form the plan in his mind.

"Do you think you could find it again?" He asked getting hopeful.

"Definitely."

"But we need to tell Draven this new information, he won't know and won't be able to get over the wall so it will all be for nothing." This is where Vincent winced slightly before he told me exactly why he had come to me with this and not his brother.

"I'm sorry Katie but if Draven were to find out then there would be no saving Ari in time."

"But why not, we could…I don't know, think of something together, re-evaluate and…"

"It would be no good. The stone would need to be destroyed before we could even step foot into the Colony. It's why we couldn't sense you, why it seemed as if you had simply vanished. It hid you as it continues to hide them. For us to even begin our plan of attack we would need that barrier down…and, well…"

"I am the only one that can make it over…aren't I?" I finished it off for him and he nodded. Now I understood it all.

"Draven is never going to let me go is he?"

"No. He wouldn't let you set foot in there alone, not even if you were willing or begged him to let you save your sister." I closed my eyes for a second and let this sink in, falling to the pit of my stomach like a dead weight.

"You can't blame him for that Katie, for if it was me and I had to let my Chosen do the same, I wouldn't allow it."

"But you're letting me?"

"Yes because it is my Chosen in there and because of that I hate to say I would risk it all, as would my brother." I nodded knowing this was something he just couldn't have helped. I didn't take it personally as it was simply the nature of love.

"Have you thought what would happen when Draven realises what you have done?" I asked knowing that I had to put the question out there. He sighed and got up from his seat, to rake a hand through his short curls. The action reminded me of Draven and I would have smiled if our circumstances weren't so dire.

"I know what it is to love my brother to the death but until now I have never known what it was like to extend that love further than him or my sister…and this I know is merely a taste, a drop in the ocean compared to how he feels for you. But to know that I too could have that, if there is only the possibility of such a thing, then I would be going against the Gods and fates in between if I ignored what I knew in my heart to be true. If he can't accept that once everything is said and done, then I will have lost my family doing what I know is right and nothing more, take nothing less with me." Once he had finished this all I knew that if there was any way I could, then I needed to protect him from this ever happening. Because I believed that Draven would forgive me. However, I wasn't so sure how far that forgiveness would stretch if he knew what Vincent had risked to get what Draven had already found.

"I will do it." I told him and he closed his eyes for a moment in what I can only say looked like great relief.

"You realise what I am asking of you?" He said making sure and I nodded knowing that this was my chance to make things right. This was my one shot at getting Ari back and erasing the night I left her. So I told him…

"It's my sacrifice to give."

CHAPTER 31

REVEALING THE HEXAD

Playing the waiting game wasn't easy but knowing what I knew since Vincent and I had made our own plans made it even harder. Knowing what I was keeping from Draven was like swallowing sand every time I was around him. Vincent knew of my struggles as I had confided in him whenever I was given the opportunity to do so. But the simple fact of the matter still stood, we had no other choice.

I was the only one who could do this as the Hexad's power had to be destroyed before any of them could step foot into the place. The problem with that was that it had to be done on the ritual night as that was when it was at its weakest and most vulnerable. Vincent told me how the power that the six evoke from it only lasts until the next full moon and if the ritual went uncompleted after this point, then the Hexad's power would vanish.

When I asked him how I was going to destroy a solid piece of stone, he just said, 'I'm still working on it.' Which was the only vague answer I could get from him. Well as long as he came up with something and damn quick as tomorrow tonight was the night we were going through with our plans. We were leaving via a helicopter, so it wouldn't take the eight hours it had taken me to get here.

Vincent kept telling me there was something we had missed but after going through it all, piece by brutal piece, we came up with nothing. Because without knowing what we were searching for then how we were supposed to see it I just didn't know.

That night after Draven and I had fallen sleep in each other's arms after making love into the small hours of the morning, I started to dream. I was back walking that lonely road to nowhere, the one I first found when making my escape. I remember my feet making the steps but my mind was solely on what felt like my betrayal. The rain pelted my skin with heavy droplets and each one that fell felt like a defeat against us all…but why?

I looked harder and then I started to run through the storm that raged on all around me. I ran and I ran like I had done that night, not knowing where I was but knowing where I would end up. Because now I knew why I was here. I knew what we needed or destroying the Hexad would never work. But before I knew how to defeat it I first needed to know what it was. I needed to know its true nature or what hope did we have? It was like Lucius had said, we first needed to learn what it was we were up against and stopping them had nothing to do with first defeating Celina but it had everything to do with the power they stole.

"Time, Truth…Life." Why was it that these words suddenly hit me just as I saw it standing there in the distance? Because there it was,

The Wall.

The whole reason I had to go at this alone and if I was going back there then I was doing so knowing what I faced. So I reached the start of it just as lightening lit the sky but I didn't flinch, not in this dream. There was nothing to fear anymore. Because this was it, this was my Time, my Truth and my Life...

And I wanted it back!

So I hit out at it like I had done in the marble room, giving it all that I had until symbols all around lit up, baring themselves for me at the same time another lightning bolt struck the night sky.

"I am not afraid of you!" I told it and the bright lines pulsated brighter as if responding.

"Tell me how...how to stop you?" I asked it but again it just flickered brighter for a second as if trying to tell me something.

"What are you trying to show me?" I asked it again but only received the same thing back.

"AHHH! SHOW ME!" I roared in anger, hitting out again without touching it. The wall hit back as great energy boomed out in a flash, knocking me backwards onto the road. I shook my head, still feeling the pain of the impact, even though I knew it was all a dream. I pushed my hair back but that's when I noticed something in the wall had changed.

"What the...?" I uttered as now the symbols had changed slightly. Instead of only seeing the light blurring the lines that were hard to read now it was as if someone had given them an outline. Framed this way I could finally make out what I was seeing.

"They're..." I never finished as a beam of light coming from my side hit me. I looked just in time to see a car coming straight for me and just before it made impact I woke with a start.

"Katie?" Draven bolted up and had his arms around me before I fully came back from the dream.

"It's okay, it was just another..."

"Nightmare?" He finished off for me and instead of telling

him no, that it wasn't, I simply remained silent, letting him think that it was.

I knew that there had to be some way that I could get word to Vincent. Because now I finally knew what we were dealing with but all I had was a name and that was the extent of my knowledge. In truth the only reason I had heard of them in the first place was when seeing one of the lads playing with a bag of stones that had symbols on. Once he was caught his punishment had been to be severely whipped in front of the entire Colony. I remember Ari telling me what they were soon after and the name had stuck. That's why when I saw them that I knew what they were. It was like fate had kept it stored away, ready for this very moment, because there it was, the word so easily found...

Runes.

"You still restless?" I nodded as he must have been able to detect my unwillingness to sleep.

"Do you mind if I get up and, I don't know, go for a walk or something."

"You mean around the manor?"

"Yeah or do you have a library or something?" I asked when I could tell he didn't like the idea of me wandering around the place, no doubt fearing the worst.

"We have a library but these days it is mainly occupied by my brother. I don't know what he hopes to find in those old texts and scriptures but I am worried about him." Hearing this made me feel like the worst person in the world. He didn't deserve to worry but what could I say. Because right now, hearing that Vincent was usually in the library and would be that easily accessible, was like someone turning on the light in the dark room when you were looking for the key to escape it.

"I'm sure he will be fine and besides, it's probably the only thing that is keeping his mind from going crazy worrying about my sister." I told him, knowing that I wasn't exactly lying. He gave me an 'Umm' sound as he thought about it that way.

"Do you think he will mind me being there…I promise not to disturb him." I asked and Draven smiled.

"We could sit together and read if you like, it has been too long since I picked up one of my old favourites and I do have quite a collection I wouldn't mind showing you." Now this made me feel like an utter bitch! But I knew I had to say it and the worst thing was that it sounded like a perfect way to spend time together as I adored reading.

"But I take it from your face that you would prefer to be alone right now…am I right?" I winced again and said,

"I'm so sorry. It's just that I can't think knowing all that could happen tomorrow, all that *will* happen. I just need a little bit of time to sort my head out before I go back there…you know?" He nodded brushing a piece of my hair back behind my ear and said,

"I understand love, and don't worry, you have mortally wounded me…well, my ego maybe." He teased before whipping back the covers.

"What are you doing?" I asked as he started pulling up his jeans over his bare behind and I swear the sight made my mouth water.

"Why escorting you, my fair lady." He said bowing in such a way he looked as if he had done this a fair few times in his life.

"Oh, of course." I said in one of those 'duh me' moments as how else was I expecting to get there. I got out of bed and redressed in what I had taken off earlier and as I was bent over sat on the bed putting my shoes on a thought came to me,

"Draven…?"

"Yes love?" He said after pulling down a plain black t shirt and unfortunately hiding all that sexy goodness from view.

"That idea you had, about me and you in the library, reading together."

"And?"

"When this is all over, promise me that we will do that." I said looking back up and over to where he stood watching me by one of the bed posts. He took two steps to where I sat, lifted my face up by my chin and said,

"I promise." Then he bent at the waist and kissed me softly.

"Seriously, how big is this place?" I asked after what felt like half an hour of walking. Okay so it probably wasn't that long at all but it certainly felt like it!

"It's bigger than it looks." He said smirking down at me as we walked side by side.

"Are you getting tired yet?" He asked and I had to laugh.

"Are you?" I teased back and then ended up losing the battle as I squealed like a girl when I was suddenly swooped up into his arms.

"Not at all, in fact, I may refuse to ever put you down." I burst out laughing and then couldn't help it when I said,

"Well that will make going to the toilet interesting, if not slightly challenging." He actually had to stop walking he started laughing that hard, probably doing what I was doing and trying to picture it.

"Seriously, if you don't stop I might throw up here, I am jiggling all over the place." I told him as his whole body shook from laughing so hard. As soon as I had said it his eyes went to a certain area on my body and he grinned down at them.

"Men!" He tried to hide his smirk and then jiggled me harder making my girls wobble in my bra.

"Draven!"

"I'm sorry, did you say something?" He said pretending not to hear me. I rolled my eyes at him and he started chuckling to himself.

"Do you think we will get there before Christmas?" I asked sarcastically.

"Right in front of you my Patient Queen." He said making me giggle. I looked to where he nodded and saw a pair of massive double doors in carved oak that resembled the front doors to Afterlife. He let my legs swing down and held me a moment longer to make sure I was steady. It was sweet the way he thought of these little things and I was grateful enough of his attentions that I noticed them all.

He walked up to them, paused and said,

"Welcome to the Afterlife library." Then he pushed the mighty doors open with what looked like little effort but the way it made his muscles stand out on his back was a delight to see. The doors opened and the sound echoed in the vast space.

"Oh...my...God..." I uttered in complete awe! The place was by far the most incredible room I had ever seen...which made me ask,

"Have I ever seen this room before?" He knew what I was asking,

"No, this is the first time." I don't know why but this made me smile as I would have hated knowing that I wouldn't have been able to remember such beauty. It was hard enough thinking about the things that I had seen in my life that I might never get back. So seeing this for the first time was a little slice of happiness I would always hold with me, for it was going nowhere this time.

"It's...Oh Draven, its stunning." I felt him come up behind me and after placing both his hands on my shoulders he whispered in my ear,

"It pleases me to hear you think so." My body reacted and a little spark tingled down my spine at both his touch and praise.

But what else would I have said in sight of it all. In fact, it was hard to take it all in there was so much to see. The floor wasn't made from stone for once and I was glad to see it, as I thought the rectangles of wood all slotted together with its high shine, instantly gave it a warm, inviting feel. The golden colour of the wood on the floor complimented the darker red of the mahogany walls. Walls that were row after row of shelves full of books. Great square pillars of the same wood broke up the shelving into sections and were embellished at the top with carved flourishes.

The ceilings rose up to two levels and at the far wall an enormous black fireplace stood at the centre. It was the biggest and meanest fireplace I had ever seen and looked more like the gates to Hell with its two iron statues that stood like sentinels guarding their realm. There were two spiral staircases that framed it either side made from fancy, delicate metal work. But both were then encased in curved wooden pillars, arched in sections like some gothic glassless windows that interlocked to create an intercut pattern.

It was stunning craftsmanship and I think if the men that made it had been here I would have shaken their hands. And then there were of course the books. Thousands and thousands of books. There were sections of old versus new and as I moved around the room, you could tell the age came down in height. The oldest of the old were kept on the second floor and the newest closest to the door. It was like an aging wave of words travelling through the room before leaving through the doors into the world of reality.

"Oh my word, don't ever make me angry in this room Draven or I will never forgive myself." Of course I was referring to my temperamental 'gift.' Draven laughed and then said,

"Nothing broken can't be fixed." I had a feeling that when he said this he wasn't solely referring to the room I had destroyed. Not surprisingly I quickly changed the subject.

"I wonder which shelf you're up to." I said tapping my lip and humming.

"What do you mean?"

"I mean I wonder how many of the books you have read in this room." Draven was still stood at my back but I didn't need to see his face to know he was being serious when he said,

"Most of them I imagine."

"What!? But that's…that's impossible." I told him, now really intrigued to know how old he was.

"When you live as long as we do, you come to realise that you have a lot of time on your hands."

"How old are you again?" I asked, knowing he probably wouldn't tell me but it was worth a shot anyway.

"I'm older than I look." He said against my neck, repeating what he said about his home on the way here and I laughed.

I looked back around the room and couldn't help but wonder how many first editions and priceless books Draven had in his collection. The rest of the room was furnished as you would expect in such a grand space, filled with antiques galore which, for all I knew, could have been bought when brand new. Wing backed Chesterfields in forest greens and tartan foot stools gave it that lovely Scottish manor vibe. Where as in another area, huge old globes of the world stood mounted in spindled wood that I doubted very much had hidden bottles inside.

There were tall golden candelabras flickering away from the many church candles they held and the same hung down from chains attached to the panelled ceiling, branching off like stars in every direction. Even the smell of the room was inviting and one that welcomed you to stay awhile, surrounding you in luxury and comfort until you'd finished with your story for the night.

"Okay, new promise, after our reading session we then lie in front of the fire and make love." I said looking back over my shoulder at him.

"Now that is a promise…actually, *I am making it a vow."* He whispered this last part in my ear making me giggle.

"I thought I heard voices." Vincent said coming from behind one of the hidden doors that blended into the vast amount of woodwork.

"I hope you don't mind, but I was hoping to read a little… you know, to settle my mind." I said giving him a look I hoped he would interpret in the right way. You know, instead of being one of those people that say, 'Uh, why did you just kick me under the table' or in this case 'Why do you look like a zombie staring at me like you want my brains for breakfast', that type of thing.

Thankfully though Vincent wasn't one of those people and simply smiled and said,

"Its fine, I am not working in this room anyway, so have no fear, for you won't be disturbing me."

"Okay, that's good, in that case I will just…" I trailed off as Draven squeezed my arm affectionately before leaving my side to go and speak to Vincent. I tried to pretend I wasn't listening and wandered over to the nearest bookshelf to pretend to scan the books for one I wanted. I grabbed one without looking and started flicking through its pages as I listened in to their conversation.

"When was the last time you slept?" Draven asked him and Vincent turned the other way before answering him.

"I will sleep once it is done."

"You're worried our plans will fail." He said, stating it as a fact.

"Of course and so would you be should the risks be as great for you." Vincent replied sternly, giving me a quick glance, one long enough to tell his brother what he meant by that statement.

"Do you not think I have had to endure my fair share of risks!?" Draven snapped back and I flinched alongside of Vincent. He released a sigh and said,

"Yes of course. Forgive me Dom, I didn't mean…"

"I know, brother. Let's speak no more of it." Draven said putting his hand on his shoulder and cutting his brother some slack. Vincent nodded and then rubbed his forehead saying,

"I am wary is all and fear that I am not sound of mind. I fear to dream in case she is no longer there, so I do what I can here in case Celina's name comes up in any of the ancient scrolls."

"I remember my times in here as well Vince, you're not alone in this, *you* should remember that, for it was you telling me the very same thing when I first encountered my own Chosen." Draven looked back at me over his shoulder and I ducked my head down hoping they wouldn't notice my eavesdropping.

"I remember." Draven nodded to him and turned back to me.

"Hey…" Vincent shouted back to him and Draven stopped in his tracks as he waited for what he had to say,

"If it helps, I no longer think you were being a whiny little bitch over it." At this Draven burst out laughing and said,

"I will get you back in the ring for that one, brother!"

"Yeah, yeah, it's what you say every time." Vincent responded before turning the other way in search of something from the row of shelves. Draven was still chuckling when he came back to me.

"Are you guys all good?" I asked as I had never seen them

like this before. But to be honest, I couldn't really remember what they were ever like, so for all I knew they were always at the pub, shooting pool and arguing about football whilst eating hot wings! Okay so I doubted it but you never know and at least one thing I did know they enjoyed doing together and that was obviously trying to beat the crap out of each other in a ring.

"Yeah. So what have we got here then?" Draven said and before I could stop him he took the book from my hands and was turning it over to read the front page,

"The History of Migrating Birds?" He said the title out loud and I had to stop myself from saying, 'Oh you are freakin' kidding me!' Thankfully instead I said,

"Uh…What, it's educational…and uh…did you know that the…" I tried to look at the page he had it open on and could just about see the words to read them out like it was something I had just learnt.

"…The Arctic tern holds the long-distance migration record for birds, travelling between Arctic breeding grounds and the Antarctic each year. Some species of tube…noses?" I said the last word like a question and then looked up to see he had one eyebrow raised, so I carried on and said,

"Tubenoses, such as albatrosses circle the earth, flying over the southern oceans…um."

"I did actually as I read that one only last week." He replied crossing his arms across his chest.

"No you didn't!" I shouted hitting him on the arm with the book. He grabbed my arm and held it up in the air, pulling me closer to say in a seductive tone,

"No I didn't, so stop pretending and go and get yourself what I know you really want to read…I have many editions of them you know." He said nodding to the far side of the room.

"Many editions of what?" I asked breathlessly. He moved that extra inch closer and then whispered over my lips,

"The Kamasutra." and then he left.

"I don't want to know." Vincent said laughing and holding up his hands.

"We need to talk." I said getting straight to the point.

"About what?" He asked placing the books he collected down on a side table.

So I finally told him what the last of the puzzle pieces was...

"Runes."

CHAPTER 32
DO I LOOK VIKING TO YOU?

" R unes?"

"Yeah Runes." I said again when Vincent obviously started to question my sanity.

"Okay, you are going to have to give me a little bit of something else to work with here." He said heaving his books back into his arms and walking back towards the secret door he had appeared from. I followed him and said,

"This is pretty cool you know." I nodded to the hidden door as it started to open on its own like something out of a James Bond movie…I wondered if they still made those?

"Yeah well sorry to disappoint but it isn't full of guns and yes, they still make those." He said walking through and making me realise that I had spoken out loud again. As soon as I walked through the door it became another one of those 'wow' moments but now for a different reason.

"What a mess!" I commented taking in the chaos around me.

"It might be a mess but it's an organised mess." He said defending himself.

"Yeah, sure it is." I muttered under my breath.

"I heard that!" He said sticking his head back over the gravity defying pile of papers, older than dirt. The room was perfectly round and instead of holding beautifully carved shelving, it was surrounded by dusty pigeon holes stuffed with rolled up parchments of all sizes. Some were in brown tubes with aging labels on the sides and others were just aging! Old cobwebs floated from one hole to another and the musty smell was starting to make me want to sneeze.

"Uh…I hate to point out the obvious but why are we stuck in this forsaken place when there is a perfectly fine and more importantly, *clean…"* I said running my finger along a line of dirt and then rubbing it on my jeans for later before carrying on,

"…space out there…no offense." I added just in case this was like his 'Special place' or something.

"None taken and the reason we are in here is because this is where we keep…"

"All the crap?" I said filling in the blanks or just plain interrupting him.

"Hard copies." He corrected as I was too busy looking up to find it was in fact a tower we stood at the base of but more shocking was that the cubby holes went all the way up until my eyes couldn't see that far. There was no ladder so I asked the obvious,

"So what if we need one from up there?" I pointed my finger up, hoping he didn't think I was referring to Heaven.

"I climb."

"Really?" I asked and he chuckled.

"No sweetheart, I'm an Angel remember, I fly."

"Oh, yeah right. So is there anywhere we can sit?" I looked around the space that only held an island in the middle that was slightly higher than your average table. There were even gaps zigzagged all the way around that with rolls of paper sticking out in every direction.

"I guess not." I said answering my own question after a quick scan of the room told me this place looked about as comfortable as a prehistoric man cave!

"Vincent?" There was no answer and it was becoming clear that he thought he was on to something as papers were frantically being flipped over.

"Vincent, I think we need to…"

"Yeah, something about Runes…go on…" He said and I could tell he was elsewhere so I shouted, finally losing my patience,

"Vincent!"

"What?" He said at last, laying down his scrolls that were the size of newspapers.

"I am going back in there, finding myself one of those comfy seats and waiting until you come to your senses and listen to what I am trying to tell you." I said calmly and without waiting for him to say a word I turned around and walked through the door. Thankfully once I was back on this side I felt like I could actually breathe again. Then I did as I said I would and found myself a seat to wait.

He took forty-eight seconds.

"Alright, you have my full attention." He said coming to sit opposite me on one of the chesterfields.

"You good?" I asked him and I could see the guilt start to come out.

"Yeah. Look I am sorry, it's just we only have tonight and I am not sending you in there with no way of destroying that stone. I know what I said about the risks but…"

"Vincent…"

"Yeah?"

"I think I found a way." This was it. I had tried casting my line as soon as Draven had left the room but Vincent had been too occupied in finding other bait.

"Tell me."

"Okay, so you know how I could barely make out the symbols on the wall, because they were so bright and blurred?" He nodded for me to continue,

"Well I woke not long ago from a dream that sent me back there. I found the wall and this time when I hit it, I started to see things more clearly…They're Runes."

"Are you sure?" I knew he had to ask, so I wasn't offended.

"Positive. A lad got punished pretty badly for having a pocket full of them. I only know what they are because Ari herself told me." This definitely got his attention.

"So what's your theory?" He asked probably praying right now that I had one.

"I think that it's not only what's keeping everyone out but also what's keeping everyone inside under control. No-one hardly asks any questions, everybody just follows orders and those who don't, well maybe it doesn't work on them, but either way I think the runes and the symbol of the Hexad are connected." He shook his head and said,

"The Hexad symbol simply means the power of six. It is rarely used and there is very little history on its origins, that's what I have been searching for all this time."

"But think about it, what if the two are connected? What if the symbols on the walls hold the clue to how to stop it? If we can somehow read the runes, find out what they mean, then maybe we can…I don't know, maybe come up with our own spell." I didn't think we were on the same page until I said this.

"You mean one to counteract it?" His voice elevated at the end in his excitement, as he too began to see my logic.

"Yes, exactly, because I don't know if you will agree with

me on this one, but unless I am going in there with the latest World's strongest man winner to break this thing, then I don't see a way to stop it." His face said it all…neither did he.

"But we don't have the runes." He stated and I smirked at him, pointed to my head and said,

"Yes we do."

For the next hour Vincent looked into my memories and drew what he too now saw from my latest dream memories. Once he thought he'd got them all, then the real fun could begin, I thought dryly as we simply both sat there and stared at them.

"Well, if it helps, you were right, they are definitely runes."

"But what do they mean?"

"I have no clue." I frowned and then looked around the place thinking how stupid we were, as we were sat in a damn library for Pete's sake.

"I know what you're thinking but unless you have some clue as to where a book on ancient runes could be in all this lot then I think that in itself could take hours."

"Google?" I asked but he grinned back at me and said,

"I have one better." Then he jumped to his feet.

"What?"

"A Viking." He answered before running out the door.

Ten minutes later he came back with a gruff and moody looking Sigurd with him and I gave Vincent a look as if to ask silently if this was a good idea. He motioned with his hand not to say anything just yet as he walked ahead of him.

"This better be important Curly, 'cause I was about to get me round two from this sweet piece of…oh hey there girly." Sigurd said not finishing the sentence as it was something I really didn't want to know. He rubbed the back of his neck awkwardly and I had to say, it was strange seeing him without his usual black hooded jacket on. Now he simply wore a dark grey vest that was tight across his large torso and loose fitting sweatpants that hung low on his hips. As a matter of fact, if I didn't now know better, I would have said he looked ready to go jogging.

"Sooo, this looks a bit cosy." He commented looking around our little space. I had hidden the drawings of runes we had done before they came just in case Draven had gotten restless with how long I had been.

"Does Captain 'Holier than thou' know we are having this little shindig?" He asked sitting down next to me.

"No." Vincent said and then added,

"And we would like to keep it that way." Sigurd didn't seem to need much time to digest this before he simply shrugged his shoulders and said,

"That's cool by me. It's no secret he ain't my choice as a dancing partner. So what are we keeping from him?" He asked and he looked from me to Vincent as we eyed each other warily. Sigurd slapped his hands to his knees and got up saying,

"Well how about you guys just get back to me when you both figure out your shit, but in the mean time I am going for a run." I knew that's what he was really up to!

"Wait!" I said reaching my hand out and grabbing his hand. I noticed all the tattooed snakes and serpents he had up one arm and they vibrated and tickled under my touch. I giggled and dropped my hand.

"They remember you." He told me softly and I smiled up at him.

"Vincent, come on, I really can't see what choices we have here and besides...*I trust him.*" I said looking towards Vincent and as soon as I declared my trust the black ink buzzed again under my hand.

"Stop doing that!" I shouted laughing and chastising his arm.

"Hey sugar, it's you not me. Now let's cut the mushy shit and you two tell me what's going on." We all sat down and we told Sigurd what we had planned and why. He stood up and said,

"Oh Fuck no! We are not sending her in there alone!" At this I had to calm him down and make him see reason before he did something irreversible, like tell Draven. In the end it took all my persuasion and yes, a little bit of pleading before he finally understood why.

"And besides, if I think I am right with this, then I won't be going in there alone."

"No?" Sigurd questioned, raising a sceptical eyebrow at me.

"No, I will be going in there with the power to destroy that thing."

"Alright, tell me what you've got." And with this came our victory and his defeat. Because the thing I also learnt about Sigurd was that we had a common ground and that was the need to save family. I didn't know the background in detail but I knew enough to know that if he could have saved his own sister, then he would have done anything.

"Well, I had a dream…"

"You know I heard this one, although I am pretty sure he was black and was into some African-American Civil Rights Movement or something." Sigurd said being cocky and Vincent rubbed his forehead like the Draven brothers tended to do when frustrated. I smacked him on the arm and said,

"That was I *have* a dream, jackass! So as I was saying…"

"Shit I forgot not to make you angry." He mocked and I carried on regardless.

"Earlier tonight I dreamed I was back at the wall that surrounds the Colony. This time I could see the symbols that will keep us out...*Runes."* I said what they were at the same time I pulled out the sheets of paper we had covered in the unknown language. Sigurd's eyes widened in surprise and I briefly noticed the snake in his eye coil round tighter.

"And you say you found these exact ones on the wall." He said picking up one sheet to inspect it in greater detail.

"Yes, with six symbols in particular always circled together. Like this..." I pulled out the sheet from the bottom that I had drawn first. I handed it to him and he frowned down at it as I continued,

"Now I believe that it has something to do with the Hexad. This symbol here..." I said pulling out yet another one for him to see but as soon as I mentioned the Hexad his eyes shot to mine.

"What...? What is it?" Vincent asked him as he also noticed the change in Sigurd.

"She's right." He uttered in some kind of awed disbelief.

"She is?"

"Yeah, but it's been mixed up."

"What do you mean?" I asked and he got to his knees and put all the pages back on the low table, laying them out for us all to see. Vincent came closer until all three of us were around the table, solely focused on the symbols.

"Okay so Runes are a bit like the alphabet. But they can also mean more than just letters, like a magical script. Arrange them in the right way and you get a gateway, like a path between different worlds." I looked down at the way he started to arrange them and then looked back to the one I had done of the runes always arranged together in a circle.

"And see this, these Runes here spell out, but wait, that's wrong...unless...of course, they have used more than one set." He quickly started to talk to himself and Vincent and I exchanged looks which said it all. We would have never been able to do this without him, that much was clear now.

"Okay so they have used both Germanic Fupark, along with both Anglo-Saxon and this, well this could be either or maybe even Danish. But this here is an H." He said pointing at one that actually looked like an H only with the centre line at an angle.

"And this one, well only in Germanic Fupark is this an E but they would need their X from an Anglo-Saxon Fuporc to get this symbol." He then referred to the one in the middle that looked a bit like a tree with three branches.

"Yes, all these combined together this way and they spell Hexad and look, even the symbol of the Hexad can be found through the Method of Tacitus."

"The what now?" I was still wondering what on earth that word Fupark was that sounded like he was saying Foot hark.

"It is a way of Divination…a way of telling the future, like reading tea leaves or crap like that! Only instead of tarot cards or reading lines on a palm, you get your Rune Staves and cast them down onto a cloth." He said getting animated with his large hands as he explained the history of his people to us.

"What are Rune Staves?"

"They're usually nine straight twigs obtained from a fruit bearing tree or hell in this day and age matchsticks would do, but at the end of it you find what runes it made and…"

"Spell out a word?" He grinned at me and said,

"Nice guess but no as I think the chances of finding true love's name or some shit like that would be more than luck, it would be a fucking miracle." Vincent coughed back his laugh and I shot him a look.

"What, he has a point."

"Alright smarty pants, what would you find then?" I snapped crossing my arms over my chest.

"Well Runes don't just mean the alphabet like I said, they

also each have their own meaning, Deity, function and association. Like this one…"

"The one that means H." I said, clarifying for myself.

"Yeah, its God is Urd and also Hella, its function is The Norn of the past and its meaning is the Wrath of Nature."

"What's a Norn?" I asked and this time Vincent was the one to answer me,

"They are the three Goddesses of fate, the Past, the Present and the Future." He said looking thoughtful about something.

"So you're saying that they got the symbol for the Hexad by throwing sticks on the ground?" I looked to Sigurd who started shaking his head.

"No, because there is another use for the Method of Tacitus and that is casting spells."

"So I was right." I muttered before he elaborated on how they must have done it.

"So you have the Method that is future told by chance. But there is also another way of getting exactly what you want. So say if you are looking for defence or a spell that you can adapt, you would use this one that they used here for an E. Then this one means protection, one they used here for an X. So when you put them all together in such a way you find this Hexad symbol doesn't just have five symbols but I can count many hidden away beneath its lines."

"You can? But what do they mean?" I asked on the edge of my seat being utterly fascinated by it all.

"Well, now all of these that you say you saw written on the wall are hidden within the Hexad symbol, but even if you were to just use the five that spell the word it would create a spell that reads 'Destruction and wrath of nature to those who fail the test or trial. Defence and protection and shields for the leaderships and power within. Awareness and awakening to those that sin against us'." I flopped back against my seat hearing all that was needed to fight against us.

"But there's more." Sigurd informed us shuffling the paper around to the others,

"See each rune has its meaning but when used for binding spells you can also use them another way, so they mean something else."

"I'm not following." It was Vincent's turn to say and I was glad because neither was I and also it was somebody else's turn to sound like they were bottom of the Viking class.

"Right, so this one is one of those you saw carved into the wall." I nodded and when he held out his hand for the pencil I had been using earlier I passed it to him.

"So this one is used both on the wall and in the symbol, see like this." He said drawing the flag shape over the symbol of the Hexad and he was right, it fit.

"This is the God of Thunder and means boundaries and self-discipline which has its uses for this spell but if you turned it like this, how it fits in the Hexad the other way, it also means, hate, rape and evil." I sucked in a sharp breath as he just described everything the Colony stood for because as much as I hated to admit it, the girl they had sacrificed looked to have first been violated repeatedly and most likely by all Six of the Fathers. Vincent saw my distress and swiftly came over to sit next to me to then put his arm around my shoulders.

"So you see, each rune has two meanings, when put together like this Hexad symbol is then it combines the two together. And also, you said the symbol you saw was carved into round stone?" I nodded not being able to speak for the moment as it all began to sink in. But then what he said next turned my blood to ice as the last of the puzzle came together and painted a dark and damning picture. Words so strong and powerful that I too had felt them come to me when facing the wall and now I knew why,

"Well in both Celtic and Germanic Wiccan symbols there are three that are all round and each mean...

"Time, Truth and Life."

CHAPTER 33
GOT ANY MATCHSTICKS?

"So, what now?" I asked as we all needed to take a minute before formulating a plan.

"To be honest, I have never seen any binding like it, even with the symbols on the wall for added strength with that Rune set in the Binding Stone, then having that in place we have no shot at ever getting over that wall...not unless we all become assholes and turn human overnight...no offense." Sigurd said and I replied in a sarcastic tone,

"Oh, none taken." I took it by this comment that Sigurd and humans didn't mix often and if they did, they didn't walk away from it feeling as though they'd just made a new friend.

"But what about the blood ritual they do on each new full moon?" Vincent asked holding his elbow with one hand as his other hand was fisted to his lips in thought.

"The blood rituals do give it its strength yes, but even if the ritual wasn't done, there is no guarantee that the binding would fail instantly. In fact, my guess is that it would take weeks to fade fully that was unless we had a powerful witch on our side to take it out completely once this had happened but that's not the point here...?" The worry and horror on both mine and

Vincent's face was enough of an answer for him. Because we knew who was next in line for that blood ritual and there was no way we were going to let that happen.

"No, that's not an option." I said for us both.

"Then I think the only way to go is to somehow create a diversion on one end of this nut job camp, whilst our girl here goes in and destroys the Binding Stone."

"That's a great plan and all but how exactly am I going to do that?" I said now being the one to rub my head in frustration.

"Well lucky for you Gorgeous, I have a plan for that as well." I blushed at the compliment and he smirked when he saw it.

"Which is?" Vincent asked firmly.

"Anyone got any matchsticks?"

Vincent did one better and I found myself in utter hysterics when a plum tree started to grow in the middle of the library, but that wasn't the funny part. What was funny though was seeing two grown men standing around a tree and asking each other, 'Is this the perfect length?' or 'Is it straight enough.' And hearing replies like, 'It could be longer' or 'Stay away from that one, it's got too much of a bend at the end'.

By the time they came back to me I had to wipe the tears from my eyes I was laughing and snorting that hard.

"What's wrong with her?" Sigurd asked Vincent jerking a thumb at me.

"Beats me." Even Vincent didn't know so I enlightened them.

"Oh my God you two were sooo cute talking about your twigs together, very sweet way to bond. Maybe we should think about in the future doing it with everyone, like a supernatural team building exercise or something." I joked making Sigurd growl.

"You know my pets do bite on command." He warned and I giggled again.

"I'm sorry, I promise not to say another word about your… um… *man twigs*." I said pausing before muttering the end. Vincent rolled his eyes but there was no hiding the humour I could see in them.

After I had finally found my composure I watched as Sigurd got ready to throw the sticks onto the huge cream rug that lay in front of the fire. But then he paused.

"What's up?"

"I think I am the wrong person to be doing this." Then he put the pile of sticks down and walked me over to where he had been stood.

"Uhh…are we sure this is a good idea, after all, you're the expert here?"

"Yes but it's your spell to cast as you're the one that will be using it." He told me and leant down and whispered,

"You'll be fine. Just breathe nice and deep." I did as instructed and took a few deep breaths to calm my nerves. I really didn't want to screw this up, because let's face it, what other options did we have.

"Now what did she used to tell me…oh that's it, okay, so having the fire here is good, it will help keep you focused." I really wanted to ask who 'she' was but I knew with these two watching they were counting on me to do this right, and I didn't want my curiosity to mess with ancient Viking Mumbo Jumbo.

He turned me slightly so I was indeed facing the roaring fire. Thankfully it was set back quite a way or I think it would have melted my face off standing so close.

"Right hold these, close your eyes and let your mind drift to a passive state…that shouldn't be too hard for you." He added and I elbowed him in the gut.

"Watch it or you get to play stick man!" I warned still with my eyes closed and I could hear Vincent chuckling.

"Then concentrate on what you're asking of the Runes, in this case, think of the Hexad symbol in your mind and see it disappearing. Fade it out in your thoughts and then when you're ready, open your eyes stare into the fire and cast the sticks on to the rug holding on to that image."

"Okay, I can do this." I said taking the pile of sticks and doing exactly as he said. I took a deep breath, closed my eyes and thought back to the night I saw the Hexad. First I stripped the room of all the nightmares that night held. The girl went, then the blood. Then the Fathers, the rope, the chains, the instruments of torture and death, everything faded away as though the room was being cleansed. Until all that remained was me facing the Binding Stone with the Hexad symbol carved into it.

I stared into it as though it could see me back and this was like some twisted, gothic Mexican stand-off. Suddenly the symbol began to blur rapidly, as if it could feel me pushing for its destruction. I fought against it trying to claw its way back, thinking more and more about it simply fading away, leaving nothing but rough stone in its place. I don't know how long I tried to do this as it could have been seconds or minutes. Either way as soon as the points started to drift and merge back into the stone, I knew I had won the battle. I let the rest of it go and just as the three centre spots where all lines crossed I opened my eyes and cast the sticks out one by one.

"Good, now finish off the ritual by repeating after me,

"We give thanks to the one that is mighty…"

"We give thanks to the one that is mighty."

"…and he who is brave and strong."

"And he who is brave and strong." I repeated again thinking this part sounded kinda corny but hey, he was the expert.

"For we show our thanks to this godly figure by baring ourselves and partaking in the act of love and worship to…"

"For we show our thanks to this Godly figure by baring ourselves and…hey, we what now?"

"…Worship to Sigurd, the most handsome of God like… Hey, you just ruined the flow." He said as I stood on his foot for making a fool out of me. I crossed my arms and said,

"Are you quite finished?"

"Well if you're not taking your clothes off and worshipping me, then yeah, nothing better to do." He said winking making his snake coil round again. I looked to Vincent and asked,

"Is he always like this?"

"Yes but not with me, thank the Gods." I giggled and looked back to Sigurd who was now bending on one knee and examining the Runes I had made.

"Did I do it?"

"You know what kid, this is not half bad, in fact I think it's just about perfect." I smiled childishly as though I had just received an A in my Viking Witchcraft for Beginner's class.

"Do you think it will work?" Vincent also asked stepping closer to the rug to see for himself.

"Yes I do. See all the Runes it has made are the counterparts needed for all those found inside the Hexad. Like this one represents mankind but combine it with this one for leadership and the one for justice and it tells you which spell it would cast if written on the Binding Stone above the Hexad symbol."

"And what about these?" I pointed to the ones that looked like two triangles together and the one that looked like an arrow.

"This means what began must now end from the Gods of order and chaos. So next to this one of chance and destiny and with both connected to the arrow, it means it is a binding agreement made. But the icing on the cake is this bad boy right here. This is at its centre, which means it is where the action is at. It determines what you want the outcome of your casting to be and in our case it means destruction."

"And that's good right?" I asked hoping the whole place wouldn't explode with me still inside.

"It's a very good thing as it will destroy the Hexad." I still didn't see how and I think my face gave it away. So he said,

"Let me put it in layman's terms for you honey, it simply means that you are casting a spell that counteracts against the injustice that the previous Symbol represents. You are taking away its power and giving it back to mankind...*you*. And by doing so, taking back the destiny you believe was stolen from you...all in all, I would say it's about a 'Hard core' on the kick ass scale, so we're definitely good." I only understood about half of it but the most important parts stayed with me and that was he thought it was 'hard core'.

"So you're telling me all I need to do is get myself a spray can, break into that cabin and graffiti all over the stone?" He looked up to Vincent and then back at me before saying,

"Actually, blood would be better."

"What!?"

"Look I am not talking pints here or to say, slit a vein...uh, I didn't mean..." As soon as he said it he looked down at my arms and then looked to Vincent.

"She doesn't remember." Vincent murmured probably hoping I wouldn't catch it.

"She doesn't remember what?" I asked frowning at him but it was Sigurd who spoke up.

"Look there's no point keeping it from her."

"Snake eye." Vincent snarled in warning...one he ignored.

"Look she has a right to know."

"A right to know what?"

"Nothing."

"Your accident." They both said at the same time.

"What accident?" I asked Sigurd who seemed to be the only one who wanted to be honest with me right now.

"Don't get yourself worked up but sometime ago you were fighting, put your arms up to defend yourself against a hit and got sliced across the arms. The girl got hit back, you got patched up, no problem." I thought about this and wondered what was so bad about it. Hell, if anything I sounded kick ass!

"Did I win?" I asked making him chuckle.

"Yes sweetness, you won." He replied ruffling my hair as he walked past. I saw Vincent and him exchange a few looks and Sigurd shrugged his shoulders whilst having his back to me.

"Well thank you for trying to spare me any horrible thoughts Vincent but it's actually nice to know in my past life that I had a backbone and could stand up for myself." Sigurd, after picking up a piece of paper and pencil, walked back to the rug but on the way slapped Vincent on the back and said,

"See, she's fine. Happy even." Vincent just scowled at him as he walked back to the rug. Then he started to draw the symbol out, no doubt ready for me to do the same.

"So you were saying blood...are we talking pin prick here by any chance?" I asked being hopeful.

"Not unless you also know how to piss blood on demand. You need enough of your blood to write the symbol with it." Eww, even talking about this was making me queasy.

"But the other one was carved into the stone."

"Yes but do you think you will find the time to whip out your hammer and chisel. What are you going to do, ask the bad guys politely to step outside and give you a minute, or a few weeks?"

"Okay, good point. Blood it is...but does it have to be mine?" Vincent's eyes widened before he raised an eyebrow at me.

"I don't mean like dragging some poor sap in there with me and using theirs! What I mean is couldn't we just say, nip to a blood bank and borrow one, or steal…hey I am up for stealing if it gets the job done." I said looking between them to find them both smirking.

"Sorry Honey, that's a no go. The symbol needs to be from the blood of the one doing the casting. Even the six Dicks would have had to have done the same, even after it had been carved."

"Right, well then, I'd better to remember to take a sharp kitchen knife and a first aid kit with me!"

"We will be there as soon as the barrier is down." Vincent told me gently.

"Yeah buck up sweetness, we won't let you bleed to death." Sigurd said patting me on the back.

"I knew there would be a bloody catch." I said flopping down into a nearby chair utterly deflated.

"Nice, I see what you did there." Sigurd said winking at me for my 'Bloody' comment.

"So we have our plan." Vincent stated and even though the worry was still there you could see the difference in him from when I first walked in here. I suppose it's the not knowing that is the worst part and considering what little we had to go on, then I would say we had come a long way since Vincent's first vision into my memories. And from the look of things, he knew this too.

"I think we do." I said assuredly.

"Then might I suggest we all get some rest, as I have a feeling we may need the extra energy come this time tomorrow."

"Yeah and the extra blood." I said sarcastically, once again making Sigurd chuckle.

"Ah come Lille øjesten, we wouldn't let anything happen to

you." He said pulling me to his side like a big brother would show affection, which got me thinking about what he kept calling me.

"Sigurd, why do you call me that and what does it mean?"

"It means 'little apple' sweet cheeks and for my people and especially in my family, it is meant as an endearment to someone we care for." I felt so touched by this that I didn't really know what to say. I didn't know what had gone on between us two in my past as it was one story Draven wasn't willing to discuss but deep down I didn't need to know. Because what I already knew in my heart was that I trusted him to my core and I knew that he cared deeply for me. He actually felt like a brother and now I knew that he felt the same way. So I smiled up at him and then gave him a hug around his waist before saying,

"Thank you for telling me."

I said goodnight to them both and started walking back when Vincent caught up with me.

"I think it's best I walk you back."

"Oh that's okay, I think I can manage." I said thinking about my plan.

"Then I think you should know you're heading towards the kitchens." He told me with a smirk and then turned me by the shoulders so I was facing the other way.

"That way would be best." He added making me blush.

"Oh...uh, maybe you're right, it probably would be a good idea to walk with me just to make sure I don't end up in the dungeons or anything." I joked and then inwardly shivered as I thought back to my dream of the prison.

"My thoughts exactly as we don't want a re-occurrence of last time." At this I stopped walking.

"Uh...come again?" Vincent stopped when he realised his mistake and by the time he turned to face me he still didn't know how to recover from it. In the end I gave him a break by holding up my hand and saying,

"You know what, I don't want to know."

"A wise choice." He said looking relieved. Then before we could go any further I grabbed his arm and said,

"I will be right back." Then I turned and ran back into the library, where it was my turn to be relieved to see the plum tree had gone. I smiled thinking how when Sigurd had left he had grabbed a plum from a branch and walked out taking a big bite out of it, saying goodnight with juice running down his chin.

Well at least Vincent had been careful enough to cover our tracks as I don't know how any of us would have explained a tree growing overnight in the middle of the beautiful parquet floor.

I ran over to the right shelf after checking it out when waiting for Vincent to return with Sigurd in tow. Then I grabbed the version that looked the most interesting and tucked it under my arm before leaving to get back to Vincent. As soon as I came close he tilted his head and read the spine. He raised one eyebrow at me and I warned,

"Don't say a word." Before continuing down the hallway back to Draven's room with my head held high, a naughty grin on my face and with me my borrowed library book…

The Kamasutra.

CHAPTER 34

UNEXPECTED GUEST

The next day was tense, to say the least. And after not getting much sleep, which yes, was partly my fault considering what book I decided to take to bed with me, I was feeling it that morning. Although to be fair I didn't know Draven was going to be awake sat at his desk waiting for me. Nor did I know that after thanking Vincent for walking me back he was going to be all sexy and demanding.

I mean it was three in the morning, jeez, didn't the guy sleep. When I asked him this he wouldn't answer me until I had submitted and walked over to him, doing as I was told. Once I was within arm's reach he grabbed me around the waist and swung me as he stood from his seat and sat me down on his desk. My bum crinkled the papers he had been working on but he didn't seem to mind. He then separated my legs and stepped into me.

"I have been forced to sleep too many nights in our bed alone and I refuse to add another to that painful number." He said running his fingertips across my shoulder and neck in a tantalising way.

"You must be tired then." I assumed being cheeky.

"Um, funny but I seem to have perked up all of a sudden." He said pressing into me and he was right, he most certainly had.

"Have you had fun reading, love?" He said picking up the book I had dropped on the desk beside us and as soon as he saw the front cover his eyes flickered purple in what looked like excitement.

"Uh, well I brought that back with me, it wasn't like I was reading it there or anything, cause that would have be weird, especially with your brother there as well, so…uh…no?" I said making him laugh because I'd got myself into an embarrassed state.

"I adore it when you blush for me." He said before bending his head to my neck and kissing and sucking and nipping at it in a way that made me moan aloud. God it felt so good.

"I'm glad to hear it." He said smiling against the sensitive skin he had been working on. I was left realising once again that I had said my thoughts out loud.

"You know I don't think I have ever received a love bite before." This time he growled against my neck and I cried out a little louder when he held a mouthful by his teeth, letting me feel the pinch of pain. It was so strangely erotic being dominated this way and I felt my underwear get even damper from the act.

"Trust me when I tell you that you have." The gruff way in which he said this was enough for me to believe his words. But if that wasn't enough we spent the next hour re-enacting not just the experience of a love bite but also some of the positions we found in the book.

Hence why I was so tired and this mixed with my nervousness about tonight, well I think by ten in the morning I was ready for an adrenaline shot! The club was generally shut in the day, unless it was a weekend, so it was decided that we all meet in the main part of the club to go over our plans. This was also a very tense time considering that I felt like a complete betraying bitch as I knew full well that not only were their plans doomed to fail, I had also gone behind his back and made secret plans without him.

I felt terrible but thankfully he took this side of me as someone that was tired and anxious about the safety of her sister. And don't get me wrong, a lot of it was, it's just that he didn't know about the sneaky, soon to be winner of the worst girlfriend of the year award!

There were points last night when he was inside of me that I wanted to scream about my deceit. Because what that man could do with his body or more importantly do to mine, was the most exquisite torture that as I was begging for him to stop, in my next breath I was telling him that if he did it felt as if I would die. At that point if he had suspected anything then all he would have had to have done was ask me once and I would have been singing like a damn canary! I would have signed sealed and delivered him my soul with a damn bow on it for the Devil if he'd asked in exchange for allowing me to come. That's what the man did to me.

"It's okay love, you can sleep in the car."

"I thought we were going in a helicopter?" I asked and it came out in an unintentional whine that made him grin.

"We are but first we have to drive into Portland where I have a few ready to go."

"What about the others?" I asked knowing we would need a convoy of them to fly us all out there.

"I also have a plane fuelled and ready to go that will take the rest. We will all meet at the Hotel and wait for nightfall." I nodded, knowing it made more sense to get us all there first and then they could plan accordingly if there were any unforeseen changes in circumstances. Well I knew right now they were going to find a big one, but obviously and stupidly, I might add, I kept my not so big mouth shut on the matter!

I was just trying to count how many of us there were in total when all of a sudden the front doors burst open and the angry sound echoed to the high ceilings. Draven stepped in front of me before I knew what was happening and it was an act so quick and precise, that it seemed more like second nature to him.

"WHERE IS SHE!?" A demonic voice boomed around the room and I instantly gripped onto Draven's jacket. I looked around his large shoulders and gasped at what I saw. A man had raged through the doors with long determined strides, his long black jacket bellowing behind him as though power swirled all around his tall body. But it was his look of fury that had me trembling in fear. His skeletal features stood out like someone screaming nightmares in your face. Translucent bone flickered above the handsome face making it hard to pinpoint where the Demon ended and the man began. The two faces were so tightly fused they seemed to battle each other with little control.

He wore tight black trousers that were ripped and full of what looked like paint splatters in varies shades of reds and greys. Big army boots that were unlaced matched the paint marks and underneath his jacket was a black vest that looked as if it had seen better days. I could tell instantly that this guy was an artist, and from the looks of it a broody one at that. He had that 'I don't give a shit what people think' look and just wore what was to hand. Even his hair was haphazardly styled.

But it was the black eyes and black on his nose that made him look like death walking the world and clearly from his entrance he did so in search of something. White eyes with their tiny dots at the centres scanned the room with little care that he was definitely outnumbered.

He moved in a very predatory manner as if trying to sense if what he was looking for was in the room.

"As I have told you before, we don't know where Aurora is, so you can continue your hunt somewhere else Pure Blood." Draven said sternly, standing like an impenetrable force in front of me.

"My hunt for that traitorous bitch continues! But I am not here for her." He informed us and I could see there were many in the room that didn't appreciate his distasteful tone directed at their King.

"Then who do you hope to find by barging through my doors?"

"Mine!" He snarled back and I heard Draven sigh heavily as this must have meant something to him.

"She is missing?" He asked.

"She went in search of *her and I want her back or I take yours from you!"* He growled at me and this went down even worse with the rest of the group. Suddenly one of Jared's men ran at him like a beast would do on all fours. He roared and just as he was about to change into his other form mid leap the skeleton man snatched out his hand. Without touching him the beast turned back into a man and was suspended in the air being choked by an invisible hand.

Then another of the beasts let out a bloodcurdling growl and started to change before he too charged the man. The newcomer simply used his other hand to flip the beast over his head and again without touching him, threw his body into the far side of the room.

I saw Lucius nod to a young punk lad that barely looked like a teenager. Then quicker than a heartbeat he pulled a blade from behind his back and threw it at the man. But without releasing Jared's man he caught the knife that flew at him by the blade and spun round on one foot, throwing it right back at the boy. I gasped only to find the young lad had himself caught it again but the surprise was plain to see.

This was the point Draven had clearly had his fill.

"ENOUGH!" He roared and opened his arms so the intruder flew backwards into the bar, smashing bottles as he landed. The beast fell to his knees, grasping at his throat and the other one that had been flung across to the other side transformed back into a man.

Draven nodded to Ragnar who was at his side and he took a step forward to stand guard over me whilst Draven dealt with the man. His long determined strides took him closer to the bar and this was the first sight of Draven's true power I had witnessed.

"You come into my home and dare to threaten me!" Draven warned in a dangerously furious voice. The man shook the glass off him as he made it to his feet. Then he jumped on the bar itself and spun round trying to land a kick at Draven's head. But he was too fast for him and ducked, grabbing his foot at the same time. Then Draven used his momentum to spin himself and fling the man up and into the VIP area above us.

"But worse still, YOU DARE TO THREATEN MY QUEEN!" Draven suddenly bellowed at the peak of his anger and his wings burst from him. His veins lit up with purple fire and for the second time I was to witness Draven in his demon form. Then he let his wings take him up so he was level with the mezzanine above and I turned to try and see what the man was doing.

"Don't do it Seth, man." I heard Sigurd warn under his breath as he too looked up. Well at least I now had a name to go with the broken body that was sure to follow. Ragnar, fearful of what would happen, grabbed my hand, swallowing it up in his massive palm and he pulled me off to one side, which gave me the advantage to see what was going on better.

I could now see that there was movement below the rubble and quickly what followed was the ground beneath us started to shake.

"What the fuck?!" Jared asked from behind us before I could ask something similar. I had to grip on to Ragnar's arm as I suddenly felt like I was on a ship in stormy seas.

"What's happening?" I asked gripping harder just to stay upright. No one answered me because no one knew.

"Wait, what is that?" Someone else asked as my eyes flew first to Draven and then back to the VIP. Draven still hovered in the air with a better view of what was coming than anyone.

"GET BACK!" Draven suddenly ordered as he must have seen what was happening and knew the destruction to come from it.

"Oh God." I uttered as first a hand burst through the mound of stone that Seth had crashed into. Then bone burst through the surface of the skin and started to get longer and longer, until it reached double the length of his normal arm. Then as if it was reacting with the air, it started to turn into black stone like some kind of infection had taken hold and was feasting on the bone like bacteria multiplying.

I jumped when I saw great branching fingers started to claw into the floor around him and drag the rest of him out. It was only when one giant stone skeletal arm was free that panic really started to set in. What if Draven couldn't defeat him or what if he got hurt trying?

"That ain't no fucking Nephilim I have ever seen." The big black guy named Orthrus said.

"He is the Son of Sammael and combined blood of the first." Another one whose name I didn't know yet informed him.

"Well that makes perfect fucking sense if you wanna spawn a walking disaster!" He commented back as the shaking ground got worse. The ceiling started to rain clouds of stone dust as cracks started to appear in the arches above.

It didn't take long before more of this Seth had dragged himself from the fallen stone and when he was finally free, I cried in horror,

"Oh my God!" Seth was no longer a man but a skeletal beast with arm bones as thick as my legs. Just as he got up he arched backwards as the rest of the Demon burst from his chest and the last remaining flesh of a man was torn from him. His head had transformed into the giant skull of a demon with ridged horns that looked like they had been hacked at with a hatchet. Big grooves and chunks had been taken out of them and it left razor edges that looked like weapons in their own right.

Draven seeing him getting ready to make his first move let massive swords come from the insides of his wrists and I could see the power firing around his arms as they were produced. I was so shocked to be seeing all this that I held my hands to my face now the floor had finally stopped shaking.

Every elongated and misshapen bone that stood waiting for the fight looked to be made from blackened stone. Eyes that had once been white had now changed to dark holes in the skull with now a tiny white dot lit in the centre. Pointed teeth and long fangs were rooted all the way from either side of the open nose bone and he snapped his jaws at Draven, goading him into making his move, so Draven didn't disappoint him. He flew at him at great speed and then spun at the last second, using the force of the move to lash out at the monster with both his blades.

A clashing that sounded like metal hitting metal vibrated around the room as sparks burst out from the contact. It was like underneath that rough surface lay uncut black diamonds that were impenetrable, even for Draven's powers. The force of the hit made the Demonic beast stumble backwards a step as Draven was also forced back from the energy that was produced between them.

I knew someone had to do something to stop this before one of them ended up dead or mortally wounded. I didn't know enough about this world to just stand here and do nothing, hoping for the best. It sounded like this Seth was simply looking for someone dear to him and now this!

They were just getting ready to go at it again when I shouted,

"Someone stop this! Do something!"

"To step in between them would be death as the challenge has been made." Ragnar informed me in a gruff, hard voice.

"Fine, then if none of you are going to do something then I will!" I said getting angry! Actually this time I welcomed the feeling that started building up inside me because I was getting sick of shit like this happening when we had far more important things to deal with right now! Oh yes, I had gone from scared to pissed in less than five seconds all because someone wouldn't do something to stop this. I knew that everyone combined would have been able to take this beast down but no one had stepped forward.

So now it was my turn.

I tore myself from Ragnar's side and ran into the middle of them both looking up at each of them.

"Now stop this!" I said but Draven ignored me and ordered,

"Get her out of here!" Again I could feel the blood coursing through me as my anger grew to new heights. That same tingling feeling started in my fingertips and I flexed them in and out as if trying to test what I knew was building. It felt like I had an investable ball in my hand as I squeezed down on the power I felt I had hold of.

Seth, or what was left of him, roared down at me and

Draven was just about to react by charging him but I got there first.

"STOP THIS THE BOTH OF YOU! I screamed, closing my eyes tight and thrust my hands out in the direction of both of them. The whole room went silent and you could have heard a pin drop. I finally cracked open one eye hoping they were both still breathing and thankfully they were. But they had also been held behind an invisible barrier that I had created with my hands which had warped the air making it look like a door of waving vapour were in front of them both.

Neither of them could move and neither looked too happy about it.

"Katie." Draven warned but there was no way I was letting these two go just to start tearing into each other again. For once I actually felt like I had some control over these powers of mine and I wanted to see how far they would reach. Seth's demon snarled down at me so I thought I would teach him a lesson by showing him I wasn't scared anymore. I reached out my fingers towards him and he howled as I slowly started to draw my fingers back in, starting from the tips. He howled again because he didn't want to let go but I could actually see myself gradually pulling the demon, dragging him out of Seth. Soon after one last yank, I ripped him from his host, leaving the human part of Seth in his place. Then the shadowed figure of his demon fought me for a few more moments until I suddenly released my fingers in a snap of power, making my hand go flat again from the fist it had been in.

This was enough that the shadow burst into black dust and Seth breathed deep, trying to recover from what had happened. As he did so, he sucked in the vapour of his Demon and the skeletal figure remerged over his skin, making him whole once more.

The power in which it took to do this was exhausting and I fell down on one knee just as my shields fell.

"Katie!" Draven cried out my name and was with me in an instant.

"What were you thinking?! You could have been hurt, you could have…"

"That was pretty cool though uh…?" I asked in a breathless tone and he took a deep breath, no doubt to calm his nerves and refrain from chastising me further.

"You are seriously frustrating, you know that." I gave him a small smile and said,

"Yeah, I imagine I get that a lot."

Suddenly I heard feet land and Draven tensed next to me. He helped me to my feet as Seth now approached. Growls and snarls came from all corners the closer he got and Draven went to take a step towards him in a threatening way before I placed my hand on his arm to stop him.

"No more fighting, please." He looked down at me and that hard face that was set in stone started to lose some of its anger.

"How did she do that?" Seth asked in awe.

"She is the Chosen and with each moon drawing us closer to the Prophecy, she grows stronger." Draven answered without looking at him and instead running a finger down my cheek affectionately.

"She is incredible. No one has ever been able to control my Demon like that." Seth said in a mixture of disbelief and wonder.

"Okay guys, gonna give me a big head here." I said getting a bit hot from blushing and feeling pretty happy with myself for kicking demon ass.

"You need to leave." Draven said as enough was enough.

"I need to find her." Seth replied twisting his words.

"You came into my home, you threaten my Chosen and

expect me to help you." Oh yeah, Draven was getting pissed again.

"I was angry and it had been building for a few days. It is no excuse and I know I was in the wrong but I am not the only one to lose his head when his Chosen is taken from him and nor do I have the feeling that I will be the last." At this he looked around the room at all the big players in Draven's world but there was only one I was looking at and that was Vincent.

Because Seth was right. It seemed to be that if something threatened who they believed to be fated to be their 'Chosen' as everyone kept calling it, then they would stop at nothing to save them and keep them from harm. They were no different from what Draven was doing now, what he had always done.

These men, these supernatural kings in their own right were all the same. Even if they hadn't found their own Chosen yet, there was still one common ground they all stood by and it was called love.

Or at the least the chance of it, I thought with a smile at the idea.

"We will help you find who you're looking for." I said speaking up and Draven shot me a look.

"Is that so?" Draven said crossing his arms and giving me his best frown.

"Yes, call it my first royal decree." I said smirking and I heard quite a few sniggers from behind me. Draven raised an eyebrow and if he hoped to stare me down in this one, he was in for a shock. I simply matched his raised eyebrow and crossed my own arms. Seth cleared his throat and said,

"Should I just give you two a minute?" And it was the first light-hearted thing I had heard out of him yet.

"Fine! But if you get out of line again then I will let her loose on you, do you understand?" Seth grinned and Draven walked back to the others behind us. I heard Vincent ask his brother,

"And what does 'letting Katie loose' on him entail exactly?"

"I have no fucking clue." Draven replied dryly and I laughed once before holding my hand to Seth and saying,

"Welcome to the team."

CHAPTER 35
CONVOY

I was just shaking Seth's hand when Pip suddenly bounced in and said,

"Ahh shit sticks! Looks like we missed all the fun, steamy buns!" She said over her shoulder at her husband Adam who was walking in behind her.

"Blame him, he wanted a quickie before we left." She added and Adam cleared his throat before walking over to her.

"Excuse us a moment." He said politely and then he picked her up and threw her over his shoulder.

"Whoopdie whoop whoop! The second train is pullin' in to the station!" She said as they walked right back through the door they'd appeared from. We could hear her singing,

"I'm gonna get me some, gonna get me some, I'm gonna get me some… awhoahhh!"

"Is that…?"

"Normal? Yeah, I believe it is." I said beating Seth to it.

"So when did you notice she had gone missing?" Draven asked getting back to business and then throwing one of the bags of gear to his brother. At this Seth looked away for a moment as if it pained him to give an answer.

"I don't know exactly as I haven't been able to watch over her as I should."

"You were hunting Aurora?" He asked and there was that name again.

"Yes but so far nothing." Draven thought a moment and informed him,

"We have heard nothing from her for a while as she believed we weren't doing enough to find her friend. She left here in anger but naturally we kept an eye on her for a few weeks, just to make sure she didn't do anything foolish. After that we gave her space to mourn for her loss." Seth looked thoughtful a moment and then asked,

"And the authorities?"

"Nothing and we would have picked up on a missing girl report. So it is either someone got to the mother or she just didn't file one." Draven answered and I was now burning to know who this girl was.

"Either is a possibility as they do not see eye to eye."

"How about the boy?" Draven asked as though he wasn't prepared to say his name.

"He has gone also, so my only hope is that they are together."

"Maybe if we found who she was looking for then we would find her…who did she go searching for?" Seth frowned at me as if I had lost my mind and suddenly it clicked,

"It was me wasn't it?"

"She has had her mind altered."

"Hey, don't put it like that! People will think I eat checkers and wear a foil hat so the aliens don't probe my brain or something!" I said hitting Draven lightly in his rock hard abs. Seth now looked at me even stranger but at least Draven found it funny.

"I had my memories taken away so I am sorry but I don't remember my friend, what was her name?"

"Rachael, but her friends call her RJ." I nodded and made a mental note in case we came across her.

"Any distinctive features so I know if I see her?"

"Yeah the chick is rocking some cool pink hair!" Pip said bouncing to our side.

"Uhh...*that was kinda quick.*" I muttered and she just scrunched her little cute nose up at me,

"Nah, I just got a spanking that's all, the guy wouldn't put out no matter how hard I tried...get it, hard!" I smirked, trying not to laugh.

"So are we ready to rock up in this small hick town?!" She asked clapping her hands and making all her many rings clash together.

"I can see why my Rachael likes her." Seth told me looking her up and down. Well if she was described as having pink hair then I could see why also.

Soon after this recent drama and with now one extra person in tow, we were on our way to Portland. My mind was on everything that had just happened and I found myself near bursting with questions. Draven put his hand on my thigh, one that couldn't stop bouncing and said,

"You wish to ask me something?"

"Is it that obvious?" I said laughing.

"Just a tad. Go ahead, ask."

"Well I was just wondering about Seth."

"What about him?" Draven asked looking straight ahead at the cars in front and without looking behind us I knew there was the same amount behind. We were sat in the back of a hugely expensive Rolls Royce being chauffeur driven to where the helicopter was waiting.

"Well he seems like kind of a loner."

"That's because he is."

"Oh come on, you have to give me more than that!" I complained and Draven turned to me slowly and gave me a handsome grin that told me he was amused.

"There is a reason he remains in hiding and alone and that is because his demon is unpredictable and cannot be tamed by his human side. They both battle against each other and frustration breeds anger and anger feeds the demon." Well that sounded like a rubbish deal for anyone.

"But what about his Chosen?"

"RJ?" I nodded.

"Well he refuses to claim her and now she is, well…"

"Pissed?" I finished for him and he laughed once.

"Yeah, that's one word for it. To be rejected when you are at the very foundations of falling in love is not something you get over lightly and let's just say that your friend knows how to hold a grudge." Umm, it sounded like the type of friend I really didn't want to piss off.

"So now she's missing."

"That's what he believes."

"But you don't think so?" I asked hearing the uncertainty in his voice.

"With RJ, well who knows? She might have taken her broken heart somewhere she believes he won't find her, to simply wait for it to mend again." He said shrugging his shoulders.

"Well that's not likely to happen, is it?" I said doubting very much the fates would pair two people together if it was possible for one to get over the other.

"No, it's not but she's not the first to do something stupid in love and I dare say she won't be the last." Draven said re-using Seth's words from earlier. Personally I think it was a simple case of getting them both in the same room and bashing their heads together! Well, that was after we found her of course.

Draven and I continued to talk a little more but at some point I must have given up the fight because what felt like seconds later we were there and I was being woken up.

"Katie, we're here." I murmured something unintelligent before rubbing my eyes and forcing them to open. I waited for my blurry vision to clear before waking to the best sight in the whole world, Draven smiling.

"Hey you." I said in my sleepy state and he laughed.

"I shouldn't have kept you up last night." This time I laughed and as I stretched I said,

"I have no regrets, stud muffin." Now this really had him laughing but also shaking his head at me.

"Come on then my little sex kitten, time to go." This had me grinning as I liked the whole 'sex kitten' thing and I got out of the car hoping that it stuck enough to become my new nickname. I saw a few helicopters all with their rotors whipping round and ready to go. I saw Sigurd, Ragnar, Sophia and Zagan and Seth get into one and Draven, me, Lucius, Vincent and Pip and Adam all got into the other. The rest of the group, which consisted of Lucius' council members, minus one named Percy, and Jared's council members along with Takeshi and a girl call Rue, who was asked to join us in case a witch was needed. I had a sneaking suspicion that this was Vincent's idea, so I tried not to react when Draven pointed her out to me.

"You ready for this, Toots?!" Pip asked, clearly getting excited.

"Hell yes! I have never been in a helicopter before!" I shouted over the noise.

"Oh yes you…"

"Pipper, please refrain." Lucius warned in a dry tone. Pip looked thoughtful for a moment and then her eyes lit up and she started laughing hysterically like a memory just hit her.

"Ignore her, thinking too hard tickles her brain." Lucius teased speaking to me and Adam smirked only to receive an elbow to the gut for doing so.

"Don't make me tie you up, my little imp." Her husband warned affectionately.

"Oh please do darling, then it will take me back to 1978 and that thing we did with my hula skirt. Oh man, that coconut bra was a killer and I had no clue that it would hit the pilot when I whipped it off like that!" Suddenly the man flying the helicopter looked back at us with panic written all over his face.

"Oh it's okay I'm not wearing a bra today, so you're all good!" She said opening her little cropped denim jacket to show us her T-shirt and I burst out laughing.

"Do you like it, I had it specially made for tonight." She said winking at Draven making him groan. It was baby pink with white writing across the chest that said, 'No Humans were hurt during this siege'.

"You should see my back!" Then she turned her back to us all and pulled her jacket down further so we could read the writing on the back that said, 'Unless you're an asshole!'

"I especially like that part, Mrs Ambrogetti." Draven said and this made her do a fist bump in the air but as was the way of Pip it finished with her opening her little fist at the end and saying,

"Boom Bitches!" And then she ended it with a little fizzle noise.

The helicopters took off when they had the okay from the control tower and after Draven made sure I was strapped in of course. I was so excited for my first flight and was thankful I got the window seat, although at first Draven looked dubious. Did he think I was going to wuss out or something? Although if this had been Ari then we would have had a few screams by now.

We had been in the air for about ten minutes when Lucius kept eyeing me in a funny way, as if he too kept expecting me to freak out or something.

"Well it's going a lot smoother than last time, Boss." Pip said nodding to me and I saw Adam shoot her a look.

"Oh yeah, my bad."

"What?" I asked looking at everyone but coming back to Lucius seeing as he was smirking.

"Nothing little Katie girl, just good memories that's all." Pip giggled again but stopped when I looked at her.

"Well think of it like this Toots, at least we can't all hear your thoughts anymore…although that was sooo funny, when Luc walked in and …uh, I shouldn't have said that should I?" Pip said as I was still processing what she *had* said. Unfortunately it soon clicked and if I had been allowed to choose when this happened, I would have said never as now knowing they could all hear my thoughts was utterly humiliating!

"You can what?!" I shouted, finally giving them the freak out they had all been waiting for.

"Sweetheart calm down."

"Calm down, calm down! Do you realise how many rude thoughts I have had about us…*and in front of people?"* I hissed this last part and he tried not to laugh but he sucked at it!

"It's okay, we can't hear now, not since Draven taught you how to block shit out but I must say, for a while there it was very entert…*no… it…* wasn't." Pip trailed off and then picked it back up again trying to rectify what she had started to say after receiving evil glances from Adam.

"I can't believe this." I said lowering my head to my hands and trying to trace back to every single thing I had thought when around people. No wonder I kept thinking I was talking out loud or I thought Draven was just really observant! Oh my God what a shmuck! This time I gave myself an actual forehead slap instead of a useless mental one.

"That's why when he walked in…" Draven growled, making me jump in my restraints.

"Uh, best let's not go there again Katie girl, I don't think the helicopter would survive it." Lucius said stopping me from going back to that delicate time and rightly so.

The rest of the journey went by quicker than I thought, well considering I now had a lot on my mind or more like going back over everything my stupid mind had come up with!

Soon we were on the ground and I must say, other than the first ten minutes I can't say it was an experience I would remember for the right reasons. There were cars waiting for us at the landing bay and they were the epitome of expensive luxury, but that was no big surprise, not considering this was the Dravens we were talking about here. I was becoming to realise pretty quickly that the Dravens didn't do anything by halves and they never paid for it that way either!

I remained quiet and Draven was getting more and more agitated with my one-word answer of 'Fine' to the question, 'Are you alright?'. I know it was stupid and the damage had already been done but it was just such a personal thing that I felt I had been violated. Why hadn't anyone at least said anything to me, although at the time I hadn't really known everyone in the room was a supernatural being of some kind. I felt like I battled against myself between finding excuses for them and feeling hurt for me. But in truth what could have been done? If Draven had told me that everyone and their Auntie could hear my thoughts I would have freaked...not like I am now, but the worse kind of freaked.

"Katie please, speak to me, shout at me, by the Gods hit me woman but no more of this silent treatment!" Draven said after finding his limit.

"I'm sorry, I am just so embarrassed right now."

"Please don't be. It is so natural of our kind to hear the minds of humans that most are blanked out. I very much doubt people heard all of your thoughts as it is something we try to avoid."

"Really?" I asked getting hopeful.

"Yes." I thought about that and if it was me with this gift and it was Draven's mind I could hack into well I know that I would have been just as guilty as him. I raised a sceptical eyebrow at him but then decided to turn it around and leave it. What was the point of questioning him if I was only going to make myself a hypocrite?

"Good, now that is out of the way come here, it has been far too long since I kissed you." And just like that my little freak out was done. We ended up kissing all the way to the hotel where Draven had booked us all in to.

"Do they have enough space for us all?" I asked as the car pulled us round to the front entrance.

"I found it easier hiring out the entire hotel for the few days."

"What?!" I screeched, admittedly not making a very nice sound.

"But what about all the other guests?"

"They were compensated and moved to another hotel."

Wow! How much has something like that cost, I couldn't help but wonder? The door to our car opened and Draven got out first then turned to help me out. I stepped out feeling a little like royalty, but this was only because I was with Draven not because I was getting out of an expensive car. He just seemed to emit power and authority and it radiated from him in everything he did. It was slightly overwhelming if I was honest and it was made more so when we were out in the real world, as I would call it.

It even went as far as the way he was greeted at the hotel's front desk. He was welcomed by the hotel manager who assured him everything was ready for him and if there was anything he could do then not to hesitate to ask.

"Do you think whilst robbing a bank for you, he would hand over his first born with one hand and sign over his soul with the other?" I asked Draven once we were in the lift alone and he laughed.

"You thought it was too much?"

"I don't know, can anyone say 'Grovel much'." I replied sarcastically.

"Money speaks its own language. The currency may change from land, to titles of grandeur and gold, jewels then to paper but greed will never stop and therefore its power will never fade."

"But surely it isn't that to you?" I said not knowing if I liked his speech. At this he laughed once and said,

"I must confess you learn very quickly to enjoy the finer things in life, it is not only human nature but ours as well. However, having my wealth is also a means for me to do what I was put here to do as money means influence and that is powerful indeed." I understood what he was saying and although to most he would have seemed arrogant, I knew he was simply stating facts.

"However, you must know that I would give up every last penny I owned just to have you in my life safe and happy, now that kind of love is more powerful indeed." And in this, I definitely agreed with him. After all,

I would rather spend my time on love.

CHAPTER 36
THE WALL

That night as we travelled to the wall you could tell there were people on both ends of the spectrum when it came to tonight's events. There were those like me and Vincent that were clearly anxious about how tonight was going to go and there were people like Pip and Marcus who seemed buzzing for the fight to come. Then I would say the rest swayed between looking bored and those that were just looking for the excuse to crack a few skulls, Orthrus' words not mine.

Either way we all made it to the wall without killing each other, which I thought was a sign of the group progressing and bonding further. But saying that, I also wasn't holding my breath that a fight wasn't going to break out at any minute. Marcus had already been put in a head lock by Orthrus and Pip had received another spanking, this time for flashing her breasts at some teenagers on a road trip. Oh and Ruto, which I found was the young lad's name, had threw his knife and killed a squirrel, much to Pip's horror.

I was actually surprised that I was able to show people the exact place I had come over the wall. To be honest I had been worried I wouldn't remember which road it was, let alone find the same spot that I had jumped over. After describing the whole thing to Draven he told me that place would be best considering we had found the road from the cabin, which must have been the same road used by the Fathers. It made sense then that this would be the best chance for us to get straight to the Colony without much difficulty.

Unfortunately for Draven, he only thought the powers the wall held were a concealment of what was inside, which was why he could never find me. Although what he also never counted on was that once I finally escaped the Wall, he wouldn't be able to find me then either as my mind had been altered. But of course he knew none of this.

In actual fact I was only found due to Lucius' witch Ness, as she decided not to try and track me down, but track my dreams down instead. I wasn't exactly sure on how this was done or what it really meant but I just know from Lucius that she found me the day I had the nose bleed in Lucy's house. After that she didn't take too much longer tracking me down and after she met me, she then went back to Lucius with her proof and the rest was history up until this point.

But now it was time to make new history and there was no room for error. I could feel my palms sweating knowing what I would have to do next, which was why in the car over here I grabbed Draven by his jacket and kissed him like it might be my last. It was hot, it was steamy but above all, it meant everything to me in that moment knowing it could be the end. Because once I was over that wall I was on my own. I had no backup other than the small blade I kept hidden in my boot and unfortunately, that was one only destined for me.

So I made that kiss count for all the others I might not get chance to receive. For all future kisses that I might be sacrificing in the name of saving my sister. Because if I didn't do this, then I wasn't worthy of them anyway…

I wasn't worthy of his love.

"What was that for?" He'd asked me when I had to tear myself away as I felt the emotions building.

"For luck." I had told him.

"I don't need luck when I have you by my side." He said before kissing me once more and then got out of the car. I then wiped the tear that finally had its chance to escape before whispering to myself,

"Then you will need it tonight."

Now we were all stood awaiting our orders and I waited for just the right moment for Draven to turn his back to me as he addressed the others. He was dividing everyone into three groups to take the wall at different points, reminding everyone of the plan to capture the Fathers for further questioning. This was when I backed away slowly, getting closer to the wall. Vincent knew what the plan was so stepped in front of me, blocking me from view.

Sigurd had been waiting in the shadows and when I looked to see him getting closer, I noticed that most of those shadows he created himself. They swirled around him, hiding him from plain view making him look even more forbidding. I nodded to him to tell him that I was ready and in one swift step I was being lifted with his hands at my waist and hoisted to the top of the wall. Suddenly the symbols lit up the wall at my connection and I gripped on in time just as Sigurd's hands left me as he was flung backwards. I pulled myself up quickly just as I heard shouting.

I knew I had no choice but to keep going as this was my only shot at this. The damaged truck was still there, twisted and bent from when Ari had slammed it sideways into the tree. I gripped the branches and jumped down onto the roof of the car bringing back horrific memories of that night.

"KATIE!" Draven shouted for me and when I turned I hated myself for what I had no choice but to do to him. The hurt, anguish, anger, worry was all there for me to see in one look.

"I'm sorry Draven, I have no choice."

"Katie, listen to me, we will figure out a way! Just come back over and we will go in there together!" I swallowed hard wishing more than anything that I could do just that. That I could simply grab the branch above me and pull myself to the safety of his arms. It would be so easy to escape this nightmare just like last time. But if I did that now then I would only be making the same mistakes that I did last time. I would be turning my back on Ari and for that I wouldn't be able to forgive myself. Which is why the second I made it over the wall my shields had dropped subconsciously so that Draven could hear my thoughts now.

"No! Katie please...please don't do this to me again!" He started to plead with me and now the tears were falling fast and free.

"I have no choice. The wall won't let you through until I destroy its power!"

"Rue! Get this shield down, now!" Draven snapped and I slowly shook my head at him.

"It's no good Draven. I am the only one that can do this now. Just promise me that once the shields are down you will come for me."

"Rue!" He shouted her name again, ignoring me as his desperation took over.

"It's too powerful...I...can't..."

"Just get me over that fucking wall!" He roared hitting out at it again making it spark with sizzling power.

"My Lord, I…" I saw Vincent walk over to her and whisper in her ear.

"Draven I don't have much time, promise me!" I shouted trying to get him to listen to what I was saying.

"No! Come back here or so help me!" He was getting so angry I knew I would have to leave him this way if he didn't calm down and I really didn't want to do that. I wiped away my tears angrily and said,

"So if something happens this is how you want it to be, you want me to walk away knowing I'm not taking your promise with me…is that it?" I said quickly chewing on my lip to stop it from quivering. At this he hung his head for a moment and then in front of everyone he laid his soul bare. For when he looked back up at me the tears in his eyes were on display for his entire world to see.

"Please…I am begging you not to do this to me again."

"And I am begging you to let me go and trust that I can do this." He shook his head and I saw a tear fall down the side of his nose. My breath caught on a sob at the sight of what I was doing to him.

"Why? Tell me why? Why you would leave me."

"Because if I don't do this now, then I won't be the person you love and I am so desperately trying to find her for you Draven I can almost taste how close we are. And you can't stand there right now and tell me that Keira wouldn't do the same if it was her own sister on this side of the wall. And you love her! You love her Draven…As I love you. So please, let me go…let me go and *be her."* I said this last part on a whispered plea that I tasted on my lips as my tears continued to fall.

He let his head fall in defeat and I sucked in a shuddered breath as his final words to me were,

"Then I promise you that I will come for you. *I will always come for you."* I cried out the breath I was holding when he said this and nodded as my voice was too thick to say more. I looked around at everyone that stood witnessing this painful farewell. The girls all cried freely as I did and there were unshed tears to be seen in some of the men's eyes as well. I nodded to them and held my open hand to my heart as my way of a 'thank you' to all of them.

"Then I...I will wait... for you on the other side." I managed to get out between my tears of heartbreak and from the looks on his face he read in between those lines and knew that I meant I would wait for him,

Even in death.

So I turned my back on my family and climbed down on to the bonnet and then down to the ground. I then looked down the lonely road of darkness to my own chosen destiny with the sounds of heartbreak erupting behind me.

Those were the hardest steps I ever had to take.

But the start of journey is always the most terrifying because you are stepping into the unknown. Or in my case I was terrified because I knew what lay waiting for me and the only thing I could hope for was that I was strong enough to survive it.

Normally I would say that the full moon above would be a bonus as it lit up the woods around me. But in this case it was simply like looking up and finding a timer ticking down the seconds on a bomb. This was it. I only had one shot at this so I had to make it count, which was why, as soon as the road started to flatten out, I started running. I let the fear that I could be too late drive me forward until my heart hammered wildly in my chest. Until my body hurt with strain and my lungs burned from taking to many wild jagged breaths.

"Okay, this is it, don't let me down Gods above and below...I have a feeling I will need you all in this one." I said to myself as soon as the cabin came into view. I decided it was best to get off the road, so I crept my way closer to the building from the back where all the logs were stored. I heard faint voices but it was the sound of a girl weeping that had my blood running cold. I snuck down low and taking small, slow sidesteps I edged my way around the side.

"Well look what we have here." My heart dropped at the sound of one of the Father's voices and I froze knowing it was all over before I had even really began.

I had failed.

"Nice of you to finally join us." I swallowed hard, closed my eyes a moment and then spun round to face the end…

To find nothing there.

"Get her inside. Now you brought the meat, the fun can begin soon and my cock has been itching for a piece of that ass since we brought her here!" I swallowed down the bile at the thought of anyone touching my sister or violating another girl. That night in the barn came flooding back to me in utter disgust and thinking about what I had done then, well I knew I wouldn't ever let it happen. No, not while there was still breath inside of me would I allow it. I would fight to the death, I knew that.

I continued down slow and when I finally reached the corner I peeked around and finally, there she was…*Ari*. She was tied with her hands behind her back and even though she had a dirty pillowcase over her head I knew it was her. Because she was next in line for the sacrifice, she knew that, which is why she told me to bring them back with me to save her…to bring back my Demons. Well I had certainly done that and I just couldn't wait until that shield was down so they could join me.

I waited for the two to go back inside, dragging my poor sister in tow. She looked weak and barely able to walk. I closed my eyes against the images of the pain she had no doubt endured in the time I had been gone. The punishments, the starvation, the humiliation and the ...no! I couldn't think of all of that now. I had to keep a clear head if I was going to be of any use to anyone. Now was not the time to lose it.

After I heard the front door swing shut I continued to creep round remembering the small basement window that was ground level, the one that Ari and I had found. The sight that became both an end and a beginning. Seeing it again now was as haunting as every single element of that night, the one I had selfishly tried to blank out was all flooding back to me. It felt like I was stood on a beach with no one else at my back just waiting for the devastating sight of death racing towards me, ready to swallow me whole in an earth shattering wave. She had sacrificed herself to save me, now it was time for me to do the same.

I got down on my front and shimmied over closer to the window, hoping to be at the right angle to see inside without being noticed. Very quickly realisation hit when I saw all six of the robed Fathers were there waiting as Ari was carried down the stairs over one of their shoulders like a hanging piece of carcass. I ground my teeth together when I knew that I couldn't do anything with all of them in there like that. I was no match for them and time was running out. I shifted my body backwards and once I was out of sight from the window I got up and ran. I skidded around the cabin walls and ran for the trees as fast as I could. I only had one option left to go on and I just hoped it worked.

See, I had my own backup plan for this very reason and had arranged it, setting the cogs in motion before we left Afterlife. I had found my phone, the one Lucy had given me and told her that I needed her help. I told her that I had found a way to save my sister but I needed friends to help me do it. Because I knew why they were driving along that road that night when they found me. Lucy had said they never went that way but they had been diverted because a truck had over turned. Well what if that driver had stopped for that coffee and never fallen asleep at the wheel. What if Lucy and her husband had never come that way, then where would I be?

Where would we all be right now? Where would Dex with his full police force be? And where would Lucy and all her friends be? And Jennifer and half the town that she had riled up? Well I can't say where, but I can say where they *wouldn't* be and that was five minutes away from the entrance to the Colony…providing me with the diversion I needed. So all I needed to do was send a text that said one thing,

'Angry Mob is a GO!'

I made sure it sent before I started running back to the cabin as I had made sure on the way to the cabin to check for the best spots for a signal and thankfully it hadn't been too far, or this might not have worked.

I got back to the cabin and waited near the wood store at the back and when my phone vibrated in my hand I looked down…

'Hounds have been released. Two minutes x'

It looked like the Gods were on our side after all. Now I just had to wait the agonising two minutes and pray to every God out there that they made it in time. I closed my eyes against the sounds of frightful screams coming from inside as I waited out this torture. I banged my head back against the wood and drummed my fist against my leg, as I waited it out. I wanted to go in there, I needed to!

"Come on…come on!" I muttered frustratingly to myself knowing that every second counted here.

"Work, come on just work...please God just work for me. Just this once, that's all I ask." I said gritting my teeth as the wait felt endless. I was so close to cracking, in fact I was too close to cracking. I could even mentally see the convoy of angry townsfolk all storming down that long dirt track, at the ready to cause their own version of Hell. The dust bellowing behind them and the comforting flashing lights of blue and red leading the way. I could see it so clearly but they were still too far away. They weren't going to make it...

"They're not going to make it!" I said to myself as I just heard the last blood curdling scream I knew it was now or never. I had run out of time.

Time to take it back.

So I stepped out from behind my hiding place and started walking around to the front of the cabin ready to do all that was needed and if that meant using my powers against them, then so be it. I stood there at the face of the cabin, raised my hands and...

"We've got a problem!" I stopped dead as I listened to one of them speaking.

"It's the police."

"I'm sure they can handle one damn police car!" I heard in response, my heart dropping at the sound that only Dex, Lucy and Denis had come to my aid.

"It not just one, it's the whole fucking police department! And half of the damn town! They're going to overrun us, there's too many of them! They will find the girls... they will find the bodies!" One of the Fathers said in panic. He had obviously been informed, hearing all of this on his phone. I felt my heart lighten knowing that all those people had come to my aid like the Gods had chosen them all for that very purpose. I could barely believe it!

"Fuck!"

"We have to stop them before it is complete!" Another one said.

"Let's go!"

"But what about the blood ritual?" One asked and I knew this was my time to move back out of sight.

"We will have time. You stay here and keep an eye on the girl. We will deal with the town." The voice sounded threatening enough to make me believe it belonged to my Uncle. I had just reached the back of the cabin when I heard the others piling out. Next I heard car doors slam shut and engines start before the sound of wheels spinning on gravel meant they had left in a hurry. I knew I had to hurry as I didn't want anyone from the town getting hurt and as much as I wanted to save Ari, it wasn't at the sacrifice of others.

I looked around and when I finally saw the taillights disappearing I ran round to the front and ducked down to see what was happening.

"They didn't say I couldn't have a little fun while we wait. And you teased me for far too long bitch." The remaining robed Father said, walking up to Ari who was now tied to one of the wooden poles that helped keep the structure of the building in place. I looked around frantically for something I could use and then spotted an old handle from an axe. It was a pity it didn't have anything sharp on the end but it would have to do.

I walked up the steps to the cabin as slowly as I could in a frantic state to get to my sister before she had chance to be violated by yet another member of the Colony. The steps creaked and I had to keep stopping to see if I had been heard. When I knew I hadn't I continued up them and thankfully they had left the rusty hinged door open so I didn't make a sound as I stepped through. I heard the murmured sounds of fear coming from below and then the slap of flesh before the scream of pain. I fisted my hands tighter around my weapon as it was the only reminder I had that I would soon be reaping my revenge upon the bastard that touched her.

Side stepping slowly across the hall I saw the basement door wide open and begging me to run to it but I had to catch him by surprise, it was my only advantage. So continuing with my painfully slow pace I made it to the door and mouthed a thank you looking up when I saw the stairs were made from concrete not wood. This way I had more chance of him not hearing me as I descended the stairs. I walked down and what I saw sickened me to my core. He had pulled her dress up and was slapping his belt on the top of her thighs, jerking himself off at the same time. She still had her face covered so I knew she wouldn't be able to give away my presence by accident.

The next few moments seemed to go by in slow motion as I raised the wooden handle above my head and then took a deep breath before I brought it down using all its force to slam it down into the back of his head. He dropped to the floor and from relief I almost followed him.

"It's okay, it's okay now. I'm here, I'm here Ari, I came back. I came back for you," I said as I pulled down her dress and held on to her as we both sobbed. Then I lifted the dirty cloth back from her head and gasped…

"RJ."

CHAPTER 37
FIRE AND ICE

"RJ?" I questioned again and the relief in her eyes told me it was for both being rescued and for finding me. I looked her up and down to see that in the time they'd had her they hadn't made things easy for her. Her pink hair was matted and by the looks of her dark roots I could tell she had been with them a while. One eye had green bruising, telling me she had been hit at least once across the face. The split lip however was much more recent as blood still trickled down her chin. Her eyes were red from God only knows how many hours of crying because if she were asked I don't even think she would have known.

Looking at her now for the first time I knew deep within my soul that this girl meant a lot to me and even though I was heartbroken at not finding Ari, I knew that saving RJ was all I needed to focus on right now...and of course stopping the Hexad!

I dropped my make shift bat and said,

"Let's get you out of here." She started murmuring frantically as I tried to untie the ropes that were cutting into her skin. I looked up at her and saw the panic in her eyes warped by the tears about to fall. She looked straight at me first and then behind telling me of the danger at my back. In the half seconds I had I noticed the shadow moving in the reflection of those terrified eyes and saw the wood coming straight for me. Instinct took over and I dropped to the ground and rolled out of the way just in time for the wood to impact the air where my head should have been. It had been mere centimetres from hitting RJ across the nose, so I wasn't the only one that had been lucky... although I had a feeling that luck was about to change when he turned to face me.

"Our use for you is done, now you can *die!*" The Father named Godfrey hissed down at me. As his hood no longer concealed his face I could see the true nature which he possessed. He no longer had the same old weathered skin of an aging man. No, now his bone structure was more pronounced with a greyish tint to his stretched skin. His eyes were dirty yellow where the whites should have been and his pupils were oval slits like a demonic cat. Long fangs grew, the same as the rest of his teeth down past his bottom lip and he snarled, growling at me before he attacked.

Once again I managed to dodge his attack but just as I thought I was free of him I felt my hair being yanked before he used it to throw me across the room. I tried to keep on my feet but lost it when the momentum was too great and I spun, tripping over myself before landing into a stack of wooden chairs. I felt the pain ripple over me and knew now was the time to use it as a strength instead of a weakness.

I tried to move and more wood snapped beneath me before I found a good enough place to push myself up. Come on, I should be feeling the tingling in my fingertips by now, I was certainly angry enough. I needed to be careful when I released my power because if I wasn't then I could bring down the whole place. I stood up as he started laughing,

"This is good, as it gives me a chance to work up an appetite before I eat your friend over there." I looked towards RJ and saw how scared and lost she looked. She kept looking to the stairs and if I didn't know any better I would say she was trying to tell me to save myself and run. Well I had done that once before and I was never going to do it again!

"That's not going to happen." I said answering both of them. Then I raised up my hands and let the anger I had coursing through my blood build up and up until,

"Oh really and how are you expecting to stop me?"

"With this!" I shouted and thrust my hands forward, only nothing happened. *I had nothing.* He started laughing at me once again and I quickly looked to the Binding Stone that was stood in the centre of the room. The Hexad symbol, it was still there so…

"My power…it won't…" I started muttering as it all clicked. I hadn't subconsciously let my shields drop earlier to let Draven hear my thoughts. He heard my thoughts because here, on this side of the wall, I was stripped of them. But in the barn? It must have something to do with being so close to the Stone now.

"My brothers are on their way now to kill each and every one of your friends! You think that by sending in your humans that they could stop us. You merely sent the cattle to the slaughter house! For we will show them the true meaning of terror! You will never stop what's coming…YOU WILL NEVER STOP THE HEXAD!" He said again before he lunged for me. Just as he was about to land on me I put my hand behind me for anything I could reach and grabbed the first thing I felt. I then held it out in front of me like a sword, not the chair leg it was and he howled as he landed straight on top of it. I felt my hands get wet as it pierced his flesh and sank into his belly with the blood now trickling down my hands as proof.

I kept tight hold as it seemed to be the only thing keeping him from taking a chunk out of me with his snapping teeth. Then my foot slid as I was trying to move away and we both tumbled to the floor. I twisted my body as we went down so I wouldn't be beneath him and ended up side on. He bellowed in pain again at the wood sticking out of his gut and I took the opportunity whilst I could. I picked up one of the biggest pieces, being the seat and swung it like a bat, hitting him as he tried to get up.

Something deep and sinister within me told me not to stop. So I listened to it. I hit him again and again, over and over until I was covered in blood splatter as if I had been outside when the Gods had bled into the sky and the rain carried their essence to the earth. I don't know where these thoughts were coming from but something told me that was what would happen again if I didn't act soon.

I finally stood up once my bloody and slippery hands could no longer hold onto my weapon. The Father's face was a mess of torn crimson flesh until it didn't really resemble anything other than a mutilated body. Looking down at what I had done should have made me feel sick and in some locked away part of me I was sure that it did. But in the primal side, the one that takes over when life is all about survival, well then all that did was assess that the danger was over and bask in the victory.

I only had one thing left to do before anything else mattered. I needed to save all those people before I found out if what he said was true, that I had only sent them to their deaths! I needed to fix this.

I needed to stop the Hexad.

Walking over to RJ I spied what I was looking for and picked up the discarded pillowcase, using it to wipe the blood from my face and hands. I didn't want any of the Father's blood to contaminate what I was about to do. I looked up to see RJ was watching me with a mixture of horror and confusion.

"You need to trust me. I have to stop the ritual or a lot of innocent people are going to die. Then I will get us outta here." She closed her eyes and nodded as more tears fell from her lashes. I took a deep breath and looked towards the huge Binding Stone seeing the Hexad symbol etched there like a beacon at the centre of all the pain, suffering and destruction it had caused.

"Time to end this." I said getting down on my knees in front of it. I then pulled the piece of paper from my back pocket, not wanting to get this wrong even though I'd stared at the symbol so many times since casting it, I only had one shot. This was my time. My time to take it back.

I went to reach for the weapon I had forgotten about in my boot when suddenly I screamed in pain.

"I'm not finished with you yet, Bitch!" Godfrey snarled grabbing me from behind and wrenching me backwards by my shoulders. I tried to scramble with my hands and feet just to stay up as I fumbled to get to my ankle. Then using a handful of my hair it was ripped to the side so my head had to follow and my neck was left open and vulnerable. He was just about to sink his fangs into my neck and I knew if I allowed that to happen then I was not only dead but then so was everyone else!

I quickly made one last attempt and finally grabbed the handle of my dagger. Then just as his head came to my neck, I bent my arm and plunged my dagger into his face with all the strength I had in me. He fell backwards in screaming agony, letting me scramble out of his way, over to the Binding Stone, putting my back against it. His mangled face had already tried to heal from my attack on him with the chair but not enough to look as it once did. Pink, new flesh was piecing itself back together, however, there was no healing to be done with the dagger that was sticking out of his eye socket.

His hands went to his face and he screamed in pain. I glanced down to see the piece of paper with my symbol on it had fallen between us and I looked up in time to see him studying it with his one good eye. Shock was easy to see, even in his mangled state as he must have known what it meant.

"No!" I shouted just before I jumped to reach for it at the same time he grabbed one of the oil burners and threw it down at the paper. I only had enough time to get out of the way before the explosion of fire could get me too. But I had been the lucky one as the oil splashed up the bottom of his robes and soon the fire ignited the oil like a wave, reaching out until it engulfed him.

"You will never stop the Hexad!" He screamed just before he twisted and spun round trying to get the fire from him. I took a step back against the raging flames and looked to see RJ's eyes were wide with panic. Then she turned her eyes to Godfrey and I did the same to see him fleeing up the stairs shouting,

"YOU WILL ALL BURN, THE HEXAD LIVES!" And from the looks of how quickly the fire was spreading he was right. I looked to the stairs and knew we didn't have long but I also knew that he was right. If we left now the Hexad was set in stone, *it would survive.*

So I made the decision, the only one I could. I ran over to the Binding Stone, knelt in front of it and without my dagger I knew there was only one option left.

"I hope this works." I said out loud, pulled up my sleeve and then bit down as hard as I could into my own wrist.

"AAAHHH!" I screamed sinking my teeth into my own flesh. It hurt, oh God did it hurt. But I knew I needed all the blood I could get to do this and what did it matter for I would most likely burn to death long before I could bleed out. I was only grateful that I had bit hard enough that it cut a vein.

Blood poured from me like my body had sprung a leak and I knew I needed to act quickly before I passed out. Now I needed to think. I had looked at the image so long, for nearly an hour whilst sat on the edge of the bath earlier. I needed to get this right. The paper was gone and I only had my mind left to guide me. Everyone was counting me, so I couldn't let them down or my death would have been for nothing.

Well it wasn't for nothing! It was for this moment. It was for this time. This was my truth and this was me giving my Life.

Time. Truth. Life.

"I'm taking them all back!" I told it before the symbol I wanted to draw appeared not only before my eyes but above the stone in shadow. I knew it was my mind guiding me, so I put my trust in that and began to draw over the shadow in my blood. The second I was doing the last line, half of the ceiling collapsed behind me. I was knocked to the side and hit my head hard against the concrete floor. My mind was foggy as something inside of me screamed for me to get up.

I was too hot, in fact my skin was burning and I couldn't breathe. I coughed and coughed but it never seemed to clear.

"Get up! Get up!" I heard my sister's voice saying and I knew it was in my mind. I opened my eyes to the fire raging all around us and saw RJ screaming behind the gag in her mouth. I knew I had to move, I had to finish what I had started. So I dragged myself over to the Stone, feeling the pain in my leg with every move I made. It was as though half my body wanted to shut down but the other half wouldn't let it...just a little further. Just that tiny bit, reach out Katie, reach out and do them all proud. Because you can do it. You can save them all.

Reach...reach for it...

I let one single bloody finger reach so far and fall down to connect my symbol, making it whole at last. The second I did I felt the power that had restrained everything in this place fall, like it was being sucked back to mother earth. I looked up just in time to see the Hexad symbol underneath start to weep away like tears of the fallen souls it had caused until it evaporated into vapour.

It had worked. I had finally done it and now I could die in peace knowing the evil had been stopped. Knowing my friends had been saved and Ari would finally get to meet her true love, as I had met mine. Because if only for a brief time in my life it had been beautiful. It had been perfect. But above all,

It had been worth it.

So with what little strength I had in me I knew there was just one thing left for me to do before I died and it was to give comfort in that death to another as we found the end together. So I dragged my body up, feeling that since the Hexad had been destroyed I had enough strength to at least get to my feet. I cried out as pain shot up my calf but I didn't let it stop me. I cradled my bleeding arm to my chest and limped my way to RJ.

I knew I would have run to her if there was any chance at saving her but the side of the staircase was ablaze with flames and we were surrounded on all sides. There was no way out and pretty soon the fire would consume us. I looked above RJ to see it also wouldn't be long until the ceiling collapsed all together and from the looks of things right on top of her...

No, not her.

Us.

"I'm sorry, RJ." I told her as I wrapped my arms around both her and the post she was still tied to. I felt her head fall forward on my shoulder and I did the same on hers as I let my hopeless tears fall. Knowing that I would never see any of them again. My sister Ari, after all this time trying to save her. To know that I would never get to meet the family that I had or have chance to fall in love with them all over again. Maybe subconsciously that was the reason for my reluctance in getting to know them. Maybe I always knew I would die as Katie before I ever got the chance to live as Keira.

But above all else it was Draven that was the last one my mind fixated on and it was not surprising. Because selfishly I knew he was my greatest loss and I wasn't ashamed to admit it. He was mine and I was his and the type of love we shared was eternal in both life and death…

And death was what now awaited me and I in turn would await Draven in his…but I guess that was the only downfall to one of you being immortal,

The mortal one had endless time to wait.

"I'm sorry Draven, forgive me… I love you."

These were my last words before the cabin caved in on top of us and we both found…

Death together.

CHAPTER 38
SACRIFICES
DRAVEN

Seeing Keira disappearing over that wall slammed me back into a place in time where I felt my heart literally being ripped open from the sight. Walking into that dressing room and seeing her gone was excruciating to find that she had yet again been taken from me. But there has to be something said for the kind of pain one experiences when seeing the person they love leaving them through choice.

"Keep trying, Rue." I heard my brother say gently as I could no longer be trusted administering orders without killing someone. Sigurd was already out of commission after I took my rage out on him for helping her get over that fucking wall! Although his injuries had already started to heal, the treacherous bastard!

Lucius thought it best if they took his unconscious body with them and I was more than happy to see the back of it! Lucius was heading his team off to the Colony entrance to see if they had the same shields up there. I was expecting to hear back from him at any minute for an update on their progress because the progress on our side was none fucking existent!

I was so enraged that I half wished they had left that damn

Snake Eye here so I could have had another go at him. I was surprised it had been my own brother who was the first one to prevent me from throwing that last punch too far. My own torn flesh and bruises had healed almost instantly, so I had to hand it to the Shadow King, he knew how to hit back and hard enough to make me bleed.

I knew in this moment that I hadn't been fair to Vincent because he was right, I was ready to do whatever it took to get in there right now and get my girl from harm's way. She had only been in there twenty-three minutes and I was already losing my ever loving mind just thinking about what she could be going through. I was so angry at her I could barely think straight yet so worried at the same time that I knew I needed to keep my focus. It was a battle my worry was winning, thankfully because I had a promise to keep and come Hell's armies I was fucking keeping it!

When I finally heard my phone go I had to control myself enough not to break it in half just by swiping a fingertip across the screen.

"Tell me." I demanded.

"You are not going to fucking believe what I am seeing."

"Lucius, the last of my patience is hopefully still bleeding in the form of an unconscious Viking, don't make me add Vampire onto that list." I informed him making it clear the level of my tolerance for guessing right now.

"She is something else, our girl." I ignored the 'our girl' comment as much as I could, my demon, however could not and let this be known.

"Stop growling and listen. I am looking at a convoy of what looks like every police car in this town and the next, but not just that half the town itself has turned up causing trouble."

"I don't care, can you get in there?!" I snapped.

"No, not yet but the spell is definitely weaker here so you're best sending Rue to our side…"

"Takeshi, take Rue to Lucius, now!" I ordered wasting no time.

"But Dom you're not listening."

"What?!"

"She sent them a fucking angry mob!" I frowned into my phone not seeing his point, so he continued as if he knew this was what I would be doing…damn know it all!

"She has a plan, Dom."

"I don't care, she is in there on her fucking own and I won't just stand here and do nothing! There has to be a…"

"Wait, I see something…" He said cutting me off and moving the phone so he could speak to someone.

"As far as we can see a truck has come out of the woods, we think it may be the Rogues I told you about and if it is then it means she might not be in as much danger as we first thought." Lucius had been almost as angry as I, needing Adam to holding him back when once more attempting to get over the wall, this after being flung into the trees on the other side of the road after his first attempt.

"Can you see for sure?"

"Not yet but who else could it be. She told you about the girls and …wait, they are getting out." He said stopping at the sight of this new information.

"How many are there?!" I asked praying to every God I knew above and below for the answer to be six. I know I would have breathed a little easier knowing that at least where she was these soon to be dead assholes were not.

"There's five, Dom." Lucius said in a dangerously low voice that I knew spoke of the murder to come. It was his tell and one I had seen in the many years he was my second in command.

"Fuck!" I snarled turning quick and putting my fist through yet another tree.

"If you get in kill them all but save the Uncle and deceitful bitch to me."

"I will inform you if we have any changes." He didn't need to tell me this as I knew he would. Before everything soured between us and our swords had clashed, he had been a trusted and loyal companion but then again so was a dog, so I couldn't give him too much credit considering the asshole was in love with my wife!

"Good, Rue is on her way to you…oh and Lucius…"

"Yes?"

"Make it painful." At this he laughed and surprised me by saying,

"Yes, my King." As though all those years doing so hadn't ever really worn off as I thought they would have. Maybe I would take the loyal mutt comment back for one slightly less insulting. And after all Keira was Keira, so who could really blame him…no, I still could!

I had hoped by the time I got off the phone I would have been appeased somewhat with the knowledge that she was not surrounded by Rogue Vampires being led by who we suspected was a powerful demon. But obviously one still remained and that was enough to make my blood boil all over again because that was still one Vampire too many.

"Try it again!" I snapped. Seth and Zagan both complied with the order and attacked the wall in tandem. This, like all the times before, was useless and all that happened was those damned runes lit up like it was a Viking's fucking Christmas show! Before I sent Ragnar away he told me what they meant and the power we were looking at every time they showed themselves to us. But after what Keira believed, I knew she had known all along and somehow got it in to her hard human head that the only way to defeat this was through her alone. By the Gods if I had only known what it was that I had been truly up against then I would have employed every powerful witch in the world to go in there with an army of every special forces to deal with it!

If only I'd seen it, if only someone had been able to foresee…that's when it suddenly hit me and as soon as it did, everything quickly fell into their deceptive places. I looked to Vincent and he looked up at the same time, knowing instantly that I knew. Vincent should have seen all of this when he looked into Katie's memories as he couldn't access Keira's, this he had told me later. However, what he had failed to mention to me was that only Katie would be able to pass over the Wall and now with much more on the line than just a sister-in-law to lose, he had risked my everything to save his own.

"Now Brother, you need to listen to me." He said backing away as my legs had already started to take me over to him. Sophia looked first to me and then to Vincent, trying to figure it out for herself.

"I didn't send her in there, it was her choice to make, not mine and not yours."

"You didn't!" Sophia shouted now discovering the level of our brother's deceit.

"And what would you do if it was Zagan?!" Vincent shouted getting angry himself but if he wanted to see anger, then he was about to!

"I would sacrifice myself to get him back, I wouldn't sacrifice my brothers!" She snapped getting in his face first because she was closer.

"Exactly! I didn't sacrifice her, she sacrificed herself!"

"And you let her!" My demon growled as I felt my wings burst free and I charged at him. I caught him in his centre and

pushed him into the wall, holding him there with an arm across his throat.

"It was her choice to make and you know that!" He said in his defence but I wasn't listening. I was too far gone in my rage to care about his reasons. All I could see was the red mist of wrath coming straight from the ultimate family betrayal.

"Uh Dom?" Sophia called my name but I wasn't listening.

"And what would you be doing to me right now if I had helped risk the life of your Chosen?" I snarled the question an inch from his face.

"The same. But ask yourself, who would you have risked to get back your Chosen?" I knew what he was asking of me, to put myself in his shoes…would I have risked this Ari to save Keira, knowing she was destined for Vincent?

"DOM!" Sophia screamed and we both turned as brothers and shouted,

"What?"

"What?"

"The wall, you're both against the wall and it's not reacting!" Sophia shouted back and we both looked to see she was right. The shields were down! I let go of Vincent at the same time he said,

"She must have done it, the Rune worked!" I ignored him because I had little time to care for anything else other than getting her back to me. I jumped over the wall in one motion and was off through the woods like Gorgon Leeches were biting at my feet.

That's when I started to smell it…

Smoke.

"KEIRA! I roared her name not giving a shit about what fucking name I used right now because no matter what she thought that was my Keira in that cabin and nothing in this world or the next would change that!

The closer I got the stronger the smell became and my fear doubled. She'd better be okay, she just had to be, she…

"By the Gods no!" I stopped in my tracks as my heart stopped beating in sight of the cabin completely ablaze. Then I really started to move. She would be okay, she would have gotten out of there…she couldn't be in there…not my girl, not my Keira! I told myself all of this over and over like some lifesaving mantra.

"Oh please no!" I heard my sister's cry behind me as I reached the front of the cabin that had been utterly consumed. In fact, the roof was ready to collapse and cave in on itself. I scanned the whole thing searching for any signs of life but the smoke and flames were a sight only reserved for my own personal Hell. She couldn't be in there!

I had never felt so helpless in all my years on this earth as I did in that moment! If I started moving anything structural it could simply mean her death from that alone. If I went in there I might also disturb too much which would only give me the same outcome.

"Where is she?!" Sophia asked appearing next to me.

"I don't know but she's not in there." I said firmly knowing it wasn't possible.

"Dom…tell me…by the Gods, please say…" My brother couldn't finish that sentence after swiftly landing next to me and folding his wings back.

"What's that?!" I looked to the black charred body dragging itself from the wreckage with its legs still smoking. It had something sticking out from its head that looked as if it could have been a small blade.

"What the hell is that?"

"Not what, *but who.*" I snarled knowing more importantly who it wasn't. I nodded to Sophia who knew what I asked of her. She flew to him, extended her demonic hands and dug in her claws making the creature cry out. She dragged him over to us and the closer he came the easier it was to see that beneath the scorched blackened flesh lay a parasite rogue.

"Where is she?" My demon demanded. But the cretin simply started to laugh, as much as his burnt lungs would allow.

"Your...your..." He coughed up black blood into the grass and I placed my booted foot onto his neck, seeing bloody cracked skin open and flakes of ash peel away from the pressure I inflicted.

"WHERE?!"

"Your little bitch and her friend are cooking as we speak!" He spat out and my Demon snapped.

"NO!" My blade impaled him in the head just as Seth cried out his own agonising howl of pain, knowing now that RJ was in there with her.

"KEIRA! HOLD ON!" I bellowed running to the cabin and with my powers pulling away piece by piece praying to every higher power I knew not to let them crumble on top of her.

"KEIRA, I'M COMING, I'M COMING FOR YOU!" I roared out, screaming for her to just hold on. Take a deep breath, keep conscious, take the heat or just hold on a little bit longer...I was coming for her.

"DOM LOOK OUT!" I heard Vincent yell behind me and I moved back in time to see first the front of the cabin fall and then I knew everything after it would follow. I reached out my hand trying to catch it in time, bursting into demonic flame myself so that my body could stand the heat. I flung my body, twisting it to make it go further, so I just reached for it before it went too far, for I knew what would happen if I didn't make it...

She would be lost to me...*forever.*

"DOM!" I heard Vincent scream just as the wall fell right past my fingertips by a hair's breadth away. My powers had been useless. I landed on the ground just as the wall landed also, blowing debris and ash in my face. I closed my eyes only for them to snap open just as quickly when I heard the devastating sound of the rest of the building collapsing.

"NOOOOO!" I thundered at the sight of the whole blazing roof crumbling on top of my entire world that was trapped inside. I felt the tears of my loss flowing freely and I screamed my pain into the night, one that was quickly echoed by the rest of us.

"No. No. No…don't do this to me! You can't do this! YOU CAN'T LEAVE ME…! Keira, please…please…" I looked up to face the cause of my anger and I lost it! I didn't even remember getting to my feet, or tearing into the flaming building like a mad man. I didn't remember the heat only the freezing pain in my heart. I didn't remember when my demon split the cabin in two, only the sound of its agonising howls cursing the Gods.

But what I did remember what how it felt when I first saw her. Back to the day in the forest where she fell at my feet and nervously mumbled her first words to me. I remember what it felt like to hold her for the first time, knowing I could never let this girl go. How I tried to deny the pull her magical spell cast on us all that is simply powered by the purest soul known to both man and being. A power she didn't understand but the rest of us did. It was beautiful and it was raw and it was life in all its terrifying glory. And I got to hold it, to possess it and most of all, I was loved by it…

And I didn't deserve it…because I had failed her. I promised her I would come for her and I…I…

Failed.

"I CURSE YOU ALL!" At this Heaven itself started to weep for their loss. The skies erupted with light and flooded the earth with rain. It hissed on the glowing embers but it answered back by becoming heavy enough that the flames died almost instantly. It wasn't enough…it was too late! The Gods had only answered her death, not her plea for life.

"Forgive me…forgive me…*I* was too late…I was…Oh God! By the Gods… *can it be?!"*

"What is it?!" Sophia asked pulling her sobbing face from Zagan's shoulder. I looked back in utter shock and even Vincent, who had fallen to his knees in despair raised his head to see the miracle that was an impossible dream made true.

"Keira?" I called her name not trusting what my mind could have conjured up in the cruellest of ways.

"It's them! IT'S THEM! THEY'RE ALIVE!" I heard Seth shouting next to me as he too now started to remove the broken cabin from around them. The rain continued to aid us in our attempt to see if it could be possible. Just that shred of hope bloomed inside of me like a flower that just wouldn't die. And sure enough, there she was. I fell to my knees just as my brother had at the incredible sight of my girl, my Keira with her arms around RJ, holding on tight as if her last thing to offer the world was as simple as comfort in death.

But she wasn't dead! And I cried as the realisation hit me like the Devil himself had delivered the punch into kick starting a heart that was so close to giving up beating without her.

She was alive.

It was the most perfect sight I had ever seen in my entire existence. Seth and I didn't quite know what to do next. We looked to each other with a mirror of relief held in front of us, letting tears flow with little care of much else but knowing the girls we loved were still breathing in this world.

"How could it be…? How can she…? Gods of truth…" Vincent said when flying up next to me on top of the rubble seeing what we were both witnessing. Because words of explanation escaped me as Keira had wrapped both their bodies in a shimmering protective bubble of light that emitted the most powerful aura, you could almost taste its brilliance in the air. In fact, I think if love had a scent or even a taste then this was it and from the looks of everyone around me now staring down at them cocooned inside it, they would agree with me.

"You know what this means, don't you Brother." Vincent said, wiping away the same tears he had shed, just like the rest of us had.

"It means that it isn't just anger that her powers stem from but it looks as though it is love as well." I thought on this and then I turned to face him and smiled before I said,

"No, to me it means…" I paused and looked back to my precious girl looking so serene in such chaos, that she was *my* sun shining through the storm. She was *my* light guiding me in the night but most importantly,

"She was my Love survived."

CHAPTER 39
LOVE SURVIVED
KEIRA

It was the strangest feeling of calm that took over me the second before we died. I wasn't scared or upset, because I didn't want those negative emotions to follow me into my Afterlife. And as I held onto my friend, one I knew I had sacrificed along with me so that many others could live, I couldn't find myself taking guilt with me either, an emotion I should be feeling for sure. Because RJ hadn't deserved to have her life taken from her, a decision I myself had stolen from her. Her only sin was the love she had for her friend, one that pushed her enough to coming looking for me. And in the end what she had found was death at my own hands.

Yes, I should have been beside myself with guilt but right now there seemed to be no room left for it. Because the only feeling I wanted to take with me was,

Love.

It was so strong I felt like my body could no longer contain it and it burst from deep within my soul in a blinding white light all around us. I didn't dare open my eyes but saw it all happening in my mind's eye. It was the most beautiful thing I had ever seen, as it encased us in its warmth and safety and I knew it had come straight from Heaven. This was it. This was our time and the Gods were letting us go together. They were granting my final wish. My way to say sorry to a friend I felt I had never met but yet loved her dearly for the life that I had known her.

The urge to open my eyes was getting too strong for me now and I lifted my head from RJ's shoulder knowing that I wanted to see as we entered Heaven. Because what else could there be for us, well the alternative was too horrific to think about and besides, being surrounded by such a powerful and Heavenly force, it was hard to believe it could be anything else.

But I needed to know.

So I opened my eyes and what I saw took my breath away. It was like thousands of sunrays were coming from me and breaking through an invisible cloud, breaching the barriers I couldn't see like I was... *the sun.* The end of the light would hit some kind of sphere that surrounded us and I wondered if this was to protect your soul as you travelled up into Heaven?

"Open your eyes RJ, its beautiful...they gave us a beautiful death." I said with tears running down my face. I felt her head lift from my shoulder and I reached up and pulled away the cloth they had tied around her mouth.

"Keira?" I nodded feeling the tears fall harder at just hearing her name. The emotional attachment I had with just five letters was hard to describe but knowing it would be the last time I heard it was even harder.

"What's happening?" She asked me and I bit my lip knowing I would have to tell her. I didn't know how people did it, doctors, nurses, policemen and anyone in the profession that had to deliverer such devastating news that would change so many lives forever. My respect for them was overwhelming and I held on to my lip, trying to find the inner strength.

"RJ, I'm sorry but you're..."

"Is that Seth and…Dominic?" She shouted interrupting me, looking up and my heart froze. I could actually feel my body tingle at just the possibility. My head turned and I sobbed out his name,

"Draven." Because he was right there. He had come for me and even if it had been too late I knew he had kept his promise.

"Oh God…*Draven I'm sorry."* I told him and I reached out my hand to him as I said my goodbye. So this was what the Gods had granted me…*my last goodbye.* He reached his own hand out to me and even through the sunlight I could see the tears running down his face, just like mine. He looked like an Angel come to take me home. He was the most perfect sight I could ever possibly witness and I cried even harder knowing I couldn't take him with me.

"I love you." I said just as our fingertips were about to touch.

"I know." He told me back and then I finally felt him break through the light and grab me. I gasped as the sphere burst around us and suddenly I was pulled into his arms, being held by him. I felt myself moving through the air and I clung on, with my face in his neck crying out all my emotions. I didn't understand what was happening to me now but I knew I never wanted to let go. I wanted to stay with him forever. I wanted to be selfish and beg for this life that I had only had a taste of but it wasn't enough. I lied before, because this would never be enough! I wanted it all! I wanted it to be mine and I wanted to keep it for all eternity!

I wanted him.

"Just let me love him, please." I muttered into his neck, hoping that my prayer made its way into Heaven. Then I felt my feet touch the ground and I couldn't bear to open my eyes and find out where my final destination would be.

"Love, look at me." Hearing Draven's voice only made me

cry harder and he understood my pain. He squeezed me tighter to him and said,

"No one is taking you from me. Do you understand, look at me Katie" He asked again and this time I did. I pulled back and his thumb wiped away my tears, tears that were still flowing freely.

"You're going to be okay...do you hear me... do you understand what I am telling you?" He said and I shook my head because I didn't understand...I didn't understand anything. He sucked in a breath, then placed his forehead to mine and whispered,

"You're alive Katie, thank the Gods you're alive and you're with me and I am never, EVER letting you go again. Tell me you understand that." His voice was thick with an emotion I had never heard from him before, so I answered him in the best way I knew how.

"Call me Keira." I told him and he knew with that one sentence that I understood not only that I would never leave him again but that I knew who I was. I may not have her memories but I had her heart and for Draven, that was all that mattered. And in turn, that was all that mattered to me.

"I love you. Keira." Draven told me and I smiled against his cheek, kissed him and then answered him the way he had answered me,

"I know."

After this emotional reunion I found myself being overwhelmed even more when Sophia ran up to me and I caught her in my arms, needing to go back a step from the impact. She too had been crying for the sister she thought she had lost...*again*. We held each other and just as Draven had

needed to do with me, I comforted her into believing I had actually survived.

I saw Zagan approach from behind and he nodded to me once which told me all I needed to know from him. He was both happy I was alive and also that it was alright, he would take over his wife's comfort now. I turned her into him and he took her back in his arms to offer the only strength a husband could.

I smiled at the sight and then felt a chill run along my spine before turning to face the man looking at me now.

"Vincent." I said his name knowing how he must be feeling and his heartbroken face said it all...he blamed himself for what could have happened. We both stood looking at each other from afar and I couldn't stand the distance any longer. I breathed deep and ran to him. He opened his arms just as I reached him and he held me so tight I could only just breathe.

"I'm so sorry, I am...oh Gods Katie, I am so sorry! I can't believe we almost lost you and it was my..."

"Ssshh. Don't even say it because it isn't true. I chose my own destiny Vincent and I knew the risks better than anyone. Now let's go and get my sister...*together.*" He nodded taking in my words and hopefully holding them with him until the guilt went away. I took one last look at the crumbling charred wreck of the cabin and I was glad it was gone. I could only hope that it cleansed the horrors that had taken place there and all those girls could find rest knowing it was no more.

Another place of Hell on Earth baptised by fire.

Fire...and ice. I now understood what those words meant. The one in my dream had spoken of this and her exact words started to replay in my mind.

"Take away their time and you take away their power. They have taken eight...don't let them take nine. Find yourself and learn of the Prophecy's seven, find the key and you will find me next time in Heaven"

Which could only mean one thing… They still had their power as we had one job left to do. So I uttered the last words she had said to me…

"To remember there is power in time and it is time for you to remember…To take time back."

"Keira, what's wrong?" Draven asked me from behind. So I turned to face him and told him,

"It's not over." To which he simply answered…

"Then let's go take back our time."

CHAPTER 40

THE PATHWAY

" Then let's go take back our time."

After Draven said this he took my hand and we walked past everyone else knowing they would follow. I looked behind to see that Seth was still with RJ who had passed out and rightly so, I had been close to doing so myself a few times already.

Draven's phone rang and he answered it in one swift motion.

"She's alive, the shields are down."

"Good, now get your fucking ass over here and bring your famous wrath with you because we fucking need it!" I heard Lucius growl from the other side and then the sounds of fighting raged on in the back ground.

"Lucius...? LUC!" He shouted his name but it was useless as his side had cut out.

"Sorry sweetheart, it's time we went for a ride." Draven said grabbing me around the waist and I screamed as he launched us both into the sky.

"Holy shit!" I said at the feeling of being shot through the air by Draven's race against time. Lucius needed us and without question the others followed in a shadowed blur. I pushed my hair back from my face so I could see as we flew towards, well I didn't yet know what. However, Draven saw it long before I did.

"Gods...can it be possible?" He uttered and I stared out into the distance to try and see what he saw. It was only when it started to come into view that at first it didn't look real... because things like this didn't happen on Earth. Hell's monsters didn't just pop up like this. Because that is exactly what this was,

All Hell had broken loose.

Draven looked where Lucius was and landed us down so quickly I was ashamed to say I almost lost whatever was left in my stomach.

"Is that what I think it is?" Draven asked Lucius who was equipped with a massive sword that he held in his gloved hand. I looked around the open space that was usually filled with long tables for gatherings and communal meals. But now the sight was unbelievable and I couldn't help but gasp in horror.

"They are preventing us from getting into the church where some ritual has begun." Lucius said just as Draven picked me up, spinning me round to protect me as Lucius thrust his sword into some strange dwarf like creature. It looked like it had dipped its hand in black oil and then dragged it down his face as its war paint.

"How long?" Draven asked once Lucius' bloody deed was done.

"Five minutes, but this is merely the first wave. They keep us out by creating pathways to the nine worlds. We stop them, we stop this..." By this he meant the chaos that was going on around us. An actual battle between us and them and by them I meant an army of dark dwarves that were angry, twisted creatures that attacked like a swarm.

"What about everyone? What about the humans?" I shouted praying that they were all still alive and hadn't been collateral damage in this supernatural war between worlds.

"Takeshi took care of them, putting them in a passive state of mind and led them to the largest barn." He nodded to the one I suspected and I sighed in relief but looking at this lot I knew it might be premature if I didn't get them out of here for good.

Suddenly I saw a pile of the creatures being tossed up and out of the way like a battering ram was hurtling through the crowded enemy. It was only when it neared the end that I gripped onto Draven as it was headed straight for us. Thankfully I recognised Ragnar's demon from that day in the marble room, when Draven and Lucius fought. He was charging his way through and knocking them clear of him with his huge, powerful form.

"My Lord, they have to be stopped before..." Ragnar said after his horned helmet twisted away so he could speak freely. His demon appearance was no longer shocking and seeing it actually brought me comfort, knowing such a strong beast was on our side.

"Tell me." Draven demanded as Lucius started to take out a group that were getting too close to us.

"The rogues have the type of Runes that when combined in certain ways it opens up a pathway to one of the Nine realms from Yggdrasil. The first was Swartalfheim, this is the army of dark Elves my Lord." Ragnar said looking worriedly back at the church entrance where I spotted four of the six Fathers all holding painted stone in their hands, chanting something.

"How are they doing this?" I asked, myself finding what they were capable of doing impossible.

"It's the blood rituals." Vincent said coming up to stand beside us. Draven and I both looked at him and he continued to explain,

"It makes sense after what Sigurd said. The wall wouldn't lose its power after the full moon went by without a blood ritual. Which means the rituals were about gathering power for this and for whatever they are doing in that church…it must be, for all they needed was the ninth."

"So what you're saying is that they had enough power gathered to bring forth the pathways to eight of the worlds, if they chose?" Draven asked and Vincent nodded.

"Yes but we might have gained some time when saving RJ because why would they be guarding the church, using all of the power to do so. Whatever it is, we have to get inside and stop them." I looked to see the Fathers just as they combined the stones they held in a certain shape, creating what looked like another pathway.

"Easier said than done from the looks of what's coming!" Lucius said fighting his way back to us and nodding to each of the runes that were lighting up on the stones one by one. They each shot out a beam of light, connecting the stones and creating a type of web until the cycle was complete. Next we saw something emerging from the centre as the circle of light grew bigger and bigger as if needing this to accommodate the immense size.

"It is Jörmungandr, the great beast!" Ragnar roared and only Sigurd, who was also fighting the dark elves, as now I knew what they were, looked shocked. The creature he shouted about he had pronounced as 'YOUR –Mun-gandr' with the 'Your' part said louder with more depth from his heavy Germanic sounding accent.

"Is…is…that…a giant snake!" I shouted this last part when a huge serpent slithered from within the portal with the head of a gigantic monitor lizard. It snarled and shook out spikes from beneath its scales and size wise I could only compare it to a line of pickup trucks all together, nose to bumper.

"Niðr, gǫrr ykkarr ofreflismaðr!" Ragnar roared to his son. ('Son, ready your superior power') Sigurd growled at the sight of the beast and had started to summon his own powers. He threw off his jacket to bare his own shadowed creatures and the dark tattooed skin started to spin and merge, taking over his body. Only this time instead of the usual two serpents that came from behind him something started to change. He seemed to draw up from beneath him, as if tapping in to some hidden power source and draining it for what he needed. It came up from the earth beneath him in streams of black smoke, adding to the power that was already there.

Then on another demonic cry he released it all at once, twisting and combining it all and shot it forward straight for the beast. The further it got the more it combined into one massive shadowed beast of his own. So when it finally reached the huge serpent it went at it with its newly formed head snapping deadly jaws.

The monster Jörmungandr twisted its head and bit into Sigurd's shadowed creature, biting through its head after only a second into the fight. I gasped thinking it was useless, only to see it reform behind its enemy and snap back at its neck, getting its revenge. Unlike Sigurd's clever beast the serpent Jörmungandr hissed in pain as black blood spurted into the sky like a mist.

"He's winning!" I shouted back to Draven who wasn't looking at the fight but straight at the Fathers to see they were opening yet another portal.

"Where is Jared and his council?" Draven asked Lucius.

"They should be coming from that side any minute, why?" He responded fighting back the last of the defeated army of dark elves that looked like hybrids between what you would have expected of dwarves and elves together. Pointed ears, short bodies, coal black matt skin and white hair braided back into Mohawks.

"Because we are going to need him if what I suspect is next through that portal." Draven said tensely and this was quickly followed by an almighty roar that would have put any lion to shame.

"He Who Dwells in the Marshes" Ragnar uttered in awe just as an enormous wolf leapt from the newly formed pathway snarling at the world. He was terrifying and I grabbed on to Draven, as it came straight for us.

"FENRIR ATTACKS! GET BACK!" Ragnar shouted to all that were making sure the last of the dark elves were dead. Meanwhile Sigurd still battled the giant serpent, Jörmungandr who looked as if he would soon be defeated.

"Where the fuck is a Hellbeast when you need one!?" Lucius said sarcastically as he held his sword out like a modern day knight.

"Come on Cerberus, now would be a good time to..." Draven was suddenly cut short as demonic howls sounded that they were near. We looked towards the trees and saw at first it looked like an actual giant was running through the woods. The trees shook and some even uprooted through the force of Jared and his council all charging into battle. Then, bursting from the trees, wild beasts of different kinds came charging through, all being led by the biggest, which I knew was Jared. He had a Jurassic look about him with hardened clumps of stone fur, pointed and tipped with razor edges.

He raged through the rest of us straight for Fenrir, whose fury was building into a crescendo. The remains of thick massive chains hung in sections from the heavy collar he wore and large links had been stretched back by brute strength. It was obvious he had broken through these but it was confusingly the single silky thread that hung down from the front that looked to be made of woven silver that I stared at. It looked to have been sheared off from whatever it had been attached to. However, this was nothing in comparison to the great sword, one the length of a two storey building that had been thrust up through his jaw. The handle curled back round, sitting under his lower jaw and the blade part had broken through to his upper jaw, sticking up like a horn or a weapon. One he used right now to charge at Jared and his men.

"What are we going to do?!" I shouted up at Draven.

"They will only bring more in My Lord and Odin only knows what is next in store for us." Ragnar told him and Draven snarled at the Fathers, at the sight of them doing just that.

"If you get the Runes, can you send them back?" Draven asked scanning the area for his people.

"Aye, me and the boy with some help from the seer." He said nodding to the girl I now knew as Rue.

"Then we kill the Fathers and take control of their power... Rue, Takeshi!" Draven shouted over to them and Takeshi led Rue, which quickly told me she was blind. She had her hands out in front of her but the eyes I saw tattooed there told me two things, one she could see from them and two, they weren't equipped enough to move quickly.

"Yes my Lord." Takeshi said surprisingly calm, considering our dire situation.

"Rue, do you think you can use your power to confuse them, to prevent them from bringing anything else through?" Draven asked her.

"No, my powers are nothing up against the four of them but I might be able to slow them down, plant some fears against them. One is weaker than the others and already fears what comes through will attack them." She informed us.

"Good, use that against him and focus all your energy there.

We only need one to fail enough to get close to them." She nodded and ran off towards the side of them.

"Takeshi, you go and protect her…and use what you have to aid in boosting her powers."

"With my life I give." He replied and was quickly at Rue's side, making sure she got there safely.

"LOOK OUT!" Sophia shouted to us and the next thing I knew I was on the floor after being pushed out of the way. I looked up to see the massive body of the serpent had landed like a falling, thousand-year-old tree in between Draven and I. Sigurd had done it but from the sounds of things the job was long from finished. This beast was down but there was another coming from the next pathway.

"You need to get out of here!" Sigurd said walking over to me, half hidden in his surrounding shadows. It was like black smoke that tried to cling to him every time he moved. Draven saw that Sigurd had me and the relief was plain to see. Draven nodded for him to take me far from here and just as he took the top of my arm ready to take me to safety the sky split from the unearthly sound of our biggest monster yet.

"Fucking Thor's hammer, what next!?" He growled looking back to the lit pathway.

"Fuck no!"

"What is it? Sigurd what is…oh my God! You have got to be shitting me! It's a fucking Dragon!" It was my time to roar as the head started to emerge.

"It's no Dragon, its worse…*its Níðhöggr!*" This is the point where I would have asked him 'who' but he turned to me and screamed one thing,

"RUN!" I didn't need to be told twice as that is exactly what I did. I started running and knowing what was at my back I did so like death was following me! I looked back over my shoulder expecting to see Sigurd running with me but he wasn't

there. He was stood in between it and me surrounded by a black cloud that was growing bigger and bigger.

I screamed as fire burst through the shadows at the same time an almighty roaring purr rose up from the belly of a mighty beast before the crackling scorch of flames travelling through the air. I ran even faster to get away and as I looked over my shoulder its head materialised through the fire. It was trying to reach for me and stopped abruptly, bellowing its anger into the sky. I looked back to see Sigurd's shadowed serpent had wrapped itself around its neck and for a false hopeful minute I thought Sigurd had him. But the Dragon, Níðhöggr was obviously a lot smarter than the giant snake Sigurd had defeated. Because he looked down and saw who the shadows were being controlled by and with one nasty wipe of his tail, Sigurd went flying into the side of one of the houses.

I froze in horror, too scared to move. I looked to Draven to see now he had his own monster to deal with, one that had a flaming sword and was bigger than Ragnar. I looked to everyone around to see they each had their own devastating force to try and control as even all of Jared's crew were still battling it out against the monstrous wolf. But nobody was left to fight the biggest of them all! If only we had our own monster to fight him, because if something didn't happen soon then all would be lost.

I don't know why but my subconscious kicked in just at the right time as the next set of flames came at me. I took a deep breath as the seconds seemed to slow down and raised my hands up. Suddenly there was no fear and there was no doubt left in me. For I knew I could do this and for the first time I didn't need anger to cast it out. I simply said,

"No." And from me came a blinding flash of light that boomed from me and I could see it travelling along in the air like a shimmering curved wall. It hit the beast like a shockwave and it whipped its head around in what looked like agony, screaming this high pitched sound so great everything stopped for a moment.

I thought for a second I had been victorious but after what felt like using all of my power the creature recovered. Now instead of being a wild angry beast, I had just given it purpose and made it a wild, angry, vengeful beast!

"Oh shit!" I said once again trying to run only this time in the direction of someone that could aid me. Because as cool as what I did was, I knew I was now all out of juice. I ran and screamed just as one of Jared's Hellbeasts rolled past me after being thrown off the back of the wolf, Fenrir. They were all going at it together and I could see little by little it was weakening from the constant attacks from all sides.

But instead of getting to safety by running this way I was only bringing more danger. I was just about to start running the other way when suddenly I was scooped from the ground and being flown backwards by Lucius.

"Stay here." He ordered and then snapped open his phone. I couldn't imagine who he was going to call at a time like this and would have asked if he hadn't snapped,

"Pip, get your ass here now!" Pip! What the Hell could Pip do?

"No I know what I said but that was before the fucking Dragon appeared, so yeah fuck it, I will take the chance of Hell breaking loose, because right now, I need a fucking Hell on my side!" I frowned having no clue what he was talking about but then my whole body tensed as it just sounded like thunder striking a volcano right behind us in the trees.

"Fuck that was quick!" Lucius said and before I could ask, Pip suddenly came racing through the trees with the whole forest shaking behind her. Even the ground started to vibrate until it felt like it would open up beneath us.

"Oh God, what now?"

"I would move your asses if I were you...my hunka train is coming through." Pip said running past us and changing direction just before she ran straight into the Dragon.

"I think now would be the time to ignore my order." Lucius said, picking me up and launching us up in the air over to where Pip had decided to stand...well out of the way. Just as we got close I looked over his shoulder to see the scariest, most terrifying beast so far! Actually he made all the others look like demonic pets you would buy at a pet store run by the Devil.

"What the fuck did you say to him to get him to change so quickly?" Lucius asked her as soon as we had landed.

"Oh nothing much, just a little female persuasion."

"Pipper!" Lucius said her name in warning.

"Okay, okay...I simply told him that if he isn't gonna turn all beasty and sex me up then I might have to just go over there and find myself a naughty little beasty to play with me...see no biggy."

"Oh fuck!" Lucius shouted dragging both his hands through his hair. Meanwhile the battle still raged around us but with one big exception, now we had our own monster, and he was kick ass! He took one look at the Dragon standing in between him getting to Pip and went crazy! He ran into Níðhöggr at a dead run, charging at him with his head down and you could just see all the skulls of other demonic creatures embedded in his thick unearthly flesh.

"How the Hell are we going to get him to come back down now!?"

"Well you told me there was a freakin Dragon for foogle sake! What else was I supposed to do, Adam wouldn't listen to me!"

"Where is Adam?" I asked looking around realising this was the first time I hadn't seen the two of them together.

"Uh…durr Toots, he's right there." She said nodding to the new beast on the block.

"Wait a second…you're telling me that's…Adam?!" I said thinking this was the time I might actually pass out.

"Ooops, sorry, our bad! …Do you think a fruit basket will help?" Pip asked as her monster husband just back handed one of Jared's crew into the forest.

"More like a free night out at a titty bar, he's a fucking biker Squeak." She shrugged her shoulders and said,

"I know a girl, she can do me a deal." Were they serious right now! I looked to Draven and saw him still battling it out now with Vincent at his side as the enemy he fought had more than tripled in size.

"The last one is coming through." Lucius said nodding towards the Fathers and he was right. But I was surprised as I thought they were getting bigger but the one that walked through now was…

"It's just a woman." I voiced this as I wanted to make sure my eyes weren't deceiving me.

"That's not just a woman sweetheart."

"Oh Shit on a stick for breakfast." Pip added causing a chill to ripple across my spine.

"Who is she?" I asked,

Lucius pulled his sword from his back, swung it round once as if testing its weight and then said,

"My next fight." He took two steps towards her before Pip grabbed his arm.

"Be careful, Boss." He pinched her chin and said,

"Aren't I always?" Then he walked off leaving Pip shouting behind,

"Well no, the last time you were in Hell you lost your hand remember!" To which he turned and saluted her whilst holding up his middle finger. She gave him a smile that didn't reach her eyes and it was the first time I had seen Pip not only serious but also worried.

"Who is she?"

"She's the Devil." She answered as simply as that and I gasped.

"What?!"

"It's true. Her name is Hel and she is the ruler of Helheim, the Norse underworld, ruler of the dead. Her name means 'Hidden' and she is the most powerful of all that has walked through the pathway." She said, not being able to take her eyes off Lucius as he might be walking to his death.

"How do we stop it, Pip? How do we stop all of this?" I asked her grabbing her by the tops of her arms and spinning her to face me.

"Hey Honey, your date just arrived." Lucius said as he got into position to fight her.

"PIP!" I said dragging her away from the sight of Lucius. I needed her to focus now on how to stop this.

"We can't, she won't go back to where she came from until the pathway is about to close. She won't risk it, not in this world. She draws her power from Helheim but if that closes then she is powerless and she will be forced back to the underworld." Pip said telling me that at this level of crisis, she could lay it all on the line just like everyone else could.

"So we can stop it!" I said and she shook her head,

"Not with those four dickheads keeping the …oh, okay yeah we can stop it." She said getting where I was going with this. I was just trying to think of a plan when suddenly the Dragon that was on its way down after finally being defeated by Adam let out one last burst of fire into the sky and then straight across the field towards the barn when its head hit the ground. The barn was set alight almost immediately and I knew my priorities had changed.

"Oh God, the people!" I shouted and started running but turned to see Pip wasn't following.

"I have to save the others!"

"From what, the Dragon's down?!" I shouted back and then she shocked me when she whipped off her top and shouted back,

"No, not from them, from my husband!" And then she was gone, sprinting towards Adam the monster, half naked. I watched for a second longer to see little Pip hopping around trying to get her pants off and at the same time waving her little arms around under the beast. The second he saw her he tried to grab her but as his big hand came towards her she smacked it away, put a hand to her hip and shook her finger at him. I could barely believe what I was seeing as it was a bit like watching the damsel in distress taming King Kong. The next second she sprinted for the trees and the chase was on. I was quickly left shaking my head and praying that she knew what she was doing with that one.

I turned and raced towards the barn, knowing there were people inside! The whole back wall was covered in flames and I had to wonder how many burning buildings a person could see in their life before they knew they were gonna have fire issues?!

I got to the barn and flung open the door to see it was packed with people. Thankfully the smoke wasn't too bad yet and the part that was burning was at the back where no one stood thanks to it being full with straw.

"EVERYONE OUT NOW!" I screamed at them and even though they all resembled zombies, they did as they were ordered. I recognised that most of the Colony was in there too but after a frantic search for Ari I knew she wasn't with them.

"That way!" I pointed to the furthest point away from here and after one started walking towards the corn fields they all followed like drugged sheep. It was heart-breaking seeing Lucy and Denis not recognising me and looking all mindless but then one look back at what anyone would think was the end of the world, and I thought it was for the best.

"Go! Go! Follow the others!" I commanded and it was only when Dex walked past me that I saw something I might be able to use. I stopped him and being a good mind controlled human he obeyed.

"I'm just gonna borrow this." I said unsnapping his gun from the holster and taking it in my hand. I pointed it down not having a clue but knowing it might come in handy. Once everyone was out of the barn I closed the doors and stepped away as more and more of it became consumed. I turned to face the cause of all the chaos and death seeing that the Fathers were once more trying to bring something else through. I couldn't let it happen!

I remembered Ragnar saying how he and Sigurd could stop it if they could take the power away from the four Fathers but no one could get close enough. Draven had tried a few times and Rue had been hit and lay on the floor unconscious. Takeshi did what he had pledged to do and was protecting her against the walking dead that Hel, the ruler of the underworld, had brought through with her.

It was only now that I could see she was only half the image of a beautiful naked woman and the other half was decaying death, with ripped grey flesh and withered bone showing through. Yet despite appearances of frailty, she was kicking Lucius' ass and seeming to be enjoying herself whilst doing it… well if the evil grin and laughing was anything go by because she certainly wasn't speaking English!

No there was only one person they weren't expecting to stop them and that was a human girl they had helped terrorise for the last eight months that had felt more like a life time! So I crept up to the church just as I had done at the cabin and keeping close to the wall I edged my way round. The four robed figures all had their backs to me and thanks to concentrating on what they were doing they didn't even see me.

Not until it was too late.

I pulled the gun from the waistband of my jeans and from watching probably too many cop shows from my other life I knew to flick the safety off. I then aimed and fired at the closest one. I heard a click and had been expecting a lot more than that!

"Oh come on!" I whispered wondering why we couldn't just get a freakin break here! I looked down at the gun wondering what I had done wrong but at least not playing the stupid blonde in this disaster movie by looking down the barrel. I looked back up to see I didn't have much time as the next beast was making its way through and I don't think even after finally bringing down the wolf that Jared and his men looked capable for another round.

No, it was up to me to try one last time because it was now or never. I raised my arm again and this time prayed for violence. Then I pulled the trigger and finally fired my first bullet. One of the Fathers dropped to the floor and the pathway disappeared. I didn't stop there as I continued to fire all the bullets I had in the gun until all four were on the ground moaning in pain. I knew that if a blade in the head didn't kill one then a couple of bullets wouldn't but this was all Draven had needed!

This was also perfect timing as Hel looked to be getting ready to deliver a few killer blows down at Lucius when her source of power she was tapping into was ripped away from her.

"My turn, bitch!" Lucius said and kicked up so hard her rotting arm was severed. Draven too finally had the upper hand as the flames from the giant's sword he had been fighting suddenly extinguished, then turned to stone before crumbling away. The giant bellowed in anger but by this time Draven had flown up in the air and landed on its back slamming both his swords into the creature's brain. As it fell forward Draven rode the body down until it was on the ground and then calmly jumped off its shoulder.

Ragnar was already taking charge of the Runes after stepping on one of the Fathers hands, crunching his bones before he willingly would give it up. He threw it to Sigurd who got started on what needed to be done. Draven flew over to me, pulled me into his arms and simply held me for a moment as if needing to be reassured first that I was real and I was alive.

"Are you alright?" He asked holding me back at arm's length to look at me.

"You know, I don't think I even have a scratch." I told him looking down at myself. He smiled down at me and said,

"I have decided that's the only thing I ever want to hear from you after a battle." Then I reached up on my toes and whispered in his ear,

"Trust me, that's not the only thing you want to hear from me after a battle." Then I winked at him and did something I never thought I would do and that was I grabbed his man package and rubbed my hand along his length. His reaction was priceless as he groaned after giving me eyes wide with shock.

"Do you know what I would do to you right now given half the chance?" He growled back and I moaned at how sexy it sounded. That was until someone cleared the voice behind us.

"Sorry to interrupt my Lord but…"

"The fuck we are! If you don't mind we have shit to do here and I think there is shit in there for you two love birds to be getting on with, don't you think?" Sigurd said after dragging one of the bleeding Fathers off the front of the church before flinging him towards one of Jared's men, saying,

"Hold that for me won't you?"

"Oh god Draven, the ritual!" I shouted remembering this was what it was all for.

"Christ alive… Monster dead shit everywhere, barn blazing to the ground, human zombies in the cornfield and all of us watching and you two are about to get it on! And I thought I could get horny at the weirdest of times…well you two can certainly take my crown for that fucked up shit award!" Sigurd carried on talking to himself and I blushed every shade of red!

"I don't think you will be needing that now, sweetheart." Draven said ignoring him and taking the gun off me. He clicked the safety back on and took my hand. I looked over my shoulder at everyone dealing with helping Sigurd and Ragnar contain the mess of defeated creatures, ready to send them back to where they belonged. Vincent ran up to us both and asked,

"Where would they keep her?" I told him about our basement and pointed to the furthest house at the back of all the others. He nodded and set off in search of my sister.

"You ready for this?" Draven asked looking down at me and I nodded back up at him. Then he said the sweetest thing at a time like this…

"Let's go kick ass together."

"Hell, yeah!" I replied and we both pushed open the door only to witness the new horror waiting for us.

Ari was dead.

CHAPTER 41
REMEMBERING LOST DECISIONS

"**N**O!" I screamed as my eyes first went straight to Ari's body lay on the altar bleeding into the grooves carved around it. I tried to run to her, not seeing anything else when Draven grabbed me from behind.

"Ssshh, she's not dead…do you hear me?" Draven said but I was too far gone to hear his words of comfort. I fought him, needing to get to my sister.

"Listen to me! Look, she is still bleeding, which means she is still alive!" I finally let what he was telling me sink in and saw what he was talking about. She was still bleeding and if you looked very closely you could just about see she was still breathing.

"You're too late! Our Lord comes this night!" My Uncle shouted raising his hands up to the ceiling.

"We need to do something." I told Draven but he was looking along the floor to see there was some kind of white line.

"Is that salt?" I asked in confusion.

"We can't cross over." He told me still looking for a way.

"Can't we just…" I went to kick it with my foot to break the line when Draven shouted,

"NO!" And grabbed me back before I could touch it.

"It won't recognise you as human." He told me and I looked up at him frowning.

"It won't let anything from Hell to pass."

"Well then I should be able…" Draven started to shake his head so that sentence tailed off. From the look on his face now wasn't the best place for confessions, although we were in a church!

"We have been together." I frowned again and said,

"Yeah but just because we have been around each other shouldn't mean…" Draven sighed, pulled me to him and decided to clear this up in the only way he knew how in a situation where time was of the essence,

"I have come inside of you, many times now."

"Oh…right, super demon seed, got ya! So how do we get past this?" I said ignoring when he rolled his eyes at my 'super demon seed' comment. Before he could answer me someone else decided to join the party. Draven and I both spoke a name at the same time, only the names didn't match up,

"Rory?!"

"Aurora!" Okay, so Draven definitely hissed this name. He looked to me and said,

"You know her?"

"Yeah, she's my cousin or at least I thought she was. Now I have no clue what she is, other than a total bitch with a baby on the way!" Draven growled turning back to face her and I could definitely tell these two had history. But wait, did he say,

"That's the Aurora chick you have been telling me about, the one who double crossed you?"

"Yes and she also left you for dead in a prison in Hell." He told me, not taking his glaring eyes off her.

"Figures…she was always a bitch to me in here too." I said

taking it all very well I thought…well that was of course until I got my hands around her scrawny swan like neck!

"It will hold?" She asked my uncle, referring to the salt line that was keeping us out.

"Yes, it has been purified in holy water before being blessed by our seer."

"Is there any way to stop it?" I whispered side on to Draven.

"In the time we have…I just don't know." I looked around just like he did hoping that answer would be staring us in the face. Come on think Katie! What would Ari do? I looked towards her and gasped when I saw she was looking right at me. She was mouthing something to me but I couldn't make it out. Then I saw her painfully lift her bloody hand just a fraction and point towards the back of the room. I saw there was nothing there but stacks of old pews and a dusty piano that was never allowed to be used, no matter how many times Ari begged with our mother. Ari loved playing…

"Oh god. That's it." I said.

"What? Wait Keira what are you…" He never got to finish as I picked up one of the tall church candles and chanted the song I had heard my sister singing in her dream…that's what I needed to see that night. That's what she was trying to tell me!

> *'It is not this salt I wish to burn,*
> *It is my lover's heart to turn;*
> *That may neither rest nor happy be,*
> *Until he comes and speaks to me.'*

"We have to burn it!" I said and used the candle to set it alight. I jerked back when it started to sizzle and burn, crackling like gunpowder all the way along. Draven gave me a look as if say, 'how did you do that?' but instead just took my hand and we both stepped over.

"You're both too late, the ritual has begun, our Lord will be born!" Draven growled ignoring my uncle but looking down towards Aurora's belly.

"Don't make another step or he's dead!" My mother's voice echoed around the room as she stepped from behind a large red curtain that was hung up, concealing the doorway behind the altar. With her she was dragging in the poor lad I saw that day in the barn bringing in the X frame when I was hiding in the loft space.

"John?" I spoke his name and he looked towards me but the confusion on his face was clear to see, especially when my pretend mother was holding a blade to his neck.

"Celina!" Draven shouted her name and what must have been out of habit, she flinched.

"You're too late, it has begun." I looked to Draven and said,

"They really need to get a new line, I'm getting bored." Aurora snarled at me and I gave her the finger.

"Let them go or else!" I demanded and Celina started laughing at me. I shrugged my shoulders when Draven looked down at me and I said,

"What, you're scary enough, I thought I would give it go." The next thing Aurora doubled over and started screaming,

"It has begun! Our Master comes!"

"Who is she talking about?" I asked but Draven took a step towards her and Celina dug the knife further into John's neck at the same time Ari screamed out.

"Ari!" I also took a step towards her and my Uncle shouted,

"Stay back or they both die!" Draven held out an arm to stop me and snarled,

"You don't have the power to do this, or the right vessel, Cronus' reincarnated soul will never survive the crossing!" This is when the image of my mother started to change. I gasped when she lifted up her hand over herself and what was left behind it was a beautiful red headed woman with an evil grin.

"You have no idea how long we have planned this. Even Sammael had no clue as to the depths of our plan right under his nose. He was always going to fail but we needed you in Hell!"

"Enough Celina!" Aurora snapped obviously not wanting to her to divulge their plans too much.

"And what does it matter now, it cannot be stopped Eos! Our Uncle comes to claim back what was taken from him!"

"Your uncle?! But that means…" Draven was piecing it together and Celina started laughing,

"You are such a foolish King and have little clue what happens right under your nose! I am Selene, daughter to the mighty Titan Hyperion who was imprisoned in Tartarus and who Cronus will release with his rebirth!" Celina or Selene told us with pride but Aurora shouted,

"Silence sister!" As she doubled over again.

"It is near, get him ready!" My uncle interrupted and all the pieces started to fit together for Draven.

"I have to stop this… I have no choice, Katie." Draven told me and I knew what he was asking of me.

"No! You can't…you…" I was cut off when Ari screamed out again.

"I have to kill the boy!" I frowned and after taking a deep breath he told me,

"He's RJ's brother Jack and he is also your friend." I inhaled sharply at hearing this and looked to him trying to dig deep and find those memories. I didn't find them but what I did find was a good soul looking back at me through those eyes. I just couldn't do it and I couldn't let Draven,

"There must be another way!" Draven looked around and said,

"Cover your head." I did as I was told and just as Aurora screamed for the last time, Draven unleashed his power. He opened up his arms and roared. A wave of energy blew out all the glass around the church but this move backfired. Celina held out her hand and drew in some of the power for herself and from the look of things this was something Draven didn't know she could do.

"My turn!" She said and then fired it back out at Draven and I, only this time it seemed more concentrated than what Draven was trying to attempt.

"Look out!" Draven said pushing me off to the side so I wasn't hit.

"Now Selene!" Aurora screamed bending double again and crying out just like someone in labour.

"Do it, drain her Galizur!" Aurora's sister then shouted to my Uncle and before he could do anything to Ari I ran at him. Unfortunately, Selene saw me coming and threw some of Draven's stolen power my way, knocking me off my feet. My Uncle took one of chalices that Ari's blood was dripping into and first drank some himself and then walked over to Aurora who drank from the same cup.

"Give me that!" Selene said then grabbed Jack by the hair and forced him too to drink. Then, at the sound of Draven's wrath, she dropped the cup, slopping Ari's blood down Jack, when his furious roar was powerful enough that the walls began to crack.

"Deal with him!" My Uncle ordered and Selene threw Jack by the hair over to her sister. He hit the ground with a thud and Aurora forced her bent body over to him.

"Give me the blade!" Aurora snapped pointing to the one she couldn't reach lying on the pulpit next to my Uncle. He grabbed it and I knew I had to stop them. Draven was busy fighting Selene and I could tell he was doing so in a calculated way so as not to slip up again and give her any more extra power to work with. I also noticed the way he drew her even further away from me, so that he could keep me protected.

"Begin the transfer!" Aurora snapped obviously being the one in control here. My Uncle nodded and began chanting over Ari, doing something to her that caused her back to start to arch off the altar.

"No!" I shouted looking around for something to use. I ended up picking up a tall candle stick and I walked up to him and said,

"Hey Uncle, why don't you preach about this!" He turned around just at the right time as I swung the heavy brass stick around, connecting with his face. I think if you could have slowed down time you would have seen the moment his lower jaw dislocated from the rest of his skull. Unfortunately, he didn't sack it to the ground as I had hoped, so just before he could seek his revenge I went to grab Ari off the altar. I was finally just within reach of her when once more I went hurtling backwards, my body slamming into the line of pews laid out ready for service.

I looked up only to see I had underestimated my Uncle and after quickly snapping his jaw back in place he carried on sucking the life out of Ari. At the same time the whole place was suddenly filled with the deafening sounds of agony coming from Jack, pleading for his life. I looked over to see Aurora was bent over him carving something into his chest with the blade.

"We are running out of time…transfer it!" Aurora screamed at my Uncle who had his hands hovering over my sister. A second later Selene's body came crashing down the centre aisle like a human bowling ball and smashed into the altar enough to leave a back shaped indent. I looked back to Draven to see him panting in anger, no doubt finding it difficult to rein in his powers and not use them against her. I stood up and ran to him.

"Are you alright?" He said lifting my chin and wiping the line of blood he saw from the cut I knew was there.

"I'm fine but we need to stop this."

"You're too late!" Aurora said picking Jack up by his hair and holding the blade to his neck.

"Now Galizur! TRANSFER IT NOW!" Selene thundered the order and he held out his hands towards Aurora's belly letting streams of light fire from his palms. Aurora could barely keep on her feet and the force knocked her back against the wall where she took Jack with her. Then she groped around for the red curtain and yanked it down as soon as she felt it, ripping it from its hoops.

It quickly revealed another set of Runes all painted on a wooden door in blood and each of the symbols was positioned around a giant Pentagram.

"AAAAHHHH" Aurora screamed just as Draven sent one last burst of power towards the door, trying to destroy it. Selene saw it and jumped in front of it just before it could hit and once again she simply absorbed it. Aurora pulled herself and Jack in front of the new pathway.

"We need the power in his blood to complete the path and then to seal it!" Selene said backing up towards her sister after nodding to my Uncle.

"You dare to double cross me!" His outraged reaction to this was proof there was no end to the deception of these two sisters.

"We don't need it, yours will do…! *Good bye my sister.*" Aurora said before yanking Selene back by the shoulders and then thrusting the blade in her back, stabbing her through the heart. Shock and confusion made her eyes go wide before she muttered,

"Sister?" Aurora didn't care, she removed the blade, lifted up her hand then dragged it down, finishing the last rune needed to complete the circle. They lit up one by one and just as the

portal opened Aurora fell backwards into the abyss, taking Jack with her and I screamed out as the last thing we saw was Aurora slitting Jack's throat.

"NOOOO!" Draven grabbed me, stopping me from racing after them as he knew what would happen next. Selene still had her hand on her heart as the blade had pierced right through to her front and with bloody hands she crawled towards the pathway, trying to follow Aurora.

"Eos...sister, don't leave me...don't leave me here...save me!" I wanted to point out the obvious at this point that she was actually the one who stabbed her so it was unlikely she would just pop her head back through and say, 'oh okay then' and give her a hand!

But she dragged her way there and just as she went to put her hand through the portal Draven roared,

"Sister, COME BACK!" Her heart breaking cry was her last words on this earth as Draven roared,

"Get down!" Then he was on top of me, covering me with his wings and all I could see was light exploding through the feathers making them glow. When he finally lifted his wing after checking it was first safe, I found myself blinking rapidly until my eyes could take the bright light.

"Fuck!" Draven swore, meaning this was bad.

"Where did they go!?" Draven demanded striding straight up to my Uncle, who I still called that out of habit...besides I couldn't pronounce the name Selene and Aurora had called him. I blinked away the rest of the dancing spots of light and was surprised to see the church didn't look like a bomb had just gone off like I would have expected.

I watched as Draven grabbed the last one standing in our way by the throat and lifted him clean off the floor. It was as if the only power stopping Draven from doing this in first place was now gone. I looked to where they had both disappeared only to see the slight remains of Selene, that were charred bones still reaching out to the door that was long gone. It was a haunting sight that spoke solely of the ultimate deception. Aurora had sacrificed her own sister, using her so she could escape. I thought back to that night at the wall and it couldn't have been more different.

A sister who sacrificed herself so that the other may escape. The differences were screaming out at me as I looked to Ari to see she was still alive!

"Ari!"

"Stop!" Draven ordered me back from getting closer. I didn't question it knowing he was protecting me and after what I had put him through at the wall, I knew I owed him this.

"Let her go...NOW!" Draven ordered and I looked again more closely this time. I sucked in a quick breath realising now that our Uncle still had control over her. Streams of energy seemed to be connected to him and Ari started moaning from having her essence drained out of her.

"I... can't!" He said struggling to form the words through not being able to breathe.

"NOW!" Draven bellowed again bringing him down to his knees and putting him in a head lock that looked as though with one twist he could break his neck.

"I told you I can't! We are connected now, as long as I live she will die."

"Then you die!" Draven snarled but before he could make the fatal move, he shouted,

"WAIT! If you kill me then you will lose your Chosen One!" Just as he said this Vincent walked through the doors at the end and took in the situation, first finding Ari on the altar. He seemed frozen unable to move at his first real sight of her.

"Speak!"

"If you kill me then you lose all chance of getting back your

Chosen One's memories. The second I die, so do her memories with me."

"Oh god." I muttered covering my mouth with my hand in horror.

"Draven please…you have to…*save her."* I said crying for what we would both lose but the sacrifice was worth making for the life we would gain. I looked to Vincent who seemed locked to his brother's eyes, displaying too many emotions to count.

"Forgive me, Keira." Draven said and I cried out,

"No!"

Then Draven looked to his brother and said,

"I do this for you, brother." Then with a sharp, violent twist snapped my Uncle's neck.

Draven then closed his eyes, against the obvious pain of saying goodbye…

Goodbye…to his Keira.

CHAPTER 42
'IT WILL BE OKAY'

Vincent fell to his knees at the same time my Uncle's body did. I burst into tears and ran to my sister as she dragged in her first breath. I wrapped my arms around her, lifting her upper torso towards me holding the back of her head.

"Ari! Oh god Ari, you're going to be okay now, I'm here." I said crying and unable to stop.

"Kay Bear…is that you?" Hearing her broken voice calling me that was the greatest of gifts I could ever have had received and the most perfect of endings to this battle against evil. Of course Aurora had escaped and poor Jack was gone but as I held my sister so close after all this time I cried for what I had gained, more than what I had lost.

"Am I dreaming?" She asked me and I pulled back to look at her. She was staring at Vincent at the end of the aisle on his knees and his magnificent white wings were stretched out in all their glory. He looked like a broken Angel begging for forgiveness.

"No, he's real Ari." I told her and she looked back at me

with wild eyes before they suddenly rolled back up in her head as she promptly passed out.

"Ari!" I shouted her name and gave her a shake as fear overtook me.

"It's okay love, she's fine. But my guess is like you, she's a little overwhelmed seeing a certain someone for the first time." Draven said laying a comforting hand on my back and looking back at his brother over his shoulder. I lowered my sister down once I realised he was probably right. Then I turned into his arms and held him tight.

"You saved her." I stated the obvious and I felt him swallow hard.

"Yes." I looked up at him and I bit my lip at the raw emotion I saw there.

"I'm sorry you had to choose." I told him softly knowing that he would never get the 'me' back that I knew he must have been hoping to find. Draven looked up and nodded to Vincent before moving us to the side so his brother could pick Ari off the altar before carrying her out of the church, safely nestled in his arms.

"I have you back now, that's all that matters to me." Draven told me before kissing me softly. Then he pulled back, held his hand out to me and said,

"Let's go home." And with that he just added the most perfect words to begin my new *perfect* life.

The next day we all found ourselves back at the hotel and this is when Draven explained a few things regarding what we were to expect next now that Aurora had escaped. First he explained all about Cronus and his plans for reincarnation, using Aurora as a foolish pawn.

She had tricked Seth, needing the power he had in him as the first blood. I didn't fully understand all Draven told me about Seth and the importance of who his mother was. But I understood that by using unknown spells she had opened up a small window of time in which she could become pregnant, nurturing Cronus' trapped soul until it was strong enough to be passed onto the right vessel.

This is where Celina, or who we now knew as Selene, came into it. In the last few days Draven had already started his investigation trying to piece together Celina's real life and information had come trickling in bit by bit already. It turned out that she had not only stalked me most of my life but also RJ and Jack too as there was something about them that we were yet to discover. Draven thought they must have been descendants of great importance no doubt for both Jack to be chosen as Cronus' vessel and also for RJ to be Seth's Chosen. Although I heard from Draven that Seth wasn't having an easy time telling RJ that her brother was still missing. It was decided and I agreed not to tell RJ what we didn't know for sure.

Yes, we had all seen Jack's throat being cut but because nobody knew who Jack really was, then we couldn't instantly assume death. Draven quickly assured me there might still be a chance but to also not get my hopes up, so I was left with trying not to think about it. This was hard knowing that they had both come here thinking they were saving my life. Seth did manage to get out some information from the difficult RJ, and who could blame her really, when she was simply worried about her brother.

She told him that Celina had contacted Jack and convinced him that I needed his help. She told him that she had helped me escape Draven after finding out about his betrayal but she couldn't go into details as there was no time. Of course being madly in love with Celina, the girl who broke his heart once and calling me a dear friend, he fell for it hook line and sinker.

RJ said she had found him packing a bag frantically and after she forced him to explain she wouldn't let him go without him agreeing to her tagging along. Of course the threat to go to Draven and tell him everything worked for Jack, which had been a shame because if RJ had done that, then none of this would have happened.

She even told Seth that Jack had heard me asking for his help as proof, over the phone but Draven hadn't seemed shocked by this. Not when I found out that it was simply done as that type of mind manipulation was easy for someone of their kind. After that they got in Jack's truck and drove to where Celina had a trap waiting for them. RJ remembered hearing people arguing over something not working on her and the decision to keep her in case she ever became useful to the cause. In other words, if they were lacking in human girl sacrifices, they no longer had to simply pick one up at the shop of horrors, also known as hitch hikers on the side of the road. Which turned out to be where they'd found most of their young 'Colony members'.

So after this, the next thing RJ knew was that she was being kept in a basement as a prisoner, only being kept alive, fed and watered for one purpose…to be a *human sacrifice.* I hated to say it but I think therapy was in RJ's future as I didn't know how someone could get over an ordeal like that without it.

We also found out that after some of the minds of the humans had been read that nine months ago this had actually been a quiet, peaceful Amish community and because of that it was the perfect place for the Hexad cult to set up base. The six 'Fathers' had easily distorted the people's minds into believing in the Hexad 'Religion' and it became the perfect hiding place to keep Aurora from being found.

The next part of their plan involved Ari and me, only lucky for me I knew my back story before they managed to steal me away through a mirror Celina had planted. Ari on the other hand had no clue who she was or where she came from. Because when Draven had killed our Uncle, now better known as Galizur, it wasn't only my memories that died with him, it was Ari's too. She struggled with this and I knew why as I too had the feeling of great loss knowing we weren't actually sisters. But for me it was easier as I already had a family waiting for me, Ari had no clue and felt completely alone.

Vincent had tried to give her the time she needed to deal with this without adding to her stress in finding out that they were actually meant to be together. It had been different for me as I had been graced with nearly a whole month to deal with all this new information given to me bit by bit over time. But Ari had been bombarded with everything all at once and it had taken me a whole day to explain it all, in between consoling her.

I will never forget how difficult and utterly heart breaking it was to have to tell your sister, who has a life time of memories together that it was all a lie. Of course the vision she had been hit with when we first found the cabin together prepared her for this, so she didn't doubt what I was telling her. But having your worst fears confirmed, no matter how ready you are, is still devastating to hear.

"What now...what is there left for me?" She had asked me breaking down into gut wrenching sobs.

"Ari, we may not be sisters by blood but we are always going to be sisters by tears as we have been through too much with each other to ever walk away. You will always have family with me." I told her as she soaked my shoulder through her grief.

After this she calmed enough to ask me about Vincent as I

knew a burning desire to know must have been nagging at her brain. But before I delved into what I thought about him first I had to tell her the whole story, starting with what happened after the wall. I told her about Lucy and Denis and how wonderful they were to me. I told her about Dex and the rest of the town that came to our aid, which I should mention all got back safely without any memory of what had happened.

As for the poor confused people from the Colony, Draven's 'clean up' team, which was code for when supernatural disasters happen like this, as a widespread mind sweep of memories is needed. He had his people erase all memories of the Hexad cult and seeing as most of the homes and crops survived, they didn't end up homeless and starving.

I then moved on to more difficult parts to explain, like meeting Draven and what they were. This she took remarkably well but considering what we saw that night, then I guess it wasn't too surprising as I had accepted everything rather quickly. Well, minus the whole marble room fight, that was.

All I could say was at least she had been spared the whole Norse monster invasion, although bleeding on an altar whilst someone sucked the life right out of you, couldn't have been fun. My favourite part about explaining things to her and my story was definitely when I got to tell her about all the wonderful people I had met. I told her about Luc and blushed when telling her about our bus journey together. And then meeting Pip and Adam, telling how much she was going to fall in love with Pip the second she meets her. Also about Sophia, reminding her she was Vincent's sister but most of all, I enjoyed telling her how in love I was with Draven.

I told her everything…well, almost everything. But most of all I told her how much he seemed to adore me, how good, kind and gentle he was with me and how loved he made me feel. Then she asked me,

"But why do you call him Draven if his name's Dominic?" I thought about it and ended up answering her honestly,

"I don't really know, it just kinda…feels right." And I knew why but I didn't tell Ari as she had too much to deal with right now. But the fact was as simple as I knew this was what Draven's Keira, my other self, had called him. I had tried to talk to Draven about what had happened and trying to find out how he really felt about me never regaining my memories but every time I tried to talk about it he would distract me by making love to me. Not that I was complaining but I knew he was also using it as a tactic to distract me from talking about it. I guess it was still raw, so I decided that if he needed to talk then he would. But I think deep down the problem was that he felt like he had failed Keira.

It was a difficult position to be in and I was hoping with time it would get better. I had even made the decision to ask everyone to start calling me by my real name, hoping this would help the transition. In truth I was a bit scared that now there was no way of the old me coming back that Draven would start backing off or decide that this was something he didn't want anymore. I would like to think of it as an irrational fear but still, a fear was fear no matter how silly it seemed to others.

Ari was the only one I could tell all this to and know that she would understand better than anyone. Which is how we finally got onto the subject of Vincent. I told her all I knew about him and that included, kindness, a good sense of humour, ridiculously handsome like his brother, but there were other attributes too, such as courageous, intelligent, fun and most of all loyal to what he believes in. She had been surprised when I told her the lengths to which he had gone to just to save her from the Colony.

"The man barely slept!" I told her and she muttered quietly,

"Then that makes two of us." I winced as she hadn't yet told me of her time there after I escaped,

"Ari, if you want to…"

"No! I'm sorry but I never want to speak of what I went through there, let alone think about it ever again. It's not worth my time and it's certainly not worth upsetting you over." She said before giving me a hug. I didn't know if not wanting to talk about it was a good thing or a bad thing but for now I knew not to push it. After this she told me she was still so tired, so I left her in her hotel room to sleep some more. I can't say I was surprised to see Vincent standing guard outside her room.

"I wasn't eavesdropping but…thank you for all your kind words." He said pulling me in for a hug and I smirked knowing that with his thanks he had been eavesdropping but no harm was done.

"I'm sorry but I still don't think she's ready." He nodded looking disappointed but not shocked as I guess he gathered as much from what he had heard.

"I'm not going anywhere, so she can have whatever time she needs." He told me and I smiled, patted him on the arm and said,

"Just a heads up, she's a speed freak, so maybe a good place to start would be your bikes." Then I winked at him and made my way back up to Draven in our suite. It had been a good job he had hired out the whole place because the state that we came back in would have frightened most guests away or at least had them calling the cops!

I took the lifts up to the top floor penthouse suite ready to crash again after such an emotional day. Last night, or should I say the early hours of this morning I must have passed out on the way back to the hotel because I woke up in the comfiest bed and surrounded by Draven's heat as I found myself locked in his arms. As was most mornings with Draven it was always the perfect start to whatever you faced in the day and I was looking forward to finding myself in those arms once again.

I didn't know what to make of my sister's emotional state, having really no clue as to where her head was at. But I knew where my head was at after it all and that was soon to be lying on a comfy pillow and passing out. I was exhausted and it had been a difficult day for all of us. In a way I would have loved to have pushed Ari into Vincent's arms, knowing secretly that was what was best for her. Because that type of comfort was like no other and far surpassed even my abilities as a sister. But if she had what I had, what I was about to receive for herself, that level of love and understanding from someone who would hold you through the night…

Well, there was nothing like it in the world.

This is why I smiled all the way up the floors and straight to the only door on this level. I was about to walk straight in but I stopped when I heard Draven getting angry at someone on the other side of the door.

"Where the fuck is she?" Draven roared and I heard his sister reply,

"Dom calm down. We don't know where she is right now, no one does." After this answer I knew his anger wasn't about my whereabouts at least.

"Well she needs to be found to sort out this fucking mess!" He snapped and I reckon if I'd been in there I would have seen Sophia flinch.

"You really think anything can be done?" She asked and I jerked back when I heard him say,

"She's the fucking fates! If she can't then tell me who can, because I won't accept that I just killed the only fucker out there that can bring her back to me!" On hearing this I felt like he'd just rammed a dagger straight through my heart. I took a few steps backwards and with each one my heart sank just that little

531

bit more. And here was me thinking he was dealing with it in his own time when really he was just biding his time until he could get 'This mess fixed!'

I couldn't help feeling betrayed by all his lies when telling me he had me back and that was all that mattered. When in actual fact he was glad I was back but just wanted a slightly less broken version of me!

"Dom! You need to calm down and think rationally, if Katie knew this is how you felt…"

"She won't!" He snapped back interrupting his sister.

"Yes but if you carry on this way."

"I wouldn't let it happen. She doesn't know how I am struggling with this and I want to keep it that way. She has enough to deal with at the moment than to know what my issues are as I very much doubt she could cope with this as well." At this I started to get angry instead of upset and the more I heard the more I wanted to give him a piece of my mind! I actually gave him the finger through the door but knew it wasn't nearly enough for what I was feeling right now.

"Have you shown her the newspaper article yet?" Sophia asked and I frowned wondering what else he was hiding from me other than his obvious resentful feelings towards me.

"Again you think this is the time?" Draven said being sarcastic and Sophia snapped back,

"Actually yeah, I do! Because I have to say, in the past Dom, keeping shit from her has never really worked out for the best for you, don't you agree?" I think at this point if I had been in the room I would have high fived Sophia for being on my side. Draven growled and said,

"I know what she can and can't handle!"

"Oh really and how do you think she is going to handle knowing you lied to her?" At this I heard a table being upturned and breaking against what sounded like the door I was listening through, which is why I jumped back in fright.

"She just handled a fucking battle!" He roared and suddenly I was lost...he was defending what I *could* handle now? Thankfully Sophia spoke for me,

"Exactly, which means she will be able to handle the article."

"You think that the best thing for her right now is reading about how her and her twin sister died in a car crash at the age of seven! You don't think that is going to fuck with her mind even more!" At this I put my hands to my mouth just to keep my cry of shock from escaping.

"No, I think it is the closure that her and her sister needs right now, so they can move on with no more doubt." I decided that biting my fist was safer at this point, especially when Draven lost his temper completely and shouted,

"It isn't even her real sister for fuck sake! She has a real one who we... *I* have been lying to for nine months now and am I am sick of messing with their minds, letting them think they see her once a week! She has a niece who I swear looks at me like I am the biggest lying asshole in all the world but thankfully is too young to speak!"

I mouthed the words 'oh my God' at hearing the lengths he had gone to just to keep my family from worrying but then it got worse,

"What else am I supposed to do? That family has been through enough the first time she was taken and they have the scars as everyday proof, do you really think Keira would want them to go through that again?"

"No I don't and I understand why you do it. We all do and Keira would want that but Dom, Keira is home now..." Sophia said and the next thing he said almost killed me,

"No Sophia, she isn't." He said quietly and even Sophia gasped,

"Dom, you don't mean that." I listened closely, desperate to hear what his reply would be, even going as far as putting my ear to the door.

"No, I…" He was cut short suddenly as Zagan appeared and said a loud,

"Katie?"

Suddenly the door opened and Draven was there and at the very first sight of tears streaming down my face, he knew that I had heard…

Everything.

CHAPTER 43
TRUST

With that one look Draven knew he was in deep shit as my face must have said it all.

"Katie I..." I held up my hand to stop him and said,

"Don't...just, don't." Then I wiped away my tears with an angry hand gesture, not really knowing what I was feeling the most...anger or beyond upset.

"Oh Katie, no." Sophia said coming to the door and looking gutted on my behalf.

"Come on sweetness, I think it's best we say goodnight." Zagan said gently, holding his hand out to his wife. Sophia gave me a small smile of regret and walked past me but before she did I stopped her with a hand on her arm.

"Thank you." I told her honestly, feeling a sense of not only sisterhood but loyalty, as it was comforting to know that someone would stand up for me that way and have more faith in what I could and couldn't cope with. She nodded in understanding and as they walked off I turned back to face Draven. I pushed myself past him into the room and walked straight over to the bed. He followed me after a big sigh and shut the door. He turned to face me and said,

"Alright, I understand you're…Umph!" Draven was cut short making this noise because I threw a pillow at him.

"What are you…?"

"You're gonna need it!" I said with my chest heaving I was that angry and ready to explode.

"Uhh…why?" Okay so it was obvious this was a new experience for him, so I snapped,

"What, perfect little Keira never threw you out before?"

"You do realise how ridiculous that sounds considering *you are Keira!*" He threw back at me and I was seriously getting emotional whiplash from this man!

"Well not according to you, buddy boy!"

"Did you just call me…?"

"Yeah and trust me, that was one very low on the list right now, so count yourself lucky!"

"Look, I know you're upset and heard…"

"Upset? Your think this is upset!? You haven't seen fucking upset! So save your damn speeches for someone who gives a shit and get the fuck out of here!" I screamed at him and now he looked shocked. Good, maybe now he would be taking this a bit more seriously.

"I'm not leaving!" He stated throwing the pillow back on the bed and then folding his arms.

"Fine then you can sleep in the tub! Lucky for you it's big enough for about ten people so you should have no problem getting your big man ass in there!"

"Big man ass?!"

"You heard me!" I said really wishing I would have gone for something a bit more insulting that 'big man ass' but I gathered men didn't really get over protective about their ass being called big.

"I am not moving." He stated ignoring my insults and no wonder, as they were kinda lame.

"Fine! Stay there all damn night if you want to, you're not coming in this bed!" Then I stripped all my clothes off in some angry attempt at proving how little I cared and I had to say, it was hard to keep in my satisfied grin when I saw how hungry his eyes got as they roamed over my body. Then I turned off the light, leaving him standing in the dark so that I could finally get away with smirking to myself.

"I can still see you, you know." I inwardly cursed at being caught and then said,

"Good, can you see this?" And then I gave him the middle finger.

"I'm ignoring that and enjoying what comes with it." He told me in a rough voice that spoke of desire so I checked and sure enough the bed sheet was around my waist, showing him my naked breasts in the dark.

"Yes well you can just go on and keep enjoying it because this is the closest you're gonna get, 'cause you're certainly not going to be getting some for a while!"

"That sounds like a challenge." He purred back and I snapped,

"More like a promise...! Ah!" I shouted in surprise as he was suddenly on top of me. He yanked me further down so I slid under him and I quickly found myself breathing heavy.

"You were saying, sweetheart." I growled back at him and I felt him chuckling above me. Fine. He wanted to play, then we were going to play! I gave him a sweet sickly smile and as soon as he raised his eyebrow I quickly brought my knee up and caught him in the ribs. I knew it wouldn't hurt but it caught him off guard enough that I could wriggle from under him. I was just scrambling off the bed when I felt him shackle my ankle and say,

"Going somewhere?" Then he pulled me back, making me slide back up the bed. I twisted my body so that his hold slipped enough for me to launch myself at him so now I was on top.

"Ha! I win!" I shouted suddenly having way too much fun and forgetting what I was actually mad at him for...well, almost.

"Not yet you don't!" He shouted back and then first got his leg over me before twisting me round so I was back to where I started. I was panting from all the effort and Mr cocky pants above me I could barely hear him breathing at all. So this was when I decided to cheat. I stuffed my hand down in between us and grabbed his obvious erection in my hand. Now this definitely got his attention!

"You're not playing by the rules." He warned and the sound of his zipper going down was my only answer to that. I reached in his trousers and grabbed the steely length suddenly hungry to play a different game. I don't know what had come over me but the urge to have him inside was getting intense. I was angry yes, I was hurt, oh hell yeah, but all of these things were never going to be enough to make me not want him. And right now, all that insecurity I felt was quickly warping into *need*.

He groaned above me as I worked my hand up and down, loving how powerful it made me feel having this control over him. Then I let him go and pushed up, tipping the scales and flipping him onto his back. I knew he obviously let me do this, probably knowing that I needed that power exchange right now. So before he knew what was happening I moved my legs to either side of his hips and lowered myself agonisingly slowly onto his length.

"By the Gods, woman!" He said gripping my thighs tight in an effort to anchor himself to me. I started to move, slowly at first up and down, then I tried rotating my hips, so that I was dragging the tip along those beautiful nerve endings of mine.

He growled below me and each demonic noise only managed to spur me on even more. I wanted to work him up into a frenzy and then just as I moved faster and faster I would then slow it right back down denying him what I knew he was so close to. Of course by doing this I was also denying myself, which was a lot harder than it sounded but if this was my only way to punish him then it would be worth it to make my point.

"Say my name." I told him and saw his purple eyes flash in the dark. He growled and took a chance by saying,

"Keira."

"And who is making love to you now?" I asked at the same time twisting my hips again and forcing myself down hard on his length. He moaned louder and gripped me tighter.

"You are, my Keira." He gritted out from no doubt the intensity of it. Because I received the right answer I rode him harder as a reward, ignoring the bite of strain in my muscles.

"Fuck!" He ground out and hearing it I could feel myself building.

"So...am...I... her?" I forced the question out through each hard push against him, plunging my body down to take him as deep as I could.

"Yes! Fuck yes! You're her! You've always been her!" He shouted and this time he couldn't help it, he needed to go faster than what my body could physically do. So he sat up, gripped my cheeks in each hand and powered me up and down on his cock so fast I came in seconds pulsating and jerking around him as I screamed his name,

"DRAVEN!" He came straight after I did this, baring my neck and biting into me like a raging animal. I came instantly again and it was a beautiful pain that merged quickly into pleasure that the feeling became lost into the world of euphoria. He was panting through his nose where he was still embedded against my neck and felt him suck me in one more time before his fangs retracted. I wasn't surprised there was no pain as the endorphins in my body were overriding all my senses.

"I love you, Keira. You are mine and I was being foolish. Please forgive me my darling." He whispered into my cheek after kissing his way up there from my neck. I didn't know what to say, other than knowing that we still needed to talk about this, now that the initial storm had passed. So I didn't agree to forgive him, not just yet because if we were going to move past this, then I needed some assurances from him. So I lifted myself off him and for a moment I didn't think he would let me as his hands momentarily gripped me tighter.

I felt the combined evidence of our love making drip down and thankfully without the blinds down I had grown accustomed to only having the moonlight to guide me. However, Draven must have been worried I could fall because I only made it a few steps to the bathroom before the soft glow of a bedside table lamp lit my way. I walked into the bathroom and cleaned myself up before wrapping myself in a robe. Then I grabbed a damp cloth and walked back into the suite.

I found Draven sat on the edge of the bed with his head in hands looking lost. I walked straight to him and he lifted his head in question when I lowered myself to my knees in front of him. I then took the damp cloth and started to clean him in the most intimate of ways.

"Keira, you don't need…"

"Ssshh." I whispered softly and by this it told him that I needed this connection right now. It was my way of showing him that I needed to feel wanted, that I needed to feel… *needed.*

Once I was finished I lowered my head knowing what was coming next. I felt his hand reach down and stroke my face and I was mesmerised by how gentle a man as big as Draven could be. With little added pressure he raised my face until I was looking up at him.

"Forgive me." He asked me and I swallowed hard before getting to my feet.

"Do you trust me?" I asked him as I sat next to him on the bed. He sighed probably knowing where this was going.

"Yes"

"And you in return want me to trust you?"

"Of course." He said looking sideways at me, making his raven black hair fall to one side.

"Then you really need to start earning it instead of demanding it from me because you don't reward trust with lies."

"I have not lied." My look said it all but my words backed it up,

"You told me you were fine. What I heard back there didn't sound 'fine' to me." He knew I had him on this one.

"You have enough to deal with."

"And you don't? What, you think my issues are greater than yours or more important?" He didn't answer me but just closed his eyes against the cracks that appeared in his logic.

"Do you think I am not strong enough to be your wife?" His head shot up and he looked at me in confusion, affronted by my question.

"Keira, I think you are the strongest woman I have ever known." I gave him a small smile and blushed slightly but then said,

"But you don't think I'm strong enough for you?"

"I don't think that at all." He told me.

"Then you should know I am strong enough to be there for you because I have to say, if you think you are protecting me by keeping things from me then I'm telling you now, you're not protecting me, you're just hurting me."

"Please don't say that." He told me looking as though I had just caused him great pain.

"But it's the truth. How would you feel if I kept things from you because I thought you couldn't cope? Correct me if I'm wrong but didn't this whole thing begin because I kept something from you."

"What do you mean?" I wasn't sure if he had put two and two together but when I found those pictures I certainly had.

"I found those pictures of Celina in my bag, one that I brought to Afterlife, so I must have brought them to show you but I didn't…now why do you think that was?" Draven looked to me and you could see all it all playing out in his head. He rubbed a hand across his jaw and he now came up with the same solution as I did and he nodded his head slowly letting me know I had made my point.

"If we keep things hidden then we are only fighting against each other rather than fighting as one. To hear how you're really feeling about all of this, when there was a door in between us was you shutting me out in more ways than one. And by you not telling me something I should have known the second you found it out then you're asking the impossible when you ask me to trust you."

"I understand what you're saying but you have to know that none of my actions were done to hurt you, but the opposite."

"I know, which is why I am not walking out that door now and never looking back." He jerked back at just the thought of me doing this.

"Look, I am going to be honest. Yes, hearing what you said hurt me but I also knew that you were angry, frustrated and you were venting it out when I wasn't around because it had built up and up until you could take it no more. I get that people say things they don't mean in situations like this." I looked to him, lay my hand on his knee and continued,

"But it wasn't what you said that hurt, it was the fact you felt like you couldn't talk to me about it that hurt. If I am going to be your wife then I need to be the first person you turn to when you are feeling this way, even if I am the cause."

"But how could I have said any of this to you, Keira? None of this is your fault yet I struggle with how I feel knowing what we lost. I didn't want to hurt you, I didn't want you to feel at blame, when the blame is all mine. I didn't want you to know how ashamed I felt at letting you down." He told me, finally being honest and it lifted my heart to know that he was finally opening up.

"But that's just it Draven, if you would have told me that to begin with I would have then told you in return, that the only people I do blame are the ones that did this to us. You saved me from them, you saved Ari from them and sacrificed our memories to do so, which if possible only makes me love you even more. I am still Keira in my heart and that is all that should matter because I hold you there." He took my hand and raised it to his lips to kiss before whispering,

"I know. As you are forever in mine."

"I'm sorry." I took his face in my hands and told him,

"I forgive you." And with that our argument was over and now we could close that chapter on our lives and start over. Because I was looking forward to making new memories with him and it was time to get over the loss of what we now knew we could never get back. I understood that it was going to be hard for Draven as he knew exactly what he had lost and I... well, it was easier to get over something you didn't know, a bit like mourning a person you never met but knew everyone loved.

At first I had thought that I would never be able to live up to her memory and in some ways I still had this fear but just because I was scared of not being good enough didn't make it true. It wasn't going to be easy but as long as we walked this difficult path together, hand in hand, then I knew we would make it to the other side, the only question was time.

Because that is all we had now. That was what we had been given. Time. Life. And now after this came the Truth.

After this he pulled me into his lap and held me close like he needed this, like he needed me. Because I was his wife. Not any other version of me. Not my other self or some girl named Keira. Because now I knew...

I was Keira.

And there was only one.

Draven stood and lowered me down to the bed before slipping under the sheets next to me. He wrapped me in his arms and whispered,

"Good night, my Keira." I smiled in the dark and whispered back,

"Good night, my Draven."

I closed my eyes and started to drift off with the visions of what my life would be like from now on. I was nervous but excited about meeting my family for the first time which had me thinking about what it would be like. Times like birthdays and holidays spent together and I looked forward to learning different family traditions and quirks. Did we all sit round and play games whilst family Christmas movies played on the telly in the background. Did we listen to cheesy Christmas tunes whilst decorating the tree and getting the men to hang lights outside, moaning about getting out the ladder. Did we bake our own birthday cakes for our family members or did we know someone that made them?

My mind was filled with silly little questions that would come to mean the world to me. Because it was the little things in life that you counted on to build the whole picture. And that picture was often the most beautiful thing in the world to you when it was the little things that made you smile.

So that night I went to sleep with a smile on my face, just thinking of all the beautiful little things that I had to look forward to. And before I knew it my peace was shattered what felt like only minutes later but the sun coming through the windows told me otherwise.

Sophia burst through the room and shouted

"Ari's gone!" My heart stopped as I tried to process what Sophia had said, quickly trying to think why, how or even who had taken her but if I thought these words were shocking then the next thing Sophia said was even more so…

"Vincent took her."

CHAPTER 44
THE HARDEST WORD IS ALWAYS GOODBYE

"What do you mean she's gone?" I shouted sitting up, happy that at least Draven had left my bathrobe on. So I grabbed the collar and pulled it closed just to make sure I wasn't flashing her my girls.

"Tell us!" Draven commanded getting out of the bed having no care that he was naked. He simply put on his trousers ready for this next drama.

"Are you sure it was Vincent?" I asked panicked that it could have even been a possibility considering he assured me last night that he would give her time. Well waiting until my back was turned and then swooping on in there and taking her off somewhere wasn't exactly something I would class as giving her time!

"Well, who else could it be? He was keeping watch outside her room last night when we left you guys to um...well, you know. We saw her open her door and ask to speak with him. He seemed surprised but I left them hoping it was at least a good sign. Then when I went to check on Vince, he wasn't there and neither was Ari." I thought about this and could only hope they had decided on leaving together and that it wasn't anything more sinister at play.

Draven fished out his phone and had it to his ear in seconds.

"He's not answering." He complained and then walked over to the hotel suite's phone. He was on to the front desk in seconds and asked them if they had seen his brother. I wasn't shocked when Draven didn't need to describe him as it wasn't like management would forget what the Draven triplets looked like, not considering they had hired out the entire hotel.

"He definitely took her. They said that the both of them came to the reception and asked for a cab."

"Did they say where to?" Sophia asked and Draven scoffed and said,

"The nearest bike dealership."

"Uh, figures." She replied dryly.

"What does that mean?" I asked as the both of them seemed to know more than I did about their brother.

"My guess, a long distance road trip."

"But where would they...wait a minute...does Vincent know about the article?"

"Yes." Draven said definitely already knowing where I was going with this.

"Then I know where they're headed." I said getting out of bed and grabbing my bag on the way to the bathroom.

"What are we going to do?" Sophia asked and I turned to face her and said,

"We're going on our own road trip." And it only took one look to Draven to tell him how much I needed this. Because there was no way I would let Ari do this by herself, even if Vincent was there with her. I knew there was only one other person in this whole world that she needed by her side who would understand exactly what she was going through.

And that was me.

I wasn't there for her once but I would be damned if I wasn't going to be there for her in this. Not when she saw it for the first time.

No, we would face our death together.

～

By the time we arrived in what was supposed to be my home state of Minnesota their head start on us meant nothing when you had a private jet. Draven knew exactly where to go having read the article himself and when we got there he finally received a phone call from his brother just as we were pulling up through the gates.

"We are here now." Draven informed him and I heard his single reply before the phone went dead,

"As I knew you would, Brother."

The second the car stopped I was out of the door despite the pouring rain.

"Keira wait!"

"Let her go, Sophia." I heard Draven say gently just before I started running. I saw Vincent sat leaning against a motorbike with his arms crossed and I pushed myself harder to get to him quicker. I didn't know how long they had been here already but just the thought of my sister upset and facing this alone was enough to have me in tears already.

"Where?" I asked him as soon as I reached the top of the path. He nodded straight on with drips of rain falling from the end of his nose and his hair plastered to his head. I looked to where he indicated and sucked in a sharp breath when I first saw her.

A lone figure stood in the rain holding two white roses hanging down from her hand and this time I walked slowly towards her. Every step was one that took me closer to my death and it was near terrifying to understand the concept of what we faced. But Ari needed this and looking at it now so did I. Because this was the closure we both needed to witness in order to move on.

I was soon taking my place next to her and I didn't say anything but simply took her hand in mine letting her know I was here with her. Looking down at the two gravestones and seeing our names there was a feeling that was almost impossible to describe. Ari passed me a single white rose, keeping one for herself and together we both lay them down over two young girls that were taken from this world far too soon.

Then we just stood there staring at the grass as all our memories sank into the ground as the rain washed away all the lies, cleansing us from the Heavens above.

"Vincent told me that white roses stand for innocence, purity, Heaven and last of all silence." I closed my eyes as more tears fell for the life we had shared and lost with these two girls.

"It also means 'I'm thinking of you'".

"That's sounds about right." I told her.

"I never thought it would be like this." I shook my head and said,

"Me neither."

"I thought we would get out and build a life together. Work at some crummy diner somewhere, moan about our feet hurting and save every penny to buy our own place." I grinned and squeezed her hand.

"Can't say I'm sad about the feet thing." At this she finally laughed. This was when I pulled her into me and hugged her.

"It will be okay, Ari." She burst into tears and sobbed,

"But I'm not Ari...am I?" She asked me this by pulling back and looking at me.

"She was Ari, and you're Keira, not Katie. And we're... we're...not..."

"Don't you even say it! Do you hear me...you are never to say that! Because we are sisters! Like I said, maybe not by blood but we survived as sisters Ari, I only survived that world because of you! That counts, it counts...it counts!" I repeated this over and over after pulling her to me so we could cry together.

"You will always be my sister, no matter what...promise me, Ari, promise me you will always be there for me. Because I need you Ari...I need you." I whispered to her holding her tight and not letting go until she told me all I needed to hear.

"I promise. I will always be there for you...

I promise you, my sister."

After this emotional farewell to our pasts we left the graveyard and Draven suggested we talk somewhere warm as we were both soaked. Which brought us to now and we smirked at each other when we both picked the crummy diner as we drove past.

"So where do you think you will go?" I asked Ari, who thankfully had decided to keep her name for now.

"I don't know but Vincent mentioned some Oracle who he seemed to think might be able to help." She said shrugging her shoulders and then she shouted,

"Oh my God! I'm getting the pancakes! Do you remember the last time we...?" She quickly trailed off realising her mistake. I grabbed her hand and said,

"Yes I do and because I always will remember, to me it happened...I thought you were gonna puke that day!" I added and her smile told me this was what she had needed to hear.

"So you're really going then?" I asked trying not to show her how sad I was about her decision, one that I knew hadn't been made lightly.

"Yeah." She said sympathetically.

"It will be okay, you've got so much stuff about to happen, exciting stuff and I… well, to be honest, I don't want to get in the way of that."

"You would never get…" She stopped me by saying,

"I know you wouldn't think so but I would. Vincent told me about your family…don't give me that face, I asked okay. I am happy for you, and I want that for you, I really do but I also might have it out there somewhere for myself and not even know it." I understood what she was saying and I really couldn't blame her as I knew I would be doing the exact same thing. And if you think about it I kinda did go in search of my family when finding Draven, without even knowing it.

"I understand and I would do the same thing. So is Vincent going to go with you?" At this she blushed and sipped her coke, probably needing it to cool down. I raised my eyebrow at her and she laughed saying,

"What?"

"Okay, okay well I am not going down that road yet, but he is helping me." She said after I gave her 'The look' but I had to admit that hearing this made me feel miles better. Even though I knew she still had a lot of stuff to sort out in her head at least I could say she was now on the right path after finding her closure.

"So I guess this is goodbye." I said trying to be brave and stuffing my hands in my pockets from fear of grabbing on to her and never letting go. In my mind that month we spent apart was the first time we had ever been separated and even though it was a life of lies, it was still all we knew. But more importantly, it still felt real, which was why saying goodbye now was so hard.

"Only for now, you're not getting rid of me that easily." She said and I could tell I wasn't the only one trying not to break.

"Why is it Goodbye is always the hardest word to say but there's nothing good about it?" I asked swallowing down my emotional lump straight after. She shrugged her shoulders and then we both turned to the Draven brothers and said at the same time,

"Take care of her."

"Take care of her." We laughed feeling like old times.

"I give you my word." Vincent said then pulled me in for a hug and whispered,

"My sister." I nodded knowing my voice was too thick to say more.

"As always I guard her with my life." Draven told Ari and she patted him on the arm in that awkward way someone does when they don't really know a person.

"No more battling monsters?" Ari said and I chuckled saying,

"No, I am thinking about taking up knitting, I hear it's nice and safe." She laughed back and then came the inevitable final hug goodbye.

"I love you."

"I love you more."

She rubbed her face free of tears before she put on the helmet Vincent handed to her and Draven tucked me under his arm for comfort. I thought it was sweet the way he made sure it was on properly before starting up the bike, kicking it into action.

And with that, they were gone. So the rest of my tears were soaked up in Draven's t-shirt all the way back to the airport…

As it was time to go home.

CHAPTER 45
TROUBLED SKIES

" I will tell ya something Tootie pop, and that is you don't make life boring, that's for damn nerdy cricket!" I smiled at Pip from across where she was sat stuffing cheese balls in her mouth and washing it down with some toxic looking soda.

We were all travelling back in one of Draven's private jets after getting back to the hotel and saying goodbye to Jared and his men and also Lucius and his. Cryptically during this farewell Draven added,

"Until you receive word." I would have asked him what he meant by it but Draven had a way of distracting you with a simple caress or in this case a mind blowing kiss as soon as I started to speak.

It had been two days since the battle and the end of the Hexad's destructive reign on humanity. But even though we had won the battle we were yet to win the war as Aurora had escaped and no-one really knew the outcome to the forging of souls.

But if there was one thing I had learnt through the short time I had been with Draven and that was, face it when it comes and only worry about it when it does, not before. I had said goodbye to Ari, but it was only the next day that she was ringing me from Vincent's phone telling me about all she had seen. I had asked her about Vincent and she murmured that he was right there and did I know that they had super powered hearing?

I laughed and told her I felt her pain, making her laugh. I think she had rung me not long after our goodbye just to let me know she was thinking about me and that even though we weren't together, we were never really that far apart. Draven was just happy to see the smile it put on my face and before hanging up with Vincent he said,

"If you could make this a regular thing I would appreciate it." This then made my smile grow to cheek aching proportions.

Now we were on our way home and I was laughing and joking with Pip and Adam, who had decided to come back with us, for reasons I still didn't know. Not that I was complaining as when you had Pip and I in the same room I found myself snorting with laughter and time simply ran away with us. So I was looking forward to that and simply getting back to start my new life with Draven. I think after our turbulent night back at the hotel he finally understood what it was I was asking of him because he started opening up more and we had a long chat about my family. I knew it wouldn't be long before I was meeting them for the first time and I was nervous about it, even after Draven tried to reassure me. Because the problem remained that I still felt like some kind of imposter.

"You know what you need…a game of angry birds Star Wars edition!"

"Uh…come again?" I said in confusion and I saw Adam grinning from behind his newspaper.

"I can feel you grinning, honey bumpkins…he's only smiling because he has more levels cleared than me but it's those stupid little pigs fault, they just don't do what they're told and you would think that by giving them their own Lightsabers they would take the responsibility more seriously and do as they are friggin' told!" She raged bouncing all over her seat with her back to Adam.

"Breathe little plum and remember, it's participating that counts sweetheart, not the winning." I had to giggle as when Adam said this Pip mimicked him, word for word.

"Yeah well he would say that seeing as he doesn't lose at any game we play…he's such a nerd, I even bought him nerd of the week underpants." Pip told me and I looked to Draven who had one eyebrow raised at Adam.

"They're very comfy, my Lord." He responded and I chuckled.

"I think I will stick to commando." Draven commented dryly which just made me laugh even harder. Then I snuggled over to him and whispered in his ear,

"I'm glad, easy access." Then I winked at him and now he was the one chuckling but there was one thing I was forgetting and that was damn supernatural hearing!

"Oh they don't take long to get into at all in fact there was this one time in Shanghai where there was this particularly huge…"

"Pipper." Adam said her name in warning and she folded her arms and slumped back in her seat.

"You know he won't let me tell any of the good stories!" She complained and I had to try to keep a straight face but I was still curious,

"What makes them nerd of the week pants?"

"Oh fairy gods they are epic! Like Mondays have a picture of Dr Who with his Sonic Screwdriver over where Adam's pe…"

"Yep, got it! So they're all like that." I said thinking this might not be the best conversation to be having with the poor man sitting right there, although I dare say being married to Pip he was probably used to it!

I quickly found out that her other favourites included, 'Release the Wookie' from Star Wars, The Periodic Table with the symbol for Iron 'Fe' over a certain area, that then in smaller letters said underneath, With the Power to 'Fuck Everywhere'. But she told me her personal all time fav...her words...were Thursdays, 'You can Klingon to my Photon Torpedo any day of the week!' Which she explained was from Star Trek, and if I wasn't a fan, then this was something that needed to be rectified immediately.

After this and a load more giggling, we started playing this game she was telling me about and I completely agreed with her, those fat little Sci fi pigs just wouldn't go the way I wanted them to! It was at this point when Draven was laughing at me getting so worked up that something unexpected happened.

"It's okay, he would totally be the same if he was playing it!" Pip said then she patted my bare forearm and everything changed. I couldn't understand it but the whole inside of the jet folded in on itself as though the walls had started peeling away to nothing. Underneath the smooth, curved white lines and strip lights were bare block walls and suddenly it looked as if I was sat in a prison cell!

"What...what's happening?" I turned to Draven to see him turn to stone and start crumbling away like he was made of ash. I screamed at the sight as one by one they all blew away with the rest of the remains of the plane.

"Stop this! Stop this! STOP THIS!" I screamed again and again holding my head in my hands and shaking it like I needed to empty my mind.

"Have you forgotten all about me...*My Catherine?*" Came a voice and I looked up to see I was back in my Uncle's basement. A dread filled thought crashed through me that I was back there and this had all been a dream. But then I really started to look and noticed the differences. The bed in the corner had been the same one in my vision that day, the last time I was locked down there. The day that kicked started events that changed our lives completely.

"Who are you?" I asked the shadows looking desperately around for a figure hiding there. I didn't recognise the voice, so knew it wasn't my Uncle coming back to haunt me.

"We were meant to be together, you and I." He told me and I looked all around in a desperate attempt to make any sort of sense out of all of this. Had I fallen asleep?

"I don't know you and my name is Katie." I said for some reason not giving him my real name.

"So many names...so many lives...but still, *not enough deaths.*" His voice took on a malicious edge in this last bit.

"Look, I told you I don't know who you are!" I shouted getting angry and looking round for anywhere I could run to.

"No but you will...you will again...*soon.*" This was finally when I knew where to look. I walked a few steps round further into the room and looked up at the staircase. There at the very top stood a black figure looming there like death waiting to take me.

"You will be happy here once again. We were so happy together, until you went and spoiled it with all your blood!" He said getting angry and I couldn't help but ask,

"What blood?"

"Pick up the glass and look for yourself." He told me and at that moment a ray of light shone in my eyes from the floor. I looked down and saw a broken piece of mirror just lying there. I bent to pick it up and somewhere inside the room a music box started to play.

"You asked for death, listening to the sound of sugarplum

fairies." I frowned knowing that the sound chilled me to the bone but I couldn't understand why. So I slowly lifted the mirror as this would have my answers and looked into the shard.

"No...no, it's not me! It can't be me! STOP IT! DON'T DO IT!" I screamed as I watched myself slashing over and over at my own wrists and with each cut I made blood dripped from the shard I held, pouring down my arm and landing in a pool on the floor by my feet.

"STOP THIS! IT NEVER HAPPENED!" I screamed again knowing that it had. Knowing this was what really happened to my arms. Because if I actually died that day in the car crash, if Katie was no more, then what else could explain my scars?

"It can't be...I would never..." I sobbed and then suddenly the world started to tip and it sounded like a jet engine was right outside the windows. The room shook and slowly the basement was falling into the ground, nose diving.

I fell forward only for the shadowed man to catch me as he was no longer at the top of the stairs but right in front of me. The face of someone I knew was suddenly there and I screamed out his name, for it was one I now remembered.

"Morgan!" He smiled his evil grin and said,

"Let him know...

I'm coming for you."

I jerked back and then fell to my side, quickly realising I was still in the plane but it was out of control. I pushed myself to my feet and looked around to see everyone on the plane was unconscious!

"WAKE UP!" I shouted pushing Pip, who just flopped over and then Adam. Alarms were going off and I looked out the window to see we were going down!

"Oh God!" I didn't know what to do but I needed to think of something and quick or we were all dead! I turned right around and found Draven slumped in his seat completely out of it. I used the seats to stay on my feet as the plane started shaking. When I made it to him I jumped on him and slapped his face once, twice even a third time but there was nothing.

"DRAVEN WE ARE GOING TO DIE!" I screamed down in his face but still nothing. I would have thought he was dead if I couldn't see his chest rising and falling.

"Draven please! Save us!" I sobbed knowing somehow this was all my fault. I had done this! This stupid power I didn't understand could end up killing everyone! Come on think, think! Fuck! THINK! Power...that was it...if my powers did this then they could undo it.

"Come on you have to work...come on!" I thought about the energy I had flowing inside of me and I pulled it to my hands, I only needed a little bit, not much or I might destroy the damn plane. I felt it starting to tingle and looked at my fingers to see it emitting little sparks.

"Okay here goes everything!"

"WAKE UP!" I screamed and hit Draven in the chest with my palm out flat. I pushed with everything I had so my power would shoot in to him and he suddenly arched his back as he shouted out, dragging air through his lungs.

"What happen..."

"Draven the plane! We are going down!" I told him quickly and half a second later I was on my feet and Draven was stumbling to the cockpit.

"Strap in!" He shouted back to me and the door flapped open, banging against the wall to show me glimpses of Draven in the captain's seat, with the captain also unconscious on the floor where Draven had put him.

"Fuck! Hold on Keira!" He said, and I felt the plane start to go up and I felt sick to my stomach as the pressure hit my body. I saw Pip flopping around and I wished I had strapped her in first before doing as I was told by Draven. I heard another alarm going off and Draven started saying,

"Come on baby! Just hold it together for me…COME ON!" He yelled out and soon it lifted enough that he could level it out. I completely refused to look out of the window, in fact by this point I had my eyes closed and I think even a little wee came out!

But he had done it! Draven had saved everyone on board and I could breathe once more. I let my head fall back against the headrest and had to hold back the urge to burst into tears.

"Keira are you alright?" I couldn't answer him as reality of what I had done sank in further.

"Keira!"

"Yes." I told him but he could tell that was a lie by the emotional way I had said it.

"Wh…what happened?" I heard a man ask and I looked round to see the Pilot waking up.

"Everything is fine Carter, you passed out so I took over." Draven told him and I then heard a long string of apologises that were only really mine to say, coming from the pilot. Draven assured him everything was fine and then I heard the door close before he came back through the plane. As he passed he touched Adam and Pip, waking them up from their forced slumber.

"Hey I napped! Honey I finally napped!" Pip said sounding excited and Adam took one look at the situation and read it for what it was immediately.

"Let's go check on the others, little Plum." Pip took one look at him and said,

"Oh, you want to give them space…well why didn't you just say that." She then jumped up and said,

"Remember kids, no nookie is bad nookie!" Then winked and skipped down the aisle off to see Takeshi, Ragnar and Rue who I had completely forgot about. I was just glad that Sophia and Zagan weren't on here as they stayed behind for some reason Draven wouldn't say.

"I don't know what happened..." I started to say as he came to stand before me. Then he got down on one knee and asked,

"Are you alright?"

"No! I could have killed everyone! The plane was about to crash and I woke up and nobody was awake and I panicked and..."

"Ssshh, it's alright now." Was he drunk?!

"Alright now! Are you crazy? Did you hear what I just said?"

"Yes and unless you shock me by telling me you knew what you were doing and this was some insane prank, then it is done now and there is little point torturing yourself over it, when what we should be doing is trying to understand it. Now tell me what happened." I nodded, feeling better that he didn't blame me at least.

"Well as you know we were just playing that stupid pig game and then Pip touched my arms and..." I looked down at my scars and Draven took hold of them as they started to shake. The memory of what really happened started to creep under my skin now the immediate panic was over.

"I was taken, wasn't I?" I looked up at Draven who still remained on one knee in front of me. He closed his eyes as if this was what he dreaded me finding out the most.

"Yes. Before we met you had...*history.*" The way he said this told me he didn't know what else to call it.

"I saw myself back there. I was scared and in the dark. I felt like I had been in the dark for so long, locked away in the shadows that it changed me." I took a minute and Draven used both his thumbs to take my tears away.

"I picked up a piece of the mirror and I saw what I did to

myself…please tell me it was wrong…please tell me I didn't try and kill myself, tell me he didn't win that way…please." I sobbed out my pleas to him, grasping on to his t shirt as if I let go time could tear me back there. I was never going back to that place!

Never…

"No. listen to me, you didn't try and take your life, you did it to save yourself and most of all your family…you were a heroine…you're always the heroine Keira, please believe that." He told me and I cried even harder into his shoulder, not understanding what he meant but hearing that I didn't give up that way was enough to comfort me.

"I will explain everything to you and you will see. But for now, I think that we hold off on long plane journeys until we have this new power figured out." I had to laugh and knew this was his way of trying to help me through this.

"I think I'd better cancel the white water rafting then." He chuckled and then said,

"Good plan and in turn I will cancel the track day and balloon ride." I laughed louder this time and said,

"And I will cancel the…" He stopped me by pulling me to him for a body tingling kiss, the kind that left me near panting at the end of it.

"Sorry, it's just the 'cancel' thing could have lasted a while." Then he winked at me when my mouth dropped in shock. It wasn't often Draven cracked jokes but when he did it was worth being teased for that grin alone.

"You're lucky you're so sexy and handsome, that's all I can say." I told him making him laugh.

"As long as you think so then that's all that matters." Again he winked and this time I hit him in the stomach making him laugh.

"So any ideas to what happened?" I asked when he retook his seat opposite me.

"I have a theory, yes."

"Care to share with the class?"

"Not really but you will only nag me I suppose." He teased again and I knew he was doing this to help keep me relaxed and my mind off feeling guilty.

"Ha ha, well I am a wife after all, isn't that what men think we all do once we get a ring on our finger?" Draven gave me a small smile and then looked down at my hand in regret. I followed his gaze to see no ring was where it should have been.

"I wish I had never lost it when they took me." Draven obviously not knowing what to say to that just shrugged and looked out the window. It was probably not something he wanted to think about right now or maybe he had something else planned and just needed the time to get me a new one. That thought certainly put a smile on my face.

"So, your theory?" I asked him again.

"I think that some of your difficult memories somehow get triggered and then try to break through. Only the block on your mind counteracts this and in turn the stress it causes comes through in a burst of uncontrollable power. Remember the mind is a powerful thing and when it has been messed with as yours has then there are going to be side effects."

"I guess so. Just like when I would pass out in the beginning."

"Exactly. Too much stress and your brain will cope anyway it needs to and this power you hold will react if it feels its host is threatened." Okay so this made sense, in a strange way at least.

"So I just need more time to try and control it...more practice I mean."

"Yes and I will be there to help you. You're not alone as

most of my kind experience the same thing when acquiring a new host as our powers develop and our new body has to grow accustomed to the changes." I found all this fascinating and was going to ask more questions when Draven suddenly stopped me with a difficult question of his own.

"I don't like asking this of you Keira, but I need to know."

"What?"

"Were you alone in your vision?" My reaction probably told him his answer when I took a deep breath but I said it anyway,

"No, there was a man there."

"Do you know his name?" I nodded and said,

"Yes, he told me…no wait, I just seemed to know it…it was Morgan." At this Draven looked ready to spit fire at just hearing the name being spoken. But then if I thought this made him angry before then the next answer he received was one of pure hate,

"Did he say anything to you?"

"Yes he did. He called me Catherine and said we were meant to be together, Oh God…"

"What, what is it, what did he say?" I looked to him, bit my lips and then said,

"He told me to tell you…"

"What?"

"That he's coming for me."

CHAPTER 46
PERFECTION

Once we were back within the walls of Afterlife I couldn't help but feel better. I was as if all felt right with the world again, well almost. I knew that it would take some adjusting to this new way of life but at least now I could enjoy it without being worried about Ari and having the Hexad looming over my head.

All the remaining 'Fathers' were awaiting trial and from what I could gather Lucius had, for the moment, taken control of the situation. I asked Draven about this and he told me that the 'Rogues' as they were known, were indeed what I first thought…Vampires. And as it passed over to the responsibility of the Vampire King, it was up to Lucius to deal with their sentence.

It was obvious that Draven was less than happy about this, if the shouting and swearing was anything to go by I could hear from the next room. Okay, yes so I was shamefully listening to it all but it wasn't like I had an empty glass up against the wall, just more like casually standing next to it looking at my feet.

Draven told Lucius that he wanted them to be interrogated and I shuddered when it was obvious through Draven's reply of

'Good' that this had already begun. Also his response of 'Make it like old times' gave me a strong sense that Lucius himself was the one doing the torturous deed. I listened for more but Lucius must have been talking because it went quiet on Draven's end.

"I can confirm they are still there." I screamed and turned round to see Draven right there behind me...oh and he was grinning.

"You nearly gave me a heart attack!"

"I'm sorry but I didn't want to disturb your in depth study."

"Uh?" He looked down at my bare feet and I realised what he meant.

"Oh, that."

"Yes, that." He smirked.

"The light was better over here." I said slipping past him so he wouldn't see my lie.

"Did you forget what they looked like or something?" He asked and I hid my smile with my back to him.

"No, I just thought I'd picked up a splinter, or something." I said, with this last part repeating his words, mocking him. The next thing I knew I was being swooped up over his shoulder and I squealed out in surprise.

"What are you doing?"

"It could be fatal. I need to do a full examination. Now hold still." He said as I wiggled to get free. He gave my bum a little tap and I huffed making him laugh.

"Put me down!" I shouted playfully.

"As you command, my Queen!" I quickly found myself being turned back upright and plonked down on the sofa. Then he sat down, picked up my feet and started tickling me.

"No! No, no stop, that tickles...please!" I begged in between snorting laughter.

"I'm sorry but it could be serious, I need to make sure infection hasn't spread." He teased again and using his arm to hold me down he tickled in between my toes and I was almost in tears at this.

"Oh no!"

"What? What is it?" I said sitting up quick at his serious tone.

"Keira, its more serious than I thought, this looks like it could be a rare disease called Sockitis. See here, it starts with the fluff in between the toes…" He said actually picking out a bit of fluff and showing me. I thought I would die of shame but then I quickly forgot about it when he carried on with,

"…then comes the next symptom called the 'snorts' and after that you pee yourself!" Then he started tickling me even more and he was right, if he carried on any longer I would have wet myself.

"It sounds like you are wrestling a pig in here!" Sophia said saving me by walking into Draven's suite.

"Oi!" I said and she smiled before saying,

"Shouldn't that be Oink?"

"Ha ha!" And actually it was pretty funny.

"Did I happen to mention a very pretty pig." I tried to hide my smile and be serious when I crossed my arms and said,

"That's better."

"Anyway I can see that you're busy so…" I snatched my legs off Draven's lap and said,

"Oh no we're not!" And this made Draven roar with laughter.

"I just wanted to inform you that we were back."

"Good. Any problems?"

"None."

"And were you successful?" I frowned at them both wondering what they were up to.

"I was." Draven nodded looking relieved.

"I could just leave if you want as it would save all the cryptic stuff."

"But where would the fun in that be." She said winking at me before leaving the room.

"So are you going to tell me what that was about?" I asked following him when he got off the sofa.

"Nope but I do have a surprise for you." My eyes widened in anticipation and I quickly lost interest in what Draven and Sophia had been secretly talking about. Then I closed my eyes and held my hands out making him laugh. He took my hands in his, gave me a quick pull and then kissed my nose when I fell into him.

"It's not here but come with me and I will show you." He told me and I had to rein in my girly shriek of excitement.

"Let me just get my shoes on and…" once again I cried out as I was lifted into his arms, only this time it was Knight in shining armour style, which I had to say was a little bit more romantic than a fireman's lift. Although, it had to be said that a fireman's lift definitely had its sex appeal as it was more rough and ready!

"You know I do still have the use of my legs." I told him grinning.

"Yes but then I wouldn't be able to do this…" He suddenly threw me into the air making me scream and then promptly lifted me up to his lips so he could kiss me.

"Well you certainly give the saying 'making a girl's head spin' a whole new meaning." I told him making him chuckle.

"So where did you say we were going?" I asked after we came to yet another corridor.

"Nice try, sweetheart." Well you couldn't blame a girl for trying.

"Not much farther now." He told me after I did one of those dramatic huffs.

"You're so cute when you sulk like that, you make me just want to bite you." His velvet, seductive voice painting that image had me suddenly wishing we were back in his room.

"You like that idea don't you?" He said and I tried to hide my blush.

"I know you do because I just heard your heartbeat quicken. I wonder, does it make you ache for me to be nestled in between your thighs, thrusting into you as far as you can take it?" I sucked in a sharp breath, instantly feeling myself getting damp just from hearing his dirty, delicious words.

"I can't wait to have you again. I want to taste you, feasting upon your intimate flesh, sucking the blood to the surface and making you more sensitive against my tongue. Then I am going to take what's *mine.*" He growled this last part and the vibrations rippled all the way down my back and to my core. I let my head fall back wishing he would just stop us right here and take me up against the stone wall like some wild beast of a man that just couldn't wait.

"We are here." He whispered and I didn't care anymore just so long as it had a place where he could push me up against. Or he could just take me standing, either worked for me right now because if he didn't follow through with his words then I would end up stir crazed, out of my mind, jump on him and attack, type of insane.

He used the power of his mind on the massive set of doors and it took me a minute to recognise where we were.

"I wanted to keep my promise." He told me as he walked us through the great library that had now been transformed. Pure white church candles were everywhere and on every available surface transforming the room into the most romantic setting I could ever have imagined. He walked further into the room and I could see dinner was set up for two with plates covered in silver domes. White flowers of all different kinds, too many to mention in fact, were also scattered around the room and the white was a stark contrast against all the dark carved wood. But with the soft candle light gently flickering against all the petals, well the effect was astonishingly beautiful.

"Did you…?"

"I had this arranged, yes."

"You're a romantic!" I said utterly shocked.

"You sound surprised, believe it or not I am familiar with the concept." He said grinning and lowering me to the ground.

"Nice touch." I said looking to the main attraction of the room, or at least I hoped after the way he had shamefully teased my body on the way over here. Because there, right in front of the enormous fireplace, was a makeshift bed with piles of white cushions, throws, comforters, and every other soft, luxurious comfort that was made to surround your naked body in bed.

"I thought you might like that part in particular." He whispered in my ear before walking past me down the centre of the vast room. I followed him, chanting in my head, 'Go to the bed, go to the bed, go to the bed' but it didn't work as he went straight to the table that had been laid for us. He then pulled out a seat for me like a perfect gentleman.

I couldn't help smile as I approached, knowing how lucky I was that I had found this perfect man, demon bits and all.

"Thank you." I told him sweetly and before I sat down I reached up on my tip toes and started kissing his neck. It was only supposed to be a little peck, but I just couldn't seem to pull away. I lifted my hand to his neck to hold him to me and then before I knew it I was sucking and biting and kissing my way up to his lips. His groans and moans told me he didn't want me to stop either but it was only when our lips touched that passion exploded between us.

"Fuck romance, I need to have you and *now!"* He gritted out the last word as he swept his arm out, smashing everything to the floor. I was shocked for the half a second it took him to yank me roughly to him and then lift me by my cheeks onto the table. Then the wild demonic side of Draven that I had hoped for earlier suddenly appeared and he was breathing heavy with need.

I was near frantic trying to get my clothes off and doing so whilst lying on a round table wasn't easy with my legs dangling off the side. Draven could see me fumbling with my top and in the end simplified it for me by ripping it into two pieces that just slipped down my arms. I yelped when I felt the pull against my skin as he did the same with everything else I wore, including the lace I had covering what he wanted to see the most. It tore easily but he made a show of doing it slowly, unlike the rest of my clothes. He just slipped one finger in the waistline and I held my breath as he looked up at me, keeping eye contact and teasing me with his eyes. The material tore away like it had been made from tissue paper and without saying a word he raised up my legs and spread them, placing my feet flat on the table's edge.

"Draven I can't do…" He cut me off with one look when I tried to close them, feeling far too exposed this way. But that one look had me rethinking my decision and I submitted to his command, with trepidation quickly seeping into a greater need. The whole thing was such a turn on I felt that if I didn't do as he asked I would regret it for the rest of my life.

"Good girl." I felt my heart soar when he praised me like this but then swallowed hard when he added,

"Now lie back and let me enjoy my meal." I looked down watching as he swung a chair round in one swift move so that he could sit comfortably whilst…well, *enjoying me.*

In fact, by the time he actually started touching me I could barely stop my legs from shaking. I looked to him to see he was grinning and there was nothing kind or gentle about it. It was bad to the demonic bone. First he ran his fingertips down my inner thigh, caressing them slowly and feather light, making me tremble even more.

"I adore the way you respond to my touch. The way your delicate pale skin blushes in that tantalising way that teases me with the promise of your blood. Do you know how much I crave you?" I bit my lip at what his words did to me.

"How much I crave your scent, the pheromones your body emits only for me, makes my mouth water at the thought of tasting you. Bringing you to your peak, soaking your thighs and getting you ready to take me when gentle just isn't an option. When I know that once I get inside you that nothing could stop me from taking you hard. That's what you do to me..." He paused from stroking the crease of my leg, where the top of the inside of my thigh meets the most intimate part of me. He also paused his words, bringing his head closer to my most sensitive part and when he continued the feel of his breath against my clit made me moan for him.

"...And that's what I am going to do to you." I abruptly cried out after he said this as his mouth descended to claim me, sucking in my clit and rolling his teeth around it. My back arched and I thought I would fly straight off the table. He became relentless and after only a minute I was ready to come. But the first time I got to this point something would happen and the feeling would fade back to how it felt in the beginning. At first I thought there was something wrong with me but then it happened again, and then a third time until I was soon begging the man responsible.

"Please, oh Draven please!"

"You will come when I am ready for you to come." He informed me and went back to his meal like it was the most civilised thing for a gentleman of high stature to do. I think I could actually feel tears running down into my hair line I was that mad with need.

"So you want to come little bird of mine?"

"Yes, yes, yes, Oh god yes!" I said out of my mind.

"Lucky for you then that I am thirsty for it." And that was my only warning. Because it came to me like lightening was striking my body…no, not my body, just my clit. Because Draven had suddenly bit down, driving his fangs into me and plunged two fingers inside me at the same time, making me go off like a firework, exploding into a star of colours. With each draw on my blood I jerked, tugging at his fingers again and again, trying to keep him there.

I had never come so hard before that the intensity of it had me reaching out to him. He knew what I needed and he didn't disappoint as he pulled me up into his arms off the table. I clung on to him as he walked me over to the bed and I knew he wasn't finished with me yet. I panted into his shoulder, with both my arms and my legs locked around him, soaking his now naked stomach with the evidence of what he had just done to me.

"I'm sorry, I can't wait." He ground out just before he lifted me up and impaled me on the length of him. I threw my head back and cried out at both the pain and the pleasure. His strength was remarkable and when he erupted into his demon form the sight sent me wild against him. I raked my nails up his back and across his shoulders as I gripped on for dear wonderful life!

He continued to lift me up and down as if I weighed nothing at all and once more the orgasm he gave me was mind shattering. I felt like I was floating and my mind was elsewhere. Even as Draven found his release, pumping his seed deep within me, he was brought to his knees with the force of it. He roared up at the ceiling with his wings outstretched and he had never looked more magnificent.

I felt myself being laid down and even after Draven left me to fetch something and then came back I hadn't been able to move. I felt him cleaning me and I sucked in the air at the first touch of my now, overly sensitive female area. Once he had finished he lay down next to me and I felt pieces of my hair being pulled from my forehead that were now soaked from sweat. I had a feeling that this new work out was going to mean aching stomach and inner thigh muscles for me tomorrow and I could only hope I didn't walk like I couldn't catch a pig in an alley way!

"Are you alright, are you in any pain?" He asked me running the backs of two fingers down my flushed, rosy cheeks.

"Wow, when you keep your promises you *really* keep them!" I opened my eyes finally to see that what I had said must have meant something else to him and I was about to ask but then I stopped myself. I knew when to pick my times in trying to get him to open up and this wasn't one of them.

"You were incredible my love." He told me and I beamed at the compliment.

"Really?" I asked enthusiastically and he laughed,

"Trust me, it is not every day a woman can bring a man to his knees after he finds his release. So yes, you were perfect." Again this had me smiling.

"Here drink this." He leaned back and brought a goblet to my lips.

"What is it?"

"It's just water. I don't want you to get dehydrated and I am not finished with you yet." He told me winking and my heart skipped a beat...which I knew he had heard from his cocky grin.

After this we talked, we laughed and exchanged parts of our lives, which must have been hard for Draven knowing that most of what I said had never happened, which is why I tried to keep most of it from the last eight months. Ari's and my antics amused him, especially when I told him how many times we cleaned the toilets using Celina's and Aurora's toothbrushes.

Draven even managed to salvage some of the bread rolls that had been discarded from the table, as one of them had flown over to one of the Chesterfields and the other I found on a shelf between The History of Politics and Tactics of War. I thought having those two books together was very practical.

After we had both picked at our recovered baked bounty Draven started to kiss me softly and then tenderly made love to me this time. The whole night was perfect and it was only when I was being carried back to our suite that I realised I must have fallen asleep straight after we came together.

Everything about it was perfect and in the end, for one of us it turned out to be the most perfect way...

To say goodbye.

CHAPTER 47
ROLL OF THE DICE
DRAVEN

After lowering my Chosen One to our bed I needed to leave. I just needed to get out of here for a time to think. Her comment about keeping promises was as though she had pulled a thread on my heart and it was unravelling fast. Just looking at her right now caused me pain and I didn't know which was harder, to stay or to leave.

So in the end I left. I was thankful that our time together had exhausted her enough to sleep heavily, as I didn't want her waking to find I wasn't with her. I brushed the shorter parts of her hair back from her forehead and leant down to kiss her soft skin, inhaling her scent once more before I left.

Everything about her was perfect but the parts I had failed to get her back and the thought of that tore me up inside. What was the point of having all this power and influence in my world if I couldn't stop things like this from happening? And more importantly what was the point having a damn Oracle when she caused half of the problems set against us. It still played on my mind how both Keira and I had been played like royals on a chess board. Ones used simply to gain other pieces for the game…the game named The Prophecy.

When Keira had heard but a slice of my anger back in the hotel room I was more ashamed of myself than ever before. I never wanted her to know my inner feelings as she deserved better than that. But it didn't detract from the facts and the reality of our situation. Keira's powers were obviously getting stronger but without her years of self-control it was like giving a child a gun, praying they control their urge to use it.

First the incident in the marble dining room and then more worryingly in the plane. They were nearly uncontrollable and dictated more by strong emotions rather than rational thought. In this new mind of hers she merely hadn't had the time to develop them in such a short space of time, whereas the Keira I knew had years of control behind her. Which meant that her life had been shaped and formed from a young age in order to deal with this transition. Memories and fears, self-doubt and each new experience faced all added to what the Gods would one day ask of her. Every single thing, the good, the bad and unfortunately the ugly had all happened for a reason. Appearing from the shadows like stepping stones taking you closer to the destination life had planned for you…that life had planned for *us*.

But now that had all been erased and my biggest fear was what if by making my choice I had somehow put her life at risk? What if the next path she had to face was something she was only supposed to face as Keira, not Katie? This was what I couldn't explain to her. This was the fear I wouldn't allow myself to admit to her.

The insane notion that my issues stemmed from lost memories on how we met, or time shared, or any other selfish reason was just not something that should be entertained by anyone, let alone feeding Keira's new form of self-doubt. Yes, I was sad and mourning the loss of the Keira I knew but she was still in there. She was still my girl no matter what, nothing could take that heavenly soul away from her. Nothing would change her and nothing and no one had the power to ever do so.

But what if in those precious seconds she'd had left on that plane she couldn't have woken me? What if a memory hits her again and her mind destroys itself trying to find its way back? There were so many 'what ifs' and I feared for them all. I couldn't let anything happen to her again, I couldn't have her taken from me. I knew this time I wasn't strong enough to survive it!

I walked the empty halls still in need of greater solace to calm the storm that I could feel brewing. I pulled out the phone I had tucked in my jeans and rang Sophia.

"You're going out again and want me to keep an eye on Keira." She told me, knowing my need to escape my own madness.

"I won't be gone long. I just need…"

"I know, Brother. Time they say can heal all wounds but what happens to those wounds when time is stolen from you." It wasn't a question so I had no need to answer but if there had been a need then my answer would have been the wrong one. Because I had killed all chances of getting that stolen time back. And although everyone involved thought it the best decision, in most cases the only one in fact, in truth only time was going to tell us if that was true or not.

"Have no fear, I will watch over her."

"Thank you, Sophia." I told her before hanging up the phone. One of the biggest gratitudes I had in this life was that I never faced it alone, not with Vincent and Sophia by my side. We stood united on most things and in that came great strength. In fact, the only time our differences ever clashed was when love was involved. For Sophia it was Zagan, brought into her life no doubt quickly for a reason. The struggle Vincent and I had in the beginning reining in our temperamental sister was not an easy feat, not when the world was your playground.

Zagan changed all that and after they met, we as brothers, felt as though our job was done...or at least the hard part. Because no matter how much I loved my sister, it did sometimes feel like being a parent, or at least what I could only imagine it to feel like. We both catered to our sister's charms and fanciful whims, like most adoring siblings do and that sometimes had its price but when it came to Keira, I never realised the levels Sophia went to in catering to *my* needs. In a word I would say that she had definitely 'grown up' since Keira came into our lives.

Thinking these thought calmed me somewhat as I made my way down to the garage level. Not that I had as much time for it now and thankfully so but during Keira's disappearance I would often lose myself down here building engines and customising projects. Anything really just to keep me sane enough ready for her return. For this was what I was eventually told and not by whom it should have come from, Pythia the Oracle. No, it was the Gods themselves that had to intervene when I not only searched the globe for her but the other worlds as well. They told me that the fates had foreseen, that like the first time, the power of the Electus will seek me out and all I was left with was the helplessness of time.

I didn't need to think about which car I wanted to drive because right now it was all about the memories. So I grabbed the key fob for the one seven seven Aston Martin and walked up to it allowing the keyless entry to work. Then I lowered myself into the sculptured bucket seat and started her up. I looked to my right thinking back to that night I drove her home and what her honesty meant to me. The way she gave me a taste of the spirited creature I would come to love and adore when chastising me on scaring her when I first drove us out of here. I watched the hidden door slide up and laughed to myself remembering her face, doubting me on my sanity.

"Let me ask you, do you really believe I would have driven us both through a stone wall?" Her response had been the first time I had glimpsed a life with someone who wouldn't be afraid to challenge me and strangely, the thought had never excited me more.

"Well, how was I supposed to know you had your very own bat cave? And considering it didn't look like a bloody door and I've had a knock to the head, maybe you could cut me some slack?" I had tried to keep my grin to myself but instead of giving into to laughter I simply ended up repeating her words,

"Bat cave?" I shook my head thinking about her humour and how much I enjoyed every aspect of it. I think if I was to add up the amount I had laughed in all my lifetimes combined it still wouldn't be half the amount that I had done so around Keira.

By the Gods how I had wanted her back, going nearly out of my mind battling with myself between what was right and what I wanted. Which was why seeing Vincent stood by those church doors with the fate of his world held in my hand, weighed against the memory of my world held in the other I knew I had to do right by the people I loved not what I wanted.

Because I had made that wrong decision once and it took Keira all the way to Hell and back twice to make me see that.

I drove the Aston hard and with little care this night. The twisted roads forced me to concentrate on something other than what I left behind. I knew the type of road I travelled wasn't suited to such a beauty but she surprised me, like the other beauty in my life was constantly doing. And like that beauty I pushed her to her limits but she never let me down. She knew what I needed and her strength got me there, just as it would this time.

I found the turning easily as this was always where I came. It had been since she was taken and even before that. Whenever we were miles apart, due to other influences or to our own senseless reasons, this was where I came. Because the first time I saw it, the first time I was here, I found Keira saying goodbye to me. She hadn't known I was there at the time that she ripped up the image of me and let the elements take me off her hands. This seemed to be the place we usually said goodbye to each other and carrying on that sad tradition, I had come to do the same.

I got out of my car after turning her side on to the cliff's edge and took in the vast space blanketed above by stars. I thought about tomorrow and the first day of the rest of our lives but I couldn't say what was to come and once this night was through I would no longer care. Because as long as we were together we could face anything. I knew that now. I had faith in that...the fates, the Gods and Keira herself had proven it time and time again. Through the storms and across the turbulent seas she would find me as it was always to be how the Prophecy begins. How it ends...no one knew but as I had discovered since meeting her...

Hope was a powerful thing.

I leaned back against the side of the hood and focusing all my thoughts on the item Sophia had retrieved for me I let it materialise in my hand. Seeing it for the first time since I had placed it on her finger hurt enough to close my eyes against the mental torture. Our wedding night and our joining had been one of the most perfect memories I had with her and at first I had thought of nothing but putting this ring back where it belonged.

But the truth was it had belonged on the girl I married that night, not the girl I am going to remarry shortly. It wouldn't feel right giving it to a Keira that didn't remember when I slipped it on her the first time. So I would find her a new ring, ready for a new memory.

So this was going to be my goodbye and when I heard her cry I knew I wasn't to do it alone. I looked up at my Ava and told her,

"My Queen is home." She responded by crying out into the night, creating that magnificent sound I always found comfort in.

I looked down, taking one last look at the ring and then said,

"I loved you then as I love you now but with a heavy heart, I...I must say... *goodbye my Keira.*"

Then I threw the ring as far as I could, turned around and didn't look back. I got back in the Aston and drove...

Back to my Queen.

~

After pulling into my 'Bat cave' I cut the engine and left the garage, this time using a different door, knowing this took me to the VIP of my club. I needed to check on things before returning back to my sleeping beauty, who no doubt was snoring her pretty little head off. I smirked knowing she didn't just snort when she laughed but this was my own treasured secret to keep and I revelled in the fact that only I knew this.

I walked through the doors knowing it would be quiet with the main part of the club closed for the night. The VIP however never really closed as there was always something that needed to be discussed between the higher ranking members of my kingdom. Without them as my eyes and ears over the world then chaos would be inevitable. Because in the end you could be as powerful as they come and it would still mean nothing without the men you lead standing tall at your back.

I continued on past my top table, walking close to the

balcony when something caught my eye. I turned and looked down into the empty club to see a lone figure sat at the bar. It was easy to know who it was when looking at those trademark boots tapping a steel plated toe on the foot rest.

"Now what do you want this time." I muttered to myself before I descended the stairs. I crossed the dark vast open space of the club that always held a kind of lost aura to it without all those souls filling it each night. As I approached I saw him tip the rest of the amber liquid down his throat and look down to the side as I stepped up to the bar.

"Quiet place you got here." He said stepping from his seat and turning round to take in the empty room. I raised an eyebrow at this, knowing this wasn't exactly his type of place. He took one look at my face and said,

"Well, being the honest man I am, it's not much to my likin' to be true with ya, as it wasn't the Shindig I was expecting."

"We're closed. What are you doing here Bill?" I came right out, cutting any bullshit I wasn't in the mood for. Bill leaned back, resting his elbows to the bar and then casually lifted the rim of his grey hat, informing me,

"I wanna buy you a drink." Again I raised an eyebrow at him, this time in confusion. What was this old cowboy up to?

"I'm busy Bill, this isn't really the time." I told him gaining a raised eyebrow in return.

"The place is empty and your little lady I'm thinking gotta be sleeping. You don't look like you got much to be troubling yourself with." I looked around the place I called home and had done for many years knowing that for once, he was right. There was nothing in this moment for me to do but get back to Keira and lie awake thinking about what the future now held for us.

"Plus I'm a'reckonin' you're gonna want to hear what I gotta say...so how abouts you and I, we get ourselves a table?"

He said pushing himself off the bar. I grabbed him by the arm and said,

"And tell me, what makes you think that?"

"Because when it's something to do with that sweet girl of yours, you won't just *want* to know, this is something you will *need* to know." I let him go, knowing I had no choice but to let this play out. He turned and grabbed the two rocks glasses, clinking them together between his thumb and fingers and with his other hand he grabbed the bottle of forty-year-old Glenfiddich single malt scotch, that he must have helped himself to from the top shelf before I arrived.

The sound of his snakeskin boots echoed in the open space and he looked back to me expectantly. When I took a moment too long for him he said,

"Got my hands full here, Big Bug." Then he lifted his small burdens to emphasise his point and I rolled my eyes having little patience for what the two of us could have to talk about. But there was a part of me intrigued enough, so I moved both my hands at the same time into the centre, using my powers to drag a table from one side and two chairs from the other.

Bill placed the bottle in the middle and nodded for me to take the seat opposite him. As soon as I did he slid the unused glass my way and pulled off the cork with an echoing pop. I decided to shed a little light our way, so with just a thought the chandelier directly above illuminated the space around us in a soft glow. Then I watched Bill pour the forty year old scotch into our glasses. Then he lifted his up and before he took a drink he said,

"To lost time." Hearing this was like someone was pulling on that damn thread again and my heart tore a little bit further. However, no matter what my inner thoughts were, I drank to the same notion.

"That's mighty good stuff." He said after whistling.

"And so it should be for over four thousand dollars a bottle." I told him calmly. This time his whistle got louder.

"A man can't have all his saddle bags in the right place to be spending that amount of coin on some whiskey...now on a horse I would understand."

"That depends on the horse." I said thinking back to those times.

"And from what I heard, you paid much more for such a horse, in blood more than coin." Hearing this I was quick to frown and let my patience slip. I banged my glass on the table and said,

"I gather you didn't come here to talk about damaged souls, so cut the bullshit Bill and tell me what you did come here to talk about." He gave me a one side grin and took out his trademark pack of cards from his grey suit pocket. I had to say he certainly looked the part of the famous lawman gambler he was renowned for the world over. Of course it was just his memory that survived not what he lived for now and being shot in the back of the head by some nobody out to make a name for himself, certainly wasn't the way any great gun fighter wanted to go down.

That was like a warrior winning every battle, coming home only to die from the common cold. There was never any victory found in death but when you sell your soul to the highest bidder there is even less victory found in the life you feel has been extended. Because you never really cheat death, you merely just end up handing it over. Which is precisely what Bill did just before he died and he did so to a man named Jared Cerberus. Yet another King brought into the fold of the Prophecy by my Electus. Our flame in the dark, where one by one the moths travelled closer, drawn in to the power it held.

He started shuffling and the sight was hypnotic, he did so with such speed and precision.

"I don't have time for cards." I told him knowing quickly where this was headed. It was rumoured the guy only ever lost once and that was to the man who now owned his soul.

"Time, it's a funny thing." He said now cutting the deck over and over with just one hand before putting the pack down in the middle of the table between us. Then he lifted his hat, scratched his head and replaced it.

"When you want it to slow down love is usually found on your side of the door, when you're trying to get out of that door, now that's when you want time to speed up." It didn't take a scholar to recognise he was referring to when he was imprisoned.

"You broke the law, Bill." I told him, leaning back in my chair readying myself for what I expected was to come but then he surprised me.

"Everything in this life and the next has a plan, some we choose, some we don't. It would do you well to remember that." I was about to speak but he held up a hand to stop me and added,

"But think for a moment on what would have happened to that little bean of yours if you had never sent me down there for crimes you believed committed…ah yes, time's a funny thing indeed." So this was why he was here.

"At last we come to it…You want compensating for saving Keira?" I asked him outright.

"Don't insult a man buying you a drink in your own establishment." He said affronted at the thought.

"Then what? You already have my thanks and my pardon, and from what Jared told me you accepted no reward, so what more is there for you to ask of me."

"I simply want your time."

"My time for what?" I asked getting frustrated and taking a long swig of my drink knowing that would help. The smooth rich flavours warmed my throat as it went down and I took a deep knowing breath when he told me,

"I want three games of chance." I looked down at the deck and said,

"And what are we playing for?"

"You're playing for the information you seek." My eyes widened in surprise. What did he know of Keira's future?

"And you?"

"Whatever is in your pocket." I was about to tell him there wasn't anything in my pocket other than my phone but when I put my hand into the fabric I realised in my emotional state I had left my phone in the garage and kept the key fob to the Aston in my trouser pocket.

"And if I win you'll tell me all you know regarding Keira?" He nodded smirking.

"But if you lose then the next thing I ask of you is a favour owed."

"What kind of favour?"

"Now that you will only find out when the day comes for me to ask it." I didn't like the sound of that but I had lost too much already not to take the risk for Keira.

"Alright, let's get this over with." I said putting my beloved car on the line when placing the key fob on the table. Then I reached out to take the cards when he stopped me.

"Before we start this, you should know that if you lose a third time there are no more chances."

"Why not?" I asked wondering why he wouldn't want to fleece me for all he could get.

"Because there are only three things I want from you and I ain't used to kicking a man when he's down."

"Then I should probably ask, what's the third thing?" Again he smiled.

"That would be a mighty fine idea and I will tell ya it's as simple as the game itself."

"Which is?"

"I want a promise." Now this wasn't something I could easily give but then again what wouldn't I give when presented with the possibility of knowledge that could potentially save her life when facing the Prophecy.

"Done." I said sealing the deal by cutting the pack. He did the same and said,

"High number wins."

"And Aces?"

"In my world Aces are always high." He replied. We turned them over together and I had the four of spades. He naturally had the Jack of diamonds. I wasn't happy about losing the car, especially one that held those memories of being with Keira but I had already made the decision to let those memories go anyway, so maybe it was for that reason I lost. Either way I slid the keys over to him.

The next turn was left to Bill to cut the pack and I took another taste of my drink before doing the same...

Again I lost but this time I lost to a Queen of Hearts.

The pressure started to get to me just knowing all the things he could know and putting things on the line without any reassurances that even if I won, that it would be any use to me. My thoughts were interrupted when Bill took out a piece of paper from the inside of his jacket. He was dressed smarter than I had ever seen him before and his grey suit, although still in keeping with his old western style, gave him an air of authority I had never recognised before.

The small piece of paper was folded and he put it down on the table and slid it across with one finger until I reached for it. On it was written a single name that I had never heard before and meant nothing to me personally.

"And what would you like me to do with this?" I asked placing it in my pocket to look into later.

"When the time comes you will need it for what I just won." So he did have some idea on the favour he would ask of me. I could only hope it wasn't another person I would end up letting out of Hell.

"Time for the last chance."

"I think this time I would prefer a flip of a coin." Bill raised his eyes at my request and started playing with the double coin attached to the cord around his neck. I knew that the bullet that held them together was the one that was loaded that day with the sole purpose to kill him.

"I don't ever bet on coins as to me they demand more respect, considering what they can do." I understood what he meant as coins in our world meant much more than just basic currency. So I came up with a different idea after hearing Keira calling it out in her sleep, the night she woke up from that bad dream. So I produced a black carved wooden dice and asked him,

"Six or One?"

"I only ever need one." He replied confidently.

"Very well. The closer to one you win, the closer to six I win." I held it out to him to throw but he shook his head,

"This is your game to win, so you do the honours." He told me and I almost wished for a second I was playing against another human so they wouldn't be able to detect my powers but sat opposite a being as strong as Wild Bill, then I knew honour was another thing we played for in this game and it meant everything to a man like Bill. Don't get me wrong I like to think of myself as an honourable man but at times like these with the woman I loved whose life might be on the line, then cheating wasn't something I would have lost sleep over. But it was by the by considering the option wasn't on the cards, no pun intended. So just needing to get it over with, I kissed the dice, threw it on the table and closed my eyes, waiting for the sound of silence to tell me it had stopped moving.

I opened my eyes and the sight of two little dots nearly devastated me.

"My promise is owed."

"And what is your damn promise?" I asked feeling my anger rise slowly.

"I want you to promise that when the time comes you will look the other way."

"Of course it is." I said dryly and before I could mention there were things beyond my power to be able to do that he added,

"It will be in your power to do this, trust me…you may even thank me for it in time." I gave him a look but it wasn't enough to get him to explain more, however his words did at least ease my mind in what I had unwittingly been forced to give up and all for nothing.

"Well I best be getting' a wiggle on." He said before draining his drink and getting up from the chair.

"Now you go and take good care of the little bean, she's a catch that one." I gave him a head tilt in acknowledgement then he started walking out of the door but stopped abruptly.

"I almost forgot but a man always pays his debts and I said I would buy you a drink." Then he yanked the coin from around his neck and flipped me the one he removed from the bullet. It landed on the table and started spinning dead centre.

"I'm a'reckonin' you show that to your little woman, she took a mighty fancy to it on the way through Hell." Then he winked at me and walked out the door whistling a song I knew, all about making it home. I couldn't take my eyes off the coin as my heart began to race. Then as the heavy front door to the club slammed shut the coin stopped spinning and I reached for it.

My fingertips made contact and the full force of what the coin held slammed into me like a gift from Heaven. I grabbed the coin tighter in my grasp, shot out of my chair and started running as fast as I could.

I needed to get to her, nothing else mattered!

So I ran to my girl now with all my hope resting in the palm of my hand. Because this was it! This was my time...

To fulfil my promise.

CHAPTER 48
OCEANS APART
DRAVEN

I ran through the halls suddenly cursing my home for being so big. I would have used my wings if they would have gotten me there any quicker but right now that wasn't an option. Could this really be happening, could it be as I hoped?! Well there was only one way to find out and that thought only drove me faster. I could see the door getting closer and it was as Bill had said, when you want through that door you only wish for time to speed up.

When I finally reached for it I nearly tore the damn thing off its hinges as I wrenched it open. Sophia jumped at my sudden entrance and ignoring her panicked questions that I couldn't hear for the erratic beating of my heart, I went straight to Keira still sleeping soundly.

"Keira, wake up." I said trying to keep my voice steady and calm.

"Dom what are you…?"

"Keira, wake up for me now." I asked her once more, interrupting my sister's concerns again. I saw a fluttering of her eyes before she reached up to rub them. Licking her lips, she yawned and stretched her arms before speaking my name in that sleepy voice of hers only reserved for when I know she really didn't want to wake.

"Draven?"

"It's me, can you sit up for me." I asked not really giving her much chance as I lifted her up against the back of the bed.

"Sophia, forgive me but I need to ask you to leave." I said after hearing my sister muttering her annoyance behind me.

"Not until you tell me what this is about." I turned to look at her and it only took a single second before what she found in my eyes told her she needed to leave. It wasn't anger she saw, or frustration or even irritation. It was pure raw emotion and hope all mixed into one and I could feel the tears ready to fall, both if this worked and if it didn't.

"Call me if you need me." Sophia said after placing a small hand at my shoulder and giving it a squeeze. I nodded and by the time the door closed my girl was more awake.

"Draven what is this about? Has something happened...? Oh, God tell me it's not Ari!?" I shook my head and she instantly sighed in relief.

"I have to ask you something." She gave me that confused little look of hers that made her nose scrunch up, which often made me smile secretly.

"Okay." I took a deep breath and prayed like never before that she gave me the answer I most wanted to hear when I asked her,

"If there was a way of getting your memories back... would you take it?" She sucked in a sharp breath and bit her bottom lip. The wait felt like an eternity and I was sure you could see the pain of every second play out on my face. If I cared little for the fact it was wrong, then I would have grabbed her hand and forced the coin into it...but this decision was hers and hers alone. I had forced a decision upon her life once before by hurting her more than what any normal heart could mend from. But Keira wasn't normal and I rejoiced in that fact daily.

"So there's a way?" She asked in a small voice and once more that thread on my heart was pulled.

"Yes, I found a way…" I had to pause before my voice broke completely before carrying on,

"…*A way to keep my promise to you.*"

KEIRA

I thought about what he was telling me after being woken up so suddenly. I had been dreaming of us being together and in it we had a family of our own. It had been wonderful and I hadn't wanted it to end but now being faced with this I was scared. I knew who I really was but I was scared for what I might lose. Would I be the same person? Or would I wake as someone else? It may have been an irrational thought but what would happen to the Katie part of me…

Would she be gone forever?

"I…I…" I didn't know what to say.

"How?" I ended up asking instead of giving him my answer. I looked down to see him open up his hand and there nestled protectively was a single gold coin with a hole in the middle. So this was it, this was the key? Wait…the key…a centreless key… what were the girl's words in the dream…

'*I will be here waiting for the Electus to come home. Find the centreless key to unlock the door to your mind, as bartering for souls is what he must bind.*
In blood and in tears and flames will be the price but that will

be nothing but a roll of the dice…so as one saved you from the depth of ice, the other will have to save you, not once but twice.'

So that was it. That was what she was trying to tell me. All this time the fates knew this moment would come but did that mean they knew what I would choose? In the end it wasn't hearing her words play back in my mind that made my decision. No, it was the love in Draven's eyes and that was a love I wasn't ever willing to risk losing.

So I lowered my head, let my tears fall and told him that I was…

"Sorry. I'm so sorry Draven." His head fell forward and it was almost like I could hear the moment his heart broke. Tears fell from his closed eyes and I whispered,

"Always remember that I love you, no matter who I am but…" I took a deep breath and said,

"I'm sorry if this doesn't work!" Then I reached out and grabbed the coin from his hand and the second I did, I lifted. I sucked in a needed breath as everything inside my mind changed and shifted like it was being overpowered. Then I cried out to the Heavens in a silent plea to let me stay. Then something started to feel safe and secure. Like a warmth taking away my fear and doubt as my inner soul felt like it rose up from my body. I reached out for the glimmer above me, like I was calling for it back. But then every memory I had lost came crashing back to me like a wave battering the shore over and over and over again. This was until it covered the sands enough to breach the part of my mind it needed to in order to embed itself there, digging deep enough to stay with me forever.

Suddenly there I was. Walking through the now calmer seas towards the shore. I looked around seeing a world of bridges heading off in every direction imaginable. Sparks of lightening ignited the sunny sky above, and white perfect clouds lit up high above me. I looked left to see a darker, rougher sea and on the right a perfectly calm, serene ocean all with their own bridges to walk. Was this what Heaven looked like? Was that where I was now? I had to ask myself until I looked straight forward and saw a door.

"Keira?" I heard Draven's voice away in the distance calling my name but then I heard another voice also calling my name. This time it came from right behind me and I turned round to face myself. At first I thought it was a mirror I looked into but this time, it was her. It was the girl I had been trying to reach all this time and finally she was right there.

"It's you." I told her and she gave me a small smile.

"He's calling for you." She told me nodding to the door that looked exactly like the mirror had, only now instead of glass it had wooden slats and iron rivets.

"Does this mean...?" I let that question trail off as she nodded her head.

"He found a way." She looked so sad and I wanted to comfort her but the more Draven called my name the more I found myself yearning to go to him.

"Go...go to him." She knew this was what I needed but I had to ask,

"But what about you...what happens now?" She looked around the cosmic space and sighed.

"I have nowhere else to go, so I guess I will be here waiting for when you need me."

"KEIRA! COME BACK TO ME!" My head shot round as the first crack appeared in the word with the sound of his panic.

"Go! Go to him! He needs you!" My other self shouted and I nodded. I took my first steps to the door and she called me one last time so I looked back over my shoulder and she said,

"He loves you, *so very much.*"

599

"I know. Thank you." I told her and then ran towards the door not being able to listen to the sound of his heartbreak any longer. I pulled on the door but it wouldn't budge but that's when I felt something in my hand. I opened my palm to find a single gold coin that I remembered well. I smiled knowing exactly how Draven had saved me and I shouted back to him,

"Draven, I'm coming, I'm coming home!" And then I bent down, slid the coin under the door and my heart soared when I heard the lock click. Then I pushed down on the door handle, opened the door and stepped through into the darkness...

And I was...

Home.

CHAPTER 49
I MADE IT HOME

I opened my eyes in what felt like the first time in nine months and the first thing that registered was that I was being held in someone's arms...no, not someone but *his*. *Draven*.

I heard him whispering softly that he was sorry and my heart broke at the agony in his voice. I felt his tears hit my skin as he cried into my shoulder. His hand was at the back of my head, holding me to him and it was only when I took a deep breath that I felt him freeze before he quickly pulled me back so he could look at me.

"Is it...can it be...?" He couldn't find his words and I had never seen him so emotional before. I gave him a smile and said,

"Hello again, Handsome." Then I cried out as I hugged him back and sobbed against him as the same emotions became too much for me also.

"By the Gods!" I heard him say as he held me to him so tight I could only just breathe but I didn't care because I was here now. I was back in his arms as I once was and how I should always be.

"Draven I love you, God I love you so much!" I could barely contain myself and so I jumped on him knocking us both to the floor. I started kissing him just to be sure he was real and when I could taste his tears on his skin I finally knew it was real. I had made it home...

I had really made it home.

"Let me look at you." He held my hair back from my face as I looked down where I was still sat on top of him and his smile told me everything.

"It worked, it really worked." He was in awe and so was I just looking at him knowing I was whole again.

"Gods but I missed you, my wife." I grinned just hearing the word, one I hadn't had the chance to hear often enough since we said our vows.

"I missed you too, my husband." I told him back and I thought that in this moment I couldn't get any happier as it just wasn't possible. So I got up, hearing his umpf as I pushed against him for aid and I giggled as I got to my feet, trying in vain to pull him to his. He got up staring at me like I was his whole world and I danced around, pulling him with me as I laughed and twirled like I used to when I was a kid. Libby! Oh my God Frank, Libby, Ella! Mum and Dad, everyone! I still had everyone, people I hadn't seen in so long.

"Draven everyone I missed, my family, your family...our family, I missed them all!" I told him looking around the room as if they were all to be found there.

"I know Love, I know but let's take this one step at a time." He said taking my face in his hands and in that moment I knew which step I wanted to take first. So I reached up and kissed him deeply for the first time in far too long and it felt...

Like he fed my soul with light.

It was perfect. So perfect I found my tears once more falling but this time I wasn't the only one and it was one of the most magical experiences of my entire life. This was when I knew now was the time. So I pulled away from him and his confused expression was one I smiled at before I winked telling him everything was okay. Then I took a deep breath, got down on one knee and said,

"Dominic Draven, would you do me the great honour of marrying me, *like a human this time?*" I said this last part whispered behind my hand and he laughed before lifting me up, swinging me round and telling me.

"The honour would be all mine and I would love for nothing more than to be united to you in every way possible. Of course I will marry you." And then he kissed me and like the last time my soul soared.

"Speaking of being united in every way possible." I said before I jumped up and wrapped my legs around him. His chuckle died in my mouth as I forced my deeper kiss upon him. He then carried me to the bed and lay me down.

"I want to savour you." He told me and these were the last words spoken between us as we made love. We simply gazed into each other's eyes and even when we undressed our hands never left each other's body. It was like we both feared the same thing. That if even one second went by where I didn't feel him there then he or I might disappear. For the moment we needed that connection as emotions were too raw and close to the surface to trust the world with anything else.

And with that first feel of him entering me I held on and knew I found home. I found my way back through the storm over lost seas and was finally reunited with…

My heart.

～

Making love to Draven this way was just what we both needed in order to re-fuse our souls back together once again. It felt like our new beginning only with the added bonus of never forgetting where we had been. Because I now knew how important in life that was. All the horrors, the sadness, the pain and the suffering simply put, added to your soul. It made it stronger, it made it fight harder for the ones you loved. It gave you your sense of duty and morals but more than anything else, it taught you how to love with everything you had and every fibre in your body.

It was love that brought me home.

It was love that lit the way

And it was love that made me a promise.

"Oh God I could murder a cuppa!" I said snuggling closer up to him in the bed after we had spent time talking about everything that had happened. We were now dressed, much to Draven's annoyance, but if I knew anything about the Draven clan, with the added addition of Pip, that once they got wind of this we would be bombarded and I didn't really want the first time I saw them all again to be me in my birthday suit.

"Yep, it's definitely you." Draven said and I laughed at the same time saying,

"Oi! I will have you know this is the longest I have ever gone without tea." He chuckled, put his hand to my forehead and said,

"I think you have a fever, I'd better get you an injection of tea before I lose you to that decaffeinated coma that is sweeping the nation."

"To most people that's just called a Monday morning." I told him making him laugh again.

"Well lucky for me it's a Sunday."

"Ah, a Holy day, well in that case that means that the Gods usually need worshipping by eating chocolate with your tea or is that just all days ending in Y...I can never remember but let's say it's the Y thing." Hearing him roaring with laughter was most certainly a sound I had missed. Because no matter how much the Katie side of me had actually been me in the flesh, in the mind that's where things got a little more complicated.

I told Draven that it was like being locked away in a room of my memories and trying to find my way out of them. I was still Keira but I was the Keira that would have been had I never had my life. Had I never grown up in a loving home. Had I never had fun, friends and strangely enough my visions. But most importantly I was the Keira before Draven and even though I fell in love with him, I had never had that time as I had done in the beginning. That desperate longing for something you wanted so badly you knew the root of obsession was taking hold. What it felt like to finally be able to grasp it and call it your own. The pain of losing it and the fear of losing it again. The strength you build in going to take it back from Hell itself. The fight for your life because you want it! Because you love your life and all the people in it! All of these things were what made a person and shaped them into who they're proud to be but most of all, into the person people fell in love with.

Draven knew this and he struggled with it just as I would have in his situation. So if you take away all of this, then you take away their core and leave them with an empty shell to fill. That's what they tried to do but I fought back at every turn. Through dreams or through visions, I pushed her to find a way to survive. To find Draven and her real family. I tried to show her the truth and guide her through the dangers of my world.

And in the end she repaid me by taking a hold of that coin and bringing me back. See Bill's coin had my whole life imprinted onto it when I touched it in that boat. I had passed out from the force of it and had forgotten about it since then, never expecting anything like that could have happened. After that it had acted as a trigger, releasing me from the spell I had been put under or this is what we assumed.

As for Katie, well I didn't really remember her life anymore as it became cloudy under the weight of my own. But I did have all the memories of the last nine months so the love I had for my new sister Ari would never fade along with it. She kept me going and she sacrificed herself to save me. No, I would never forget Ari not as long as I lived.

But having Katie brought out a new power in me, one that was growing in strength but unlike her I knew I could control it. I remember what happened on the plane and how close we had all come to our end. I thought this would have brought me fear but strangely it didn't. Because something deep within me knew nothing like that would ever happen again because I wouldn't let it.

"So we get to have our other wedding after all...but wait, my ring...oh that's right, we never found it did we?" I looked up and the second I saw Draven's face I knew something was wrong.

"Draven...what is it?" He looked deep in thought for a moment and shouted,

"Ava!" Then he shot from the bed and was out of the double doors before I could stop him. I scooted to the end of the bed and held on to the end post as I watched Draven calling for his bird in the wind. He looked magnificent out there and for a moment I was simply struck by his masculine beauty. His black hair blew in every direction and the muscles on his back tensed as he raised his hand to his mouth, making his call travel further. I decided to find out what he was doing so I swung my legs round, found Draven's large man socks and put them on. I looked a bit like a clown as they flapped around but they kept my feet warm, so it was worth looking silly.

I walked out into the cold and right up to the back of him,

"What are you...?" My question died as he stepped out of the way to reveal Ava in all her wonderful glory sat perched on the balcony railings. But it wasn't just the sight of her that had me gasping it was what she had clasped in her talons that had me believing in miracles.

"My ring." Draven took a step towards her and said,

"I owe you, old girl...thank you." And then after stroking her down her sleek body he pulled the ring, unhooking it from her talon and nodding to the sky, telling her work here was done.

"But how...I thought it was lost?" I asked as he turned back to me. Then he reached out for my hand and I extended the finger it was only ever meant to live on. He slipped it on and said

"Not lost, just buried with memories I tried to say goodbye to." And without asking him to explain I knew what he meant and I knew where he had gone. It was the same place I had gone to when saying goodbye. When I thought all hope was lost.

So I went there to bury memories that could never be forgotten, because no matter how we try...

Sometimes, memories just find their way home.

EPILOGUE

That night I couldn't sleep even though Draven was passed out beside me. I smiled down at him knowing that this was most likely because he had not slept properly in the whole nine months I had been gone. All that worrying had to catch up to you sometime, even for one as powerful as Draven.

I decided to get up and use the bathroom as after Draven had lovingly bestowed me back my ring, I had then drunk my body weight in tea and was now paying for it. I had also had an emotional reunion with Sophia, running at her as soon as she walked through the door in fact. We both soon found ourselves in tears and I dreaded what it would be like when I finally saw my family again. Draven had been forced to make them believe I was fine, spoke to them often, was busy travelling the world. But it became harder to make them believe they were still seeing me and Draven couldn't stand lying to them much longer as it was taking its toll out on him morally.

However, he had continued to do so because he knew this is what I would have wanted. And he was right. My family had been through enough worry over me and I didn't want that for them again. But this simply meant that my emotional visit tomorrow was going to be one sided but that was alright, I was a girl, we can easily explain it by just saying one line… 'Time of the month' which I am not gonna lie, most of the time was just an excuse that said, 'I just want to cry alright!'. What can I say, some of us were sensitive creatures but this didn't make us weak, just the opposite in fact.

In the end I said goodbye to Sophia after finding out that Pip and Adam had been in the middle of something, which being Pip could have been anything. And Vincent I knew was with Ari and I was happy for him. Which brought me back to now and staring at myself in the mirror. It was strange now having a different perception of myself and for a second I stared so hard I thought I saw her. I thought…but wait,

"Katie?" I whispered testing the question out first in case I was just freaking myself out for no good reason.

"Hello again." She said in a quiet kind voice, probably so as not to freak me out.

"But…but how is that possible?" I asked her hoping Draven wouldn't hear me whispering to myself in the bathroom.

"I'm not sure…but, I knew there was something you needed to know and it just brought me back to our mirror." She told me and I thought that this would have freaked me out enough to go screaming back into the room. But I didn't do that and nor did I want to. I guess if there was only one way to explain it, then it was like seeing a ghost you weren't scared of…one, evidently that was just trying to offer me some advice.

"Are you…alright?" I asked fearing for her locked away in my mind or maybe it was just me going crazy from it all. Like I would start seeing her every day and we would end up fighting on how I did my hair, going to the gym or eating too much chocolate. Christ I hoped not!

"Yes, I am fine. Your memories bring me great solace in

times of sadness but I needed to warn you that there is someone of great importance waiting to speak with you in the prison. She told me in…"

"Our dream." I uttered remembering it as if she had just passed it over to me to keep.

"Yes. 'Take away their time and you take away their power. They have taken eight…don't let them take nine. Find yourself and learn of the Prophecy's seven, find the key and you will find me next time in Heaven…do you know what this means?" She asked and I thought about the one place that had the Heavens above.

"I know where she is." I said quietly.

"Where?"

"She's in the Temple waiting for me." I had defeated the Hexad, stopping them from taking the ninth, being Ari. I had found the centreless key now there was only one thing left on that list.

"But who is she?" She asked looking side on in the mirror as I started to walk away.

"Pythia."

"But what does she want?" And this was it. The final answer to why I was chosen and more importantly what for? So I looked over my shoulder now knowing I was finally coming to the end of my quest. I told her in my heart what I now knew was finally here.

"She wants to tell me about the Prophecy." Then I walked from the bathroom after the image of myself nodded her farewell.

I stepped into the bedroom, gave Draven one last look before going in search of the answers I had been looking since I first met him. I could feel something coming. I had waited for it for too long and come too far to reach the end without knowing what was waiting for me behind the door. The first time it had been my memories back and my test had been taken and I had passed as Pythia knew I would. That's why she was asking for me.

Time. Truth and Life.

Well in this life it was time for the truth to be heard.

It was my time. It was our time. It was...

Time taken back.

To be continued...

ABOUT THE AUTHOR

Stephanie Hudson has dreamed of being a writer ever since her obsession with reading books at an early age. What first became a quest to overcome the boundaries set against her in the form of dyslexia has turned into a life's dream. She first started writing in the form of poetry and soon found a taste for horror and romance. Afterlife is her first book in the series of twelve, with the story of Keira and Draven becoming ever more complicated in a world that sets them miles apart.

When not writing, Stephanie enjoys spending time with her loving family and friends, chatting for hours with her biggest fan, her sister Cathy who is utterly obsessed with one gorgeous Dominic Draven. And of course, spending as much time with her supportive partner and personal muse, Blake who is there for her no matter what.

Author's words.

My love and devotion is to all my wonderful fans that keep me going into the wee hours of the night but foremost to my wonderful daughter Ava...who yes, is named after a cool, kick-ass, Demonic bird and my sons, Jack, who is a little hero and Baby Halen, who yes, keeps me up at night but it's okay because he is named after a Guitar legend!

Keep updated with all new release news & more on my website

www.afterlifesaga.com
Never miss out, sign up to the
mailing list at the website.

Also, please feel free to join myself and other Dravenites on my
Facebook group
Afterlife Saga Official Fan
Interact with me and other fans. Can't wait to see you there!

facebook.com/AfterlifeSaga
twitter.com/afterlifesaga
instagram.com/theafterlifesaga

ACKNOWLEDGMENTS

Well first and foremost my love goes out to all the people who deserve the most thanks and are the wonderful people that keep me going day to day. But most importantly they are the ones that allow me to continue living out my dreams and keep writing my stories for the world to hopefully enjoy…

These people are of course
YOU!

Words will never be able to express the full amount of love I have for you guys. Your support is never ending. Your trust in me and the story is never failing. But more than that, your love for me and all who you consider your 'Afterlife family' is to be commended, treasured and admired.

Thank you just doesn't seem enough, so one day I hope to buy you all a drink! ;)

Also an extra special thanks goes out to all of you that came to our joint Hen and Stag shindig! It was epic and I can't thank you enough for all the effort from those that came. It was a fabulous weekend, one never to be forgotten.

Thanks to the Dravenite Council for arranging it all.
You Girls are Awesome!
Also a shout out goes to Carrie Anne Gosslin Wyman who has kindly arranged the New York book signing. And to Jenn Won and Renee Krueger, for kindly arranging the Las Vegas book

signing. I am extremely touched and grateful for all of your help and can't wait to meet you all.

To my family...

My sister who gives a face and soul to the vision of Afterlife.

To my amazing mother, who has believed in me from the very beginning and doesn't believe that something great should be hidden from the world. I would like to thank you for all the hard work you put into my books and the endless hours spent caring about my words and making sure it is the best it can be for everyone to enjoy. You make Afterlife shine.

To my wonderful crazy father who is and always has been my hero in life. Your strength astonishes me, even to this day and the love and care you hold for your family is a gift you give to the Hudson name.

And last but not least, to the man that I consider my soul mate. The man who taught me about real love and makes me not only want to be a better person but makes me feel I am too. The amount of support you have given me since we met has been incredible and the greatest feeling was finding out you wanted to spend the rest of your life with me when you asked me to marry you.

I love you dearly Blake Hudson.

My very own Draven

ALSO BY STEPHANIE HUDSON

Afterlife Saga

Afterlife

The Two Kings

The Triple Goddess

The Quarter Moon

The Pentagram Child /Part 1

The Pentagram Child /Part 2

The Cult of the Hexad

Sacrifice of the Septimus /Part 1

Sacrifice of the Septimus /Part 2

Blood of the Infinity War

Happy Ever Afterlife /Part 1

Happy Ever Afterlife / Part 2

The Forbidden Chapters

*

Transfusion Saga

Transfusion

Venom of God

Blood of Kings

Rise of Ashes

Map of Sorrows

Tree of Souls

Kingdoms of Hell

The Devil in Me

OTHER WORKS FROM HUDSON INDIE INK

Paranormal Romance/Urban Fantasy

Sloane Murphy

Xen Randell

C. L. Monaghan

Sorcha Dawn

Sci-fi/Fantasy

Devin Hanson

Crime/Action

Blake Hudson

Mike Gomes

Contemporary Romance

Gemma Weir